Squaring
Circles

Squaring Circles

Carolyn Mathews

Winchester, UK
Washington, USA

First published by Roundfire Books, 2014
Roundfire Books is an imprint of John Hunt Publishing Ltd., Laurel House, Station Approach,
Alresford, Hants, SO24 9JH, UK
office1@jhpbooks.net
www.johnhuntpublishing.com
www.roundfire-books.com

For distributor details and how to order please visit the 'Ordering' section on our website.

Text copyright: Carolyn Mathews 2013

ISBN: 978 1 78279 705 0

A CIP catalogue record for this book is available from the British Library.

Design: Stuart Davies

Printed in the USA by Edwards Brothers Malloy

We operate a distinctive and ethical publishing philosophy in all
areas of our business, from our global network of authors to
production and worldwide distribution.

CONTENTS

A Note to Readers

Those of you who have met Pandora Jay, alias Armstrong, alias Fry, in *Transforming Pandora*, will already be familiar with some of the characters in this book. For the benefit of readers old and new, I have listed the main cast members in this production below.

The action takes place in early spring, 2008.

Dramatis Personae

Ashley – Jay's 22-year-old son.
Cassiel – Enoch Society Correspondence Course administrator.
Charles – Frankie's partner.
Cherry – Jay's daughter, 19.
Clarrie – Rowan's girlfriend, 18.
Cynthia – Circle of Isis member.
Dido Bull – founder of the Circle of Isis.
Enoch – big cheese in the Cosmos who showed Pandora the way to enlightenment.
Frankie – Pandora's mother.
Gaby Laing – singer.
Gavin Bull – Dido's husband.
Hugh – Four Seasons garden produce manager.
James Jay – Pandora's first husband, known as Jay.
Jenny – farmer Steve's wife.
Linden – Ashley's twin brother.
Max – Rosemary's son, 19.
Mike Armstrong – Pandora's second husband, deceased.
Pandora – narrator.
Pete – friend and confidant of Charles.
Polly – editor of an online magazine.
Portia – personal assistant to Zac Willoughby.
Ralph – Circle of Isis member.

Rosemary – friend of Frankie's.

Rowan – Jay's son, 15.

Ryan – farmer Steve's son.

Sharon – Jay's mother.

Sonia – crystal shop assistant.

Steve – Glastonbury farmer.

Tegan – healing client of Pandora's.

Theo Johnson – visitor from Los Angeles.

Tom – Rowan's friend.

Willow – Jay's daughter, 17.

Zac Willoughby – CEO of Oven Ready Productions.

Anubis – Frankie's cat.

Beau – Poitou donkey rescued by Theo.

Bonnie and Clyde – the Jay family's goats.

Flossy – a pony belonging to farmer Steve.

Fritz – Jay's dog.

Midnight – the Jay family's cob mare.

Milo – Tegan's dog.

Oscar – Pandora's dog.

For it is in giving that we receive.
From the Prayer of St Francis of Assisi

Acknowledgements

Grateful acknowledgment is offered to Damian Nola, spiritual teacher, author and artist, dedicated to serving the awakening of all beings to the true nature of reality, whose channelling inspired the manner by which Pandora received her epiphanies.
http://sourcematrix.co.uk

And also to Odile Wolff, doyenne of the gong.

Chapter 1

Losing Grip

Chilled to the bone, gathered in the soggy paddock behind my mother's home with fifty or so other mourners, I watched in horror as her rainbow-striped wicker coffin pitched sidelong into the grave.

The culprit, a young man I'd never seen before, had allowed his lowering rope to slip too quickly through his fingers, thus causing my partner, Jay, at one end of the second rope, to be somehow dragged into the grave with my mother.

You'd have thought the perpetrator would have been the first to dash to Jay's rescue, but he stood rooted to the spot, a look of dazed disbelief on his face.

Once Jay was pulled to safety by the efforts of two men, one proffering a hand, the other holding on to his pal so he wouldn't slip on the grass as Jay had, I threw my arms around him, trying to avoid the muddy patches on his full-length, black leather trench coat. As we hugged, he whispered, 'I reckon the old bat was trying to take me with her.'

'Better not speak ill of the dead,' I said softly, 'she might be listening.'

Actually, I had a feeling Jay might be right. My mother Frankie had never come to terms with us getting back together. I silently reproached her, hoping the message to lay off him would get through.

That coat cost a lot of money, Mother. Far too much for it to go anywhere near a real trench.

Her reply came immediately, as clear as a bell in my left ear.

If he calls me an old bat again, Pandora, mark my words, I will come back and haunt him.

Mercifully ignorant of this threat, Jay nodded towards the

other side of the grave. 'You better go and check on Charles.'

Charles, who'd been the other end of the stranger's rope, was now on his feet, after falling backwards when the coffin had gone into freefall. I picked my way towards him, trying to avoid the worst patches of mud, and found him examining the welts on his hands.

'Are you all right?' I said, taking his hands in mine. 'You took quite a tumble.'

'Blast this weather, makes the rope slippery,' he said. 'Don't worry, Pandora. I'm okay.'

But his eyes looked red and watery and his bottom lip a bit trembly. At that moment the young man appeared and started apologising for letting the coffin fall.

'The lads dug the hole too wide. If it'd been a snug fit, the coffin would've fallen into place,' said Charles. 'Wasn't your fault.'

But it *was* his fault, I thought, as I peered into the grave and tutted my disapproval at the sight of the coffin resting at an angle against the wall of the dugout. I could only hope my poor mother had been packed properly, and hadn't been flung too wildly around like a Christmas parcel in a sorting office.

Someone in the crowd, of mostly old hippies, shouted, 'Frankie won't mind. She was always one to go widdershins.'

'Very droll,' muttered Charles.

All eyes were focused on him now, this being a DIY job with no proper funeral director present, but he seemed to have lost the will to lead.

'Not sure I'll be any good with these hands, boys. Think I'll have to bow out and leave it to you.'

One wag then declared that whoever righted the coffin would have to be careful that Frankie was facing up, as only those suspected of witchcraft were buried face down. This drew a few titters, and someone shouted, 'Heads or tails? Best of three?' which caused even more hilarity.

2

It was plain from the clench of his jaw that Charles, like me, was not amused, so Jay's intervention was very welcome.

'Hold my coat, Andy, I'm going in again.'

(Jay always dropped the initial letter of my name, for which I was grateful. Otherwise, horror of horrors, my nickname would have been 'Pandy'.)

Lobbing his good coat in my direction he jumped into the hole, closely followed by none other than the stranger, and they set about manoeuvring the coffin. Finally, two men took the weight at one end, allowing Jay and his helper to clamber out. Thus my mother was laid to rest at last – facing skyward, as custom decreed – to the accompaniment of raucous cheers.

Once order had been restored, my mother's friend Rosemary delivered the eulogy, declaring what a loss her sudden passing was to the Glastonbury community, how much she'd be missed, and so on.

While Rosemary was singing my mother's praises, my thoughts turned to our first meeting – a Harvest Moon ceremony in her garden. How conventional she'd seemed in comparison with the rest of the supernaturalists, with her short, fair hair and immaculate house. And, despite terming herself 'Energy Healer and Practical Alchemist', how down to earth, and not at all fey.

Her voice cut into my reflections as she invited family members to take a symbolic clod of earth from the great pile of excavated soil, situated between the dugout and the boundary of the paddock, and cast it on the coffin. Charles took the trowel from her with shaking hands, then had a change of heart, going instead to the heap of flowers to one side of the excavations to find the posy he'd placed there. His face twisted in grief as he flung the pure white anemones, their black centres like huge eyes, into the pit.

I'd been holding myself together until then, but the anguish on his face made me want to weep. I knew if I broke down, so would he, so I concentrated on tossing soil on the coffin without hitting the flowers, which was illogical, as they were going to be buried anyway.

Once Charles and I had performed our rites, I expected Rosemary to extend the invitation to Frankie's friends, but before doing so, she asked, 'Are there any other family members who would like to assist Frances to return to the earth?'

To my great surprise, the errant rope bearer who'd caused all the trouble, loped forward, scooped up some soil and sprinkled it self-consciously on to the coffin beneath, smiling at me tentatively on his way back. I looked enquiringly at Charles, wondering if this person could be related to him, but he wouldn't return my gaze and had an expression on his face that seemed to say, *I've had enough today. Don't go there.*

I turned back to Rosemary in time to see her adopting the Orans posture, her arms outstretched, palms opening to heaven.

'Receive the body of our sister back into thy bosom, O Mother Earth,' she intoned, 'the circle of our beloved Frances' life being now complete. We call upon the undines of the waters that fall and flow, the sylphs of the winds that blow, the salamanders of the fire that cleanses and the gnomes of the earth that seeds and consecrates. May the elements carry her spirit safely to the Light for her soul to spin in eternal bliss.'

Then she looked in my direction and uttered the prayer of the departed one.

'Blood of my blood, bone of my bone, flesh of my flesh, keep my spirit alive. I will live on in your hearts. O remember me.'

How could I forget you? I thought, tears breaking through and racing down my cheeks. Beside me, Jay put a consoling hand on my back. Behind me, I heard the stranger blowing his nose and wished he'd go away.

Rosemary concluded by reading a long poem about the mystery of death, which she'd barely finished before an impatient volunteer backfiller determinedly picked up a shovel and set about moving clods of clay from the great pile into the grave.

The sight of his dearly beloved's interment was too much for Charles, who strode off towards the cottage, shouting, 'Anyone who wants to come in for refreshment is welcome.'

Intent as I was on drying my tears, I was slow to notice Jay leave my side, but when I caught sight of him advancing towards a shovel, I hurried to intercept him. His beautiful boots had seen enough action for one day; the mucky ground around the grave was no place for Gucci.

'Let's follow Charles inside, Jay. He probably needs some help setting the food out.'

He didn't even turn his head, so appealing was the industrial-sized spade in front of him.

'You go, babe. This needs doing now. Otherwise the donkey might fall in and break a leg.'

Presuming he was making some weird joke about what had happened earlier, I didn't give what he'd said a second thought. Reluctant to go into the cottage on my own, I hung around for a few minutes, and that was when I witnessed the stranger coming into the paddock, through the gate which led from the lane, with a shaggy brown donkey the size of a horse. He was leading the beast to a shelter which, like the donkey, was another recent addition to the pasture.

'What's going on, Jay? Who is he and why's he keeping a donkey in my mum's...' I faltered, remembering she was no more. '...In Charles' paddock?'

Jay was by now well away with the earth moving and had gone deaf, as men do when lost in manly pursuits, so I decided to find out for myself.

I strode towards them, hampered by my high heels, which had begun to sink a good half inch into the earth. By the time I'd hobbled over to them, still clutching Jay's coat, the pair had reached the shelter and were locked in an embrace.

'Love you, man,' he crooned, as he tickled the beast's enormous white nose and nuzzled his giant neck. They were oblivious to me until I uttered a rude word when my shoe stuck fast in the earth, while my left foot catapulted out of it on to a patch of muddy grass. At the sound of my voice they stood to attention, the donkey's ears extending to their full height.

'Sorry to interrupt your love-in, guys. I haven't seen you before. I'm wondering why you're here.'

I didn't know why I was being quite so unfriendly. Maybe it was the fact he'd thrown soil on my mother's coffin, and been given the honour of carrying it, even though she'd never ever referred to him during any of our phone chats.

Being of above-average height, his skin the colour of vanilla toffee, with sun-bleached dreadlocks skimming his strong shoulders, this individual wouldn't easily have slipped anyone's mind. The same could be said for the donkey, whose hair mimicked his master's, hanging in cords so long they obscured his belly.

'Hi. Beau's been visiting with the pony down the road. Just till, you know, the coast was clear.'

'You mean when my mother was finally safe underground,' I said frostily, the image of him letting go of the rope flashing before me.

I positioned my eyebrows into a shape I hoped would prompt a straight answer to my enquiry, but he responded with more prevarication.

'I guess Charles didn't tell you about me?' The beast gave him a gentle nudge. 'About us?'

Jay and I had seen Charles only briefly before the burial, so hadn't yet had a proper chinwag with him. We'd booked into a hotel and planned to take him there for a meal once all the revellers had gone – I kept mistaking this funeral for a party, considering the majority of them were sporting bright colours and cracking jokes.

I examined the stranger more closely while he was waiting for me to reply. He had a wide face with a high forehead. What appeared to be a diamond stud flashed in one ear and an expensive watch encircled his wrist below the sleeve of his sheepskin bomber jacket. His orange sweatshirt and blue jeans were unremarkable, given that only a handful of people had on any vestige of black. Charles himself was wearing a cream suit and a panama hat, reminiscent of the Man from Del Monte in the canned-fruit ad.

'No he didn't tell us about you,' I said, when I'd finished giving him the once-over. 'We haven't had much chance to speak to him yet. That's why I'm asking you who you are now.'

His bottom lip jutted out, like a sulky child.

'My dad and your mom used to know each other.' He examined his boots, then continued. 'Just before my dad died last year, he asked me to look your mom up. I came over in December, called to see Frankie and she invited me to stay. When I mentioned Beau she told me to bring him as well.'

An image of him and the donkey plodding round the West Country searching for lodgings was abruptly replaced by the memory of my mother's voice on the phone cancelling her Christmas visit to us. Struggling to keep my resentment under control, I nodded for him to go on.

'I'd kinda rescued him. I was staying with my cousin. He was in a field close to the house. He'd been left on his own...'

At this, the beast nuzzled the corner of his lips – yes, his actual *lips*, and then leaned forward, prodding the brim of my alpaca fur hat out of the way, so he could blow in my left ear.

His breath was warm and fragrant from sweet barley straw and my heart melted like marshmallow. I stood there, rapt, as he moved his enormous head, using his nose to lift my hat off entirely, to gain access to my right ear as well.

'That's his way of saying "hi".'

Retrieving my hat from the soggy ground, I felt a rush of affection for this enormous, gentle creature.

'Can I stroke his head?'

'Yeah, go ahead. He likes his ears being scratched,' he said, taking my hat and Jay's coat so I'd be able do the job properly.

Beau lowered his ears to horizontal, and I worked my way along them with both hands, giving every last inch a proper good scratch.

'You're a handsome boy,' I said, in a goofy voice. 'Just like your name.'

'His name?'

'We used to have a goat called Beau. He was handsome too.'

His expression was still vacant.

'The word "*beau*" is French for "handsome".'

He looked startled.

'When they told me his name I assumed it was short for "bodacious".'

Now it was my turn to look blank.

'It means gutsy.'

'Well, he's certainly got a gut on him,' I said, still using the same goofy voice so Beau wouldn't know I was being rude about his figure.

'Yeah. People used to stop by and feed him. They meant well, but...'

'And he could do with a haircut,' I crooned.

I finished scratching his ears and he nudged me, so I cuddled his great head.

'You fallin' in love with him? Most people do.'

Come to think of it, that was just what it felt like. But I was getting sidetracked. My mission was to gather intelligence on these two, and all I'd got so far was this stranger with a transatlantic accent had taken advantage of a tenuous connection with Frankie to provide himself and his donkey with a squat. I began to wonder whether he was a con-man who used his creature to inveigle ingenuous folk like Charles into subsidising him. What else, I wondered, was Charles providing him with?

I held out my hand.

'Pandora Armstrong.'

'Theo Johnson.'

He fumbled to shake my hand, his own being occupied with my hat and Jay's coat. I paused for a beat, giving him the chance to elaborate, but by then he'd handed the hat and coat back to me and walked into the shelter to pick up a large plastic bucket.

'He needs fresh water...'

So I took the hint and left him to it; it was too cold to stand around chatting, anyway. I lurched back to the grave to see how Jay was doing, to find all the backfilling volunteers gone, except Jay and a man I recognised as a friend of Charles.

When he saw me, Jay gave the soil one last thump with his shovel and addressed his companion.

'Coming over to the house with us, Pete?'

Pete shook his head.

'Nah. It'll be heaving in there. I'll get off home to clean up. Be back tomorrer, first thing, to lay the turves.'

'Cheers, mate.' Jay seemed to be enjoying the camaraderie of his fellow manual labourer. 'I'll let Charles know. Reckon he owes you a drink.'

Chapter 2

Fragments

When we finally got into the cottage, having crossed the paddock, opened the garden gate and entered the kitchen through the back door, we found there was standing room only. This was worrying, as the living room and study were packed with knick-knacks, crystals, and books in teetering stacks on every surface.

Charles had set up beer, wine and cider in the kitchen, with sherry, as he put it, 'for the ladies' (his little joke). He'd also spread the dining-room table with a buffet of sandwiches and savouries, almost every last crumb of which had been snaffled by the time we got there. Leaving Jay to get us a drink from the rapidly diminishing stock, I fought my way over to Charles and tugged at his sleeve.

'How are you doing?'

He had the look of a drowning man.

'Miscalculated on the catering front, I'm afraid. Do you think I should go and get more supplies?'

This idea, to me, was madness. We needed to get shot of these locusts, not encourage them with further wining and dining. If a queue formed for the downstairs loo, we might well have a peeing-in-the-garden situation on our hands.

A sharp crack, followed by shocked 'oohs' and 'aahs', silenced the hubbub and all eyes turned to the wreckage of an ornamental skull in smithereens on the wooden floor of the living room. Rosemary was standing over the fragments, one hand clasped to her mouth.

'I'm so sorry, Charles. It just slipped out of my hands.'

She then burst into tears, which surprised me, as I'd only ever known her as capable and composed.

Further concerned murmurs ensued, a woman with a multi-coloured turban squawking, 'It wasn't Mayan was it?' with a man in a paisley waistcoat adding, 'Damn. There goes the last chance to save the world,' which provoked a few sardonic smirks.

'Can't be helped,' said Charles wearily. 'Sentimental value, that's all. My birthday present to Frankie on her sixtieth.'

Looking as if she'd been responsible for smashing a human cranium rather than a carved crystal one, Rosemary did her penance on hands and knees with a dustpan and brush, the assembled company overseeing operations until the last crystal tooth had been collected. Finally, she got to her feet, making miserably for the kitchen bin.

Charles followed her. 'Crystal goes back to the earth,' he hissed, forgetting the rawness of his hands as he made a grab for the dustpan. Flinching, he snapped, 'I'll bury the fragments.'

Rosemary coloured and said, 'Of course, sorry,' but by then he was on his way through the back door and into the garden.

Luckily for Charles and me – but not for Jay, who complained afterwards he'd been in the middle of an interesting conversation about Joseph of Arimathea with the turbaned lady – the combination of the accident and a lack of booze brought the party to a premature end.

'Anyone for the Flying Horse?' shouted the paisley waistcoat. And bit by bit they filed out, stopping first to find Charles and pat him on the back, hug him, or shake his hand, before making their escape.

One of the last to leave was Rosemary, who looked beseechingly at Charles as she leaned in to kiss his cheek. I noticed he moved his head when she did this, so her kiss landed more in the region of his upper ear.

She started to apologise again, offering to pay for a new skull – Charles owned Gaia's Cave, a crystal emporium, so there'd be no trouble getting a replacement – but he just took her arm and walked her to the front door, like a bouncer escorting her off the premises. As he opened the door, a woman appeared at the top of the wooden stairs which led down into the living room. I presumed she'd been using the bathroom, although now that everyone had gone, she could easily have used the downstairs loo.

'Wait, Rosemary, I'll come with you,' she called.

The speaker was petite with long, raven hair. Unusually for Frankie's friends, she appeared to be the right side of forty. Over her ankle-length, grey velvet dress she was wearing a black cape with a cowl hood lined in cream silk. As Jay remarked later, she had the look of a sexy abbess.

I watched her descend the stairs and wave airily at Charles, making sure she didn't notice me standing further back in the room.

'Bye, Charles. Don't forget, if you find anything that belongs to the Circle, let me know.'

As she said this, Rosemary threw her an enquiring glance and the woman returned serve with an almost imperceptible shake of the head.

In reply, Charles simply stood at the open door, closing it on their heels almost before they'd crossed the threshold. I went to the window and studied them as they walked down the short path to the street. Rosemary's body language suggested remorse – presumably at breaking the crystal skull. Except...there was something more that I couldn't put my finger on. Her companion, on the other hand, exuded self-assurance and determination.

I was straining to pick up their conversation when Jay came up behind me and whispered in my ear, making me start.

'You've got that look. What's cooking?'

'I don't know,' I said, stroking his craggy face, which I found absurdly attractive. 'We need to talk to Charles.'

* * *

The waiter brought our drinks and the three of us clinked glasses. Our hotel restaurant was warm and inviting and we were all glad the ordeal of the funeral was behind us.

'It went well,' said Jay, being kind.

'Apart from your mother's crash landing,' said Charles, looking guiltily at me. 'We should have used another rope. Two weren't enough.'

'You should have used another rope bearer, more like, donkey-boy was hopeless.'

He patted my hand. 'Pandora, don't be too harsh. Grief often makes people lose concentration.'

'But why would *he* feel grief, Charles. And when exactly in December did he knock on your door?'

Charles sensed I was on to something and pretended not to be quite sure.

'I bet it was just before Christmas, wasn't it?'

Bowing under pressure, he nodded. My mother and Charles had been supposed to come to ours for a few days, but she'd made an excuse at the last minute that Charles was ill.

'You didn't really have the flu, did you, Charles?'

He studied his vodka tonic, avoiding eye contact.

'Did you?'

'Crikey,' said Jay. 'This is better than *Judge Judy*.'

'Well,' shrugged Charles. 'He turned up the day before Christmas Eve, without warning, to deliver a letter from his father to Frankie. What could we do?'

'You could have given him a glass of Drambuie and a mince pie and sent him on his way,' I snapped.

I was fuming. Typical, I thought, a personable stranger turns up out of the blue followed by an even more charming equine, and Charles and Frankie throw their doors wide open to both of them, turning their backs on me and mine.

In a bid to break the tension, Jay cut in.

'He told me about the donkey when we were turning your

mother in her grave.' At Jay's mention of Beau, my heart gave a little hop and I leaned forward. 'He found him in a field. No fresh water, no proper feed, just grass. So he asked around and it turned out the landowner had died and the place was up for sale. The other livestock had been sold but nobody wanted the donkey, so Theo rescued him.'

'He said something about staying with a cousin?' I said, having calmed down a bit at the thought of Theo rescuing Beau.

'Yes,' said Charles. 'His cousin was renting a house near Stonehenge. Making a documentary, I think Theo said. He's back in the States now. Theo made us his next stop. He'd already placed Beau in a sanctuary but when he saw our empty paddock, he asked if he could bring him here. I'm glad he did. That gentle creature...' Charles' grey ponytail quivered with emotion, '...he's helped me through these last few days. No doubt about it.'

Jay and I both nodded. We'd had enough assorted animals in our time to know the truth of that.

'It was so sudden. I thought Frankie would go on forever...'

A couple of tears trickled down Charles' cheeks which set off my energy depletion alarm, so I took his hands in mine to give him a boost. He and Jay knew what I was doing and we all stayed quiet for a little while, until the waiter brought some bread and broke the spell.

Charles had been in a state of shock since my mother had died in her sleep ten days before. *Cardiac arrhythmia* was what the death certificate said, but she'd had no medical history of heart trouble; in fact, she'd been the picture of health. Some would say it was the perfect way to go: no painful seizure, no traipsing to hospitals for her next of kin. But the impact of losing her so suddenly was like being hit by a truck. It had hit me hard, and Charles harder. They'd been together for nearly twenty-five years which, considering Frankie's previous track record, was something of a miracle.

My mother and I rarely saw each other more than three or

four times a year, but we spoke on the phone at least once a week. I'd actually spoken to her the day before she died, and yet she'd never mentioned her house guest and his four-legged friend.

'Why didn't Mum tell me about Theo and Beau, Charles?'

He started massaging his forehead, with a frown of trying to remember, but I sensed he was faking. He greeted the steaming bowl of carrot and coriander soup the waiter brought him with relief, avoiding my question by praising the freshness of the rolls and the flavour of the soup a little too fulsomely.

I exchanged a glance with Jay. He saw I was irritated at being left out of the loop and his eyes held an amused, *chill out* message. I contained myself until we'd progressed to dessert, when I said, in what I hoped was a casual tone, 'So how long are you going to let your lodgers stay?'

'As long as they like, my dear. Theo pays his way more than generously. Would you have me throw them out on the street?'

His curtness took me by surprise and it was my turn for a few tears. Charles was too busy scoffing his plum tart to notice, but Jay did, and patted my hand.

'Too right. It's company for you, man,' said Jay, giving me a soft look so I'd know he was still on my side. 'It'll help you get over the worst of it.'

I felt ashamed then of the jealousy I'd been feeling, for that was what it was. Not of Beau, naturally, but of Theo.

'Yes,' I said, trying to make it sound true, 'I'm glad you've got someone here with you, so you won't be lonely.'

In response, Charles raised his head and stretched back in his seat as if a weight had been lifted from his shoulders.

'I'm so glad you feel that way, Pandora. Your mother wasn't sure you'd approve, and that was why she didn't tell you. You're not rushing off tomorrow, are you? I'd like you to come round after breakfast and have a proper chat with Theo before you go.'

We said of course we'd come, and he beamed at us both. My

puny *volte-face* had put him in such an expansive mood that he began to deliver a sermon on the blessed Beau. He told us he was a rare Poitou donkey, a variety farmers had crossed with working horses to produce giant mules to work the land, but when the mules were replaced by tractors, French farmers had no more use for the Poitous.

'They're very large, very friendly and very hairy,' he finished.

'He could do with a trim, in my opinion.'

'Who? Beau or Theo? smiled Charles.

'Both.'

'Theo said traditionally they're left ungroomed. But I agree with you, Pandora.'

'We'll have to ask him.'

'You can ask Theo tomorrow when you come over.'

'I meant ask Beau,' I said.

* * *

On the drive back to drop Charles home, I realised I still didn't know why he, usually the most forgiving of men, had been so cool with Rosemary when she'd dropped the crystal skull. But hearing him tell Jay how dog-tired he was, I decided to leave this interrogation until the next day.

The cottage was in darkness when we got there, so I assumed Theo had gone to bed. But Charles surprised us by making an odd request.

'Could you just hang on for a few minutes? Let me make sure everything's okay. I'll come to the door and wave.'

It was wholly out of character for Charles to be nervy. A favourite quote of his had always been, 'The only thing we have to fear is fear itself.'

'Do you want me to go in with you?' said Jay.

'If you wouldn't mind, old man.'

'What's going on?' I asked, as Jay opened the car door five

minutes later.

'Can you believe it? He had a break-in last Sunday. They searched the drawers and cupboards, but they didn't take anything. I asked him what he thought they were looking for but he clammed up. Bit odd, that.'

I tried to visualise a figure searching the cottage. But my 'super powers', as Jay liked to call them, had been wearing thin lately.

Once upon a time I'd been in touch with a sort of supernatural life coach called Enoch who told me that I had the gift of inner knowing (he called it claircognisance), and I should meditate regularly to keep it functioning. But what with my mother dying and Jay's youngest son, Rowan, going through a tearaway teenager phase, I'd been neglecting my meditation practice lately. And without that charge, my battery was dangerously low.

I started the engine up, being the designated driver (to leave the gentlemen free to take a drink), but Jay didn't get in.

'He shouldn't be left alone, Andy. I'll have to crash here tonight.'

'But isn't Theo there?' I wailed, not wanting to be on my own, either, on the night of my mother's funeral.

'He hasn't come in yet. Charles says he sometimes stays out all night.'

I opened my mouth to whinge some more, but closed it again when I saw the concern on Jay's face.

'But you haven't got any of your stuff.'

'Don't worry.' He smiled. 'I'll borrow Charles' toothpaste. You go back. At least you'll get a good night's sleep.' He ruffled my hair as if I were a pet poodle. 'See you tomorrow, hon.'

I kissed him goodbye, waiting until his long-limbed frame disappeared back into the cottage before I drove away.

Chapter 3

Opening Up

Having spent a lonely night in a king-sized bed, I'd overcompensated by consuming a king-sized breakfast and was lying on the former, waiting for the latter to go down, when my phone rang. It was Sharon, Jay's mother, who lived with us.

Some women might baulk at sharing their home with a former mother-in-law, but with Jay's five sons and daughters coming and going, having Sharon around was a godsend.

'Hi, Sha. I was going to ring you...'

'Hello, honey. How was the funeral?'

She allowed me a brief 'Not too bad,' before she galloped on.

'You are coming back today, aren't you? I tried James' cell phone but it's switched off.'

Sharon had taken to calling Jay 'James' having called him 'Jim' for most of his life. He was convinced she did it to annoy him, but you could never tell with Sharon.

Willow, the swot of the family, had looked up the meaning of our names. I already knew that mine meant 'all giving', a name that was proving difficult to live up to since I'd joined the Jay clan. She and her brothers and sister were clearly all named after trees. But Rowan's also meant 'little redhead', which was vaguely appropriate, because he had the lightest hair.

Their mother, Debbie, had been blonde, and I sometimes wondered if she'd ever looked at her young and wished they'd resembled her just a little bit. Shades of Sharon there, I thought, who was as fair as Jay was dark. *And me*, whispered a familiar voice, which I thought I recognised as my mother's. But it couldn't have been, as I *had* inherited her dark hair and green eyes, if not her hourglass figure.

Willow found that her father's name, James, meant

18

'supplanter' which he wasn't too keen on. So he asked her to look up Jay, and it turned out that in Hindi it translated as 'victorious'.

'That settles it then,' he said, looking pointedly at Sharon.

But Sharon had refused to budge. She probably didn't like the idea that her son preferred an Indian name over a British one, even though fifty per cent of his DNA was entitled to it.

'It boils down to the same thing, doesn't it?' she'd huffed. 'The victor supplants the loser...'

Sharon barking down the phone bumped me back to the moment.

'Pandora. Can you hear me? You're coming home today, aren't you?'

'Yes, of course we are. We've got to say goodbye to Charles first.'

She didn't reply immediately and I sensed she wanted to talk to Jay.

'Jay's not here,' I said, slightly queasy at the scent of trouble. And the fried bread I'd had wasn't helping, either.

'Gone outside for a smoke, I suppose.'

It wasn't the time to go into the highways and byways of the night before, so I didn't contradict her.

'I'm just finishing the packing. Is everyone all right?'

The 'everyone' principally referred to Rowan, who'd been caught in the act of underage drinking the previous weekend and grounded until further notice.

'Well, I don't want to worry you, but he went out last night and his bed hasn't been slept in. *His* phone's switched off as well.'

At nine o'clock on a Saturday morning that didn't surprise me.

'Don't worry, Sha. He must have stayed over at Tom's.'

I tried to sound unconcerned for her sake, but inwardly I was seething. He'd been expressly forbidden to go out in the evenings but he'd ignored this and upset his grandmother in the process. Jay would be furious.

'Is Willow there?'

Willow was in her last year at school, the only other offspring at home at the moment. Cherry was at university and Ashley and Linden occupying our flat in Fulham – Ashley still slogging away at his medical studies, Linden an unpaid intern.

'Yes, I'll put her on.'

'Hi, Mum. You and Dad okay?'

It was four years since I'd come to live with them, but I still got a thrill when Willow or Rowan called me 'Mum'. This was what Jay had wanted, but seemed a bit hard on dead Debbie, their real mother. The older boys called me 'Andy' and Cherry veered between the two.

'We're fine, darling. But what's happened to Rowan? Do you know where he is?

She lowered her voice. 'I don't think he's at Tom's.'

'Where is he then?'

'He's got a girlfriend. He might be with her. But you didn't hear it from me. Okay?'

My blood ran cold. Out all night with a girl. And him with his adolescent hormones at full throttle.

'Is she a girl from school?

(Not that that would guarantee any degree of rectitude, as her hormones would presumably be uploading at the same speed as his.)

'No, she works...'

Willow broke off at that point as Sharon's voice pierced the air, making it all the way to my eardrum.

'Where on earth have you been without letting anyone know? You'd better speak to Pandora. She's on the phone and she knows you've been out all night.'

There was a bit of a pause and then, 'Hi, Mum.'

Hearing his easy-going drawl, my anger evaporated; irresponsible and thoughtless he might be, but he could charm the birds off the trees.

'Rowan,' I said, trying to sound stern. 'Why did you go out last night? You know you weren't supposed to.'

'I thought you and Dad wouldn't mind me going to a friend's party. But it got late and I didn't have the money for a taxi, so I slept on the floor in a spare bedroom. A few of us did.'

This sounded feasible, but was it true?

'Whose party was it?'

'Oh, just a girl we know.'

'Were her parents there? Where does she live?'

'She lives...'

He stopped in mid sentence.

'So how did you get home, in the end?'

'I got a lift.'

I waited for him to tell me who from, but again, silence.

I decided to defer the cross-examination until later. He might tell me more if there were only the two of us. For now, I needed to check out of the hotel and be on my way.

'I've got to go now. We'll talk when I get home. And you must say sorry to Grandma. Imagine how she felt when she saw your bed hadn't been slept in.'

'You won't tell Dad, will you?' he said, in a husky whisper. 'You know he'll freak out.'

I pictured the pleading in his big brown eyes and nearly caved in, but who was I to deny Jay authority over his own bloodline?

'I have to, darling. Grandma will tell him anyway.' I lowered my voice. 'Make sure you're nice to her and then she'll stick up for you.'

* * *

When I finally reached the cottage, I found all three men in the kitchen, chatting over tea and bacon sandwiches. I kissed Jay and Charles and joined them at the table.

Jay leaned forward and put his head on one side, so I knew something ironic was coming.

'Did you miss me, wife?'

'What do you think? I had a king-sized bed all to myself. And breakfast in my room. Heaven.' I flashed my eyes at him so he knew I was joking about it being heaven without him. 'Where did *you* sleep?'

The cottage had one double and one single bedroom, plus what could only be described as a box room. Assuming Theo occupied the single room, I guessed that Jay's lanky frame had been overhanging a Spartan folding bed with the skinniest of mattresses, no doubt accounting for his bleary eyes.

Jay gave me a wink.

'I got the dodgy bed. Theo was out all night, but he made it back in time for breakfast.' Jay glanced at Theo, who shifted his eyes away from Jay's. 'At two o'clock this morning, my back was giving me so much gyp, I nearly hijacked his bed.'

I laughed.

'He would have got a surprise if he'd come back and found you in it.'

Theo gave a nervous smile.

'That's usually the cat's trick.'

'You would've been better off in the donkey shelter with Beau,' I laughed.

'Funny you should say that. I went out in the garden to have a fag in the middle of the night, and I must say, I was tempted.'

Charles cleared his throat and we took that as a sign to settle down and be quiet. He'd put his cream suit trousers back on, despite them being muddied from his fall and sprinkled with black cat hairs, and I felt a pang of compassion for a man who no longer had his woman around to monitor what he was wearing.

'First, I'd like to thank you for the support you all gave me yesterday. And I must apologise for keeping Jay here. He insisted on staying, even though I told him I was fine.'

'So what about this break-in, Charles? Any idea who it might have been?' I said, my curiosity knowing no bounds.

His forehead creased at the memory and it didn't surprise me when, with a noncommittal shrug, he changed the subject.

'Theo has something to tell you, Pandora.'

Bemused, I sat in silence while Theo proceeded to reveal his secret, or rather, my mother's secret.

'My dad used to be a movie actor. You may have heard of him. Earl Cramer?'

I shook my head. Theo spoke in a subdued tone, as if breaking bad news.

'In 1975 your mother worked in a pub in Chelsea? Is that right?'

I nodded. In February of that year I'd married Jay and she'd come to the wedding alone, being between boyfriends. By that time my parents had got divorced and she was living and working at the Unicorn in the King's Road.

'My dad was over here making a movie. When they met he'd just finished filming; he stopped off in London before he went back to LA – to his wife and family.'

My mother Frankie had left my father when I was seventeen and gone on to cut a swathe through a steady succession of boyfriends until she'd finally settled down with Charles. I had a feeling that Theo intended to reveal an illicit romance between his pa and my ma. Hadn't Charles said something about a letter? I was not at all surprised and more than a little intrigued. Maybe the movie star had written to her declaring she'd been the love of his life. Although getting his son to deliver it would have been a little bizarre, to say the least.

Theo had paused, probably to let the words 'wife and family' sink in.

'Go on,' I said. 'I have a feeling you're going to tell me they had a fling.'

'You got it. My dad went back home.' He paused, watching me intently. 'And nine months later I was born.'

My brain refused to accept this piece of information and I heard myself saying, 'That's impossible. Don't you think I'd have known if she'd had a baby?' I did a quick calculation. 'Anyway, she'd have been forty-seven, for goodness' sake.'

Three pairs of eyes surveyed me, each with varying degrees of pity.

'It is medically possible for a woman of that age to give birth,' said Charles, always the clever clogs.

'As it goes, I don't remember Frankie being around much the first year we were married,' said Jay, joining forces with him.

'She did confirm to me she was my mother,' chipped in Theo. 'That's why my dad wanted me to find her. So we could meet up before she...before it might be too late.'

Two large tears rolled down his cheeks and he brushed them away with his shirt sleeve. And then it was my turn to pity *him*, so I suggested he removed himself to the sofa in the living room and while he composed himself, I searched my memory banks to see what Frankie had been doing in 1975 because I still found it hard to believe what he'd told me.

But my brain-combing was interrupted by a hammering on the back door, which turned out to be Pete. He looked surprised to see us all there. Maybe he thought Jay or Theo should have been helping him place the turves on the grave, now that the earth had settled. He shifted from one foot to the other, wringing his hands.

'There's no easy way to say this, folks. It's a terrible thing. Some bastard's interfered with the coffin. They've dug out the soil and opened it up.'

Charles immediately leapt up. I could see he was trembling, so I stood beside him.

'Have they touched the body?' I said.

I couldn't believe how normal my voice sounded when I felt so distraught.

'Doesn't look like it. I'd say they were trying to find something. Did she have anything valuable buried with her, Charlie? Jewellery or some such?'

Charles had begun pacing up and down.

'Only her wedding ring.'

My mother had been married just once – to my father, which meant that Charles must have placed this ring on my mother's finger after her death, a gesture which I found incredibly touching.

Jay moved towards the back door and we all took his lead and walked quickly through the garden to the eastern side of the paddock where we found a pile of earth beside the grave. The coffin lay in the hole, wedged to one side with its lid removed.

Jay lay flat on the grass beside the grave and Theo squatted behind him, holding his legs while he leaned over to check if our poor mother's body had been interfered with. Charles and I clutched each other's hands as we waited for Jay's verdict.

'No sign of any disturbance to the body. And she's still got her wedding ring.'

As one, Charles and I took a great gulp of relief.

Jay got to his feet and said softly to Charles, 'Do you want to call the police?'

Pete thought he should and Charles looked as if he agreed with him, but changed his mind when Theo said, 'If we put the earth back now, who's to know any different? If the police get involved it'll be in the papers and your privacy'll be invaded, man.'

'But who would have done this. And why?' I demanded. 'And what if they come back again? We should report it to somebody.'

Jay came over and hugged me, whispering, 'Let him decide, Andy. It might be connected to the break-in. But he never reported that either.'

Charles gave a deep sigh. 'Best fill it in. Whoever they are, they've seen what they want isn't here. No point in getting the police involved.'

'The Man from Del Monte, he say no,' said Jay, in a voice so low only I could hear, and I had to turn away so the others wouldn't see me smiling through my tears.

Leaving them to bury my mother for the second time, I went into the cottage for a think. Once they got back, Jay found a bottle of brandy and we all had a shot. But when he reached for the bottle again, I had to stop him.

'You'd better not. You're driving.'

He grinned. 'Thought I'd let you drive.'

'I can't come back with you, Jay.' Seeing the disappointment in his eyes, I wavered, but I knew where my duty lay. 'I need to stay here for a couple of days. It'll give me a chance to get to know Theo. And...' I sent eye signals to him, hoping he'd understand that I wanted to try to get to the bottom of what was going on. '...I think it's the best thing to do in the circumstances.'

I don't know if he cottoned on, but his answer indicated he had my best interests at heart. 'If that's what you want, but there's one condition. You get the guest bed, not the camp bed.'

I knew from experience that the guest bed wasn't much better, but Jay needed to win this battle, so I gave Theo an entreating look.

'No problem,' said Theo, 'I can stay at a friend's.'

'Is that all right, then, Charles?' I said, aware that I'd invited myself to stay.

'Of course it is, Pandora. Life is full of mysteries. Theo can explain the mystery of his birth to you. Frankie never told me she had a second child. I don't think she ever told anybody. It seems that no one knew her completely.'

Chapter 4

Secrets Unearthed

As soon as Jay roared away, the atmosphere relaxed slightly. The way he'd immediately got my overnight bag out of the boot of the car and plonked it at the bottom of the stairs when I said I was staying, indicated that he minded more than he'd let on.

I put his bad humour down to the recent trauma of a birthday ending in a zero. I purposely hadn't got him a card with the dreaded number, nor a hot air balloon ride, as suggested by Sharon. She'd lived in Canada for most of her adult life and her ideas tended to turn to the great outdoors.

He'd often joked about wanting a Cartier Tank watch. I'd like to have surprised him with one, but he had more chance of playing the O2 Arena than receiving a designer timepiece from a woman who was still paying for her latest garden installation.

I'd actually solved the problem of a present by contacting the editor of a women's magazine, months earlier, with an idea for a feature on men approaching sixty who were still hot. I gave her a list, my top three being: Jeff Bridges, Richard Gere and Jay, providing her with his most flattering photograph and a suitably embroidered update on the state of his career. Luckily, she took the bait. As a result, the birthday boy was well chuffed with the latest issue of *Barbarella* tied up with a big red bow.

On the other hand, the joke inflatable Zimmer frame from Rowan found its way straight to the dustbin, along with various mugs emblazoned with the forbidden number, and a barbecue apron saying, *Now I'm 60, can't somebody else do the cooking?* The only reference I made to his age, was the dedication on his card: *To my sexy genarian.* He didn't seem to mind that.

I'd walked with him from Charles' cottage to the car to say goodbye and he'd regarded me mournfully, his frame still hunched from its recent trauma.

'I froze to death last night with no one to keep me warm. Now I've got two more nights on my own.'

I kissed his stubbly cheek.

'At least you'll be sleeping on a pocket-sprung memory foam mattress.'

My other birthday gift to him had been a four-poster bed, so I was familiar with the terminology.

'It won't be the same without you, babe.'

'Hasn't there been enough earth-moving for you lately, darlin'?' I said, mock seductively, as he got into the car.

He usually smiled when I imitated the way he said 'darling', but this time he put his foot down and zoomed off. It was then I realised I'd forgotten to tell him about Rowan, so he was going home unprepared, which made me feel even worse.

When I came back in, I found Charles preparing to leave for Gaia's Cave. He'd arranged for Sonia, his trusty assistant, to be in charge today, but after the morning's drama he'd decided to get away from the house for a few hours. As they left, I heard him and Pete arranging to meet up when Charles finished work, and I began to wonder what I'd do with myself if Theo decided to abscond as well.

'I'm going for a walk. You wanna come?'

Theo's invitation prompted a rush of relief and I was ready in a flash. The day was bright, so we decided to climb to the top of the Tor. When we started out, I was still full of agitation at the unearthing of my mother's remains, but as we passed the Chalice Well Gardens, my mood began to lift.

By the time we reached the summit, where St Michael's Tower stands, the weather had worsened to wet and blustery, but the panorama below us of knolls, levels, hills and downs, made the gale-force conditions bearable.

After our eyes had their fill of the views and our ears their fill of the winds, Theo suggested taking the other path down, which in due course led us through a green meadow. From there he took us over stiles, down lanes, past a campsite, across the levels, eventually to arrive, via a quiet back lane, into town.

Once there, Theo suggested having lunch at the Flying Horse. This suited me, as I was in no hurry to return to the scene of the crime.

Up to then, our conversation had been pretty run of the mill, mostly about the Tor and the town. It had become plain to me that I'd get nowhere if I waited for *him* to spill the beans regarding his life thus far, so once our ploughman's lunches were placed in front of us, I got down to business.

'So, Theo, where were you born and who brought you up?'

His face assumed the shy smile he was so good at.

'I thought you'd never ask.'

My heart softened, for the first time feeling a connection with him.

'That's why we Brits know so little about each other. We're too polite to ask and too reserved to tell.'

'In that case, I'll be calling on my California genes to reveal all.'

He chewed on a mouthful of crusty bread for a few moments and then began.

'The bald truth is that my dad, Earl, and your mom, Frankie, probably had a one-night stand. It wasn't much more...he was only in London for a few days. When she found out she was pregnant she contacted him via the studio and they passed on her letter. She said she couldn't keep the baby – due to her age, circumstances, no proper home. Earl said she also told him she had a daughter in her twenties who'd just got married...'

I felt a thought-bubble appear above my head containing a notion that had only just germinated. *Why didn't she offer you to me?*

And then I pictured an alternative reality, where Jay and I had brought up Theo. We didn't know then I couldn't have children, but we'd both been dying to start a family, so we'd have taken him like a shot. Having him would have kept us on the straight and narrow, off the drugs and booze. Being unable to have our own children wouldn't have mattered so much. We'd probably have adopted more kids so he wouldn't be an only child, as we both had been.

Before I got totally carried away with this scenario, my mother's voice butted in.

But how would I have felt? And you'd still only have been a pretend mother...

She was right, the situation would have been impossible, but it didn't stop me feeling sad and angry that she'd let him go so easily.

Theo had paused for my comments and I wondered if he'd been thinking the same as me. Growing up in the UK would have produced an alternative version of Theo, one with a British accent, different education, memories – the result of being in touch with a very different strand of his genealogical DNA.

'Anyway,' he continued, 'she said that as she didn't agree with abortion, she'd go ahead and have the baby and then put it up for adoption, but she needed to be supported financially through the pregnancy. Luckily for me, Uncle Earl – I grew up calling him that – arranged for Frankie to come to LA when she was three months pregnant.'

He'd resumed his attack on his ploughman's and I reined in my curiosity until he finished.

'Where did she stay?'

'He rented a house for her in Hollywood Hills, near his sister, Martha. He opened up to her, and she volunteered to take care of me. Her son Felix was named as father on my birth certificate. That way, it didn't create a problem for Earl.'

'So that's why your name's Johnson?'

'Yeah.'

'How old was Felix?'

'Twenty-three.'

My nose wrinkled in disgust at the thought of my mother, as a mature *gravida*, linked in a public document to a youth of twenty-three.

Theo's eyes were full of sympathy.

'I always assumed my mom to be roughly the same age as Felix. I only found out myself a few months ago. From Earl. When he told me *he* was my dad.'

I found it incredible that he hadn't discovered the truth before that.

'So who did you think your mother was?'

'I knew she was British and her name was Frances. She used to send me birthday cards and gifts, but they stopped when I hit eighteen. I never met her all that time. That was the deal.'

'The deal?'

'Earl made a deal with her that she wouldn't see me in his lifetime.'

I gasped.

'But how could he stop her from seeing you?'

His eyes hardened, quashing my indignation with his words. 'The deal was financial.'

I felt my face colour. To discover that my mother had signed away all access to her son for monetary gain made me ashamed to be her daughter. No wonder she'd kept Theo's arrival a secret because she thought I wouldn't approve. She'd got that right. I didn't.

'And did you ever contact her?'

Theo blinked, and stared at his beer.

'I wrote the occasional thank-you letter. But she said she never got them.'

'How come?'

'I guess I was naive. The family had a PA that dealt with all that. Martha would take the outgoing mail to her. Earl probably told Martha to tear the letters up.'

'But why did they give you the cards and stuff she sent?'

He shrugged.

'I don't know. Maybe because it was my birthday. Maybe to stop me asking about my mother...who knows? Martha's long gone. There's no one left who'd know the answer.'

He looked sad for the first time and I experienced a rush of sorrow for him. And, unexpectedly, for Frankie, too. I was glad that she'd seen him before she died, so he'd been able to explain that he *had* written to her.

'When were you born?'

'December 1975.'

'Did Earl visit Frankie in LA?'

'I don't think so. It wasn't just his marriage he was protecting, he was worried any bad publicity might rock the boat with the studio. And the public.'

I pictured my mother hidden away in an ivory tower, knowing no one, killing time for six months, and then having to abandon a tiny baby. My eyes filled with tears at the thought of those intense postnatal hormones screaming out to cherish and protect him. By now I was weeping and Theo was looking rattled. Luckily, our table was tucked away in a corner.

When my tears had calmed down, I heard myself ask, 'Did you have a happy childhood?'

'Yeah, I guess. Did I mention that Earl's wife was white? Their kids are mixed race like me, so I fitted right in with that part of the family.'

'Didn't she ever suspect anything?'

'Why would she? Far as she was concerned I was Martha's grandson. Earl had two brothers with kids...it was open house at his place. He had the biggest pool, the latest home cinema. Us kids had a great time.'

The little green monster on my shoulder whispered that my half-brother's childhood had been a sight more privileged than my North London one. And less lonely.

He talked some more about those times, and how he'd seen little of his surrogate father because Felix moved to New York shortly after his birth.

'Did you ever call him "Dad"?' I asked.

'No. He told me to call him Felix.'

'Didn't Earl's wife and the others think that strange?'

'They never mentioned it. I guess they thought I was a young guy's mistake and it was best to let his mother take over. When you're a kid you don't question stuff. But he was cool. Always took me to a Lakers game when he came to town.'

All at once he seemed to run out of steam, gulping his beer and staring into space. In the silence, I tried hard to recall what Frankie had pretended to be doing, when all the time she was actually in the States, pregnant with him. After a while, I resumed my inquiries.

'Your birthday's in December, so she must have conceived in March.'

'Guess so.'

Understandably, the topic of his conception caused Theo to blush.

'She didn't have a regular boyfriend at that time. Her previous one, Richard, had gone to prison for fraud. She'd had to move out of their apartment, because he'd bought it with stolen money. That's why she was living above the pub.'

Theo raised his eyebrows.

'So when she met my dad she was down on her luck...until she got pregnant.'

'And turned herself into a cash cow,' I finished.

We stared at each other in disbelief.

'Do you think she might have got pregnant on purpose, Theo?'

'Your guess is better than mine. You knew her. What do you think?'

I uttered a laugh which can only be described as hollow. I

wouldn't put anything past Frankie. At the time, she'd been stuck in a dead-end job, in accommodation well below what she was used to and, worst of all, no man.

'Well, it does make you wonder why she didn't use contraception. Or ask Earl to.'

Both of us made yuck-faces at the thought of it.

'Maybe being in her late forties, she assumed she was safe,' I said.

Theo shook his head, as if refusing any gynaecological speculation to sully his ear canals, and voiced what had been puzzling me, too.

'So, how come you didn't wonder about her all the time she was away?'

'I don't know. I vaguely remember she wasn't around at Christmas. I'm just trying to think what reason she gave.'

Theo got up to get some drinks and I mined deeper into my memory banks, to no avail. For Jay and me, December1975 had been our first Christmas as man and wife. Where had we spent it? Trouble was, by then we'd slipped into a drug habit and there were periods which were just a blur. I'd have to ask Jay the next time I spoke to him. His blurs might have occurred at different intervals from mine.

The thought of him made me feel guilty. He'd be getting home about now and here was I, on the lash at lunchtime. Just like the old days.

Theo placed four bottles of beer on the table.

'Saves going back,' he grinned, pushing a bottle towards me. 'Have you remembered how your mom explained away the second half of 1975 yet?'

A bunch of neurons must have fired deep in my hippocampus, because a memory of my mother enthusing over a job at sea flashed into my mind.

'Wait. I think she said she'd got a job as a floating croupier.'

'I'm sorry?'

Theo was probably imagining her swimming around with an inflated rubber roulette wheel.

'On a cruise ship. She said she had to go on a training course first, and then she'd be off to the Caribbean.'

'Neat.'

Theo obviously approved of our mother's ability to lie convincingly.

'So that solves that mystery.'

We both took a good swig of beer. I would have preferred a gin and tonic, a pleasure I'd sacrificed to get down with my kid brother. I didn't want him thinking his big sis was too uptight to drink from a bottle. But I still had work to do. We'd dealt with the distant past, what about more recent events?

'So tell me about her reaction when you turned up here.'

'It was tough for her at first. When she read Earl's letter she got a bit emotional, but she was fine after that. And Charles was really chilled, considering it was the first he'd ever heard of me. They invited me to stay. You know the rest...'

'What did the letter say?'

'I never saw it but I got the impression it was a sort of apology. Y'know? For keeping us apart so long. And an introduction, so she'd know I was her son.'

At that moment a waitress appeared with a speciality of the house, a Bambi burger made with ground venison, along with some French fries. Theo was proving to have as big an appetite as Rowan.

'*Bon appétit*,' I said, smiling, as he reached for the ketchup. 'So what's next for you?'

I wasn't sure what I wanted to hear. I'd warmed to him, but being kept in ignorance of his existence had left me feeling duped. This meant that part of me hoped he'd tell me he was leaving for the States imminently, and another part hoped he'd say that now he'd met Jay and me, he liked us so much he wanted to hang around for a bit.

'I'm staying on for a while.'

He studied my face to assess my reaction and I found myself grinning.

'Good. You should come to our house. Meet the kids. Although, technically speaking, you and I aren't actually related to them by blood.'

Now it was my turn to check out *his* reaction.

'Yeah, that'd be fun. We'll have to do it some time.'

Disappointed, I told him a little about Jay's children, but he'd become engrossed in his Bambi burger and simply nodded distractedly from time to time. Reluctantly concluding that he wasn't interested, I changed tack.

'We've got an organic fruit-and-veg business.'

Theo took a slug of beer to wash down the deer, but still didn't reply.

'And we've got a few animals as well...'

'Are you kidding? What, you slaughter them?'

I don't know whose face wore the more horrified expression, his or mine.

'Of course not. I never said I lived on a farm. I mean we've got pets.'

He had the grace to look apologetic.

'Sorry. So what do you have?'

'There's my dog, Oscar; Fritz, Jay's pointer; two goats; some little chickens called silkies; and a couple of rabbits. Oh, and Midnight, the Welsh cob.'

'The Welsh what?'

'Cob. A small horse. Small but strong, with the head of a lady and the backside of a cook.'

My words had the desired effect of grabbing his attention.

'Nice,' he grinned. 'Where do you keep her?'

'In a farmer's field at the end of our garden. There used to be some ponies as well when Debbie, the children's mother, was alive.'

After a pause, he said, 'Frankie told me that Jay used to be in a band and you two were married, then you split, now you're back together. But she said she didn't...'

He hesitated and I guessed why, so I finished his sentence.

'...She didn't like him. She made that perfectly plain to me, don't worry. It's because he got Debbie pregnant. That's why we split up. And she thought he was a bad influence.'

Theo nodded as I said this, as if he'd heard all about the drink, drugs and über-partying that had gone on.

'When my husband died, we hooked up again. That was four years ago.'

'Your husband? Now I'm confused.'

I always had this trouble explaining the sequence of my relationship with Jay, which was marriage, divorce, my marriage to Mike, widowhood, and full circle back to living with Jay.

'I got divorced from Jay when I was thirty-three. I married my second husband, Mike, in 2000 but he died suddenly, in 2003. And Jay's children lost their mother, Debbie, around the same time.'

'So you and Jay both suffered tragedies.'

'Actually, mine *was* a tragedy. Jay and Debbie split up two years before she died, so it was more their children's tragedy than his.'

'Why did they split?'

I hesitated. I didn't want to blacken Jay's reputation, but neither did I want to lie.

'She found out he'd slept with the girl who helped with the ponies.'

Theo's eyes widened in shock, so I leapt to Jay's defence.

'Not a girl really, he said she was in her late twenties. Anyway, Debbie left him, he bought her a place down the road and they shared the kids. Sharon's husband had died a year or so earlier so she came back from Vancouver to help Jay.'

'So when you guys got together it kinda spread the load.'

It was clear what he was getting at. Having me around the place had eased the burden on Jay and Sharon, for sure, but in return it had given me the family I'd always wanted. And (something Theo would find hard to understand) it had been my duty as a graduate of the Enoch Society Correspondence Course to take them all on.

'Believe me, Jay's a good guy. Frankie and I didn't agree on a few things, and Jay was one of them.'

I wondered what else Frankie had said about me and Jay, what spin she'd put on it. Theo was lost in thought, as if sifting through what he'd already been told.

After a short while, he raised his eyes and asked, almost shyly, 'Are you a churchgoer?'

'Not now. They say "Once a Catholic, always a Catholic" but it's not true in my case. I'm a great fan of Christ, but not of most of the organisations set up in his name.'

He seemed reassured when I mentioned the C-word.

'Uh, Frankie was really into the supernatural, wasn't she? It's not something I'm used to. I was raised a regular Baptist.'

He looked hurt when I burst out laughing.

'If you believe in God, you believe in a supernatural being, Bro.'

'I know that, *Sis*, but I had esoteric stuff in mind.'

'You mean crystals and angel cards?'

'More than that. I'm talking about the group she joined with Rosemary.'

I thought back to the Harvest Moon ceremony I'd attended in 2003 when she and Charles and their old hippie friends had danced around Rosemary's garden under the influence of cider, while Rosemary, part-time dentist and 'energy alchemist' had channelled the Goddess of Plenty, or whichever deity presides over such high jinks.

'It's all harmless stuff. They just celebrate the ancient festivals taken over and renamed by the Christian Church. They might be called "pagan" or "Celtic" but they're honouring nature basically. That's why Rosemary calls it "natural magic". She means the magic of nature.'

Then I remembered the one-to-one session I'd had with Rosemary that same weekend. 'Rosemary's very switched-on and I can recommend her healing sessions if ever you...'

I stopped, because he'd abruptly excused himself and made off in the direction of the men's loos.

While he was gone, I thought through my next line of enquiry. I had no idea of his occupation, or if he had one at all. Maybe he'd led the life of a rich kid. So when he got back, I wasted no time.

'What do you do for a living, by the way?'

He relaxed, probably relieved that I wasn't still trying to push him in the direction of Rosemary's therapy table.

'Not much at the moment, apart from being Beau's groom.'

I softened at the mention of Beau, but kept my focus.

'What do you do in LA? You're not a professional donkey wrangler, that's for sure. Are you in the movie business, like Earl?'

'I *was*.'

'Did you get much work?'

'Uh, yeah. Until I fell off a horse. I did stunt work mainly.'

'That must have been dangerous.'

He shrugged. 'Well, I was good at sports, into martial arts, fast cars, motorbikes. Earl knew the right people and he got me trained.'

'So you don't do it anymore?'

'Had to retire a year ago. Insurance company wouldn't cover me after the accident.'

'I'm sorry,' I said automatically.

'Don't be. It had its highs but it could get boring. Most of the time I was hanging round the set.'

'So, are you still recuperating?'

'I guess so.'

'All the more reason to try some of Rosemary's therapy.'

He didn't respond to that, or offer any further details, so I slogged on. As his big sister, didn't I have the right to ask intrusive questions?

'Have you got any ideas for an alternative career?'

'Not really. I always planned to train stunt horses, but I'd have to be fit enough to ride.'

A shadow passed across his face and I put my hand on his arm in sympathy, which seemed to embarrass him.

'Money's not a problem, so I'm having some time out.' He stifled a yawn as if all this talking had tired him out. 'I can stay here up to six months. I'll head home then. My uncle's an agent. He'll find me something when I'm ready.'

I had a feeling he was fobbing me off and wondered why he showed such little appetite for work. I took a swig of beer, giving him a chance to make the next conversational move.

'Why don't you tell me a bit more about yourself and Frankie? And about *your* dad?'

So we passed the rest of the time on my potted autobiography, and an edited version of Frankie's. I chose to drop the names of a few of her better-known suitors: a psychedelic artist, two authors and a sculptor, omitting to reveal the assortment of tradesmen she'd hooked up with. Jay used to say she ricocheted from the sublime to the cor-blimey. I had to admit that the snob in me had been glad Theo had sprung from the loins of an exotic variety, rather than a common-or-garden plumber or roofer.

Tiring of the Flying Horse, we made our way to the abbey, where we walked past the cider orchard to the ponds and back to clear our heads. We sat on a bench in the fading light until they closed the grounds. On the way home, Theo's attention was caught by something on the notice board of a church. I followed him to the side door, which was answered by a housekeeper, who left us in a small waiting room while she checked if the vicar was free. A few minutes later, she returned and conducted Theo to a room deeper within the building. He came back looking pleased with himself.

'Have you suddenly been struck by a religious vocation?' I asked.

The day had such a surreal feel that I didn't even know if I was joking.

'Nah,' he said. 'They're looking for help with one of their services. I put my name down.'

When we eventually got back to the house, we found Charles and Pete drinking whisky and eating pasty and chips smothered in brown sauce. The kitchen smelled of stale cat food. Charles had said that Anubis had been pining for Frankie and was off her food. A closer inspection of the cat's dish revealed it to be encrusted with the remnants of last week's offerings, so that didn't surprise me.

'There's some in the oven for you two,' Charles slurred.

This weekend I'd seen a new Charles. Was this really the man who'd been a devout vegetarian, making soup from scratch and insisting that only organic matter passed his lips?

I declined his offer, so Theo devoured the remaining pasties and then excused himself to go to stay the night with his friend.

When he'd gone I asked Charles who the friend was, but he pretended not to hear me, so I asked him again. Waving his hands, he said, 'I thought it rude to ask, Pandora. But I have a feeling it might be a *wench*,' the explosive emphasis on the last word being the result of a hefty belch.

Having had my fill of males guzzling and gorging, I took myself up to the guest bedroom to watch the small TV in peace, leaving the pair of them downstairs, cackling like two old hyenas.

Chapter 5

Quantum Healing

Lying in bed the next morning, I thought of another Sunday, in the autumn of 2003, when I'd woken up in this room, little knowing it was to be one of the most important days of my life. After an energy healing session with Rosemary, I'd confided to Frankie and Charles that I had a supernatural friend, Enoch, who I communicated with via automatic writing. And that a disembodied voice (who turned out to be Archangel Cassiel, whose lesson for humans was, wait for it, selflessness), had enrolled me in the Enoch Society Correspondence Course for soul transformation and enlightenment.

At the time, I'd been trying to decide whether to go ahead and complete the third and final level of the course. According to the blurb, if I followed the instructions, I'd be reborn like a phoenix. This new, improved self would then automatically be charged with the task of raising the energy of any person or situation that crossed her path. In other words, after submitting to reprogramming, I'd be locked in to what amounted to a lifetime of all-singing, all-dancing, all-giving piety with no get-out clause.

As dedicated New Agers, Frankie and Charles had been encouraging on that count. But I'd also been rash enough to divulge to Frankie that I was thinking of ringing Jay, and she'd been dead set against me making contact.

In spite of her opposition – or, who knows, maybe because of it – as soon as I got back to Phoenix Cottage, I made the call. I hadn't spoken to Jay since our divorce, eighteen years before, but Zac, the man I was seeing at the time, had recently told me that Debbie, mother of his five children, had been killed in a car accident, and I was gripped by a compulsion to contact him. I wish it had been possible to feel sorrier about her death, but her hostile takeover of my husband wasn't something I'd been readily able to forgive. When Jay let on that he and Debbie had split up a couple of years before she died, I'd struggled to stop myself cheering.

On discovering that I was single too, Jay came to see me, declaring he'd like to try again. I acquiesced, and by the spring of 2004 we'd merged and I'd acquired a readymade family of saplings, as Jay called them.

As for the spiritual shenanigans, I talked it through with Jay and he was all for it. I suspect that the vision of me wielding a high-voltage lightsaber, in a skin-tight, super-heroine catsuit, turned him on. In the end, I had serious second thoughts about proceeding with the final unit. Enoch had warned me that 'taking on the mantle' brought with it responsibilities. And that I'd have to devote my life to helping others, often in ways that would go unrecognised. But the benefit, he said, would be the fulfilment of my true purpose in life.

I went ahead mainly because Jay had sacrificed a proper honeymoon so I could spend an hour or so every night for two weeks in guided meditation, culminating in a final download at the full moon, which sealed my fate.

When I emerged from my study in Phoenix Cottage after that last session, I think Jay expected me to fly around the room like Tinker Bell. But I hadn't grown wings. I didn't look any different at all and, to be honest, didn't really feel much different.

Shortly after that, I moved in properly with Jay and family life turned out to be so all-consuming that there was little chance to sit like a yogi intoning 'Om'. So I decided to trust what my former tutors Enoch and Cassiel had told me: energy always follows thought, and by consciously keeping my thoughts and feelings positive, I was supporting and entraining others. And that's what I tried to do.

But I still felt in need of more guidance, and in the first months after what the correspondence course had called my 'enlightenment ceremony', I made time to sit with pad and paper in an effort to resume contact with Enoch. I wanted to ask him if there was anything else I should be doing, but he never turned up at Four Seasons, our family home, and I was always left staring at a blank sheet of paper.

In the autumn of 2004 my former home, Phoenix Cottage, was expecting its first tenant and needed a spruce-up, so I used that as an excuse to spend a night there, in the hope that my celestial correspondent would prefer a familiar venue. I settled in my study with Oscar at my feet and sat in meditation for fifteen minutes or so. Then I spoke Enoch's name, poised my pen over the paper, and he finally came through.

Congratulations, dear one. You have chosen well, both in your decision to activate the ascension process and your undertaking to love and cherish six souls.

Assuming he was referring to Jay and his five saplings, I thanked him and he continued.

The ascension process raised your very atoms to higher rates of vibration, allowing you to connect with new levels of your Higher Self. You now have the power to gather sacred knowledge without my presence as an intermediary. My work with you is done. Go well, beloved one.

The pen stopped writing and I experienced the panic of a child on her first day at school, seeing her parent disappear.

'No! Don't go, please! I feel there's something else I should be doing...'

My voice broke on the last word and Oscar raised his head and licked my ankle. The pen twitched and began to scrawl.

Be assured, dear one, you will find your next step by accepting the truth of your purpose. Do not limit yourself by doubt. You have every-thing you need within yourself. Simply ask, and you will receive guidance.

But I wasn't letting him get away that easily.

'Enoch,' I beseeched, 'one last question, please.'

A tick indicated I could go ahead.

'Can you be more specific on how I can assist others? Just in case my higher self has trouble getting through when I'm back at Four Seasons.'

A smiley face appeared, and I was glad that Enoch hadn't lost his sense of humour. The pen danced across the page.

Your divine purpose is to heal on a quantum level. To transform cellular disorder by assisting beings to heal their atomic blueprints of the patterns of distortion they hold, in order to restore the sacred geometry of their form to their original, flawless patterns.

The writing stopped. But the words hadn't meant anything to me. As if reading my mind, the pen explained.

In your parlance, restoring mental, physical and spiritual health to those you treat.

I'd never seen myself as a hands-on healer but it sounded as if that's what he had in mind. I'd done a Reiki course once. Could that be what he meant?

Now he'd started, Enoch kept my writing hand busy with yet more 'science'.

The human body is composed of atoms which form into molecules and thence into cells. Within the atoms are electrons that spin as they orbit the heart of the atom, the nucleus, releasing energy in the form of light. All energy comes from God. So you all carry the Essence of God in your very cells.

The speed at which the electron travels is its rate of vibration, or frequency. The higher the vibration, the more light your body holds – hence the expression 'enlightenment' – and the closer you get to God's original blueprint of Humankind, which He made in His own image.

The pen stopped, allowing me time to absorb the information. I felt I had to respond, so I said the first thing that came into my head.

'So when people talk about raising their vibration, is that what they mean?'

Exactly so. Vibration rate is also affected by negative feelings and thoughts which accumulate in the spaces between the electrons and the nuclei of the atoms. This space then becomes dense with discordant energy, slowing down the rate of vibration.

'So how can people's atoms be cleaned up so they can go faster?'

My hand sprang into action again, the pen impatient to explain.

Saint Germain's Violet Flame of Perfection is a powerful means of transmutation. During your initiation you visualised the blue flame of the Divine Masculine and the pink flame of the Divine Feminine, with the intention of bringing them into equilibrium. When this you did, the two combined to form a violet flame, thus activating the qualities of forgiveness, compassion, and transmutation. This sacred flame, acting as an atomic accelerator, consumed the distortions in every cell of your body, replacing them with patterns of perfection, therefore raising your vibration on the atomic level. Your very essence became filled with light.

You must continue to visualise this flame in meditation, dear one, to keep yourself in your ascended state so you can fulfil the task you have undertaken – to assist others to connect with the Violet Flame and thus restore the sacred geometry of their beings as you have yours.

While this esoteric explanation would no doubt prove helpful once I'd read it over a few times, I still felt the lack of some more concrete instruction, prompting me to wail, 'But how exactly do I do that? I haven't got a manual.'

Did Prince Cassiel not include a teaching for Saint Germain's Violet Flame?

'I don't think so. Otherwise I'd be doing it, wouldn't I? And who's Saint Germain when he's at home?'

I wasn't usually so terse with Enoch, but I was still feeling like a peevish schoolgirl who'd been absent on the day of the biophysics lesson.

Calm yourself, Pandora. Saint Germain is an Ascended Master and Keeper of the Violet Flame. When he trod the Earth in human form he was a master of Alchemy and formulated an Elixir of Life which kept his body youthful. Now ascended, he has gifted his Violet Flame to Humankind to rejuvenate their cells and thus connect them to their Higher Selves. Now take up your pen.

The blank pages in front of me soon became filled with affirmations and invocations to the Violet Flame. The pen drew a line under the final instruction and then added a sort of postscript.

The greater the number of beings who increase their spiritual energy, and thereby their light, the greater the advancement of Humankind, for the enlightened carry others with them. Helping many souls to evolve spiritually is important work indeed, dear one, enabling the whole planet to benefit exponentially. Blessings on your endeavours.

I joined my hands in prayer position and bowed my head in thanks. Healing on a quantum level was a concept I needed to grasp, so I could direct others to use their minds to heal their bodies and souls.

I was beginning to realise what the term 'energy alchemy' meant – it was more or less what the Violet Flame did – transmuting dense, negative energy into positive, light energy at a microscopic level.

Enoch's final tutorial had given me plenty of food for thought. But he hadn't quite finished with me yet. The pen gave a tiny jerk prompting me to grasp it again.

It is your destiny to manifest forth unto the world sound codes of light to assist all beings to remember and return to the original pattern of their atomic structure. This is the gift you hold through your presence.

The pen paused and I groaned.

'Enoch, this is information overload. I'm only just getting used to the Violet Flame. What on earth are sound codes of light?'

But the old gent wasn't giving any more away and the next line was his last.

You will be guided in this, never fear. I wish you Godspeed on your journey, dear one.

After that, the pen didn't just come to rest, as it usually did when Enoch evaporated, it actually propelled itself into the waste basket beside the desk. He'd bolted so quickly, I felt as if I'd been dumped.

'Okay, I get it,' I said. 'It's the end of the road for us.'

Something in the finality of my tone alerted Oscar and he bolted into the kitchen and out through the flap to sprinkle the lawn in readiness for bed.

So that was how, three and a half years ago, my ethereal guru Enoch and I had parted company as penfriends. As it turned out, though, I hardly had time to miss him, what with the twins, Ashley and Linden, coming home from their different universities most weekends, and Rowan, Cherry and Willow permanently on the premises. The girls were fourteen and sixteen at that time, their hormones checking in just as mine were checking out – making for a few explosive situations even Wonder Woman would have found tough to handle.

Since our handfasting ceremony (Jay and I had thought another legal wedding unnecessary), I'd tried hard to master being a mother, ably supported by Sharon, who ran a tight ship. She was often bad cop to my good cop. In contrast, Jay had lately been veering a little too wildly between *laissez-faire* and rod of iron, depending on his increasingly mercurial moods. Rowan would probably be bearing the brunt of his father's displeasure this weekend, what with the staying-out-all-night incident and me being unable to intercede for him.

The faint ringing of my mobile phone had me jumping out of bed and running downstairs. I found it under the cat, who was lounging on Charles' coffee table. I just managed to get to it before it stopped. It was Jay.

'Hi, doll. How you doing?'

'Fine.' I paused so we could enjoy our moment of reconnection. 'I had a good chat with Theo yesterday. But Charles went to work and Pete was here last night, so I didn't have a chance to talk about the break-in. Did he tell you anything?'

'No, just that he could tell the place had been searched but nothing seemed to be missing. How is he?'

'Not too bad. He seems to be coping by drowning his sorrows and eating junk food.' Hearing a footstep, I turned to see Charles coming towards me with a cup of tea in his hand.

'I was just going to take this upstairs to you, Pandora. Give my love to Jay. And if you want to talk to me, you'll find I'm entirely sober.'

He disappeared into his study and I hissed down the phone, 'Did you hear that? He heard what I said.'

Jay chuckled. 'Good luck with your little chat, then.' He paused. 'Hold on a sec.'

I heard him say something in an undertone, probably to Rowan, as the word 'grounded' featured more than once. Then he resumed speaking. 'You ought to have warned me about Rowan. Sharon's not too happy.'

'Sorry, it slipped my mind. I shouldn't have let my mother being turfed out of her coffin and being introduced to an illegitimate sibling get to me...'

Sweetly allowing my sarcasm to wash over him, he said, 'Sure. No worries, babe. We'll talk when you get back. Any idea when that might be? And how?'

That was another thing I'd been considering that morning. Charles didn't seem to need me. And I'd prefer to be getting to know Theo at our house rather than here, where everywhere I looked, I was reminded of Frankie.

'Not sure. I'm going to speak to Charles now. I'll have to get the train home, won't I?'

'Probably best. Gaby's coming over tomorrow. She's booked me for the whole week. But if you really want picking up...'

What could I say? Our home was almost a hundred miles away. And yet I was disappointed he hadn't insisted on coming to get me. Especially as Gaby was a bubbly blonde with a stunning figure. I'd never met her but I'd seen her picture in magazines and tabloids, although not so much recently. She'd approached Jay to co-write some songs. Sales for her last album had been low, and she needed to prove herself to the record label before they'd give her another contract. Jay and his band had split up long ago, but he still wrote for other people in his studio at the back of the house.

The idea of Jay closeted with a beautiful woman for a week sorely tested my powers for dealing with negative emotions. As Enoch had taught me, I tried hard to imagine my heart as a chalice, the bad emotion being consumed by violet fire and replaced by a much higher vibration, like love or joy. Producing love proved a bridge too far, so I made do with sending appreciation to her for giving Jay some work.

I didn't feel a whole lot better immediately, but I knew that if I kept it up, my mood would sooner or later improve and with it, my attitude towards her. Fully aware that this dense emotion of jealousy just clogged up my cells, like bad cholesterol, I forced myself to say something positive to Jay.

'Don't worry, I'll make it home. You concentrate on writing hits for Gaby.'

'Thanks darlin'. I love you.'

'I love you too.'

As my heart filled with love, I realised I'd got there in the end.

Just before we rang off, I remembered something I'd wanted to ask him.

'One thing, Jay. Where did we spend our first Christmas after we got married?'

He thought for a moment.

'Bermuda. Frankie was supposed to join us, but she never turned up. We know why now.'

A few moments later, Charles appeared from his study and sat in the rocking chair opposite me. He took off his glasses, breathed on the lenses, polished them with his slightly grubby hankie, and regarded me with sympathy.

'I couldn't help overhearing, Pandora. Let me elucidate. After Theo turned up, your mother told me he came two weeks later than expected. He was born on Christmas Day. If he'd arrived on time, she would have joined you.'

'It's coming back to me now,' I said, feeling my lips tremble. 'She said she was working on a Caribbean cruise liner and she'd be with us in Bermuda on Christmas Eve, but just after we got there she rang to say she couldn't get the time off. I was so disappointed...'

'When did you eventually see her?'

'She came and stayed with us a few weeks after Christmas. I don't remember noticing anything different about her. That's what's so awful. You'd have thought something like that would have changed her. Leaving a newborn baby and being told she couldn't see him...'

Talking about mothers and children was always a risky business for me, as it tended to bring out my maudlin side.

Charles spotted I was getting weepy, so he nipped it in the bud. 'If it's any consolation, my dear, she told me she wouldn't have changed anything. Theo had a good life and at least he grew up near one of his parents and his wider family. Turning up here, as he did, just before Christmas, meant he and Frankie were able to be together on his birthday at last.'

Theo celebrating not only Christmas, but also his birthday with Frankie, hadn't occurred to me before. And try as I might to feel happy for them both, a swell of disappointment at being left out flooded my heart.

Charles rocked back and forth gently in the chair.

'She would have found the whole middle-aged single mother situation embarrassing, to say the least. And I think you and I would agree, knowing Frankie, far too restricting.'

I was strangely cheered at this. Behold the paradox. Yesterday

I'd been angry at my mother for abandoning her son, yet today, here I was relieved that she hadn't spent years pining for him. Is this, I wondered, how older siblings feel about younger brothers and sisters – acutely jealous in case they're stealing their mother's love? As if on cue, Theo chose that moment to return from wherever he'd spent the night.

'Hi, Charles, Sis. You don't mind if I call you that? I'm not mad on "Pandora".'

'Join the club,' I said. 'It's the story of my life. That's why Jay calls me Andy. Think yourself lucky you're not called Zeus.'

'Yeah, right.' He went into the kitchen and started filling a bucket with cold water.

'Are you going to see Beau?' I called to him, over the noise of the gushing tap. 'Because if you wait for me to get dressed, I'll come with you.'

Chapter 6

Cutting Off

Lock by lock, Beau's matted corkscrew curls fell to the ground, as Theo and I worked either side of him, me with a pair of kitchen scissors, and Theo with shears borrowed from Steve, who had the farm down the lane.

'Glad you suggested this. Their skin gets itchy under all that hair, been meaning to do it ever since we got here. Big Guy needed a trim, huh?'

This last remark had been addressed to Beau, who had turned his head towards Theo and was nuzzling his shoulder as he bent down to clip away the soft, gingery coils. I resisted the urge to drop my scissors and hug Beau's magnificent neck, having already petted him half to death when we first brought him fresh water.

That was when I'd whispered in his enormous ear, 'Would you like a haircut, sweet boy?' And he'd lowered his magnificent head, as if giving a nod, fluttering breath through his nostrils as he did so. When he meekly allowed us to fit his head collar, I took that as a yes.

We worked on until the pile of hair was the size of a large molehill. Theo then produced some impressive clippers, also borrowed, and soon there stood before us a donkey whose full conformation could be admired in all its perfect symmetry. Perfect in my eyes, at least.

'You've lost a few kilos without giving up a single carrot. Even your belly seems to have shrunk,' I cooed, as I brushed him.

Beau gave me a gentle tap with his huge foot in appreciation, just as Theo reappeared after disposing of the hair clippings.

'He looks great, doesn't he, with his spring cut?' I said, retrieving the scissors from the ground and waving them in

Theo's direction. 'How about you? D'you fancy shedding your dreads as well?'

Tossing his head as if trying to get rid of a troublesome mosquito, Theo took hold of Beau's lead rope. *Uh-oh*, I thought, *looks like I've hit a nerve.*

'Come on, boy, time for your date with Flossy. We're done here,' said Theo.

Flossy was a pony belonging to Steve. As Beau had no playmates, he'd said he could visit her any time, for company and a change of scene.

'I'll tag along with you two.'

So the three of us walked sedately out of the paddock, along the lane and into the farm. On the way, I broached the subject of Theo coming home with me the next day but his expression told me that he wasn't too keen.

'It's not a great time to leave Charles alone.'

'He's okay with it. I've already sounded him out. He said he'd take care of Beau.'

Theo's face had the expression of a teenager who'd been told he had to visit his great aunt Mildred instead of going clubbing with his friends.

'Uh. Let me think about it.'

Annoyed that my brother wasn't jumping at the chance of us spending some quality time together, I let my tongue run away with me.

'What do you do with yourself all day, anyway? It's not as if you've got a job.'

'Why would I have a job when I'm over here on vacation?'

Technically, his answer was correct, but if he was treating this trip as a vacation, why had he taken Beau out of a perfectly good sanctuary and plonked him in my mother's paddock? By doing so, he'd put paid to any Grand Tour of Great Britain in favour of being a stable lad. It seemed to me he wanted an excuse to hang around Glastonbury. But why?

I was unable to trust myself to go any further down the *why are you here?* route. My jealousy about how close he'd grown to Charles and Frankie in such a short space of time would have been all too obvious, so I changed course completely – and disastrously.

'Where do you spend the night when you're not at Charles'?'

Theo stopped dead in his tracks and Beau with him. We'd just reached the gate to Flossy's field and she was trotting over to greet us, her foal close behind, so he busied himself getting Beau through the gate, then turned to me, his eyes as hard as stone.

'What the hell freaking business is it of yours?'

Anger rose so rapidly in me that it was way beyond being annulled by the Violet Flame.

'It's my freaking business, as you put it, because you're a Johnny-come-lately,' I shrilled, 'who's acting as if he owns the place. Coming and going as you please...has it ever occurred to you that the shock of you turning up might have contributed ...'

By that time I'd started sobbing, so the words 'to Frankie's death' mercifully remained unspoken. Theo just stood there, saying nothing, offering no comforting word or gesture. So I turned on my heel and half ran back to the cottage where I found Charles on the phone.

'All right, Rosemary. Yes, yes, we'll come. No, there's no hard feelings about the breakage. We'll be there at two.'

I managed to escape to the bathroom before he'd finished speaking, where I patted my puffy eyes with cold water. When I came downstairs he said, 'Rosemary's asked us all to lunch today.'

His tone wasn't enthusiastic but I was pleased to be invited out.

'Good-oh. There doesn't seem to be much in the fridge.'

He closed his eyes and sighed loudly but I ignored his irritation. Now that the subject of Rosemary had come up, it was an opportunity to delve deeper, so I gritted my teeth and probed.

'You seemed very off with Rosemary at the funeral, Charles. Did the skull mean a lot to you?'

His eyes grew damp as he shook his head without speaking and my heart went out to him. He looked strained and I sensed there was more to it than my mother's death, so I joined him on the sofa where I took his hand and willed him silently to open up about what was worrying him. After a few minutes he started talking.

'You see, I didn't approve of the group she and Frankie got involved with. It all started when that woman Dido arrived last year. She bought an empty barber's shop in the High Street and turned it into a beauty salon. She started a circle. Called it the Circle of Isis.'

He paused, so I persisted.

'Why did you disapprove of it?'

'Because it was so secretive. I wasn't used to your mother keeping things from me, but she'd scuttle off every week and never say what they'd been doing or discussing.'

'Why didn't you join in, Charles? You used to before.'

'It seemed to be a woman's thing. I called them "the coven" which made me less than popular. That fool Ralph went along to keep guard on the door, and...'

He stopped as if not sure whether to continue.

'I suppose an Isis Circle would be for women, wouldn't it?' I said, gently.

He looked grim.

'Yes. All in search of eternal youth...'

He seemed on the point of telling me more, but when Theo came in the back door he immediately clammed up.

'Hi folks,' said Theo, as if nothing had happened.

Fine, I thought, *if you want to play that game, so can I.*

'Hello,' I answered. 'Did Flossy approve of Beau's makeover?'

'Guess so.'

He looked at his watch and then towards Charles, as if waiting for him to speak.

'We've been summoned to Apple Blossom Cottage for lunch,' Charles announced. 'All of us.'

Theo tried to look as if this was news to him but something in his manner told me that it wasn't.

* * *

Two other guests, already halfway through their glasses of wine, were in Rosemary's conservatory when we got there. It was spacious enough to contain a long, glass-topped dining table with chrome and leather chairs, and still have room for two modern sofas and some easy chairs. Her house was the polar opposite of Charles' in its orderliness, being almost minimalist by comparison.

I recognised both of the women, who got to their feet when Rosemary showed us in.

'Pandora, this is Cynthia.'

The woman, who gave off a faint smell of patchouli oil, extended her hand.

'Call me Cyn.'

'The last time I saw you, you were wearing a turban, I believe.'

She patted her long, grey hair with a plump hand. 'Probably. I've got a selection. You should get one. They're handy when one's hair needs washing.'

Wondering what Jay would say if he saw me in a turban, I turned my attention to the smaller, younger woman next to her.

'This is Dido,' said Rosemary, in a voice almost deferential.

'I saw you both at the funeral,' I said, recalling Jay's description of this one as 'a sexy abbess'.

'Yes, I remember your husband falling into the grave.'

With most people I'd have made a joke at this juncture, but her eyes were aloof and humourless so instead I offered her my hand without comment.

The milky-white hand she held out in return bore a gold ring in the shape of a winged goddess, the head and body forming the crown of the ring, with the wings stretching all the way round the shank. These dug into my hand as she grasped it a little too tightly.

You meant that to hurt, I thought, as I quickly withdrew it.

Half-closing her eyes in an imitation of sympathy, she said, in a throaty voice, 'So sorry about Frankie. Such a great loss to the community.'

Charles harrumphed at this, turning it into a cough. I translated that as a comment on her being in Glastonbury for five minutes, yet talking as if she'd been born there, knew everyone, and owned the place.

Giving him a cold stare, Dido added, 'And, of course, to her family and friends.'

When she said 'family' I noticed she glanced not at me, but at Theo, whose face wore an expression I hadn't seen before: that of a lovesick teenager.

'I'll let Max get you a drink,' said Rosemary, 'I've just got some finishing touches to perform in the kitchen...'

Her son Max and I were old friends, even though we hadn't seen each other for ages. He'd come with Rosemary to our handfasting and developed a teenage crush on Cherry. It was perfectly innocent – Jay and I had seen to that – but he'd spent quite a few weekends at Four Seasons until his visits had gradually fizzled out when the travelling got tedious. He was at university now, studying physics.

At his mother's command, he appeared in the doorway and strode forward, giving me a bear hug which crushed my bones.

'Pan-lid, how are you?'

He was the only person I'd ever let call me this and live.

'All the better for seeing you, my dear,' I said, marvelling at how tall he'd become. 'Seems you're living up to your name.'

I'd asked him once what his full name was, expecting Maximilian or Maxwell. But he'd told me it was Maximus, because his parents had wanted him to be great.

'Yup. In height, at least. How's Cherry?'

'She's fine. She loves being a drama student. I've got some pictures of her, and the others, on my phone. I'll show you later.'

Soon we were all seated round the table enjoying Rosemary's perfectly cooked beef Wellington. Cynthia, the only vegetarian present now that Charles seemed to have given it up for Lent, was demolishing a mushroom strudel.

Rosemary sat at one end of the table, Charles at the other, and Max and I sat opposite the other three, Theo having made a beeline for the seat next to Dido.

The wine had been flowing and Charles' colour had heightened. I wanted his resentment against the Circle to be given full rein, as I didn't have very much longer to get to the bottom of what had been going on. I thought a toast to my mother might set the ball rolling.

'Here's to Frankie,' I said. 'May she rest in peace and never be disturbed again.'

An uneasy silence fell as, one by one, they raised their glasses. Perceiving this to be a good time to throw a grenade, I added, 'And may the bastards involved in vandalising her grave rot in hell.'

Of course, a person in my position would no more believe in hell than in flying pigs, but I crossed my fingers under the table, just to be on the safe side. I'd only said it to see if anyone twitched.

'Steady on,' whispered Max.

As I was mouthing *Don't worry* to Max, Charles cried, 'Amen to that, Pandora,' thumping the glass table till the dessert spoons rattled. 'Amen to that.'

Visibly shaken by what she'd heard, Rosemary was a picture of perplexity. Clearly, this was all news to her. Opposite me, Dido smoothed her napkin, Theo stared at his plate, and Cynthia bobbed her head like a startled hen.

'In what way was it "vandalised", Pandora?'

It was Dido who had spoken, and Charles answered for me.

'Someone came like a thief in the night, broke into the coffin and searched it, leaving my life-partner's body open to the elements. Whoever it was made no effort to cover their traces. If that's not vandalism, I don't know what is. Our *feelings* were vandalised as much as the grave, don't you see? But no doubt white paint would've had to be daubed somewhere to conform to *your* definition.'

The sneer in his tone was unmistakeable and wasn't lost on any of us. But Dido simply sat there, her features composed, not a hair on her raven head disturbed.

Rosemary had turned pale at Charles' words.

'Who found it like that?'

'Pete. When he came back yesterday morning to lay the turf. He wanted me to call the police, but I haven't reported it...yet.'

Rosemary's lower jaw was quivering with emotion by this time.

'That's awful. How could anyone have been so crass?'

'Are you thinking of contacting the police, Charles?' asked Cynthia. 'Because actually, if the grave has been refilled, and I assume it has, what evidence would you have?'

'Probably none, Cyn,' he said, emphasising her name. 'But the perpetrator, or perpetrators, were obviously sending some sort of message along the lines of: *We're looking for something and we won't stop till we find it.*'

I was pleased that Charles was fighting his corner and looking forward to an escalation of conflict with accompanying revelations, when Dido's phone rang. She rose from the table and left the room to answer it, followed by Rosemary, who said she was going to get the pudding.

Charles seemed to have lost his impetus at their departure, so

I decided to ambush Cynthia while her sidekicks were absent.

'What's so special about your Isis Circle, Cynthia? What's the point of it exactly?'

Shifting uncomfortably in her seat, she flung me a look of dislike.

'I'd have thought any daughter of Frankie's would know the value of a circle. We use it for healing and improving ourselves,' adding as an afterthought, '...and healing others.'

I adopted a puzzled expression.

'It's just that Frankie never mentioned it to me. And this circle's being going on for how long?'

Before Cynthia had a chance to speak, a husky voice behind me answered, 'Five months, actually. And each member takes an oath of confidentiality when he or she joins, so you'll forgive us if we close the subject.'

I glanced at Charles to see if he'd challenge Dido. I sensed that an accusation of some wrongdoing was very much in the air, but from his expression, he was undecided. Then his mouth tightened and he called out loudly, 'Come in, Rosemary, please. There's something I want to say to you all.'

Rosemary appeared in the conservatory carrying a large jug of cream and an equally outsize lemon meringue pie. Her face was shiny and her manner flustered. As she placed the dessert on the table, she spoke in a low tone, but because the room had gone deathly quiet, we all heard.

'Please don't spoil the day, Charles. The Circle of Isis is a virtuous circle for the ben...'

Charles interrupted her with a scornful reproof.

'*Vicious* circle, more like!'

Rosemary closed her eyes and through tight lips, continued.

'It celebrates the Divine Feminine. There's absolutely nothing to disapprove of...'

She was interrupted again, this time by a loud knocking on the door. Everyone except Dido looked surprised, and Rosemary hurried to answer it. I surveyed the diners. Charles had thrown his head back, his jowls quivering in irritation. Cynthia had turned away from him towards Dido, an exaggerated expression of outraged innocence on her face, while Dido was looking at Charles with an expression I can only describe as loathing.

Beside her, Theo fidgeted in his chair, like a child desperate to escape from the quarrelling grown-ups.

I turned to Max, widening my eyes and shrugging my shoulders, so he'd know I had no more clue what was going on than he did. He leaned towards me and whispered, presumably so that Charles wouldn't hear, 'Do you think this is a case for Miss Marple? Is that her at the door?'

But the person Rosemary brought into the room at that moment bore no resemblance at all to a silver-haired sleuth. This man was tall, muscular and bronzed, his highlighted, russet hair draping fashionably over his collar. His tan was intensified by the whiteness of his shirt, over which he wore a close-fitting, grey cardigan, the type that few men can carry off. His blue-green eyes alighted on Dido, causing him to break into an incredibly white smile.

'Your wanderer's returned. Come and give Gav a kiss, pussy cat.'

Fascinated, we watched as Dido returned his smile with one of equal brilliance and moved into his arms. When they finally parted, she beamed at everyone.

'This is Gavin, my husband. He's been working away, but now he's home for good.'

Chapter 7

Four Seasons

As I watched the cows whiz by from my window seat on the train to Reading, I went over the events of the day before.

The surprise appearance of Dido's husband had put paid to any attempt at further investigation of possible duplicity on the part of the members of the Circle of Isis. When he and Dido had eventually unglued themselves from each other, he took the seat Cynthia offered and she sat next to me. Luckily for my little brother, the happy couple only had eyes for each other, and were oblivious to the silent movie of astonishment, hurt, anger, and misery, that flickered across his features. As for the others, Cynthia wore a Cheshire Cat smile, presumably glad of the interruption, while Charles' face had become a mask of indifference.

Rosemary sat down at the end of the table and nervously began serving the dessert.

'Great timing,' said Gav. 'I'm starving.'

'So, have you met Gav before?' I asked, addressing Rosemary as she handed me a portion.

Rosemary glanced at Dido, who was still ogling her dish of a husband.

'No. This is the first time.'

'Gavin's been in Australia, helping an associate set up a hair salon,' broke in Cynthia, full of herself now that their gang outnumbered Charles and me two to one. 'That's right, isn't it Di?'

Without tearing her eyes away from her man, Dido uttered a bored 'Mmm.'

This irritated me. In fact the whole only-eyes-for-each-other nature of their reunion was getting my goat quite considerably, so I forced her hand.

'Did you know Gav was coming home, or did he surprise you?'

She gave me a silky stare, like a cat who'd been interrupted stalking a bird.

'Yes and no...' she said finally, having paused so long before answering that I wasn't sure she would.

I turned to Gav, forcing myself to sound chirpy.

'Come on, I bet it was you who phoned just now.'

He stopped shovelling lemon meringue pie in his mouth for long enough to confirm it. 'Yeah. Di left a note. I rang to tell her I was on the way.'

My face burned at this proof that the scheming siren had planned for him to turn up here, knowing what a kick in the teeth it'd be for Theo who, I was ninety-nine per cent certain, she had been sleeping with. If she wasn't the 'friend' he regularly spent the night with, I'd eat the Man from Del Monte's hat.

While this revelation had unfolded, Theo had been glaring at his pudding. I attempted to catch Charles' eye but he, too, seemed to have subsided into a mere spectator at the feast. We continued working our way through the meal. Once Gav had polished off most of the cheese and biscuits, leaving his speech organs free, the conversation focused mainly on jet-lag and which of Rosemary's herbal potions would help him cope with it, followed by the vital issue of what might be done to alleviate the shock to his system of coming from the southern hemisphere to a cold, English February.

When we'd drunk our coffee, in Cynthia's case, nettle tea, I got up from the table, suggesting to Max that we went into the living room.

Max looked across at his mother, so I provided a cover story.

'I've got some pictures of Cherry and the others to show him.'

Rosemary signalled her permission with a limp wave, so he and I left them to it, paying no heed to the suspicious expressions of the other women. Once inside the room, I closed the door.

'I'm not sure what's going on, Max, but I'm worried about Charles, and I don't trust Cynthia and Dido.'

He looked relieved. Maybe he'd thought I was on a mission to matchmake him and Cherry back together.

'Yeah, talk about a really weird atmosphere.'

'Can you shed any light on that circle they're involved with?'

'Sorry, haven't got a clue. What you said about the coffin – was that true?'

'Yes, and there've been other things, too. There was a break-in at the cottage and Charles was very unfriendly to your mum and Dido at the funeral.'

Max was frowning and looking solemn at this point, so I left out the bit about Theo being my half-brother and probably Dido's lover. I didn't want to frighten him off the case at this early stage.

'Mum's been different lately...sort of nervy. It probably does date back to when Dido came on the scene.'

I waited for him to elaborate, but he shook his head.

'I'm in Manchester most of the time, so this is all news to me. I came home because I thought you and Jay would be around. Sorry I missed the funeral, by the way, had a lecture on Friday morning. When Mum said she wasn't planning on having you and Jay and Charles here, I was surprised. I persuaded her in the end, but I didn't expect anyone else to be invited.'

Hearing that he'd come home specially to see us, I immediately felt happy.

'Thanks, Max. Jay will be so sorry that he missed you, but he had to go home – something to sort out with Rowan.'

He grinned when he heard Rowan's name.

'How old is he now? Fifteen, sixteen? It's tough being that age. Your head's all over the place.'

I passed him my phone so he could see the pictures I'd taken at Jay's sixtieth birthday bash. He laughed at the one of Rowan wielding the inflatable Zimmer frame.

'I hope he turns out like you,' I said, remembering the regulation stroppy teenager Max had been, who, somewhere along the line, had transformed into this delightful young man.

During his terrible teen phase, whenever he'd come to stay with us, he'd always sought out Jay. After he'd gone home, Sharon would inevitably declare, 'That boy lacks a father figure, that's why he's such a handful,' which was the cue for Jay to roll his eyes at me when she wasn't looking.

When we were on our own, Jay would have his usual rant.

'This from the mother who let me think she was my sister, then emigrated when I was two. What fucking father figure did I have? My granddad died when I was three.'

'You haven't done badly as a dad yourself, though, have you, my love?'

I would say this to calm him down – and because it was mostly true.

Max and I sat in silence for a moment. I'd begun to think that there was no more he could tell me about the circle and its members, when he said, 'There is one thing. When Dido first moved here, Pete said something about a slimming scam. And he mentioned she had a husband who was involved in it too, although there was no sign of him then.'

I shook my head blankly and watched while he went to a table in the corner of the room and opened a laptop computer. As it slowly came to life, he told me that Pete had recognised her picture from an exposé in the *Daily Mail* in connection with some sort of rip-off involving a weight-loss product which turned out to be useless.

He finally found the web page he wanted and beckoned me over.

'Come and see this.'

Tina and Gavin Bull are being forced to close their hair and beauty salon in Guildford due to a boycott from clients after their slimming pills were found by Trading Standards to be composed of nothing more

*than corn starch, lactose, cayenne and saffron. The tablets, manufac-
tured for the couple privately, had not passed any safety, quality or
effectiveness standards even though they had been priced at £60 for a
month's supply. The couple traded online as T&G Slimming Club
offering a free trial of slimming tablets. When requesting a free trial,
however, consumers found they had unwittingly signed up for regular
monthly payments that could not be cancelled.*

It was while we were reading this together that the door
opened and Charles peered in.

'Pandora, if you don't mind, I'd like to get going now. I'm
suffering from a bit of indigestion.'

'Okay, Charles, we're just looking something up. Be with you
in a minute.'

As he backed into the hall, I whispered to Max, 'Email me the
link.'

Max nodded and handed me a pen and Post-it note. As I
jotted down my email address, I said, 'Are you sure they're the
same people?'

So he clicked on to another site, this time with an image of
Tina getting into a car with Gavin at the wheel. She was using
her bag to cover her face but you couldn't mistake that sweep of
black hair and the goddess ring on the hand holding the bag.

'I wonder when Tina reinvented herself as Dido.'

'It has to be some time between June, when the salon closed
down, and September, when she turned up here,' said Max,
getting up from his seat.

'Thanks, Max,' I said, standing tall to kiss him on the cheek.
'I'll keep you posted on any developments.'

'Okay, Pan-lid.' He usually grinned when he called me that,
but today his expression was serious. 'If there is any funny
business, you will keep Mum out of it, won't you?'

'I'm sure your mum would never be involved in anything
illegal. Don't worry, it's only the baddies I'm gunning for.'

I said this to reassure him, but for the life of me I still couldn't imagine why Rosemary, of all people, was in thrall to a woman like Dido.

'I won't mention any of this to her,' he said, pointing towards the computer. 'She's stressed enough as it is.'

I found Theo and Charles in the hall, but there was no sign of Rosemary. I didn't want to go back into the conservatory, so I asked Max to thank his mother and we headed back to the cottage.

Theo walked slightly ahead of us, looking glum, while I made small talk with Charles. I wanted to tell Charles what I'd discovered about the Bulls, but I couldn't in front of Theo, in case his allegiance to Dido was still in force. Come to think of it, Charles had probably already heard about the couple from Pete anyway.

The appearance of Gavin Bull was another no-go area. Discussing that would be twisting the knife in Theo's wound, so we soon lapsed into silence and my mind became occupied with the next day's journey home, and whether to go early or later, to avoid the Monday-morning crush of bodies heading towards London.

We arrived at the cottage to be greeted by Anubis, who ran towards her bowl, mewing. After giving it a good scrub and opening a new tin of food, I was pleased to see her devouring her dinner. Charles watched from the doorway.

'That's the first good meal she's had since...'

He stopped short and I felt his pain.

'Can you manage Anubis, Charles? If not, I'm sure Sonia could find her a good home...'

He turned pink, a colour his complexion had become all too familiar with lately.

'I never put you down as a cat expert, Pandora. Thanks all the same, but rehoming Anubis won't be necessary. I'm quite capable of opening a tin of cat food.'

Stung by his tone, I snapped back.

'Animals like clean bowls and fresh drinking water. You don't need to be an expert to know that. Her bowl was filthy, no wonder she's been off her food.'

Stomping out of the kitchen, I went upstairs for a long bath, adding some of Frankie's essential oils of lavender and rose, which helped soak away the bad vibes of the afternoon.

Slipping on a dressing gown, I went into Charles' bedroom to replace the oils in their wooden case, when a picture of an Egyptian goddess-figure, on the wall behind the bed, caught my eye. She was sitting cross-legged on the ground, her winged arms outstretched, her head in profile, wearing a headdress shaped like a throne. On closer inspection, it proved to be a painting on parchment which had been framed and glazed.

Charles had asked me if I wanted anything of Frankie's, but her jewellery was a bit too clunky for me and her clothes far too big. This painting, on the other hand, was drawing me to it, and I resolved to drop a hint that I liked it.

Back in the guest bedroom, I decided to meditate for a little while. Nothing miraculous happened anymore during these quiet times (now that my former mentor, Enoch, had left the building), but often, some time later in the day – or week, or month – a problem would be surmounted, a difficult situation resolved.

I'd acquired the habit of listening to my higher self, who would sometimes give me messages which arrived like emails in my brain, and sometimes put words in my mouth which I didn't expect. I was still getting to grips with this, not always being able to differentiate between my own thoughts and the sager guidance of my spirit.

When I'd finished meditating, I put on some expensive pink and white striped silk pyjamas, which Jay said made me look like an inmate of a secure unit, and went downstairs, where I found Theo leafing through the supplements. Charles was on the sofa, squinting sideways at the main newspaper, the cat refusing to budge from his lap.

The scene melted my heart, so I immediately forgave him for his earlier rudeness, when I'd only been trying to help a dumb creature. Not that Anubis was so dumb – Charles had pushed the sofa closer to the woodburner, securing her the warmest seat in the house.

'Charles, I couldn't help noticing that Egyptian picture in your room...' He gave me a *What were you doing in my bedroom?* look over the top of his spectacles. '...When I got some oils for the bath.'

'You mean the papyrus painting of Isis,' he said, resigned to his reading being disrupted by females of the species. 'The goddess of magic and medicine with the power to heal or destroy. A clever trickster who always maintains her power at any cost.'

He was obviously still in a bad mood, so I decided against telling him I wanted it, and concentrated instead on something else that had come to me.

'Oh, so it's Isis,' I exclaimed. 'That explains Dido's ring. It was in the shape of a goddess with wings.'

At the mention of Dido's name, Theo raised his head from the magazine and became very still.

'The wings of a vulture,' responded Charles. 'Rather appropriate when you consider who was wearing it.'

Charles heaved a sigh, giving me a glare which said: *Why did you have to mention that woman's name in my house?*

'Pandora, would you put the television on, please? If I can't read in peace, I might just as well watch the *Antiques Roadshow*.'

I did as he asked. Then I remembered my other concern.

'Have you got the number of a taxi service, please? For tomorrow.'

Irritated at this further interruption, he said curtly, 'I'll give you a lift, don't worry.'

'But I want to catch the twelve-thirty. You'll be at Gaia's Cave, won't you?'

'No. I've decided not to go in. I'm feeling a bit off colour.'

I was just about to ask him what was wrong, when Theo said, 'Is that invitation still open, Sis?'

I could hardly believe my ears. I wanted to dance with delight that he didn't think the Jays too boring to be with after all. Then a small voice, suspiciously like Frankie's, whispered: *Don't get too excited, Pan. He's running away from trouble. And you're his get-out.*

Refusing to be brought down, I flashed my little brother a big smile.

'You bet. That's great. I'll ring Jay now and tell him you're coming.'

* * *

Theo was sitting opposite me on the train, his eyes closed. Having no 'friend' to sleep with anymore, he'd spent the night on the box-room mattress, which might have accounted for his fatigue. Or maybe he'd had a sleepless night nursing a broken heart. He'd been quiet all morning, grieving, no doubt, over losing Dido. I wondered if he'd known that she was married.

After changing trains, we reached Maidenhead, where we waited for our last connection. On arrival, we headed for the station car park and found the people-carrier waiting.

My heart fell when I saw Sharon's familiar cropped blonde hair and pink face behind the windscreen. I'd left a message on Jay's phone as soon as we pulled out of Castle Cary, giving our ETA, and an hour or so later he'd texted me: *Message received and understood. Pick-up in station car park. xx*

Even though I hadn't forgotten that his time belonged to Gaby this week, I'd been hoping he'd leave her to it, and come and get us himself.

Sharon got out of the vehicle, pecked my cheek and swiftly turned her attention to Theo.

'So you're Frankie's boy,' she twinkled, offering a plump hand sparkling with some impressive rocks. 'You look nothing like her. Or Pandora. But, then, I suppose your father's genes would be dominant. It was the same with my James.'

I'd warned Theo earlier, on the third and final train, that Sharon didn't always engage her brain before she put her mouth in gear, but he still looked shell-shocked.

'Yeah. I guess so.'

Sharon, fair and blue-eyed, had produced Jay, dark and exotic-looking (until he opened his mouth to reveal his Shepherd's Bush roots), after a teenage encounter with a man from Kashmir, who'd been passing through and never knew he'd impregnated her.

I'd met her for the first time on the day of my marriage to Jay. She'd been slim, vivacious and attractive and she and Frankie had flirted with the Italian waiters at our wedding meal. This well-upholstered woman standing before me was totally unrecognisable as the person she'd been then.

'Get in, you'll get cold,' she ordered.

She patted the front passenger seat for Theo to sit next to her. I sat behind. As soon as she started the engine, Sharon targeted Theo.

'What part of the States are you from?'

Once he'd answered that, she proceeded to tell him how she'd spent most of her life in Canada but her husband had died, so when James needed her to care for his kids, she'd come straight over.

'...Never gave it a second thought. Family first, that's my motto.'

Hm, I reflected. So how exactly does emigrating and leaving him for your mother to bring up fit with that?

Sharon had resumed talking at him.

'James said you didn't have any contact with Frankie growing up. Why not?'

There was an embarrassed silence from Theo, so I stepped into it.

'Theo's aunt brought him up, and his father and Frankie agreed it would be confusing for him to have two "mothers".'

I knew I was stretching the truth but it was none of Sharon's business anyway.

She gave a snort and looked ready to continue disapproving, so I decided it was time to take the heat off my little bro or he might be tempted to make a break for it. I pictured him sliding open the door and jumping out at the next red traffic light, never to be seen again. Besides, there was something I needed to know the answer to.

'Did Gaby turn up this morning?'

Struggling to restrain the stirrings of jealousy which clutched at my vocal cords, I managed to keep my tone neutral.

'Sure. She booked into the Carlton last night so she got here bright and early. I asked if they wanted lunch but they said they'd have something in the Feathers. Hadn't come back when I left.'

It was now four-fifteen.

'Whose car did they go in?'

'Hers. She's got a cute little silver coupé.'

She said this as we drew into the drive, adding, in the next breath, 'Welcome to Four Seasons'.

'Formerly known as Jay's Nest,' I said, hoping to raise a smile from Theo.

When Jay and I were together, the first time round, we used to refer to the house by this name. Jay had even painted a pair of jays and a nest full of blue eggs on a slice of wood, which he nailed to the gatepost at the entrance to the drive.

My mother's boyfriend at the time was a sculptor – very much down on his luck. They were living in a leaky caravan in Devon, so we bought the biggest piece of statuary he had, which turned out to be the maidens of the four seasons on a single base, each facing a different way. It had been in his yard for so long, it appeared as ancient as any Greek sculpture. Once the statue was

installed, we reluctantly took down Jay's work of art and obediently put up the Four Seasons sign, hand-carved by Frankie's
boyfriend. An omen, perhaps, that we'd never manage a clutch
our own.

I asked my mother once how they'd spent the substantial
amount of money Jay had paid for the statue, and she said it'd
been a cold, wet winter so they'd moved into a hotel and lived it
up until the money ran out. I suppose replacing the old caravan
with a luxury model had never occurred to them.

Sharon decided to drop us at the front door before driving on
to park in the courtyard at the back, where Jay's studio was
located. I badly wanted to see if the coupé was there, but I put a
brake on my curiosity and took Theo into the house instead.

'Nice place you got here,' he said, looking surprised and
pleased. Seeing that his most recent guesting experience had
been quaint and draughty, our late-nineteenth-century, eight-
bedroomed country home, built of honey-coloured Cotswold
stone, must have cheered him up no end.

'I'll take you to your room and give you a tour of the rest of
the house,' I said, as I began to climb the stairs, but we were interrupted by the patter of eight paws on the parquet, coming in our
direction.

'Hello, Oscar, Fritzy. Oh, my good boys.'

'Hey guys,' said Theo, as he joined me in making a fuss of
them.

I liked the fact he was an animal lover. And I was touched that
he was wearing his hair tied back in a sort of exploding bun
today. When he'd appeared at breakfast, I'd badly wanted to tell
him how much it suited him, but remembering his reaction
yesterday to hair-talk, I'd hushed my mouth by distracting it with
a piece of toast.

The dogs were soon followed by Sharon, who hove into view
like a galleon in full rig, breathing heavily. Since she'd put on
weight, she'd taken to wearing baggy blouses and full, dirndl

skirts, which only served to emphasise her generous proportions.

'The dogs need a walk, Pan. I let them out this morning and they hung around outside the studio, whining, so I've had to keep them in.'

'I'll come with you,' said Theo. 'I could use the exercise.'

So, after quickly depositing his bag – Sharon had prepared him a room at the front of the house with a view of the Four Seasons maidens – we made our through the house to the courtyard. To my dismay, there was no sign of a silver coupé anywhere.

I opened the boot of the battered hatchback we used for dog-walking and both dogs jumped in. I'd lent my beloved little red MX-5 to Ashley and Linden a year ago and never got it back, which was a shame, as I suddenly wanted to impress my little bro. Not that the two of us and two dogs would have fitted in it, but its presence in the courtyard would have added a certain *cachet* to my profile. I was conscious that just as I was fitting together the jigsaw of Theo, so he'd be fitting together the jigsaw of Pandora – whoever she was. I still wasn't entirely sure myself.

We'd reached the bottom of the drive and I was waiting to turn right, towards the common, when a silver car approached from the left, indicating at the last minute that it was turning into our driveway. As I pulled out and the other car pulled in, the man in the passenger seat gave us a lazy wave. It was Jay. His companion was laughing, seemingly oblivious to us.

A couple of miles further up the road, we passed the Feathers pub, where Jay and Gaby were supposed to have gone for lunch. Try as I might, I couldn't silence the Greek chorus in my head: *Why were they coming from the other direction? Where have they been?*

Chapter 8

Falling Out

We rarely used our dining room, preferring the informality of the kitchen. Sharon liked to take care of the weekday evening meal and, today being Monday, she served up sausages, fried onions and mash, drizzled with Sunday's leftover gravy.

Rowan and Willow would sometimes dine before us if they had other things to do – in Rowan's case almost certainly perfecting his computer game skills, whereas Willow would be doing schoolwork or mucking out the barn where the horse and goats took shelter. But today, in honour of Theo, they'd turned up at seven to give him the once-over.

Earlier on, I'd managed to have a separate word with them. When we'd got back from walking the dogs and Theo had gone to his room with his tablet PC, I found Willow in the sitting room, reading. ('That girl's always got her nose in a book,' was Sharon's usual line, followed by, 'No wonder she has to wear glasses.')

I wasted no time in bringing up the subject of Rowan with Willow. I explained that if he'd started a relationship with someone, we'd have to talk to him about taking precautions, so if she knew any more she should tell me. Willow blushed.

'I heard him on the phone to Tom. He'd left his bedroom door open...he said he fancied a girl who worked in the Feathers.'

'Wasn't that where they got caught?'

'Yes. On Fridays loads of people from school go there. Him and his friends were openly drinking beer. They were unlucky, really. Maybe someone from school had it in for them.'

Jay had got a letter from the school saying that Rowan was part of a group seen drinking alcohol in the pub and that all the miscreants' parents had been informed.

'So does the girl know he's only fifteen?'

'No idea. And he's sixteen soon anyway, Mum.'

'Yes, but how old is she? You have to be at least eighteen to work in a pub.'

'I don't know. I've never seen her. All I know is, her name's Clarrie and it was her party he went to the night he stayed out.'

My imagination took flight, as I visualised a buxom barmaid leering at Rowan as she pulled him a pint of mild and bitter, or whatever schoolboys drink to seem grown up.

'Hi, Mum.'

I turned to see Rowan looming in the doorway, both dogs swooning at his feet. He'd easily pass for eighteen and so would his friends, most of them being on the tall side and athletic. I approached him at a trot, ready to sweep him across the hall into the study. It was rarely that anyone else used this room: its shelves held all my books and papers. But even though I'd lived with Jay in this house before any of the saplings were born, I still hesitated to call it mine.

'Step into the study, young man, I want to ask you something.'

He looked apprehensive.

'Said the spider to the fly,' he muttered.

I motioned him to sit down and tried not to seem too anxious, even though I felt totally clueless about what to say or how to say it. I took a seat opposite him and strove to compose an opening statement, but Rowan got in first.

'If this is about staying out, Mum, I'm sorry. Dad's grounded me but he said Tom could come here. He'll be round later – we're doing homework together.'

Our eyes met and we both started laughing.

'Yeah, right,' I said. 'Wha'evah.'

He laughed. He liked it when I did my impression of a disaffected teen.

Taking a deep breath, I tried to think of the best way to convey to him that he was too young for a sexual relationship –

not to mention the fact that it was illegal until he was sixteen. But it would have been foolish to discount the possibility that he'd started having sex.

'Rowan, you know your dad and I always have your best interests at heart, so what I'm going to ask you is important, for your sake.' He seemed all set to interrupt but I galloped on. 'If you've been seeing someone...' A memory of my mother having a similar conversation with me dropped like a stone into my mind, distracting me for a moment. 'We hope you haven't taken any risks...' I stumbled around for something else to say, '...Especially if she's older than you,' I finished, lamely.

At the mention of the word 'risks' Rowan's face had turned bright red.

'Who's been talking? I bet it's Willow. What's she said?'

'Hardly anything. Don't start blaming her, Rowan, I forced it out of her. She said there's a girl called Clarrie who works at the Feathers that you like.'

'Her name's Clarissa, actually. And her dad owns the place.'

Even though my inner snob felt better when he said that, I didn't deviate from my line of questioning.

'Were you with her when you stayed out all night? All we want to know is that you're not being irresponsible.'

I used the word 'we' but actually Jay didn't have the faintest idea I was having this chat. As far as I knew, neither he nor Sharon was aware of any girl, and that's the way I intended to keep it at the moment. The last thing I needed was a family drama with a guest in the house.

Rowan's dark eyes, so like his father's, were blazing at me.

'I told you, I slept in a sleeping bag on the floor. What do you want me to do, take a lie detector test?'

Having no stomach for further grilling, I got up, holding my arms open wide, and we hugged.

'I'm sorry, darling. Of course I believe you. Just promise me that when the time comes, you'll ask Ashley or Linden...'

Making a humming sound so he wouldn't hear what I was saying, he put his hands to his ears.

'Mum, please, I'm not an idiot. You're embarrassing me. Enough.'

* * *

Rowan's friend Tom joined us for dinner and they fired questions at Theo about his stunt work which he answered in some depth, probably grateful to have found something he could talk about easily. Willow was shy with him, as she was with most people she didn't know well, but she clearly liked him. Jay's mood was expansive. Normally this would have pleased me, but I couldn't help linking it to Gaby.

After dinner, I suggested going to the Feathers for a drink. I usually preferred the smarter bars in the town, so Jay was surprised. Sharon declined on the grounds that she should stay home 'to keep an eye on things.'

As Theo, Jay and I walked into the pub, my eyes were drawn to the bar where a young woman was serving a customer. She was attractive, with bouncy blonde hair, but too heavily made up. Worst of all, the span of her gold, hooped earrings was too wide to be anything but flashy.

'Why don't you sit down,' I said to the men, pointing to a table by the window. 'I'll get these.'

Theo moved obediently towards the window-seat while Jay turned to me with an exaggerated expression of surprise.

'Are my ears deceiving me?'

I couldn't say I wanted to go to the bar to check out Rowan's love interest, so I made something up.

'I've just got my royalty cheque.'

Jay grinned.

'You think it'll stretch to three drinks?'

I gave him a playful punch in the solar plexus.

'It's still in print. Where there's life there's hope.'

'Well, if you insist, my flower, I'll have my usual,' he said. Adding softly, 'I'm feeling rather *lively* and *hoping* you are. Hold that thought.'

I brushed the corner of his mouth with my lips, looking forward to some connubial action later on. Jay sat down at the table, opposite my brother.

'Do you fancy joining me in a pint of real ale, Theo?'

'Hell, no.'

Theo's reply indicated that he'd tasted real ale in Glastonbury and didn't want to repeat the experience in Great Marlow.

'I'll have a Bud, please, Sis.'

The pub was busy for a Monday evening. There were two other drinkers in front of me, which gave me time to study the blonde. She'd been chatting and flirting with a man in a denim shirt and a mullet haircut, and was now doing the same with the next customer. I was straining my ears to hear what they were saying when I heard a voice ask, 'What can I get you?'

A slim, fresh-faced girl with short, dark hair had appeared so I gave her my order. As she got the drinks, the man behind me struck up a conversation with her.

'How are you, my darling? Had any fleabags in lately?'

That's a bit rude, I thought, imagining he was referring to the clientele, but the girl laughed.

'No, but I had to remove a couple of ticks today.'

'Hope you got the heads out. Buggers, they are.'

On seeing my puzzled expression, she explained.

'I'm a trainee veterinary nurse.'

At this point Jay arrived to help me carry the drinks and the man moved forward to place his order.

'I'll have two pints of Old Hoary, please, Clarrie. And a lager top. Where's your dad tonight?'

It came to me in a flash that Rowan's love interest was called Clarrie so this must be his girl. She most certainly passed inspection, I thought, basking in a warm glow of relief as I followed Jay to our table.

We stayed in the Feathers till closing time. Jay seemed happy to fill us in on his day in the studio. It had gone well and they'd made progress on a new song.

'Where did you go for lunch?' I asked, trying to sound unconcerned.

'We came here.'

His answer sent my stomach into spasm. I wanted to play it cool, but my doubts got the better of me.

'Then why were you coming from the other direction when we saw you?'

Jay gave me a searching stare, glancing at Theo and shaking his head. His eyes narrowed in the way of a detective sizing up a suspect.

'If I didn't know you better, Mrs Armstrong, I'd say you had one of those overly suspicious minds.'

Elvis Presley immediately burst into song in my head, crooning the ballad of that name, and making me feel sad. Armstrong was the name I'd taken when I'd married Mike, and I wondered if that was Jay's not so subtle way of putting me in my place – of reminding me that, technically, we were both free agents.

You'd have thought I'd have heeded the stop signals and screeched to a halt, but aided and abetted by four cosmopolitans, I kept my foot on the accelerator.

'She didn't offer to show you her room at the Carlton then?'

Jay's eyes flashed, exactly as Rowan's had in the study. No doubt in deference to Theo, however, Jay simply said coolly, 'How very dare you?' proffering neither argument nor explanation.

When we got home, Theo went straight to bed and we joined Sharon for a chat in the sitting room. Jay excused himself after a few minutes and went upstairs. He was usually the first in bed anyway, because it took me so long to complete my beauty regime – cleansing and moisturising being essential for that dewy morning look.

Sometimes I sat in the dressing room for a quiet few minutes at the end of the day, but not tonight. Tonight I wanted Jay to make love to me. I needed reassurance that he was still mine.

I took off my dressing gown and slipped into bed, expecting to find Jay as naked as me. But as I curled myself around his back, the only top and bottom I made contact with were his Queens Park Rangers pyjamas.

It usually took only a touch from me to rouse Jay from sleep, but tonight he remained facing away from me, still and unresponsive. I could tell he wasn't really asleep because his breathing was too quiet.

I stayed in spoons position for a little while, and then turned over in a silent huff. Normally three nights without sex would have overruled any falling-out. But instead of being consumed by coital bliss, here we were with our backs to each other in holy deadlock. *Oh God,* I sighed. *Don't tell me my lovely, laid-back husband's turning into a grumpy old grudge-holder.*

I was getting heartily fed up with Jay's birthday blues. Admittedly, I'd reacted in the same way when I turned fifty, but all it took was a few people telling me I didn't look my age for me to snap out of it. I kept telling him the same, but he still had a face as long as a fiddle most days. We'd always been able to rib each other and not take offence, but this evening, after what I'd said about Gaby showing him her room, he'd scarcely spoken to me, addressing his comments almost exclusively to Theo.

There was definitely something bugging him. Sharon had suggested he might be feeling the strain of supporting the saplings, none of whom was financially independent yet. Let's face it, most men of his age had reared their families and were winding down at work – playing golf, doing whatever men do when they ease up. Jay was still involved in the music business, but the scene had changed: commissions were harder to come by. I suppose that's why he'd been so keen to work with Gaby. It made him feel valued.

Last September, we'd met up with an old friend of Jay's who was in London for a gig. He lived in Florida, and he'd gone on at length about the global financial market crisis, and how banks and pension funds in the United States were saddled with huge stocks of subprime mortgages, plummeting in value. He was convinced his country was heading for a recession.

'It won't happen here,' was Jay's verdict, on the way home.

But within a week, the Northern Rock bank hit a liquidity crisis. Other banks wouldn't lend to it and the directors had to go cap in hand to the Bank of England for emergency funds. Images of panic-stricken customers queuing for hours outside the branches to withdraw money dominated the front pages.

Rowan had wandered into the room during a financial news item on TV. 'What's the credit crunch all about, Dad? I've got to write an essay on it.'

'I didn't know economics was on your curriculum, Row.'

'It's not. Old Jarvis caught me and Tom playing basketball with apples. That's our punishment.'

Jay released an involuntary snort of laughter, but managed to keep a straight face.

'Well, basically, the credit crunch is the result of greedy bankers, greedy borrowers, greedy investors, crap credit-rating agencies and crap regulators. Does that answer your question, my son? If not, you can always write: *It's not a good idea to waste fruit by throwing it about during a credit crunch,* two hundred times and hand that in.'

Rowan sat down on the floor between us, his back resting against the sofa.

'Will it make any difference to us, Dad?'

Jay ruffled his hair.

'Don't worry. I've got some investments I can always cash in. As long as your mother knocks out another bestseller, we'll be all right.'

* * *

It took me ages to get to sleep and when I woke up the next morning, I was alone, having overslept; the clock showed twenty past nine and I had a client coming at ten. Leaping out of bed, I got dressed at double speed and ran downstairs to grab a cup of rose tea and a blueberry muffin. I found Sharon in the laundry room, up to her ears in ironing, and asked her where Theo was.

'In the garden. I told him to take a look at the labyrinth. I gave him the leaflet the builders left and he said he'd have a go.'

I tried hard to suppress my exasperation. It needed more than a leaflet to properly explain how to get the most out of the labyrinth walk and I didn't have time now because I was expecting Tegan. I consulted my watch. Ten-fifteen. It was unlike her to be late. 'I thought you were taking him on the fruit and veg run, Sharon?'

Trading as 'Four Seasons Organic Fruit & Veg', we supplied our produce (supplemented by supplies from a local organic farm) to shops, restaurants and individual customers throughout the county. Sharon liked to help with local deliveries if she had time, and Theo had seemed keen yesterday when she'd suggested they did the run together.

'Hugh said the boxes wouldn't be ready till later.' Hugh was our produce manager. He'd subcontracted the bulk of deliveries, leaving the smaller, local ones to himself, the family, or a cast of casual workers he drew on from time to time. 'Theo'll be out of your hair then, don't worry.'

'It's not that, Sharon,' I said, smarting at the suggestion that I'd palmed my brother off on her. 'I'm expecting someone, and I don't want him wandering past the dome while I'm working.'

'Well, if you mean the girl with the pink hair and the little dog, she arrived half an hour ago. She's probably in there waiting for you.'

Chapter 9

Finding Tegan

There was no way to get to the garden other than via the courtyard, so I let myself out the back door and crossed it at a canter, experiencing a sting of embarrassment as I passed Gaby's car. I shouldn't have said what I had to Jay and it was no good blaming it on the cocktails. I was supposed to be wise enough to know better.

But as soon as I'd elbowed that memory out of the way, the space was filled with irritation and guilt at Sharon's remark. Had she hit the nail on the head? Had Theo really become an extra burden now I was back on my own turf? What did we really have in common, apart from the same mitochondrial DNA?

I was running all this past my inner critic when I reached the centre of the garden, where two crossed paths divide our grounds into four. The massive, organic garden, resembling a giant allotment, spreads from the lower right into the upper quarter. The upper left section of the garden, once set aside exclusively for the children, has been taken over by a croquet lawn. In one corner stands an ancient wooden playhouse; in another, a tree house built by Jay, resting in a big old oak tree, with several ropes dangling from its branches. The geodesic dome, where I was headed, lies in the lower left quarter, so I turned left at the crossroads, passing the sweet little periwinkle blue shepherd's hut, which Jay had bought me as a writing retreat when we got back together.

On the outside my hut looks suitably bucolic: it sits on iron wheels and sports a curved tin roof. But inside it's beautifully fitted out. There's even a stove and a built-in bed, handy for snoozing while waiting for the muse to call. It also makes a useful waiting room if healing clients come early, with the added benefit of tea-making facilities and a loo if they feel the need.

I checked inside, but Tegan wasn't there, so I continued on till I reached the geodesic dome.

My workplace always reminds me of a flying saucer, come to rest on Earth before journeying onward, which explains the illogical relief I feel when I see it's still there, and has not boldly gone where no man has gone before.

Apart from its solid base, it's composed of a grid of glass and aluminium triangles, so always filled with light. It forms the perfect space for healing because its structure keeps the temperature even, so the client needs only a single blanket. And the acoustics are marvellous. If I stand in the middle and sing or tone, my voice hits all the notes, miles better than singing in the bath. And the ringing and chiming of the instruments bounces off the geometry like there's no tomorrow.

* * *

It was Enoch who pointed me in the direction of healing with sound. Once I'd mastered life with Jay and his brood, I began to search for something meaningful to do with my spare time and found myself rereading Enoch's last words before he disappeared.

It is your destiny to manifest forth unto the world sound codes of light to assist all beings to remember and return to the original pattern of their atomic structure. This is the gift you hold through your presence.

Every morning for a week I spent time meditating on his words without feeling any the wiser. But I should have had faith, because on the eighth day I got a flyer in the post for a Mind, Body and Spirit event in London. My eye was drawn to a workshop on sound healing, so I booked a place to see what it was all about.

The speaker started off by telling us that sound healing is an ancient, natural form of healing which works on the principle of resonance.

'Every atom in the body produces sound as a result of its metabolic processes and also absorbs sound. Our body organs and systems have different frequencies at which they naturally resonate, known as their prime resonance.'

He explained that our cells, organs, skeletal system, etc., can heal and harmonise themselves by entrainment, which means pulsing at the same rate as sounds which match their prime resonant frequency. He added that, being composed of up to sixty per cent water, the body is a good conductor of sound.

My attention was captured even more when he added that sound can heal the spiritual anatomy as well as the physical by energising and balancing the chakras (the energy centres in the subtle body). It was then he showed us a selection of instruments he'd picked up on his travels: crystal bowls, tuning forks, cymbals, Tibetan bowls, bells, rattles, gongs, drums, in all shapes and sizes.

When he opened the floor to questions, I put up my hand. I wanted an explanation of Enoch's phrase.

'I've heard the expression "sound codes of light". Can you explain that, please?'

He raised his eyebrows slightly.

'Some healers channel the language of light with their voices. People like me channel it through instruments.'

I was comforted to hear that. I'd been worried that Enoch expected me to speak in tongues. If a similar effect could be achieved by banging a tambourine, bring it on.

The sound healer smiled, probably sensing my relief.

'Today's just an introduction. I cover that in more detail in my training programme.'

During the last part of the session he encouraged us to play with the instruments, producing a weird cacophony. At this point I still wasn't absolutely sure whether sound healing was really me, but when he described it in a more esoteric way – 'It encourages the atoms of the body to recover their soul memory in order to realign themselves back to health,' – I had a sense of Enoch adding, *into their original, flawless patterns*, and from that moment, I was hooked. I signed up for his course, completed my apprenticeship, and had been sound healing in my garden for the past two years.

* * *

I could see there was no one in the geodesic dome. I always left the door unlocked when at home, but the place was empty save for my bowls, chimes and other paraphernalia.

I took a sheet and blanket from one of the cupboard-seats which followed the curve of the sphere and put them on the low bed in the centre of the space. After that I reminded myself of Tegan's progress by consulting her notes.

She'd been coming to see me ever since we first met by the Grand Union Canal, a short distance from Chace Standen, where I'd been living before Jay carried me off to the Thames Valley. I'd come to check on Phoenix Cottage; it was between tenants and I needed to inspect it before returning their deposit. I'd hit some traffic on the way and Oscar and I had been stuck in the car for well over an hour, so I stopped off at the canal to stretch our legs.

It was a lovely day and it felt good to be alive. I even joined Oscar in a little jog, despite my summer dress and strappy sandals. As we ran, we passed narrow boats moored beside the towpath. In the distance, next to one of them, stood a pink-haired girl who appeared to be juggling. The closer we got, the more interested Oscar became in the balls she was throwing in the air.

As luck would have it, she dropped one when we were within a few feet of her. Making a lunge for the ball, Oscar locked it between his teeth and made a run for it. At the same time, a wiry Jack Russell leapt off the narrow boat barking at top volume, in hot pursuit of the thief.

'Oscar!' I yelled, breaking into a sprint.

'Milo,' trilled the girl, overtaking me, her tanned legs topped off by a pair of cropped denim shorts.

By the time we got to them, Oscar had sensibly dropped the ball and Milo was guarding it, his upper lip drawn back to show the full length of his gleaming fangs, in case Oscar got any wrong ideas.

The girl picked up the red and black ball and shook her head. 'Another one bites the dust.'

There were several puncture holes in it and the stitching had started to come away between two triangular pieces of leather.

'I'm sorry,' I panted, being a bit out of condition. 'How much is a new one?'

'That's okay,' she said, in a lilting Welsh accent. 'I shouldn't have dropped it. I'm supposed to be professional standard, see.'

She'd started to walk back towards her boat and, for some reason, I did too, even though our walk should have continued in the other direction.

'No, I insist,' I said, rifling my shoulder purse.

She rescued the rest of the balls, abandoned on the towpath in her haste, and jumped on to the boat, followed by Milo, who gave a final yap as if to say, *Beat it, you two*.

Feeling as rejected as Oscar looked, I called him to heel so we could continue our walk.

'You can buy me a cup of tea at Woody's if you like.'

Her words had floated ahead of her as she emerged from the galley, having thrown a blouse over her bikini top, which she'd tied under her bust in a bow. I noticed a tattoo of a delicate flowering vine on the outer edge of each foot as she stepped on to dry land and hoped, irrationally, that she hadn't allowed the tattooist's needle to travel any further north.

She bobbed her head in the direction of a restaurant, close by the marina. Oscar and I didn't need to be asked twice and the four of us strolled down to Woody's Place.

We sat outside, sipping iced coffee, while the dogs shared an organic ice-cream. Tegan was easy company, happy to tell me about her life. She'd been a member of a circus skills club at university and was brushing up her talents, having signed up to teach stilt-walking and juggling classes at a summer camp. The boat belonged to her boyfriend. He'd left his wife and it was all he could afford.

I suppose some involuntary tic must have signalled my disapproval, because she added, quickly, 'I met him after they split up.'

I nodded, as if that's what I'd assumed, and waited for her to ask *me* something if she wanted. Since accepting my mission impossible (trying to help people heal themselves) I'd learned it was more beneficial to let the other person do the talking, rather than compete for airtime. Occasionally, though, being receptive could be interpreted as being overly reserved. It wasn't always easy being the friendly ear.

'And what about you?' she said, finally, indicating the fashionable townhouses and apartments surrounding the marina. 'D'you live round yere?'

'No. I used to live ten minutes away, but now I live in Buckinghamshire.'

'It's a long way to come to walk your dog,' she said, laughing.

Her accent had the unfortunate effect of generating in me an impulse to exclaim 'yacky da' or 'bach' in the same way the hint of an Irish brogue would trigger 'begorrah' and a Scottish burr 'och aye the noo'.

Giving myself a mental slap, I explained I was checking my property. Then we got to discussing work and she said she did supply teaching because she valued her freedom too much to commit to a permanent job. Given my erratic CV, I recognised a kindred spirit, and I told her how I'd finally settled on a little light sound healing which blended easily with family life. She was interested and asked how it worked. I told her about resonance and quoted my teacher.

'Our body's like an orchestra. If any instruments are out of tune it affects all the others, so it's important to retune where necessary, to get back into harmony.'

We could have talked for longer, but I needed to do the inventory. As we parted, something prompted me to give her my card.

Two weeks later I had a call from her to say that her boyfriend had gone back to his wife and she wondered if she could come for a session, as she'd never felt so devastated in her life and needed someone to talk to.

At first she'd come to see me once a week; now she was down to once a month. The first part of every session was dedicated to her report on how her life had gone since we'd last seen each other and we'd discuss what she could do to improve things. After that, I'd talk her through a Violet Flame visualisation so she could zap the discord out of every atom of her being and replace it with what she wanted to create in her life. Then she'd lie down while I gave her a 'sound bath' using any instrument that felt right.

Despite the noise, clients usually fell asleep, and for this reason, I never arranged appointments back to back, preferring to let them sleep on if they had time. And that, along with my sliding scale of charges (usually descending) according to what people could pay, meant that I didn't make much. In fact, I still hadn't recovered the cost of the dome, so I wasn't in profit at all. On the other hand, I'm sure Enoch was proud of me, wherever he was.

There was still no sign of her, and all I got from her mobile was voicemail, so I decided to wander over to the labyrinth to see if Theo had seen her.

I joined the straight path and walked up towards the top of the garden, veering off to the right, where I found the two of them deep in conversation and Milo having a great time sniffing round the rabbit holes.

'So this where you've got to,' I said, trying to keep the lid on any simmer of impatience.

They both stopped speaking and regarded me benignly. I expected it from Tegan, but I hadn't seen this expression before from my little bro. Something seemed to have pleased him. His eyes held a softness that I'd only ever seen directed at Beau – apart from that awful occasion at Apple Blossom Cottage when he'd aimed it at Dido.

'I was trying to figure out the labyrinth and your friend helped me out,' said Theo, serenely.

I wanted to check what she'd told him, but I was impatient to get back to the dome, so I uttered a cursory, 'Really?'

'Theo tells me he's your brother, Pandora. And you only just found each other.'

When you put it like that, I thought, *it sounds as if we fell into each other's arms, instead of the opposite.*

I nodded, deliberately sidestepping that particular conversation with a *non sequitur.*

'I like your hair.'

The colour had been lightened from hot geranium to a more delicate shell pink, and her shaggy bob shortened to a pixie cut, which suited her large eyes and small features.

'Oh, you know. New life, new look.'

Pleased to hear that, I took hold of her arm and steered her in the direction of the dome, Milo at her heels. Theo tagged along as well, much to my annoyance.

'Hey, Sis, mind if I take a look inside?'

What could I say? No, go away and leave me in peace?

'Okay. You two go in and I'll put Milo indoors.'

When I got back, I discovered Theo doing all the things I'd done when the dome had first been installed. He stood in as many different places as possible to check for the best acoustics. He played with all the whistles and bells he could get his hands on. He even managed a few bars of *The Star-Spangled Banner* – no mean feat. Tegan giggled at all this while I tried to appear unconcerned at our precious healing time being whittled away.

I sat down on a 'talking chair', which was Tegan's cue to sit opposite me.

'Would you like Theo to leave now?'

She looked startled and shook her head, so I cracked on.

'How have you been? Did you speak to Jeremy?'

My quick scan of her notes had reminded me that her ex-boyfriend had been in touch, wanting to give it another go.

She lowered her voice. 'Yes. After I said I didn't want him back he said he had a buyer for the boat. So he wants me and Milo to find somewhere else.'

'He's changed his tune, hasn't he? I thought he promised you could stay as long as you liked.'

'He was feeling guilty when he said that. But I suppose you can't blame him. His wife knows I'm still living there...'

Theo was still tinkering in the background; he'd moved on to the suspended gong and was stroking the padded striker along its surface as if he'd been priming gongs all his life.

'So what are you going to do?'

She smiled and her face became pretty in a way it hadn't been since last summer. She reminded me of the girl I'd first met – a free spirit rather than a tortured soul. *What we do to each other in the name of love,* I silently lamented.

'I'm not sure. I rented a room in a friend's flat before I moved in with Jeremy but I didn't have Milo then. I only got him because I thought our relationship was...' Her smile disappeared and tears started to spill from her eyes.

'So you can't go back there because you've got a dog?'

'Mm. But lodging at Jane's would be like going backwards anyway. I liked living as a couple. You know, cooking together, that sort of thing. I suppose I'm old-fashioned really. And a bit broody. That's what might have put Jeremy off. He hasn't got any children and he said he didn't ever want any.'

'Do you have you any idea where you'd like to live, Tegan?'

I asked her this in a soothing tone. I'd come to learn that this was all part of healing. It's the same as animals responding to a soft voice when they need calming down.

'I'm still not sure. It can't be anywhere too expensive. My work isn't always regular. And I've got Milo to think of. I don't think he'd like being shut in.'

I judged it time for her to visualise the violet flamethrower, and once I considered she'd had long enough to blaze away the sadness and pain her relationship with Jeremy had brought her, I led her to the low bed, covered her up and started working with the instruments, going with the flow and trusting that the vibrations her trillions of cells were receiving would resonate with them to the greatest effect.

Theo had taken some cushions from the cupboard-seats and settled himself a few feet from the bed. When I saw his eyes closing, I put a cover over him. By then, he'd fallen asleep and didn't even notice.

They made an engaging sight – the two of them lying close to the floor, like large toddlers having a nursery nap, their faces in repose, smooth and trouble-free. I gradually reduced the volume and regularity of my sound effects, put a Bach lullabies CD on low, and waited.

Theo opened his eyes first, scanning the space to see where he was. I waved to him from my chair and whispered, 'Can you leave us alone for a few minutes. We'll see you in the house.'

Reluctantly, it seemed to me, he left, and I waited a few more minutes. It was getting on for half past twelve and with the distraction of Theo, I'd forgotten to check with Tegan how much time she had, so I exchanged the lullabies for *Malagueña*, a lively fandango, which did the trick.

'Wow,' she said, stretching and yawning like a cat. 'I feel as if I've been somewhere but I've got no idea where.'

'Take your time...unless you've got to go?'

'No. I'm not in a hurry. Where's Theo?' she asked sleepily.

'He's gone but he was here most of the time. I thought you deserved a little privacy.'

'I didn't mind him being here at all,' she said. 'He's great. Like a friendly bear.'

I'd never thought of him like that before, but I suppose his tangly hair was reminiscent of the matted tufts on an untidy grizzly. Come to think of it, Tegan, with her youthful, boho air, made a far better match for him than Dido, the haughty ice queen.

Chapter 10

Restoring Harmony

As we walked into the Carlton, Jay took my hand and said, 'Promise me, Andy, no more cracks about hotel rooms.'

'I promise,' I said, making my eyes as large as possible, at the same time fluttering my eyelashes ironically. I knew how to make him laugh.

He'd been cool ever since I'd spoken out of turn at the Feathers. And his coolness had offended me so I'd reacted by being even colder towards him. As a result, the temperature had dropped to the lowest on record since we'd got back together. That is, until earlier this evening, when he'd come back from his day in the studio with Gaby and, seeing me primped and polished to perfection, taken me in his arms and whispered, 'I forgive you, for you know not what you do.'

To which I'd replied, 'I bet I forgive you more.'

He'd laughed and bent his head so our foreheads gently touched.

'You can kiss me as long as you don't smudge my make-up.'

I'd spent too long in front of my illuminated mirror to risk getting it smeared. So he'd glided his lips lightly across mine and gone off to get ready.

Gaby had invited us to her hotel for dinner to mark the last night of her stay and I'd dressed up for the occasion in a Stella McCartney tuxedo suit with a white scoop neck top and spiky heels. My hair had been fashionably dishevelled by Franco, in return for which he'd extracted a large amount from my bank account. While the lowlights were brewing (so subtle I could hardly detect a difference), I'd been manicured and pedicured to within a millimetre of my cuticles by a beauty therapist. Add to that the full body massage and facial I'd had the day before, and nobody could say I hadn't done my prep.

When Jay appeared, he had on his midnight-blue Boateng suit with a white, collarless shirt, and I fancied him like mad. As we left the house, he patted my bottom. 'Make sure you behave yourself, or I might have to take you to task, woman.'

We both giggled and Jay got into the driving seat.

'You sure you want to drive?'

'Yeah. Early start tomorrow – Gaby's last day here. Lot to do.'

* * *

I was a couple of glasses into the meal and beginning to feel like a gooseberry. This was the first time I'd met Gaby but I wasn't surprised at how seamlessly her silver and cobalt bandage dress clung to her – the bodice consisting of two giant silver bandages, crossing from each shoulder to the back of her waist – or at how impressively her butter-blonde hair gleamed. I'd seen enough of her in celebrity magazines to know what to expect.

What I hadn't anticipated was her accent. Maybe that explained why Jay, who hated pretension, was hanging on her every word.

My opening shot had been unimaginative.

'So you're from Liverpool?'

'Yeah, I'm a Scouser through and through.'

That was the cue for Gaby and Jay to perform a Scouser joke for my benefit.

Gaby: 'Why wasn't Jesus born in Merseyside?'

Jay: 'Because God couldn't find three wise men and a virgin.'

On a roll, they delivered a few more, which was my cue to put on a *They're funny but I shouldn't be laughing* face, all the time inwardly fretting at how relaxed they were together.

When they finally ran out of steam, I said, 'So that's what you've been up to all week – practising your comedy routine.'

'Among other things,' said Jay, cryptically, and I felt a tiny jab of fear.

They followed their gag routine with an inventory of the songs they'd been developing, from a mixture of Gaby's half-finished scores and some ideas of Jay's. They glanced at me every so often, their gazes returning to each other.

'Honestly,' Gaby said, twinkling at Jay, 'the time's just flown by. I've just loved it. Four Seasons is *so* peaceful.'

Jay was twinkling right back at her and I suffered a deeper stab of anxiety.

'And the evenings? You haven't been bored here on your own?'

'No way,' she said, directing her answer to me for five seconds before switching to Jay. 'I had dinner in my room, then I got comfy in my PJs, went over the lyrics...watched a bit o' telly. It's been great. This is the first time I've eaten in the restaurant.'

It was plain why. There were a number of necks craning in our direction and it certainly wasn't for a better view of James Jay, singer/songwriter, or Pandora Armstrong, novelist *manquée*.

'So you didn't miss home?' I said, hoping she wouldn't see through my attempt to discover if she had a 'significant other'.

Gaby blinked slightly. I sensed she'd detected a certain wifely unease and I kicked myself for being too obvious.

'Just the cats,' she chirped, 'but I talk to them on the phone every evening.'

I had a vision of a troupe of performing cats answering the phone and miaowing into it.

'Sounds like something off *You've Been Framed*,' said Jay.

She laughed. 'My ex moved in to look after them. He holds the phone and I talk to them. Daft, isn't it?'

I bared my teeth in a smile, my disappointment at her boyfriend being an 'ex' rather than a gorgeous hunk she loved with all her heart and soul, rendering me temporarily speechless.

'What'll happen to them if you go on tour?' said Jay, with more concern than I thought necessary.

'Well,' she said, looking dejected, 'if Rog can't be there, I suppose I'd have to board them. But I'd be worried sick. They're Burmese and they need to be round people...'

There was a pause and Jay finally dragged his eyes away from Gaby, towards my direction.

'We'd have them, wouldn't we, Andy?'

Since when were we a cattery, I thought. And what if Oscar and Fritz objected? But good manners got the better of me and I smiled as sincerely as I could.

'If you think they'd be all right with the dogs...'

They exchanged a glance and the gooseberry effect intensified to the extent that I almost felt myself turning green and hairy. Gaby leaned forward and let the silver bandages take the weight of her voluptuous breasts.

Neither Jay nor I could take our eyes off them. For me, it was admiration for the designer's feat of engineering. For him, giving him the benefit of the doubt, I'd say involuntary desire, which I couldn't really blame him for. She knew what she was doing all right.

Gaby's smile blasted me between the eyes.

'We've been sending demos of the songs to my record label and they love them. With the ones I've already written, there's enough for an album.'

'Fantastic,' I said, thinking of how much this must mean to Jay. 'I can't wait to hear them.'

There was a pause, which can only be described as pregnant, and I regarded them expectantly.

'We'll both need to go to the studio next week,' said Jay, speaking faster than normal. 'They want Gaby to get a shift on.'

'Which studio?'

'Abbey Road.'

I was puzzling out why Jay needed to be present at Gaby's recording, when she answered my question.

'Two of the numbers are duets. And he's playing on most of

the other tracks.'

She sounded apologetic, which made me suspicious.

'Oh, I see,' I said tartly. 'You're doing a Dolly Parton and Kenny Rogers.'

Jay gave me his 'I am not amused' Queen Victoria stare and I bit my lip to stop myself venting any further spleen. Red wine always did this to me. My fault for having the steak instead of the sea bass, I suppose. Gaby rescued the situation with a gurgling laugh.

'Not quite.'

The waiter appeared with the dessert menu and I ordered a death by chocolate sundae. The prospect of Jay disappearing through the looking-glass into a writing and recording wonderland with Gaby had set off a sugar-craving that could not be denied.

The other two hesitated for so long, that I almost expected them to order one with two spoons.

'You can have some of mine,' I said lamely to Jay.

Without taking his eyes off the menu, he said, 'No thanks, just coffee.'

He glanced at Gaby who was still reading hers.

'I'll just have coffee, too.'

'We have a special praline *tartufo* which is small, but very delicious, signorina,' responded the waiter, ogling her bandages.

Gaby sat up straight and winked at him.

'Go on then. I can resist everything except temptation.'

Flashing his teeth and giving a little bow, he moved off pronto to carry out her wishes. As nobody had asked me if I wanted coffee, I had to shout my request to his retreating back. I wasn't used to being ignored, but I seemed to have morphed into the Invisible Woman this evening.

On the way home, I asked Jay about his plans for the coming week.

'I'll go up on Sunday night, probably stay till Friday.'

He turned his head quickly to see my expression. I kept my face impassive, even though the thought of him spending all that time with Gaby was killing me.

'Will you be staying with Ashley and Linden?'

'No.'

'Where then?' I asked, trying to sound composed.

'A hotel in St John's Wood, near the studio. The record company's organising it.'

I wanted to wail, *That's how all our troubles started in the first place*, but fearing a return to the glacial state of the last few days, I made a massive effort.

'I'll miss you.'

He didn't say anything then, but the atmosphere in the car definitely warmed up a couple of degrees.

Later, as we made love for the first time since the night before Frankie's funeral, his tongue gently exploring the nooks and crannies of my left ear, he breathed, 'Will you really miss me, babe?'

I never knew where he'd kiss me, which is why I spent a fortune at the Xanadu Salon de Beauté on body-firming, exfoliation and multifarious skin treatments. Jay always said he liked my natural look, with not a clue of the time and money it took to achieve. They say the fifties are the new thirties but not without a substantial beauty budget they're not.

Jay owed his honey-coloured skin and dark hair, with just a sprinkling of grey, to his Asian father. It was only his face which was lined, but I'd given him permission to use my top-notch moisturiser and every so often he'd let me apply a collagen-boosting face mask, so he actually looked better than he had in 2003 when we'd rediscovered each other. He certainly didn't look sixty.

'Of course I'll miss you,' I gasped, as he journeyed south. Jay had been reading about tantric sex on the internet and our love-making had slowed down, being nothing like the vigorous sex we'd had in our twenties and thirties. He sometimes delayed a bit too long on his way to the finishing line for my liking, but crossing it was always worth the wait. Then we'd fall asleep together, him lying on his back and me lying across him, my head resting on his chest. Which, funnily enough, was the opposite of how it used to be the first time round.

* * *

The next morning, Sharon couldn't disguise her surprise as she came into the kitchen in time to see Jay kissing me goodbye.

'Hi, Sharon,' said Jay.

He never seemed comfortable calling her 'Mum'.

'Gaby's already here,' she said. 'Have you had breakfast?'

'Yeah. Andy gave me the full works.' I knew he'd said that to make me blush, and it did. Jay had woken up pretty rampant and had gone for frantic rather than tantric, which had seemed reassuringly like old times.

'See you later,' he called as he left. 'We'll take the dogs out when Gaby goes.'

Once he was out of earshot, Sharon said her piece. 'Glad to see you two are okay now. Was it Gaby caused the trouble?'

I felt myself colour up again. Had my distrust of Jay been that obvious? And who would blame me for worrying? After all, he had a historic track record for infidelity in and around recording studios. Sharon made a pot of tea and we sat facing each other across the kitchen table.

'It's my fault, Sha,' I said, my voice breaking slightly. 'I made a stupid remark about her showing him her hotel room, and he took offence...'

Sharon huffed her disapproval.

'Is that all? You'd have thought he'd be flattered. Anyway, you did right to ask him...they were gone a long time on Monday...'

She took my hand across the table.

'I think he's having a late-life crisis. No wonder you're in pieces. What with him being moody, and your mom dying – not to mention finding a brother you never knew you had. My sympathies are with you, honey.'

As usual, when someone felt sorry for me, my eyes filled with tears and out they spilled on to the multicoloured checked table-cloth. When they'd stopped flowing, I told her everything that had happened when we were in Glastonbury, and how unsettled I'd felt when I found out about Theo. And how much Charles had altered, and my mother's friend Rosemary, too. And how awful Dido was and how she'd hurt Theo.

Sharon listened intently. Apart from Dido, she knew the cast of characters and was relishing the drama. When I'd finished, she peered at me with some concern.

'Jay already told me about the grave being opened, but I didn't mention it, because I didn't want to upset you.'

I got up to get some kitchen paper to dry my tears, which had started again, and she came over to hug me. That set me off even more and I began to sob so much I couldn't even speak.

'That's right, honey, let it all out. Whoever did that to the grave will get what's coming to them, one way or another.'

Feeling better for the hug, I broke away and saw that Theo was watching us from the doorway, an unfathomable expression on his face.

'Don't you think, Theo?' Sharon went on. 'Flogging's too good for them.'

'I'm thinking more of cutting off their extremities,' I snarled.

Theo winced and put some bread in the toaster.

'Maybe best to put it out of your mind, Sis.' He bent down to retrieve a butter knife he'd dropped. 'You heard from Charles lately?'

'No. I was going to ask you the same thing. Are you worried about Beau?'

'Yeah. Think maybe I'd better give Charles a call to see how everything is.'

Sharon winked at him.

'You've had other things on your mind since Tuesday, haven't you?'

Theo looked blank for a moment and Sharon prompted him.

'Pink hair? Welsh accent? Cute ass?'

I don't know if Sharon had said that to shock me out of my slough of despond, but it worked, obliging me to suppress a little snort of laughter. Theo brought his toast to the table and feigned an astonished expression.

She was referring, of course, to Tegan, who, after her sound healing on Tuesday, had stayed until the evening, hanging out with Theo and eating Chinese takeaway with all of us. Sharon had spent all afternoon delivering the fruit and veg boxes accompanied by the two of them, so we'd ordered in.

'Oscar and Milo get on well, did you see them playing together?' I said, maintaining the Tegan theme.

Theo nodded, concentrating on his toast and marmalade.

I studied him, wondering how best to ask how long he was staying. I'd pretty much exhausted the local places of interest and Jay hadn't been much help, being sequestered every day with the pneumatic Gaby. Next week he'd be in London, therefore about as much use as a chocolate teapot on the entertainment front.

'Have you any plans for the weekend, Theo?'

My brother stopped chewing and nodded.

'Yeah, I'm going over to see Tegan tomorrow. Wondered if you'd lend me your car?'

My heart lifted. Being with Tegan would be good for him, give him something to occupy his time.

'Of course. Are you okay driving on the left?'

He waved his hands as if swatting flies.

'No problem. I been driving since I was fifteen.' Seeing our surprise, he added, 'On my folks' property.'

'Talking about the weekend,' said Sharon, archly, 'you haven't forgotten what Sunday is, have you, Pan?'

I mentally ran through the birthday list, starting with Sharon's, but March 2nd didn't ring any bells. I grinned at Theo.

'Have you got any suggestions?'

He rolled his eyes.

'Get a diary?'

'Come on, Sharon,' I said, 'put me out of my misery. What *is* Sunday?'

'Mother's Day. Ashley rang last night when you were out. The boys'll be here for lunch. And Cherry's coming home tomorrow, so you'll be able to meet the whole gang, Theo.'

Suddenly excited at the prospect of us all being together, I studied Theo's face for a reaction, but he gave nothing away. I'd learned it was often hard to guess my brother's true feelings. Maybe he'd spent a lifetime trying to conceal them.

I got up and performed a little jig of happiness, then caught hold of Sharon and led her in a polka. Before long we ground to a halt, Theo clapped us, we curtsied, and he sprang up and put an arm round each of us. This was unusual behaviour for him, as he wasn't one for kissing or hugging at all.

'I'm happy for you girls. You'll be all together with your – whaddaya call 'em – saplings?' He paused, shuffling his feet. 'Trouble is, I'm staying over at Tegan's...so I can have a few beers. And we'd planned to spend Sunday together.'

It had patently taken an effort on his part to divulge his personal plans, and I wondered again what made him so secretive. Had it started with his nocturnal visits to Dido, or was he just furtive by nature? I had a lot to learn about my brother. But, I asked myself, did I have the energy and inclination to find out? The hills I'd had to climb in the last few years with Jay's brood had put me off tackling any more. Just when I felt I'd cracked being a mother, along comes a brother requiring me to learn how to be a sister. The mere thought of it was enough to give me altitude sickness.

'Well, that's no problem,' said Sharon. 'Bring Tegan on Sunday. The more the merrier.'

I held my breath, realising how badly I wanted my brother to want to meet the rest of the family.

'Okay. I'll be here. Can't speak for Tegan, but I'll tell her she's invited.'

Sharon, braver than me, gave him a big sloppy kiss on the cheek and patted him on the back.

I stood and savoured the moment for a few seconds. Jay and I were back on track and the people I loved most in the world would all be here on Sunday. *Today I'm going to live in the present,* I thought. The Glastonbury business and the Gaby problem would be put on hold until Monday.

The day was bright and not too cold.

'Would you like to do the labyrinth walk this morning, Theo? We never did get round to it.'

My brother, still reeling from Sharon's assault, looked interested.

'Yeah. You said you need to talk me through it first?'

I pictured my bedroom, in a state of disarray after the connubial action Jay and I had recently enjoyed. This called for a tidying-up operation before I went anywhere, in case Sharon's vacuum cleaner was tempted to make a guest appearance.

'Okay. I'll let you finish your breakfast. See you in half an hour.'

Chapter 11

Pan's Labyrinth

Theo sat waiting for me on the hall bench when I came downstairs. The sweeping staircase was one of the features I loved about the house. I sometimes imagined the girls descending in their bridal regalia to join proud father Jay, who'd be waiting at the bottom in full morning dress. Then off they'd go in a classic Bentley to the village church, where the pews would be decorated with tulle swags and pure white roses.

I led Theo into the study where he took a seat by the window while I got my notes on the labyrinth out of the desk drawer, giving him a shortened version to use as a prompt if he wanted to do it again on his own. I noticed when he held it, that a slight tremor caused the paper to shake, which he quickly disguised by resting it on his knee.

I'd had the labyrinth installed as a place of meditation, doubling up as somewhere to take problems and seek a solution to them. Conscious that Theo had been a stranger to the esoteric before meeting Frankie, I didn't mention that it was built on principles of sacred geometry and said to have magical properties. I'd become familiar with the term 'sacred geometry' through Enoch, and from reading about Egyptian temples and pyramids, so I wasn't surprised to see it attached to descriptions of labyrinths in the installing company's brochure.

I consulted my notes and started to read out loud.

'A labyrinth is an ancient religious tradition, a way of communicating with God.'

He seemed okay with that, so I carried on.

'There's a labyrinth in the nave of Chartres Cathedral. It was originally installed at the beginning of the thirteenth century and became the symbolic equivalent of a long journey to visit a holy place, *like Jerusalem.'*

Theo was staring out the window, like a schoolboy waiting for the lesson to end so he could go out to play, so I took the hint and introduced a subject I thought might interest him.

'Did you walk round the labyrinth with Tegan, by the way, Theo?'

At the mention of her name, he resumed eye contact.

'Yeah. I thought it was like a maze but the path took us straight to the centre – well, not straight – you know what I mean. More a winding road.'

Hearing that phrase, a response mechanism in my brain compelled me to deliver some bars of an old song. If I'd been with Jay, he would have joined in, but Theo simply looked alarmed.

'You were saying?' he prompted.

'Sorry, I was brainwashed with the Beatles from an early age. Anyway, the idea is that moving in a spiral on the way to the centre affects your brain in a positive way, helping it come into balance.'

Theo sat up straight, a wry smile on his lips.

'You think I'm unbalanced?'

'Most people are when they're stressed. I know I am at the moment. We've both lost Frankie. And you've...'

I nearly said, 'lost Dido', but stopped, remembering I wasn't supposed to know about that. A shadow passed across his face so I swiftly returned to my notes.

'The inward path winds clockwise, drawing the walker deep into himself. After spending time in meditation in the centre, the walker returns in an anticlockwise direction, integrating the connection with his inner self.'

No doubt subconsciously influenced by the clock references, Theo yawned and looked at his watch, so I summed it up in simpler terms.

'Walking the labyrinth symbolises finding your soul and returning with a deeper understanding of who you are.'

'Far out, man,' he said sarcastically.

Choosing to overlook his impertinence, I yanked the labyrinth into the twenty-first century.

'As well as a place for meditation, it can be used as a problem-solving tool. That's what you've got those instructions for.'

I hated calling it a 'tool' but it made it sound less medieval. He'd returned his gaze to the window, so I raised my voice an octave and said, brightly, 'Do you want to read out the first bullet point?'

He dragged his eyes to the printed sheet and read out the first line mechanically.

'Before you start to walk, decide on what you want to change, resolve or clarify.'

From the look on his face he was having difficulty choosing what to go for.

'There's nothing to stop you walking it every day, if you like. You could sort out everything in time,' I said, smiling in a way I hoped would encourage him to love the labyrinth.

He shrugged.

'Time's something I don't have right now. I rang Charles while you were upstairs. He didn't sound so great. I guess I'll be heading back on Monday...'

Theo misinterpreted my expression of dismay as being solely for Charles.

'Don't worry, Sis. I guess he's just lonely. I should get back anyway. I need to check on Beau.'

'Okay,' I said, conflicted with regret at his going and relief at not having to keep him entertained. Added to that, was the new worry of Charles being lonely.

I made an effort to focus on the here and now.

'You could work on something emotional, like healing a relationship.' His eyes flickered at this. 'Or a physical or mental problem...'

He tilted his head slightly.

'So, let me get this straight,' he said, a hint of interest in his drawl. 'If it's a physical problem I concentrate on whatever's wrong with me and it helps?'

'That's the idea.'

He closed his eyes and lapsed into silence. To keep things moving, I read out the second point.

'Release all the emotions connected with the issue you've chosen to deal with, as you make your way to the centre of the labyrinth.'

'That's not so easy,' he said, opening his eyes.

'How about visualising them dropping away, like stones?'

Nodding, he consulted the list and read on.

'When you reach the centre, stop and wait for guidance. Open yourself to receive insights and healing. Stay as long as you need to.'

He looked up.

'So can someone walk out of the labyrinth totally cured?'

I hesitated. The matter of cures was always tricky. That's why I never promised any of my sound-healing subjects instant results. Humans are such complicated organisms that the timing of a breakthrough is unpredictable.

'I wouldn't think so. Not instantly. Most illnesses don't miraculously disappear. That's because they're not merely physical, they come from other parts of our consciousness as well. The labyrinth has the power to shift awareness, so the walker is open to healing on all levels, but that might take time.'

I could see I was in danger of losing him, so I went for a more positive spin.

'Of course it's possible that a condition could eventually clear up. For example, you might be guided to consult a certain practitioner who'll help you...'

Worried that we were concentrating more on the end product and less on the process, I sprinted to the last bullet point.

'The last stage is walking back the way you came. This is when you consider how you can integrate the guidance you have received and manifest it into your everyday life. As you leave the labyrinth remember

to express your thanks.'

Theo folded the piece of paper up tightly, put it in his back pocket and got to his feet.

'Do you want to try it, then?' I said uncertainly.

Again, I was unable to figure him out. Maybe I'd frightened him off with the consciousness stuff. Or with the idea that it might be a long haul. Perhaps he simply wanted to see for himself without me acting as director.

'Why not? Let's go.'

* * *

We'd first set eyes on a garden labyrinth at the Hampton Court Flower Show and had immediately commissioned the company to construct one in the upper right section of our grounds, which the boys and their friends had used as a makeshift football pitch when they were growing up. Knowing that Jay was fully stretched financially, I insisted on paying for it, which was why he always called it 'Pan's labyrinth', after the fantasy film.

He went along with it, thinking I still had savings, but they'd been exhausted by the cost of the geodesic dome and credit-card bills. Because I absolutely *had* to have it, I arranged to pay by instalments and was only just breaking even every month.

I'd taken a camping chair with me to the labyrinth, to allow me to watch in comfort while my brother made his pilgrimage. Having completed seven circuits, Theo had reached the centre, and looked as if he was concentrating hard, his eyes closed and his head bowed. I focused on the pattern of the labyrinth, admiring the colour of the sandstone paving blocks we'd chosen: white and grey for the paths and pale blue and purple for the background.

The labyrinth builders had explained that there was a 'Golden Ratio Option' which would increase the energy of the labyrinth and give the walkers 'a heightened experience of unity with nature, the inner self, and God'. This would mean first creating a pentagram within a pentagon as a base.

Naturally, we went for it like a shot. After marking out the star-shaped design and its surrounding border, the builders set marker stones to indicate the points and sides. Finally, they laid the pattern of the labyrinth itself, starting from the centre. The seven spiral paths, they said, corresponded to the body's seven main chakras.

We planned to landscape the surrounding area with garden benches and potted shrubs when the weather improved, lining them up with the points of the star, but in the meantime it was simply surrounded by grass and reminded me of an aerial picture of a spiral crop circle, created by extraterrestrials.

As I watched over Theo I heard a familiar whinny. Midnight had spotted me and come to the wire and post fencing, which separated the garden from the adjoining field. She reminded me of Sharon – short-legged, stocky, and as strong as an ox.

Leaving Theo to it, I approached the field, climbed over the stile and started stroking her neck, while she wiggled her ample backside in appreciation of the carrots I'd brought with me. Always on guard for treats, Bonnie and Clyde leapt down from the climbing platforms Jay had made them, and dashed over to get theirs.

As I was wearing trainers, I decided to have a jog around the perimeter of the field. I'd done four full circuits and was debating whether to force my weary legs round again, when I noticed that Theo had finished his walk and was sitting in the chair, so I joined him, collapsing on the grass beside him.

I could see that he'd been crying.

'How did you get on?' I said, in case he wanted to bare his soul.

'My head aches a bit. But it was good.'

He raised his eyes and looked deep into mine.

'You have the same colour eyes as Frankie.'

I nodded, unsure where this had come from. He'd hardly mentioned her since we'd left Glastonbury; maybe his walk had set off a belated grieving process.

'Although she used to say hers were the colour of aventurine and mine more like dill pickle ...' I said, going for the flippant approach.

He smiled but said nothing, so I pressed on.

'Some people find unexpected things coming up when they do the walk, that don't seem to be connected to what they'd been focusing on in the first place.'

He sat slumped in the chair, seemingly unable to say any more, and then I had an idea. Maybe if I took him into the dome, he'd be more inclined to talk about whatever was troubling him, because something sure as hell was.

'Come on,' I said, jumping to my feet and touching his back lightly to get him to stand. 'We'll go to the dome and I'll give you a sound bath. That'll sort you out.'

When we got to the dome he went straight to the low bed to lie down. After covering him up, I started with the gong and continued with the Tibetan singing bowls, gradually reducing the volume. Although his eyes were closed, he wasn't asleep, so I took him through a guided relaxation. At the end of this I told him to open his eyes, and asked him to come to sit opposite me in the 'talking chair'.

'Theo, tell me what's worrying you.'

I wouldn't normally have been so direct but I justified it on the grounds that firstly, we were related, and secondly, he was getting a free session. He appeared slightly groggy, which I put down to all the weaving back and forth in the labyrinth, topped off by the vibration of the singing bowls. Although he was facing me, his gaze seemed to be fixed on a point in the space between us and I realised he was in a state of mind akin to being hypnotised.

I seized the advantage by slowly repeating what I'd said.

'Tell me what's worrying you, Theo.'

'Losing my motor skills,' he said, almost in a monotone. 'Ending up in a wheelchair.'

His answer made me gasp. I'd expected it to be delayed grief over our mother's death or a broken heart. Not this.

Trying to keep my own voice calm so he'd remain in this semi-trance, I asked him to explain.

'The fall injured my spine. Then my fingers and toes started going numb. The doc did some tests. Said they weren't conclusive but there was some neurological damage. Six months later, he said it was progressive and he couldn't guarantee a good outcome. That was it, the end of my career, plus the end of my relationship...wasn't long before my girlfriend moved out. Said she couldn't stand my moods. Seems to be getting worse. I drop things...'

A memory of the rope under Frankie's coffin slipping through his fingers flooded into my brain, followed by a groundswell of guilt at how I'd reacted.

Biting my lip, I continued. 'Is this what you were concentrating on when you went into the labyrinth?'

'I guess so, yeah.'

'And did you receive a message?'

'It was weird, more like a dream. My head was aching. I put my hand to my head and touched what felt like a crown of thorns. I kept tugging at it, trying to get it off, but it wouldn't move. The blood was dripping down my forehead into my eyes. Then Frankie appeared and told me to finish what she started.'

Disregarding the gory stuff, my ears immediately began flapping when he mentioned our mother and I felt my eyes getting greener. Why had she appeared to him and not me?

Elbowing aside this unseemly sibling rivalry, I said, 'Did she say anything else?'

Theo hesitated.

'No, but I think she was pointing at something...'

I knew I had to work quickly, while Theo's mind was still in a receptive state.

'At what, Theo?'

'Maybe a door...'

Out of the corner of my eye I saw Rowan approaching the dome. Once a fortnight he had a free Friday afternoon, and this must be it.

'...It's like a hidden door...'

I waved to get Rowan's attention, so he wouldn't interrupt us, but it was too late. At the sound of Rowan's hearty 'Yo,' Theo's eyes widened and he came out of his trance.

Quelling my irritation at being interrupted, I put my finger to my lips and mouthed a request to Rowan to sit down. Then I poured Theo a glass of water.

'How do you feel?'

He drank the water down in one and wiped his mouth with the back of his hand.

'Great. Don't remember much, though.'

He glanced across at Rowan who had started speaking quickly.

'Clarrie's waiting for us. We're going for a pub lunch today. Remember? She's driving, so...'

Giving me a sideways look, he let his sentence fade.

'Oh yeah, yeah,' said Theo. 'You want me to meet your girl.' He checked his watch. 'We better get going then.'

The thought of Rowan knocking back pints in some pub and possibly getting reported by another busybody agitated me, in view of the upset the first offence had caused in the Jay household.

'I don't think so, Rowan. It's too soon after getting caught.'

His face fell and so did mine. Nobody had prepared me for the resentment that a mother had to endure.

'Come with us, then. You can keep an eye on things.'

These words came from my brother's mouth, delivered,

what's more, in a friendly tone.

Wowee, I thought, as I walked back with them to the courtyard where Clarrie waited in an ancient Citroën deux chevaux. *Give the combined power of the labyrinth and the dome a big hand. It seems to have worked a treat on my brother.*

Chapter 12

Mothering Sunday

As soon as I got in the car I set about persuading the others that it would be much better to go to a hotel in the town for lunch, rather than a pub.

'What do you think, Clarrie?' said Rowan.

'That's fine with me. But,' she lowered her voice slightly, 'it'll be more expensive.'

'My treat.' I called from the back.

'Okay. In that case, the champagne's on you, Mum.'

'Why?' I said, unable to resist. 'Are you celebrating something?'

From where I sat I couldn't see his face, but his ears gave off a crimson glow, reminding me how sensitive boys could be in the presence of a girl they're keen on.

When Rowan had introduced us earlier, Clarrie and I had behaved as if we hadn't met before, although, technically, we had – she'd served me on Monday night in the Feathers. I don't know if she recognised me, but I wasn't about to bring it up because I didn't want either of them to suspect I'd been giving her the once-over.

Later on, when they were choosing from the à la carte menu with plenty of side orders and I was hoping my credit card would cope, Theo said to Clarrie, 'You seem familiar. I feel as if I've seen you somewhere before.'

'Possibly,' she smiled. 'I help out at my parents' pub some evenings.'

'You do? I thought you worked for a vet.'

'Actually, I'm training to be a veterinary nurse – I'm at college two days a week and the veterinary centre the rest of the time.'

'When you're not bartending,' said Theo, with admiration in

his tone.

Clarrie laughed. 'I enjoy it.' She looked sideways at Rowan, 'I get to meet some cool people.'

It wasn't until well into the main course that Rowan brought up the subject of Beau.

'Clarrie's got to do a case study. I suggested Midnight, but when I told her about Beau, she got really interested.'

I smiled at the thought of a girl her age getting excited by a beast of burden.

'Have you ever seen a Poitou donkey, Clarrie?'

'Yes, on holiday in France, ages ago. We were walking along and this enormous donkey followed us. He was in a big garden, the other side of a wall. He said...'

She stopped, suddenly self-conscious, but I don't think anyone had really noticed except me.

Then Theo told her the story of how he'd rescued Beau from a field where he'd been virtually abandoned and placed him in a donkey sanctuary but taken him away from there when he found my mother had a paddock going begging.

'Was that wise, Theo?' I asked, when he came to that point in the story.

Giving me a look that would curdle milk, he demanded, 'Would you put Oscar or Fritz into a dogs' home if you found an alternative?'

My brother's goodwill was disappearing as rapidly as Rowan's scallops and chorizo starter, but my mouth paid no heed.

'But what's going to happen to him when you go back to the States?'

Pointedly ignoring me, he droned on about the history of the Poitou breed and how rare they are now.

When he'd finished, Clarrie got her diary out of her bag.

'Do you think I could meet Beau? I need to take some pictures and spend a day with him to log what he eats and what he gets up to.'

Theo nodded in my direction.

'You better ask the boss,' he said, with more than a hint of sarcasm.

'Well, *Charles* is really the person to ask,' I retaliated. 'You'd need to stay the night, wouldn't you, Clarrie? When are you thinking of doing it?'

Clarrie looked uncomfortable.

'I don't want to put anyone to any trouble. I've got a study break the second week of March. I'd like to get it all done then. I could always stay at a B&B.'

'Hey, Mum, I'll be on exam study leave then. I could go too.'

In response, Clarrie gave a wiggle of delight. In the face of all this enthusiasm, I could hardly object, and I said I'd ask Charles about places to stay.

'Steve has rooms,' said Theo.

Seeing that this drew a blank with me, he elaborated.

'You know, the farmer who has the field that Beau visits? He had an annexe built last year for his wife to do B&B. I can give you his number.'

'Fine. Let me know which days, and I'll book two rooms,' I said, emphasising the 'two'.

When we arrived home, I noticed that Gaby's car had disappeared from the courtyard and wondered whether she and Jay were having another long lunch somewhere.

'You're coming in, aren't you, Clarrie?' I said.

She glanced at Rowan for reassurance.

'Are you sure it's all right?'

'Sure what's all right?'

We turned to see Jay striding towards us with both dogs in tow.

I winked at Clarrie to let her know he was harmless.

'Clarrie's a friend of Rowan's. You might have seen her working at the Feathers.'

Seeing him frown, I added, 'She's a veterinary nurse in the daytime.'

Jay took the hand that Clarrie offered him.

'Any friend of the animal kingdom is a friend of mine. All I ask is that you treat my son with the same care you treat your patients. He's like a highly-strung colt at the moment – reckless, untrainable, and unpredictable.'

Sharon had come to the back door to eavesdrop. I knew she'd be dying to check Clarrie out, so I told Rowan to take her in to meet his grandma.

Jay was in the process of inviting Theo to come with us on our walk, but he wasn't keen.

'Nah. Guess I'll get some shut-eye. I'm beat.'

'How come?' said Jay. 'A young bloke like you, going to bed in the afternoon?'

A totally unexpected, protective response rose in my breast which told me I did have some sisterly feelings after all.

'He's done a lot today. The labyrinth *and* the dome.'

'Ah, Pan's labyrinth and the pleasure dome,' said Jay. 'A heady combination guaranteed to knock your socks off. See you later. Enjoy your nap.'

So Jay and I headed out to the common with Fritz and Oscar, who forged ahead, while we trailed after them, hand in hand. I broke the news to him of Rowan and Clarrie's planned trip together, which he took surprisingly well. But I didn't divulge what Theo had revealed. It was too personal and private, not to mention the 'patient confidentiality' aspect, even though he wasn't officially a patient at all.

* * *

Ashley and Linden arrived at ten-thirty on Sunday, bearing Mother's Day tulips and lilies – the tulips for me and the lilies to put on their real mother's grave. Cherry had been out carousing with friends the night before, so was still in bed.

Pleased as punch to have all his saplings home at once, a rarity now they were older, Jay presided over his progeny in the sitting room, quizzing Linden on which celebrities he tweeted and Facebooked for, in his capacity as intern for a company which managed the social-media profiles of any celebs unable, or unwilling, to do it themselves.

Meanwhile, I quizzed Ashley on his fourth-year medical studies.

'So do you think you might specialise eventually?'

He smiled. 'I thought you were all for the holistic approach.'

'I am. But that's not how it's done in the NHS, is it?'

'Actually, I'm doing a project on genomic testing. In an ideal world, treatment would be personalised according to the patient's genetic blueprint.'

Hearing the word 'blueprint', I was transported back to when Enoch had tried to explain cellular healing to me. In fact, his words 'appeared' in the air in front of me.

Your divine purpose is to heal on a quantum level. To transform cellular disorder by assisting beings to heal their atomic blueprints of the patterns of distortion they hold, in order to restore the sacred geometry of their form to their original, flawless patterns.

Jay paused in his conversation with Linden. Showing himself capable of using each of his ears independently, he called out, 'Is that connected with the human genome project and DNA sequencing?'

'That's correct, Father,' said Ashley, with a grin. 'A giant step forward in diagnosis and treatment.'

Jay grinned back, and continued chatting to Linden.

Ashley turned back to me.

'It's about looking at the *whole* person.'

'So it *is* holistic, then. Yay!' I cried, high-fiving him – happy to hear Enoch's words confirmed by medical science and wondering if the day would ever come when the health service introduced genetic testing as a matter of course.

* * *

Theo arrived back from Tegan's just in time for lunch, which Sharon had decreed should be conducted in the dining room, as there would be nine or ten of us, depending on whether Tegan came.

Jay loved making soup from our Four Seasons vegetables, which took care of the first course. He was a good cook. Indeed, the children's mother, Debbie, had left most of the catering to him. I thought of the first meal he'd ever made me – a greasy spaghetti Bolognese which I'd almost gagged on. He'd come on a lot since then.

'Did you tell Tegan she was welcome to come?' Sharon asked, when Theo turned up on his own.

'Yeah,' he said, blushing slightly. 'She said thanks for the invite, but she didn't want to gatecrash a family occasion.'

Our eyes met and I thought he must have read my mind: that although I hadn't known Tegan long, it was longer than I'd known *him*. I looked away quickly and called everyone to sit down.

I hadn't planned how to present Theo to Cherry, Ashley and Linden. I suppose I trusted that they'd just accept him. But Jay had prepared a welcome speech without telling me, and I died inside when he called for silence in the lull between the soup and the lamb.

'I'd like to say how fantastic it is to have everyone together again. When was the last time?'

'Your sixtieth, Dad,' said Cherry, yawning. 'All of two weeks ago.'

Jay smiled disarmingly.

'It seems longer than that. So much has happened.'

'Have you got over it yet, Dad, hitting the big six-o?'

Rowan was obviously banking on his father having drunk enough to see the lighter side of being a sexagenarian.

'Why?' said Linden to Rowan. 'Has he been in denial?'

'I've never even been to Egypt,' said Jay, and everyone groaned. 'Anyway,' he went on, 'I'd like to welcome Andy's long-lost brother into the family.'

He glanced at me to check he was saying the right thing, but by then I'd gone crimson with the embarrassment of my newly discovered sibling being the result of a one-night stand and subsequently abandoned by our mother.

'So,' said Cherry, her sleepy eyes widening. 'Have you two only just met?'

'Yup. Just over a week and already she's given me an ear-bashing in the dome. Twice.'

The kids all laughed when he said this.

Theo looked bemused.

'That means she told you off.' Grinning, Linden added, 'It's usually Grandma that does that around here.'

Sharon was across the hall in the kitchen but there was nothing wrong with her hearing and she came to the doorway brandishing a spatula.

'And none of you lot are too old for a good spank when you need it, so don't think it,' she said, winking away like a pantomime dame.

I decided to play along with the mood.

'I forced him to do the labyrinth walk as well. He'll be glad to get back to Glastonbury tomorrow.'

After lunch, all of us except Sharon went outside. It was cold, so once I'd given Midnight her daily apple, I headed back. I found Sharon loading the dishwasher.

'Sit down, Sha, I'll finish that.'

'Okay, honey,' she said, sitting down at the kitchen table and giving a contented sigh.

'Where's Jay?'

'Playing croquet. It's really windy out there but nobody seems to mind. He's trying to teach Theo how to play.'

Smiling, she raised her eyebrows at the thought.

'He's happier today than he's been for a few weeks.'

'I hope it lasts. The last time he was moody like this was when he started sleeping with Debbie.'

Jay's collaboration with Gaby had revived old wounds I thought had healed – namely, those he'd inflicted on me when he got together with Debbie. I was beginning to conflate the two women: Debbie had been blonde and busty just like Gaby. And I detected a ruthless quality in Gaby that Debbie had possessed in shedloads. I could no longer think of one without the spectre of the other lurking in the background.

Sharon stopped smiling and looked stricken. *Damn*, I thought. Why hadn't I kept my big mouth shut? My insecurities were my problem, I had no right to inflict them on others. I'd burdened Sharon enough already with all the Glastonbury goings-on, without adding further fuel to the fire.

'Sorry, Sha, I don't know why I said that. It's lovely having the kids here, let's enjoy the day.'

She frowned slightly. 'Don't worry about Jay. He adores you...'

She didn't mention Gaby's name but we were both sure as hell thinking of her.

* * *

Cherry had saddled up Midnight and taken her out for a hack, with Willow behind them on her bike, so they came back quite invigorated. They found Sharon and me in the sitting room and sat between us on the sofa.

When Jay walked in, he beamed when he saw the four of us snuggled up in front of the log fire.

'Who won the game?' Sharon said.

'It hasn't started yet,' said Jay.

'Not the football, I'm talking about croquet.'

'Oh. Me and Linden beat Theo and Ash. A complete massacre. Best of three, and we won all three.'

'Why did you play the last one, then?' I said.

'Just to rub it in, darlin',' he chuckled, bending down and kissing me on the cheek.

'When are they taking the flowers to Debbie's...'

I searched without success for another word for 'grave', which would have sounded too depressing, so I stopped there.

'Already have,' said Jay softly. 'We've just come back. The girls said they'd rather not.'

I glanced at Cherry and Willow and their pale faces told me how painful a subject it still was.

'Did Rowan go?'

I was never sure how much he missed Debbie, as he hardly ever spoke of her.

'Yeah. He was fine. He seems more together since he's met that girl.'

Willow and Cherry giggled at this.

'She's two years older than him,' said Willow.

'He's trying to impress her, that's all,' added Cherry.

As he made his way to the door, Jay said, 'You may well be right. But on a sporting note, us lads'll be watching Everton versus Portsmouth in the TV room if anyone wants to join us. Bring your own cans.'

'Don't worry,' Sharon called after him, 'my Mother's Day DVD of *Hairspray* and Pan's chocolates will keep us going in here.'

Four hours later, our perfect day came to an end, when Linden and Ash departed in the little red sports car that had once been mine, given to me by Mike, my interregnum husband who'd died so I'd be able to get back with Jay. Well, it hadn't been quite like that. I'd happily have stayed with Mike until my dying day, but a dodgy ticker carried him off, which led me to my spiritual penfriend Enoch, then back to Jay. I'd come full circle, so to speak.

Jay left soon after the twins, dropping Cherry off in Southwark on the way to his hotel. He rang later in the evening to say goodnight, admitting that he couldn't wait to get back inside a proper recording studio the next day.

'Sleep well, J-J,' I said, trying not to feel so down in the dumps now that four of my loved ones had left all at once, with my brother due to leave tomorrow.

'I'll try. I wish you were here to rub my back.'

I felt so deflated I couldn't even manage a spicy riposte, just a weak sigh.

'So Theo's going back tomorrow,' he continued. 'You won't know what to do with yourself.' Actually, I knew exactly what to do with myself. I'd be in the shepherd's hut composing my weekly dispatch, of which Jay knew nothing. Ashley's genetic screening studies had alerted my secret column antenna. This week's offering was definitely going to include something on the pros and cons of having one's genetic profile mapped.

Jay was waiting for an answer.

'Yes,' I said. 'It'll be quiet.'

'Don't worry, kid. I'll be home before you know it. Love you. Sleep tight.'

I climbed into bed but couldn't sleep, so I found myself at my computer, printing out information on DNA testing to take with me to the hut the next day.

Before I closed the computer down, I automatically checked my emails. Among the spam and the mailshots, I found one from my editor, Polly.

Hi Pandora,
Hope you're feeling better after the sad loss of your mother.
Breaking news! A company called Oven Ready Productions has contacted me. They're making a new daytime TV programme –

current affairs, interviewing celebs, that sort of thing, and they're scouting for female panellists. A researcher picked up on your column and wants to know who's writing it. Don't worry, I haven't revealed your name, but I did tell them you'd had a successful book published.

Anyway, they want you to audition.

Let me know if you're interested, and I'll pass your details on to them.

See you soon, much love,

Polly xxx

Chapter 13

Straight Talking

Theo left bright and early for Glastonbury, so by the time I reached the breakfast table he was already on the train.

My night had been anything but restful: Polly's email had set my mind racing, stirring up memories of the pre-launch publicity for my novel three years earlier. The marketing and publicity people had spun the book as a *roman à clef*, having a field day with Pandora and James Jay's unusual history. Subsequently, every interview had referred to our former rackety social life and the contrast with how relatively sedate our lives had become since we'd reconnected.

Sales had rocketed, but I knew that this had been achieved mainly by me riding on Jay's coat-tails. That was why I felt so excited now at being 'discovered' through my column – knowing that this time it was down to my efforts alone.

As I tossed and turned, I thought of Rupert, a literary agent Jay had met on a retreat when he'd been 'finding himself' after Debbie left him. Rupert was sympathetic to the genre – he called it 'mainstream fiction with a dash of the paranormal,' and had taken me on.

I'd written it as the second assignment of the Enoch Society Correspondence Course when I'd been instructed to write about my life and loves for the purpose of examining the events leading up to, and following, the triumphs and disasters of my life. The point of it all originally was to identify any negative behavioural patterns which led to me making the same mistakes over and over again.

In effect, it was a memoir of much of my life, featuring the male romantic leads with the names and locations changed to protect the innocent. Rupert made the most of my partner being leader of a former chart-topping band when he hawked it round the publishers – and on the back of that, secured me a contract and a sizeable advance.

Naturally, he'd pushed for another book, but while the first had flowed, the second barely trickled and he eventually gave up on me. They say everyone has one book in them and I found, to my frustration, that I wasn't the prolific novelist I'd hoped to be. My inspiration had sprung from my life and experiences, most of which I'd used up in the first book.

From force of habit I still spent time in the writing hut, where I kept the pages of automatic writing received from dear Enoch. One day I took out the file and started reading. I'd half-forgotten most of it and read the words avidly, reliving my worries and fears, and getting a warm feeling from recognising that the woman who'd been writing then was no longer the same person. Enoch was right. I had no need of him now because I'd taken charge of my own life.

Gradually my visits to the hut tailed off, but I'd recently returned as a result of Polly, a former client, asking me to write a piece for her weekly online magazine. Its target audience were women of forty plus – that's age, not hip size – and my remit was to write about anything that caught my interest. She wanted it to be 'mildly confessional' and since everything I'd written up to then (in short, my one and only novel) had been just that, it suited me down to the ground.

The original article, combining an appraisal of the most popular weight-loss diets with a critique of the eccentric size labelling on women's clothing, got enough 'likes' and comments to more than satisfy her, so she offered me a regular slot. This proved to be much easier than I'd thought. All I had to do was keep my eyes and ears open and tune into the *zeitgeist* of the gripes, likes and insecurities of middle-aged women, and out it flowed, on to the page. I always wrote in longhand first and typed it up afterwards, in the house. If I attempted to do it on the computer from scratch, for some reason, it never worked.

Polly ended up calling the column: 'Dispatches from a Shepherd's Hut', minus a by-line, as I wrote on condition I'd remain anonymous. I didn't want Sharon pouncing on my weekly outpourings with a retrospective blue pencil, just in case one day I'd be moved to get 'confessional' on the subject of sharing a house with my partner's mother. In fact, I didn't tell anyone about it. It was my secret and all the sweeter for it.

I finally got to sleep about three a.m. But not before the telegram from my inner critic had arrived, telling me why I shouldn't even think about spreading my wings.

Hold on a minute, girl, what if by some fluke you did get the job? You think it'd fit round your healing work? The work that's supposed to be your so-called 'divine purpose'? Plus, your nearest and dearest would wonder why you hadn't mentioned the column you'd been writing for the last six months. And if you thought having your name attached to that was too exposing, why go on TV to voice your opinions publicly to the world at large? That's assuming you've got any opinions worth hearing.

'You okay, Pandora?'

Sharon had just walked into the kitchen and was peering at me from behind her Dame Edna glasses.

'You look as if you've been up all night.'

'Oh, you know. Some nights it's hard to get to sleep. Did Theo get off all right?'

'Yup. Just dropped him at the station. He said to tell you goodbye. Got any plans for today?'

My heart sank as I wondered what Sharon had in mind for me. All I yearned for was some quiet time in the shepherd's hut to compose my column and decide whether to email Polly with a yes, neither of which could I disclose.

I racked my brains for a watertight excuse.

'I'm going to check my client list and send out reminders.'

The waggle of Sharon's head indicated she didn't consider that at all urgent.

'Then I thought I'd do some mucking out. It'd be a surprise for Willow.'

Blast, I thought. *Now I'll have to get down and dirty with my wellies and wheelbarrow.*

'Rather you than me, dear. I'm off to Bicester Outlet Village with Fran. We're aiming to blitz Curvy Girls. You're more than welcome to come with us...'

I had a vision of the three of us trying on a variety of voluminous kaftans and I lowered my eyes, hoping she hadn't seen my horrified expression.

'Of course,' she said haughtily, reading my mind, '*you* would be shopping in Temperley, or wherever all the *thin people* go.'

I got up and kissed her cheek, sorry for accidentally hurting her feelings.

'I appreciate the thought, Sha, but I'm not really in the mood for shopping. I'll cook tonight, if you like, then you can stay out longer.'

Her expression relaxed.

'Okay, honey. I just didn't want you to be lonely...with Jay and Theo both taking off.'

'Oh, I can always talk to the animals. At least they don't answer back.'

Laughing girlishly, she sailed out, allowing me to retreat to my hut on wheels. It looked like being a busy day now I'd added stable hand and cook to my list of duties.

* * *

Back from the garden and seated at my desk, I typed the last word of my dispatch and began to compose its accompanying email.

Hi Pol,

Attached is this week's offering.

What remarkable news. You can certainly tell Oven Ready I'm interested and give them my mobile number. BUT THIS IS IMPORTANT please say only that I'm Miss Fry (my single name). I want to remain a woman of mystery for a little longer. J

Must dash – catering to attend to.

Love,

Pan xx

As I pressed send, my stomach performed a half-somersault. If I got this job it would inevitably put a strain on the family life I'd chosen and committed to. It felt as if I was preparing to break my present contract in favour of a better one.

But there's more to it than that, isn't there, Pan?

It was my mother speaking.

I hated to admit it, but she was right. And now was the moment, at last, that I was allowing myself to type 'Oven Ready Productions' into the search engine, to see if my former lover, Zac Willoughby, whose uncle had founded the company, was still *in situ*.

And there he was, pictured with his production team. Fair and tanned, he appeared a little fatter in the face than before but his cheekbones were still high and wide, his aquiline nose giving him a patrician air. He was undoubtedly the best-looking man I'd ever been out with.

I suppose my failure to check his whereabouts before sending the email had been my attempt to prove that applying for the job had no bearing on him being a part of it. And the fact I'd withheld *my* real name was meant to ensure that *he* wouldn't be influenced either.

Whether or not he'd want to see me again was a mystery to me anyway. We'd parted on bad terms initially when I'd stopped going out with him after Jay reappeared. But his attitude had subsequently softened, and he'd come to our handfasting and wished us well.

It was never going anywhere with Zac anyway, I told myself. A six-year gap is a big deal when it's in the wrong direction.

The sound of my ringtone, which I'd moved to top volume, brought me back to reality with a bump.

'Hello. My name is Portia, of Oven Ready Productions.'

'Blimey, that's quick,' I said, Portia's upstairs accent triggering my cockney impersonation.

'Ha, we don't hang about,' she said, adjusting her delivery in a downstairs direction.

'Wondered if you could come and see us sometime this week for a screen test? We've got a small studio we use for auditions.'

I said I'd check my diary, but I already knew I had clients on Wednesday and Thursday but nobody on Tuesday.

'I'm free tomorrow.'

'Fantastic.'

She began to give me directions to the office and I had to listen patiently and pretend to write it down, even though I already knew the address.

After she'd rung off, I started fretting about what I'd tell Sharon, but when she sat down to her evening meal, her multiple carrier bags unpacked, she solved the problem for me.

'Pandora. I've had a great time.' This was her third glass of wine and her mouth was sagging. 'Get yourself out tomorrow. Hit those shops, honey. I *insist*. You've shovelled enough shit today.'

I rolled my eyes at Willow, who giggled as Rowan said, 'Don't pussyfoot around, Gran, say what you really mean.'

* * *

'So, Ms Fry,' said Portia, her beautifully made-up eyes gleaming from the other side of the desk. 'Are you ready to tell us your first name?'

Now I'd proved to myself I could get an audition without the help of the boss I had slept with, I came clean.

'Pandora,' I replied, flashing my own beautifully made-up eyes back at her. I'd been thirty minutes in hair and make-up and it showed.

Trying to disguise her surprise at my name being as posh as hers, she typed something into her computer, beetling her brows at the result.

'Polly said you'd written a book.'

'Search for Pandora Armstrong.'

She found what she was looking for on the Amazon website, then lingered while she read my author profile.

'It says here you live with James Jay.' She studied me more closely for a moment. 'I do believe I attended your second wedding,'

'Handfasting,' I corrected her. Zac had, indeed, brought a girlfriend with him and I seem to remember she was an Oven Ready employee they'd just taken on.

'It's a small world,' I said. Politeness would have left it there, but curiosity got the better of me. 'Are you still together?'

'With whom?'

'Zac.'

'No. We never were.'

I must have looked doubtful, because Portia bared her perfect teeth in a steely smile.

'I have a girlfriend. I was just being a dutiful employee. He asked me to act the part, so I did.'

I found this hard to take in.

'Why would he do that?'

'He told me he didn't want to go on his own, but I guessed it was because he needed to show someone that he'd got over them.'

While I was rearranging the past in my head, there was a tap on the door and a man called out, 'We're ready now.'

Portia escorted me to a small studio and seated me at a table with three other people. She'd already explained that these were actors, who'd be playing the parts of the other panellists. A minute later, a woman in her late forties, who I recognised as a minor TV presenter called Kay Sullivan, came in and took a seat at the head of the table. Then a voice issued from the sound system: 'Roll cameras,' and we were off.

Kay got under way with a reference to the current, very costly, inquest into the death of Princess Diana, who'd died more than ten years earlier, in 1997. Could we take seriously, she wondered, Mohammed Al Fayed's allegations that MI5, MI6 and Tony Blair, among others, had been involved in her death? And was Al Fayed right to insist on a jury, thereby turning the inquest into a public spectacle, where witnesses discussed her alleged lovers?

When it came to my turn I questioned why anybody was taking these conspiracy theories seriously. The inquest was peering into corners of Diana's life that should have remained private. Her life was being dissected, even down to whether she was pregnant. This must be especially upsetting for her sons, William and Harry, who'd been teenagers when she died. I mentioned that my stepchildren had lost their mother early in their lives, and how deeply affected they'd been. Bringing these painful memories back, more than a decade later, in such a public way, must be torture for her sons and wider family.

As I said this, I thought of what Willow and Rowan's reaction would be if this was an actual broadcast. They'd probably say, 'Don't mention us again on TV, please, Mum.'

After half an hour, a voice crackled over the speaker to say the session was finished, cutting into a discussion on whether the nationalisation of Northern Rock could have been avoided. Adjusting his salty language accordingly, I'd recycled Jay's line about greedy bankers, greedy borrowers, greedy investors, rubbish credit-rating agencies and rubbish regulators, which seemed to go down well with Kay.

The door opened, and Portia beckoned me. I followed her back to her office, where I'd left my coat and bag

'We'll be in touch,' she said.

'Is that the same as, "don't call us, we'll call you",' I answered, feeling deflated. 'I'm sorry I'm not much of an expert on anything.'

'Don't worry,' she said, squeezing my hand. 'We watched you from the viewing room. You were fine. If we need experts, we'll cab them in. Panellists are meant to represent the public. You know, the woman in the street.'

This was the first time, to my knowledge, that I'd been called a street woman, but I felt strangely cheered that I had. I couldn't help but focus on her use of 'we', though.

'Was the whole assessment team in the viewing room?'

'Do you mean – was Zac there?'

This girl was good.

'I suppose I do,' I said, blushing.

'No, he's out of the office. But he'll see it tomorrow. We've been running these tests all month. You're the last one. They'll be shortlisting soon.'

* * *

All day Wednesday and Thursday, apart from when I was in the dome, I kept checking my phone for voicemail. I was in the sitting room with Sharon, having a mug of cocoa and watching a DVD about a serial killer – Sharon liked her movies bloodthirsty – when the call finally came. I thought it would be Jay at that time of evening, but it wasn't.

'Hello. Pandora?'

As soon as I heard those beautiful vowels, I knew it was Zac.

'Yes, this is she.'

Jay and I used to giggle when people in old movies answered

the phone in that way, and we'd sometimes say it to each other, putting on a false accent. But I knew, as soon as the words had escaped my lips, that Zac wouldn't get the joke.

'You sound incredibly formal.'

I laughed nervously. Sharon was craning forward to hear what Jake Gyllenhaal was saying, so I used that as an excuse to go across the hall to the study. I decided to get straight to the point. Sharon was bound to ask me who was on the phone, so it'd be best to keep it brief and pretend the call was from a client.

'Put me out of my misery, please. Is this a "thanks, but no thanks", call?'

'No. I was going to ask how you were but something tells me you're in no mood for small talk.'

He paused, and I relented.

'I'm not too bad. How are you?'

His voice mellowed.

'I'm good. Are you still enjoying country life?'

'Yes. Nothing wrong with the country, it's life that's been a bit weird lately. My mother died and I found out I had a half-brother, can you believe? I'm still feeling, um, kind of churned up.'

'I'm sorry to hear that.' He sounded genuinely concerned and a ripple of fondness for him stirred my heart. 'How's Jay?'

'Okay. He's at Abbey Road Studios this week, working with Gaby Laing.'

'Good grief. Is she still around?'

Zac's reaction gave me a little lift. Most men would have said, 'Phwoah!'

'He isn't very happy to be sixty, though.'

'Tell me about it. I'm fifty in August and having panic attacks at the thought.'

'I'd love to be fifty again,' I said, inserting an oblique reminder of our age difference.

'From the clip I saw of you yesterday, you don't look a day

over forty-five.'

I blushed. How I'd love that to be true, but I had a suspicion that Zac had put his Oven Ready hat on, and was buttering me up like a trussed chicken, ready to pop into the oven.

'I was amazed when I saw it was you,' he continued. 'What an incredible coincidence.'

'Yes, a true coincidence. My column's anonymous.'

'I know. Portia was most intrigued with the mystery woman who wouldn't reveal her full name.'

He stopped, as if waiting for an explanation. Having paced enough of the floor, I sat down.

'Ah, that. I didn't want you to be influenced by...'

I faltered. By what? Having slept together, or having unfinished business?

Zac finished my sentence for me.

'By our having biblical knowledge of each other?' He chuckled. 'If that was a problem, the whole entertainment industry would grind to a halt.'

'Come on, you know what I mean,' I said, joining in the chuckles. I was pleased that the elephant in the room had been shown the door, but a small corner of my heart wished that he'd sounded just a tiny bit regretful.

'To get to the point,' he went on, 'we'd love you to be a panellist on *Straight Talking*. We're trying to sort out the rota at the moment. I'm giving you first refusal, as a mate, so you can choose to do a minimum of two days, maximum four days a week. Filming's at the Southbank Studio. You need to get there by eight.'

He must have heard my intake of breath.

'We'll send a car, don't worry. Then into wardrobe, etc., ready for filming at ten-thirty. We broadcast at one o'clock. You can be away as soon as filming's finished. Does that sound do-able?'

To me it sounded wonderful. I imagined the joy of perfectly coordinated clothing and jewellery laid out ready. And the delight of being primped and powdered by experts, just so I could sit in comfort and contribute to an animated conversation in front of an enthusiastic audience who would, no doubt, have been primed by a warm-up comedian to clap at the drop of a hat.

'It's tempting.' Then I remembered the night Jay had appeared at Phoenix cottage and proposed to me in front of Zac, who'd walked out. 'I'll have to talk to Jay. He doesn't know about the column, so it'll come as a surprise...'

The lameness of what I'd said wasn't lost on me. It smacked of the little wife having to get permission from her husband before making a decision. Then there was the unspoken difficulty – the baby elephant momma had left behind. Would Jay be happy with me being employed by the man he'd sent packing?

'Of course you should talk to Jay,' said Zac, speaking in such a gentle, understanding tone, that I felt like a skittish horse being pacified. 'When do you think you'll be able to tell me? Filming starts April 14th.'

I did a quick calculation. That was only six weeks away.

'He'll be home tomorrow. Can I ring you some time over the weekend, or would you prefer Monday?'

'No, the weekend's fine. You won't be interrupting anything. I haven't acquired a partner and five kids since we last met.'

His unexpected gibe at my situation hurt me.

'Pandora? Are you still there?'

'Yes.'

'If you decide to go ahead it might be an idea for me to show you where the studio is. Give you an orientation, so to speak.'

The last sentence, for some reason, struck me as *risqué*, and I gave an involuntary titter, which set Zac off too. I was listening to his protests that no *double entendre* had been intended, when I sensed someone else was near. I swivelled round in my chair to see the shadow of Sharon in the doorway and wondered how long she'd been there.

When she realised she'd been spotted, she came in and put

my mug of lukewarm cocoa down on the desk.

'Thanks,' I mouthed to her and she smiled tightly.

'I have to go now,' I said, briskly. 'I'll get back to you regarding that appointment.'

Chapter 14

Bad Tidings

Theo rang the next afternoon with the news that Charles was in hospital, after losing control of his car and colliding with a parked van on the opposite side of the road. He'd badly bruised his ribs and hit his head, so they were keeping him in for tests.

'How awful. What happened, Theo? Did his foot slip or was it the steering?'

'He can't remember. The car's a write-off so no clue there...'

I thought about how out of sorts Charles had been and wondered whether he'd had some sort of seizure which caused him to black out at the wheel.

'Is it serious? I mean, should I come?'

Even as the words left my lips I already knew the answer. How could I expect Theo to take charge – he was just the lodger. But he surprised me.

'He wasn't too bad when I left him. No call for you to rush over, maybe wait till after the weekend?'

'Okay then,' I said, relief flooding through me. Jay was coming home today and I'd been happily anticipating helping him unwind after his busy week.

'I suppose he hasn't got any toiletries with him, has he? Or a dressing gown?'

'Nope. Shower gel wasn't exactly the priority when I got the call. More a question of whether he was alive or dead.'

No need to be cheeky, I thought.

'Will you be going in to see him later? Would you be able to take him in some things?'

I knew I was clucking but couldn't stop. Ever since I'd become a surrogate mother, I'd acquired a mother-hen gene which was hard to control.

'I guess so. Or maybe tomorrow. They gave him some hospital-issue pyjamas.'

'Have you told Pete yet?'

'Uh, no. I don't have his number.'

'In that case, leave a message for him at Chalkie's café. He can tell whoever needs to know.'

Then I thought of one visitor he wouldn't be best pleased to see.

'Don't tell Rosemary. It would only upset him if she turned up.'

There was a silence at the end of the line and I began to think we'd lost contact, but he finally drawled 'okay' and said he'd keep me informed.

I just had time to say, 'Give him my love, and tell him I'll be over to see him soon,' before he rang off.

* * *

I found Sharon in the garden getting some fruit and vegetables for dinner from Hugh, and I told her the news about Charles.

'Gee, that's awful. That can happen with seniors. One dies and the other one turns up their toes as well. You said he was taking it hard.'

'He's not dead yet,' I protested, the thought of facing another funeral almost too much to bear.

Sharon linked my arm as we walked back to the kitchen, patting my hand to soothe me.

'You're not thinking of rushing over to see him this weekend, are you? With James not even back yet?'

'Theo said there was no need. Any other time I would have gone...'

'I get it, honey. Don't beat yourself up. You need to spend some quality time together, otherwise...'

It was her turn to leave a sentence dangling, but we both knew what hung in the air – a four-lettered word beginning with G and ending in y.

Just at that moment we saw Jay loping towards us – he must have left London early to avoid the Friday-evening traffic.

'My trusty gatherers,' he said, enveloping us both in a hug. 'I see you've been foraging for roots and berries for the tribe.'

I'd been in a dreamy mood all morning after Zac's call, reliving our brief but passionate affair. But the sight of Jay moved Zac firmly into the folder marked 'fantasy'. Jay was my here and now – a flesh and blood man: a man I loved.

I buried my face in his sweater and breathed him in. He smelled faintly of roll-ups and bergamot. Sharon always gave him cologne for Christmas and filial piety demanded he put a little on his person every so often, just to keep her happy.

After a decent interval, I furled my arms round his waist, edging Sharon out of the way. It was unusual for Sharon to give ground but on this occasion she did, allowing me to move in for the sort of welcome-home snog guaranteed to keep a red-blooded male coming back for more.

When we reached the kitchen, Sharon put the garden produce away while I put Jay in the picture. The expression in his eyes, when I said I'd have to go and see Charles, indicated that his mind had wandered down the same track mine had earlier. *Does that mean another night in a lonely bed?*

Before I had a chance to put him out of his misery and tell him that Theo was coping for the time being, Sharon intervened.

'The best thing we can all do is pray for him.'

So saying, she put her hands together, bowed her head, and began to intone, finishing with the lines: 'The Lord Our God have mercy on our dear brother Charles. May the Lord's healing touch raise him up, body and soul, in perfect health, to walk amongst us once more. Amen.'

We echoed her 'Amen'. It would have been impolite not to.

Sharon had been married to a Jewish Canadian and (so Jay

reckoned) just to annoy him, had attended an Evangelical church when she was living over there. She hadn't practised since her return to England but was a great believer in an interventionist God, keeping a running list of requests for the Almighty to grant. She was convinced that the power of prayer had got the children through all their major exams, putting any failures down to them not praying hard enough.

I never argued the point with her, but logic led me to doubt the existence of some distant God who favoured some people's prayers over others. I also mistrusted the assumption that it's okay to pray for personal favours, like winning the lottery or your football team getting promoted.

I preferred the idea of prayer being for the benefit of others in distress, and embraced the theory that our spirits are part of a great Divine Body. So it's actually up to us, as divine beings, to send healing thoughts to humans, plants, animals, the planet – whatever or whoever needs them – to help their mental, physical and spiritual bodies recover, or to help their spirits return home to the great Divine Body when their physical body expires. So in that sense, we're all God.

And if everybody believed that, they'd surely feel they had more control over life because they wouldn't be at the mercy of some unreadable, unreliable, external god-figure. And the question: *Why did God let that happen?* would never arise.

Jay caught my eye at the final 'Amen' and I had to bite my lip hard to quell a giggle.

'Poor old sod. But Theo's around, isn't he?' he said, taking my hand, out of sight of Sharon, and placing it lightly on his thigh. 'You can wait till after the weekend before you go, can't you?'

Rowan, who'd wandered into the kitchen at the sound of his father's voice, had been calculating the possible repercussions of Charles' untimely collision.

'This won't affect Clarrie and me going to see Beau on Monday, will it?'

Fiddlesticks, I thought. I'd forgotten all about that arrangement. I glanced at Jay, to find he was smiling.

'There's your answer, Andy,' he said, giving my hand a squeeze. 'Go with the kids. You can see Charles and keep an eye on them at the same time.'

Rowan reddened, even though his dad winked at him as he said it.

'You won't be coming with us in Clarrie's car, though, will you, Mum?'

The idea of being stuck in the back of Clarrie's old banger, with Britney Spears and Justin Timberlake at top volume, provoked from me a shriek of horror. The simple thought of it made me long for my little red roadster – just me, Oscar, and the open road – the way it used to be.

Jay laughed at both of us.

'Why don't *you* take *them*? It'll give you an excuse to come back when they do.'

Rowan's face went sulky and I had trouble stopping mine from doing the same. I'd had a basinful of playing gooseberry lately with Gaby and Jay, so I was blowed if I was going to do the same with Rowan and Clarrie.

I pretended to consider this suggestion.

'Mm. Maybe...' Now it was my turn to wink at Rowan. 'But I'll be making trips to the hospital. That means they'd be stuck without transport. It's best we go in separate cars.'

Rowan immediately cheered up, so I turned my attention to Sharon, who'd have to hold the fort again sooner than expected.

'Is that all right with you, Sha?'

I felt pretty certain it would be. For her it would be like old times, when she'd ruled the roost, although there'd only be Willow, the animals and Jay to see to.

'That's fine with me. Maybe we could go into London one day, James. I'd like to take a look at our old house in Shepherd's Bush, see if it's still standing. I haven't been there in thirty-five years.'

'Ah,' he said ominously.

I recognised that tone. He used it when he couldn't do something he knew you wanted him to.

'Have you got some work in?' I asked.

He often got requests to compose advertising jingles or film music. His default mode would be working on songs to pitch to suitable artists, but he wasn't keen on spending all day and every day in his studio, which is why he'd put himself on the rota for delivering the veg boxes. He'd also got into the habit of working with Hugh in the garden – he called it 'going to the allotment', so he could be flexible, time-wise, if he wanted to be.

'No, it's the same old, same old. I'm back at Abbey Road next week. Haven't quite cracked it yet...Gaby needs at least two more numbers.'

He stopped when he saw the look on my face, and on Sharon's.

'What?' he said, letting go of my hand while he hunched his shoulders and spread his palms upwards, in a gesture which announced: *Why are you being unreasonable? I have a living to earn.*

'I thought it was only gonna be for a week,' said Sharon, delivering my line for me.

'The record company are paying the bills – if they want us there longer, who are we to say no? It's all money.'

Determined not to blot my copybook by voicing any objection, I got up from the table and started washing up the tea things.

'Anyway,' he went on, addressing his mother, 'it'll be less work for you with me away. Plus Rowan and Andy'll be in Glastonbury. Just enjoy the rest.'

I felt for Sharon. She was being faced with one of those perverse situations that life deals you: giving with one hand and taking away with the other. Instead of having Jay and Willow to herself, it would just be Willow, a quiet little soul. Sharon was probably feeling more abandoned than I was. At least I'd be on the go in Somerset, rather than mooching around at home wondering what Jay and Gaby might be getting up to.

Grabbing a tea towel, Sharon started drying the cups vigorously and I found myself saying, 'I wish you could come too, Sha. But with me *and* Theo there, the cottage bedrooms are taken.' Directing my gaze at Rowan I added, wickedly, 'Shall I check if there's room at the B&B?'

Sharon put down the tea towel, looking as if she was considering my proposal.

'But what about Willow, Gran?' said Rowan desperately, no doubt aghast at the idea of his grandmother sharing breakfast with him and Clarrie.

'Willow can't be left here on her own!' exclaimed Jay.

'She could come too,' I said. 'It's the school holidays.'

Rowan almost choked on his biscuit, while Sharon and I exchanged secret smirks.

'Thanks, Pandora, honey, I'd like that. But not right now. Maybe some time over Easter. It'd be good to see Charles again.'

'When is Easter?' said Jay, sounding slightly put out that his Abbey Road bombshell had mutated into a squib and the females had rapidly moved on to making arrangements of their own.

'Good Friday's the 21st – two weeks today,' said Sharon. She always read her horoscope so usually knew what the Cosmos was up to. 'There'll be a full moon and it's the spring equinox as well.'

* * *

It was Sunday night and Jay had just left for London. I have to confess, I never did get round to broaching the tricky subject of my job offer with him. I'd chickened out, being too scared of his reaction to Zac being involved. So now I had to decide what to tell Zac.

I called his number and he answered immediately. Maybe he'd been waiting for my call the way I'd been waiting for his, earlier in the week.

'Hello, Zac. I'm calling as promised.'

I paused, still unsure.

'Pandora, hello. Good news I hope.'

His voice was assured but I sensed an underlying tension.

'Yes, I'd like to join the panel. With a proviso.'

He didn't speak, so I continued.

'I didn't tell you about my healing practice, did I?'

'No,' he said, a note of relief in his voice (which made me wonder what he thought the proviso would have been. Some condition Jay had imposed, perhaps?). 'You'd better tell me now.'

'I don't have clients every day, by any means. But I don't want to give it up.'

'Uh, no. That's understandable. So how much of your week would be free?'

'Probably two days, to be realistic. Jay's mother's getting on a bit, so she can't run the house the way she used to.'

'Get some help in,' he teased. 'If you do four days with us you'll be making enough.'

I thought of the loan I'd taken out for the labyrinth. And how I wanted to buy Ashley and Linden a second-hand car for their twenty-third birthday so I could reclaim my beloved MX-5. The bottom line was, that I needed as much dosh as I could get. Maybe I should start with the maximum, then reduce my appearances once I was solvent.

'Let me think about it. So what happens next?'

'Ah, that is the question. What happens next is, that you come into the office tomorrow and Portia gives you masses of forms to fill in. Most important of all are your vital statistics, so wardrobe can kit you out. At some stage, you'll need to have a medical. Anyway, once Portia has finished with you, we can have lunch. That suit you?'

That would have suited me excellently. With Jay away, it would have been perfect timing. I sighed deeply. The depth of my disappointment surprised me.

'I'd love to, but my mother's partner's had an accident, and I have to go to Glastonbury tomorrow. I'm staying over...not sure how long for...'

'No problem. Call me when you're ready and we'll get together.'

'I will.'

'Give me a ring when you're down there, if you like. Tuesday evening would be good. We can have a longer chat...'

'Yes, I'd like that. I'll speak to you then. Bye, Zac.'

Chapter 15

Visiting Charles

When I arrived at the cottage there was no answer to my knock, so I went round the back and got the key from under the stone Buddha. I noticed the flowerbeds had been cleared and dug over, and wondered if Theo had asked Charles' permission. He was known to prefer a wild garden, although Frankie used to say he just couldn't be bothered to tend it.

Anubis must have been dozing in the undergrowth because no sooner had I let myself in the back door, than she was right behind me, mewing and rubbing herself on my legs.

'Hello, little girl,' I crooned, flattered that she was paying me so much attention. She'd never been particularly friendly, probably because I'd always had Oscar in tow, but today she seemed pathetically so. I wondered if she sensed I was her dead mistress's flesh and blood.

I called out to see if Theo was home, but there was no reply, so I took my holdall upstairs to the cramped box room, then wandered into Charles' room and sat on the bed. It was no contest. Why suffer the rigours of a folding bed when there was a perfectly good double divan going begging? Retrieving my holdall, I started to unpack.

I needed to hang the creases out of my things, so I inspected each of the two wardrobes to see which had space for them. The first was packed full of Frankie's clothes, just as she'd left them, so I mentally added *Ask Charles if he wants help sorting out Frankie's belongings*, to my to-do list. The second, containing Charles' clothing, was only three-quarters full, so I used that one.

Feeling like Goldilocks, having picked the best bed, I went downstairs to have a rummage round the larder. Finding nothing much more than a few tins of baked beans, some stale bread and a piece of desiccated cheese, I began a shopping list. At that moment, Anubis appeared at the doorway and deposited the head of a mouse, still bleeding at the neck, on the kitchen floor.

I let out a scream, searching wildly around for something to scoop it up with, but had to resort to a tissue I found in my pocket. As I carried it to the dustbin, I heard Charles' landline ringing, but by the time I'd dumped the poor creature's brains and scrubbed my hands clean, it had stopped.

Hearing the phone prompted me to rummage through my shoulder bag for my mobile.

I wanted to ring Rowan to see if he and Clarrie had managed to find their way to the farmhouse. I'd purposely left home later than them, in the hope they'd have settled in and made contact with Theo before I arrived. He'd told them he'd be around to introduce them to Beau and give Clarrie the information she needed for her assignment.

I emptied out my bag, but there was no phone to be found. What I did find was the number of the farmhouse which Theo had originally written down for me, so I dialled from the landline and asked to speak to Rowan. After a short interval, he came on the line.

'Hi, Mum. Snap! I just rang to see if you'd arrived. I couldn't get you on your mobile.'

'Hi, darling. No, I can't find it. Are your rooms okay?'

'Yeah, great. Steve and Jenny are really friendly. Steve said he'd take us on a tour of the farm tomorrow.'

'So where's Theo? Is he with you?'

'No. He texted me that he's helping out at the shop today, so you'll be showing us the ropes. He's left some stuff on the kitchen table.'

I stepped into the kitchen and found some dog-eared pages stapled together entitled: 'Le Baudet de Poitou'. Next to it was a note for me, scrawled on the back of a leaflet advertising tree-felling, with a salt cellar as a paper weight.

Dear Sis,

I've had to go to the Cave to help Sonia unpack some new stock, so here's the info I got from the sanctuary for Clarrie to look at. T.

P.S. Bo's shelter and the paddock need a bit of a clean-up – maybe Rowan and Clarrie would help with that. And I can't find any cat food in the cupboard. T.

P.P.S. We can go see Charles later. Maybe after dinner?

Charming, I thought. *There's me imagining an afternoon at the hospital ministering to a wan and grateful Charles, finally getting to the bottom of whatever it is he's keeping from me. Whereas, in reality, I'll be supervising the kids and the donkey (whose name Theo still can't spell), rescuing the cat from starvation, shopping for food, and no doubt, cooking it as well.* Seems my brother had time for guerrilla gardening but very little else.

'Are you ready to come over now, Rowan?' I said, forcing myself into cheerful mode. 'I can introduce you to Beau, but after that I'll need to go shopping. Anubis is starving. She's had to resort to slaughtering mice.'

At the mention of her name, the cat fixed me with a piercing green gaze. A gaze that said: *I'm hungry. How many signs do you need before you take action?* For a split second, I imagined I was gazing into the eyes of my mother.

'That's nature for you,' said Rowan, 'red in tooth and claw. We'll see you in ten minutes. Will there be something for lunch?'

* * *

It was getting on for seven o'clock before we finished our evening meal and Theo and I were finally ready to set out for the hospital in Yeovil where Charles had been taken.

Rowan and Clarrie had gone back to the B&B to change. After that, they planned to go down the town to see if they could find a pub with live music. They'd spent the afternoon mucking out and bonding with Beau, the bonding being by far the easier task, Beau being anybody's for half a carrot.

'How'd you manage to get here without a car?' I asked Theo, on the way. Now I'd seen how far away it was, I was feeling guilty in case he'd had to use taxis.

'I got the bus on Saturday and Rosemary brought me yesterday.'

I bit my lip so I wouldn't swear.

'But I didn't want her involved. You know Charles can't stand her at the moment.'

I shot a sideways glance at him to see his reaction, although, being a master of the poker face, he was hard to fathom.

'I don't know how she found out,' he said, smoothly, 'but she called and offered me a lift. The bus service isn't great on Sundays. What was I gonna do?'

'So how did Charles react when he saw her?'

'He was polite.'

I imagined Charles being frostily civil, lying in bed in his NHS pyjamas at the mercy of Rosemary, practical alchemist, energy healer, and in his eyes, public enemy number one.

We arrived at the hospital and I hurried Theo out of the car; we had barely an hour of visiting time left and he'd told me it was a bit of a route march to the ward. When Theo turned into one of the bays I obediently followed him to the bedside of a pale, supine old woman whose long grey hair spread out on the pillow to frame her sleeping face.

'What do we do?' whispered Theo. 'Should we wake him up?'

Charles, for it was he, opened one eye and smiled faintly.

I'd rarely seen him with his hair down, hence my confusion. But it was more than that. His naturally plump face was now sunken and drawn. The real Charles seemed to have been replaced by someone much older and feebler.

'Theo, Pandora, how lovely to see you. But you needn't have come all this way. There's nothing wrong with me 'cept a bit of bruising. I'll be out of here in no time.'

As he struggled to sit up in bed, the red mark on his forehead seemed to deepen and spread. Theo jumped forward to help lift his torso while I arranged pillows to support his back. His face twisted in pain as Theo moved him, so I took hold of his right hand. The back of his left hand was stained a livid purple beneath the cannula which protruded from it.

He motioned me to sit down on the chair next to his bed, and pointed to a spare chair which Theo carried from beside the sink to the other side of the bed. There were two other visitors, chatting quietly to an elderly man who nodded every so often but hardly spoke. The other patients were dozing.

I kissed Charles gently on the cheek. It felt smooth and cold. *At least someone's shaving him*, I thought.

I pointed to the cannula.

'Is that thing uncomfortable?

'Slightly. They use it for pain control. I think they leave it in till you're discharged. I'm not sure...'

He sank into silence, so I asked him if he was in much pain and he shrugged.

'It was quite bad at first, but it's getting easier. Had the wind knocked out of my sails, that's for sure.' He looked pensive, then rallied. 'Anyway, enough of me. How's everyone at home?'

Charles' voice sounded as if all the air had been squashed out of it. It was obviously an effort for him to speak, so I took hold of the conversation, telling him about Jay working with Gaby, and Sharon intending to come at Easter, and how she wanted him to know that she was praying for him. He nodded his head at this, but his expression was guarded.

'I'm happy to accept any good wishes anyone wants to send my way, and I'm sure they'll help me on the road to recovery,' he rasped.

Given my own views on who to pray to and what to pray for, my interest was piqued.

'Have you got reservations about prayers, Charles?'

'Not about prayers for wellbeing, Pandora, only those for personal gain. Sharon has a habit of blurring the line between the two.'

'You mean praying for healing's okay but praying that you'll make money on your investments isn't?' broke in Theo.

'More or less,' said Charles, 'but that's my personal take on it.' He paused a moment. 'If I remember correctly, the *Devil's Dictionary* defines the word "pray" as: "to ask that the laws of the universe be annulled in behalf of a single petitioner, confessedly unworthy." You should read the whole dictionary some time. It's fascinating.'

'Is that Shakespearian English?' said Theo, frowning in his effort to unravel the gist.

Charles gasped out a faint gurgle of irritation. 'It was written a bit later than that, by a man called Ambrose Bierce – three hundred years later, in fact.'

The gurgle had brought on a coughing fit. When it subsided, I reclaimed the conversation by telling him about Rowan and Clarrie coming to stay at the farmhouse for the case study on Beau. I managed to get a few smiles out of him, but the way he clutched my hand, and the uncharacteristic trembling of his lip while he listened, made me want to kidnap him there and then and take him home with us.

We were interrupted by a nurse doing the rounds with the medication. She tipped two pills into a small plastic tub and placed them on the over-bed table.

'How's your head today, Charles?' she smiled.

'Not too bad, still feeling a bit muzzy.'

But she was already wheeling her trolley out of the bay.

'I hope you've told the doctor that,' said Theo.

I found myself touched by my brother's concern, especially as Charles had been so tetchy with all of us since the funeral.

Charles stared down at his bed cover in confusion.

'Um. I'm pretty sure I did.'

Theo and I exchanged glances and I made a mental note to speak to a doctor tomorrow.

* * *

When we got to the car I put the key in the ignition, but something stopped me from turning it, so I sat in contemplation for a few moments, trying to decide what to do.

Seeing Charles so frail and helpless had roused my latent lioness, making me even more determined to find out what was troubling him. The poor old thing was in no state to be cross-questioned, so there was only one other option – I'd have to risk asking Theo if he knew anything.

I'd been wary of my brother ever since he'd told me to mind my own business where he spent the night. In the meantime, it had become obvious he'd been sleeping with Dido. So surely he'd have some idea of why Charles was so angry with her and Rosemary.

'Theo,' I began, turning in my seat to get a view of his body language, and making my voice soft, with no hint of disapproval. 'I know you don't like discussing your private life, but you've clearly had a relationship with Dido.'

His body tensed and he gazed at the windscreen, but he didn't contradict me, so I went on.

'If she told you why Charles took against Rosemary and the Circle, I want to know what she said. All this upset and bad feeling is affecting his health.'

He shook his head, but I persisted.

'People can't play games with other people's lives. Something's stressing him. I've never seen him so worn down. And it's not just Frankie's...'

I found it hard to say 'death', so I didn't, although the thought of saying it still made my voice break. I told myself to keep calm but agitation had got the upper hand and I almost shouted the next words.

'Whatever's going on has got to stop! He could have been killed! He's a good man, devoted to our mother...he doesn't deserve this.'

I lapsed into sniffles and Theo reached for the box of Kleenex I kept on the back seat. As he passed me a whole handful, he clumsily patted my back. Despite my outburst, he seemed unruffled.

When I'd finally finished blubbing, he asked, calmly, 'Didn't Frankie ever mention the Circle to you?'

'Not a word. How did you meet Dido, by the way?'

'I went along to a Circle meeting with Frankie and we hit it off.'

'You went to a meeting?'

'Yeah. She said she was separated from her husband. I thought she meant the marriage was over...'

He paused and I finished his sentence, '...but it turned out to be just geographic.'

He gave a deep sigh, and I felt a surge of pity for him.

'So what went on at the meeting, Theo?'

'Good question. It mostly went over my head. They chanted and Rosemary spoke in some weird language. They sent healing to the earth...Rosemary and Dido concocted herbal stuff...tinctures they call 'em. A lot of it was making potions to stay young. That kinda shit.'

After that last sentence he looked sideways at me and shrugged, as if in apology.

'Did you go again?'

He nodded.

'I didn't like to say no when Frankie asked.'

'Not to mention the lovely Dido,' I said with more than a hint of sarcasm. 'Any other men there?'

'Just Ralph,' he said steadily, 'the guy with Cynthia at the funeral.'

'Paisley waistcoat?'

'Yeah, that's him. He acted as gatekeeper. I think he just tags along after Cynthia.'

This information corresponded to what Charles had told me, except he hadn't seen fit to mention that Theo was a member too, which prompted the question: why not?

On the other hand, this Circle of Isis was beginning to sound like any other pagan goddess gathering the locals were apt to frequent, and I found my interest waning. It was time to hit the road, so I gave the engine full throttle and soon we were back at the cottage, sipping cocoa and letting a soppy film on the TV wash over us.

During an ad break I asked, as artlessly as possible, 'Do you plan to see Tegan again?'

A slow smile spread across his face.

'I'm ahead of you. She's coming on Saturday. We're taking Beau to the Palm Sunday service at the church down the road. The vicar wants him to be the Jerusalem donkey.'

A rush of affection for the three of them engulfed me as I imagined them trotting down the road together and into the churchyard – Tegan with her pink hair and ear piercings, Theo his dreadlocks and Beau his massive ears.

'So *that's* what you put your name down for. Why didn't you say so?'

'Didn't think he had much chance. Guess being a rescue donkey swung it. The Rev came to see him, said long as he was friendly, he'd be fine. So he got the job.'

'That's such an honour. Is it a re-enactment? Who's going to play Christ riding into Jerusalem?'

Theo wrinkled his nose.

'Poitous weren't bred for riding. I'll be leading him.'

My chest swelled with pride.

'You'll be great – especially as you've got the same birthday as

Jesus.'

He grinned, putting on a hokey accent, 'And the same as Isaac Newton, but I ain't no astronomer.'

An attack of 'mother-hen' overpowered me.

'How are you going to wear your hair?'

He shook his head in pretend disbelief. 'I'm gonna go to the barbershop and ask for a "Redeemer". How'd you think?' Seeing my face fall, he added, 'Don't worry, I'll tie it back.'

'Good man,' I said patting his hand. 'And will Beau be allowed inside?'

'Doubt it. One dump, and he'd clear the place.'

I laughed. Beau and Tegan certainly brought out Theo's lighter side.

'At least the churchyard's got some grass. But you should take a bucket and shovel, just in case.'

'No need. The vicar's got volunteers for that. Any manure's going straight on their roses.'

'Will Beau stay till after the service?'

'Yeah. For the kids, mainly. They can pet him and ask questions.'

'Ah, so he's there as a crowd-puller. Fair enough. He'll definitely put a few bums on pews.'

My thoughts turned to Christ riding into Jerusalem on the back of a donkey a week before he was put to death, being welcomed by a cheering crowd waving palm branches. I hoped the good people of the parish would give an equally warm reception to a dreadlocked Angelino leading a giant donkey with no sign of a cross on his back.

Chapter 16

Incommunicado

'Where did you find it?'

'In your bedroom, in your black bag.'

'Oh, that's right. I changed my mind and brought the brown one. Okay, Sha, thanks for locating it. I'll give you another ring from here later in the week. You've got this number if you need to call me.'

'Bye, honey, give Charles my love. Stay as long as it takes. Everything's fine here.'

Clarrie and Rowan had just ambled over from the farm, packed to the gills with fried food. Theo almost drooled when they described their breakfast – he'd had to make do with toast and Marmite, as my shopping yesterday hadn't extended as far as a full English.

'Now I know why you never answered my text, Mum,' said Rowan, when I came off the phone. He'd moved on from bacon, egg, sausage and mushrooms and was now praising Clarrie's super powers with animals.

'What did it say?'

'I described our breakfast and said we'd be over soon.'

'Well you're here now,' I said, trying to keep a straight face. 'I can always read it when I get home.'

Clarrie smiled and I took a seat next to her on the sofa.

'So,' I said, 'can you really talk to animals?'

'It's nothing, really,' she blushed.

But I could tell from her intense expression that it was something very important to her. I'd brought a few of Jay's roll-ups with me, to remind me of him, so I used that as an excuse to get her on her own. I figured she might be more forthcoming with just the two of us.

'Come into the garden while I have a ciggie, I'd like to hear about it.'

It turned out that Clarrie was able to connect telepathically with animals. Her first experience had been with the family cat when she was seven.

'Sometimes he'd tell me something was wrong, like he'd hurt his paw or had a stomach ache. Or he'd say he was hungry.'

I had a vision of a young Clarrie dancing attendance on an enormous cat, clicking his claws and giving her orders.

'What do you mean by "say", Clarrie?'

'He didn't actually talk. It was a combination of pictures that came into my mind, or words in my head. And sometimes I could sense what he was thinking and feeling.'

Inclined as I was to the weird and wonderful, I fully accepted this. Wasn't it anyway just an extension of the relationship we all have with our pets? They read our body language and we theirs. I had no doubt that Clarrie was telling the truth.

'So does it work with all animals? I mean, if you go to the zoo, can you pick up how they're feeling?'

'Actually, in zoos, a lot of them are incredibly bored.'

I felt rather glum then and made a note to spend some time sending compassion to institutionalised animals, fed up to the back teeth at being denied the freedom to roam the plains and ice floes.

'I want to qualify as a veterinary nurse because I'm interested in the intuitive diagnosis side of it, although I haven't said anything to my course tutors, in case they think I'm deluded.'

I identified with her immediately

'Too right. Keep it under your hat. It won't stop you doing it, but it'll protect your reputation.'

She looked pleased that someone else understood.

I'd only told a handful of people about my 'phoenix rebirth' (when I signed up to metaphorically don a super-heroine cloak and fight the good fight). I'd found it best to keep quiet about the spiritual stuff and do my energy boosting in the background when no one was looking. Trouble was, since my mother's death, and all the complications that had come with it, I was fighting hard to keep myself energised, let alone other people.

I stubbed my cigarette out in the earth – ashes to ashes and all that – and my eyes were drawn to the small, white wooden cross Charles had placed at the head of my mother's grave in the paddock just beyond the garden. Frankie would have approved of Clarrie.

'Clarrie, when we get back, will you do a check on the animals at Four Seasons? I want to know if they're all healthy. And other things as well, like if Midnight's happy. She's got the goats but I'm sure she misses the two ponies we used to have.'

'Yes, sure,' she said, beaming. 'I've had a chat with Beau, by the way.'

As usual, my heart leapt at the mention of Beau.

'What did he say? Is he okay?'

'Yes. By nature he's loving and outgoing...'

'I sense a but,' I said, suddenly gripped by guilt. 'He's not feeling the cold after his clip, is he? Did we overdo it?'

'No, it's not that. There's something bothering him but it's not physical, it's emotional. He's confused about someone...about something this person did.'

'That sounds like a complex emotion for a donkey to have,' I said, surprised. Then a thought struck me. 'Maybe he felt abandoned when his previous owner died.'

'I don't think it's that.'

I was intrigued now, but at that moment Theo and Rowan appeared.

'So what have you got planned for today?' I said, hoping Theo would be going to the Cave so I'd be able to visit Charles on my own this afternoon.

'We're taking Beau down to Flossy's field,' said Rowan. 'Is that okay, Theo? Steve's going to show us round the farm this morning.'

'Yeah, that's great. He loves it there. I'm helping Sonia out, so I'll see you later. Maybe if you're going to the store, you could get some bacon and sausages for breakfast tomorrow, Sis?'

And off he rode on an ancient bike that Charles must have dug out from the back of the shed.

'He's in a good mood,' I said.

'We're going out for a drink with him tonight, Mum.'

After a pause, Rowan added, 'You're welcome to come too, if you like...'

Happy to have the evening to myself, I told him I didn't mind staying at home at all.

Tonight was the night I'd arranged to ring Zac, anyway. Then I remembered I didn't have my mobile with me, or Zac's number. Damn! That's what happens when technology fools you into thinking it's all you need and leaves you stranded without it.

In response, my subconscious played the *I know better* card, whispering that its security application had kicked in, causing me to leave the phone at home, because what might start with an 'innocent' conversation could lead to something much harder to control.

* * *

I went to the hospital early, to talk to someone about Charles. I wanted them to know that he still felt woozy. The doctor, a man in his forties, with the rugged air of a rugby player, led me into a side office. His tone was breezy and reassuring.

'Slight concussion, needs bed rest. Same treatment for the ribs. But don't worry, he's on the mend. Is there anyone at home with him?'

Technically, Theo was, but he was pretty much covering for Charles at the shop so he'd be out all day.

'I suppose I could stay for a few days,' I said, pushing the prospect of the box room to the back of my mind. 'When's he likely to be discharged?'

'We're looking at end of this week, beginning of next.'

'I don't live locally and I won't be here this weekend, but next Monday would be no problem,' I said, in a slightly wheedling tone.

The doctor scribbled something on Charles' notes and held out his hand.

'I'm sure that can be arranged. Good to meet you, Ms...'

I paused because I was technically still Armstrong even though I felt more like a Jay.

'I'm Mr Lockwood's unofficial stepdaughter,' I said, making a funny face at how ridiculous that sounded and adding, 'but he has no other close relatives.'

He took my hand and gripped it for a second too long. I held his gaze for a moment and saw, with surprise, that his blood was up. Startled, I withdrew my hand, but not too soon for me to have felt a mutual *frisson*.

I should have made a quick exit but instead, I found myself asking if they'd found any medical reason for Charles losing control of the car in the first place. This was despite Theo having already told me that no obvious cause had been identified, apart from the stress of losing a loved one.

He shook his head.

'No. The CAT scan didn't show anything...'

He stared at me enquiringly, perhaps sensing that I was prolonging our conversation.

'Thank you, that's put my mind at rest,' I said brightly. 'I'd better...'

Without finishing my sentence, I tip-tapped out of the office in my Saint Laurent ankle boots, conscious of his eyes on my derrière.

As I sat in the hospital restaurant, nursing a cup of weak tea, I considered how I felt about still being an object of desire. Since

I'd got back with Jay, I'd lost the habit of sizing men up and being sized up in return. Actually, now I'd got over the initial surprise, I was feeling a warm glow of appreciation. The doc had boosted my morale no end, just as Zac had when he'd suggested lunch.

I began to rerun the conversation we'd had on Sunday night, and started to feel even more frustrated at being powerless to get in touch with him.

But another matter was clamouring even louder for my attention. There was a wasp of an idea dive-bombing my brain and every time I got near it, it buzzed away. It was infuriating, because I knew if I could only connect two elusive thoughts, something would in some way become clearer.

Half an hour later, after the grand opening of the ward doors, I was delighted to find Charles sitting up in bed reading a newspaper, looking a different man from the fragile figure of yesterday. His face broke into a broad smile when he saw me, and he even managed a careful hug. I told him what the doctor had said and he cheered up even more when he heard the words 'on the mend'.

'With a bit of luck you'll be out by Monday. Theo and I can look after you until you're mobile again. But you won't be able to go back to work for ages. You do know that, don't you, Charles?'

'Yes, yes, my dear. I do know that. It's good to see you.'

Something prompted me to tell him that I'd cleared the air with Theo.

'I asked Theo about Dido last night and they *did* have a thing together. He thought she was separated, but once her husband turned up, that was it. Anyway, he's seeing a girl called Tegan now. She suits him much better. They met at my place, and they're taking Beau to a Palm Sunday service at the Anglican church.'

'Mm. I'd have thought Beau would be more at home in a Disney Parade.'

Charles' reply had been dismissive. Assuming that he didn't

want to discuss people's messy love lives, I let it drop and concentrated instead on what he needed in the way of beauty treatment.

Someone had tied his hair back with an elastic band but I had a proper ponytail band in my bag. I'd also brought some shampoo with me but thought it best to wait till later to mention that.

'You're looking so much better today, Charles. I can't believe the difference.'

'Ah, well. Shortly before you came, I'd dozed off and had a bad dream. That might explain it.'

His eyes grew watery at the thought, so I took his hand and asked him what he'd dreamed.

'I was staring into your mother's grave, but the corpse resembled a woman of ancient Egypt. She rose up and came towards me, closer and closer. Her eyes were dark brown and heavily outlined in kohl. I wanted to ask what she'd done with Frankie but the words wouldn't come. She was carrying an ankh and she had a snake wrapped round her shoulders; it was writhing and flicking its tongue. She towered over me, the snake poised to strike. I couldn't move...my feet seemed to be stuck in mud. Have you ever had a dream and woken up terrified? It was one of those.'

I shuddered, but put on a brave face for his sake.

'I expect it was the medication. It does funny things to your system.'

'Or too much cheese in the macaroni,' he said, with a weak smile. 'But we'll never know what happened that night, will we, Pandora?' He seemed to shrink as he sank back into the pillows with a heavy sigh. 'Better let sleeping dogs lie.'

Then I said something which came out of nowhere. The brain usually works in unison with the voice, but this time the words bypassed my grey matter, so I could only assume it was my higher self speaking.

'The only person who witnessed what happened was Beau.

We'll have to ask him.'

And then the light dawned. That was the answer. Now I knew which two thoughts I had to connect. Beau was a witness, and Clarrie could communicate with animals. Ergo, Clarrie had to ask Beau what he saw that night.

Like an old wolf scenting a new trail, Charles narrowed his eyes and gave me all his attention.

'You said something like that before.'

'I don't think so. It's only just occurred to me.'

'I mean the bit about asking Beau. The subject of cutting his hair came up and you said you'd ask him.'

Our conversation in the restaurant after the funeral gradually came to mind. Charles was right, I had said that. And before proceeding with the great trimming operation, I'd asked if it was okay, and the dear creature had given me the go-ahead by lowering his head and blowing through his nostrils, as if to say, *That's fine with me.*

I felt as if I'd been given the kind of sign that Enoch used to talk about. Deep down, I must have known that Beau would have the answer, but the realisation had taken all this time to surface.

Charles was waiting for me to explain further, so I told him what Clarrie could do and how I was planning to ask her to commune with Beau and see what he remembered of that night.

This course of action would probably have been met with cries of 'Nonsense!' by your average seventy-three-year-old, but Charles had been a student of the esoteric for at least fifty of those years, so I didn't anticipate any scepticism.

'She's already intuited that something's bothering him,' I finished, 'so witnessing the grave opening might be the "something".'

'I hope you're right, Pandora.'

I'd been hoping for a little more enthusiasm.

'What you're expecting of him is a sight more ambitious than asking him how his joints are. For a start, will Clarrie be able to take him back to the night in question? Animals live far more in the present than humans.'

The elastic band that had been holding Charles' hair back chose that moment to give up the ghost, so I seized the opportunity to suggest a shampoo and blow-dry, having had the foresight to bring a travel hair dryer with me. The way Charles lowered his head and sighed through his nose, told me he was bowing to the inevitable, so I drew the curtains round his bed, filled a bowl with water from the sink and proceeded to restore his locks to their former glory.

* * *

When I got back from the hospital, I went straight out to the paddock but there was no sign of Beau, so I walked down the lane to see if he and the youngsters were still on the farm.

As I passed the field, I saw Flossie and her foal grazing, but no Beau, so I continued on to the farmyard where I found Steve demonstrating to Clarrie and Rowan how to pick out Beau's feet. Beau was standing patiently on three legs and turned his head as I approached, lowering his ears in greeting.

'Hello,' I said. 'You've got yourself a job there.'

Steve gently lowered Beau's back foot to the ground.

'All done now. They needed doing all right. I do Flossie's once or twice a week but this big boy needs checking every day. His old pins are carrying a fair bit of weight.'

'This time next year he'll be super slim,' I said, putting my arms round Beau's neck and kissing his cheek, 'now he's on the hay diet.'

Beau nuzzled me back and I caught Clarrie's eye. I needed to talk to her on the subject of you-know-what.

'What are you two up to now?'

'Nothing much,' said Rowan. 'What's for dinner, Mum?'

I'd prepared it that morning to leave myself free for our experiment.

'Lasagne. Are you taking Beau back soon?'

I was conscious that there was only about forty-five minutes of daylight left.

Clarrie glanced at Rowan and he nodded.

'Okay. We'll eat when Theo gets back. Can you last till then, Rowan?'

Rowan had the bottomless stomach of your average teenage boy, but it was a rhetorical question really, because I had no intention of leaving the paddock until we knew whether or not Beau could reveal the identity of the grave opener.

Before we left, I asked Steve to show me the accommodation, which was in a self-contained annexe close to the farmhouse. The unoccupied room was clean and well-furnished, so I booked one for me from the following Monday and the other two for the Easter weekend. While there, I asked Rowan to show me his room. When he reluctantly opened the door, there were no clothes or towels strewn about; it appeared to be as tidy as the one Steve had shown me.

'Where are your things?'

He blushed to his roots.

'In the wardrobe. Mum, please don't fuss.'

He exchanged a meaningful glance with Clarrie, who was looking worried.

As we led Beau to his shelter, I asked Clarrie to stay behind. Rowan seemed happy to leave us to it and headed for the cottage. Knowing him, he probably had a pressing engagement with a Nintendo DS and a giant bag of crisps.

From the way her hands trembled as she removed Beau's head collar, Clarrie evidently sensed that something was up.

'I wonder if you'd do me a favour, Clarrie. Quite an important one. I want you to ask Beau what happened after my mother's funeral.'

My head jerked in the direction of the small white cross on the eastern side of the paddock, and I experienced a sharp stab of grief.

'It was held here,' I went on, shakily. 'And that night someone opened her grave. Beau might have seen who it was.'

'Yes, Rowan told me about it.'

This took me by surprise. I hadn't discussed it with him, so he must have heard Jay and Sharon talking about it.

'It doesn't freak you out, does it? My mum being buried here?'

'No, no.'

'You seem a bit anxious.'

She stopped stroking Beau.

'I thought you were going to ask me to stop seeing Rowan. I know I'm a bit older than him, but we really click. And I like you and Theo as well. I can be myself around you.'

I moved towards the girl and the donkey and we engaged in a group embrace, Beau nuzzling us in turn. Once our hug-fest was over I felt much better, but as the subject had been raised I felt impelled to take it to its logical conclusion.

'Clarrie, I think you're good for Rowan. And so does Jay.' I paused, not sure how to put it. '...As long as you take precautions. That is, if you're...'

I stopped, because Clarrie's hands were waving back and forth in a *Don't go there, everything's taken care of*, kind of way.

'We have nothing to worry about then?'

She nodded vigorously, so I willingly left it at that.

'Shall we get down to business?' said Clarrie, slipping briskly out of stepson's girlfriend into animal intuitive.

I watched as she stroked Beau's neck, slowing her movements until his head rested on her shoulder. His eyes were gazing directly into mine, so I sent him love and he blinked love back. Clarrie wasn't using any words, so I had no idea whether any communication was taking place between them. I moved to where I was able to see her face and, after a few minutes, observed an expression of shock. Then she opened her eyes and motioned me to take her place.

She gently put Beau's head on to my shoulder and whispered, 'Close your eyes, empty your mind and see if any images or feelings come through.'

At first, I saw nothing, but gradually a hazy picture formed – a view of the grave, as if through the wrong end of binoculars. What followed was a series of pictures with a commentary, which appeared in my head as I 'watched', describing what Beau had seen.

He comes into the paddock from the lane, comes towards me, whispers to me and strokes me. Then he takes up the spade at the side of the grave and starts digging, jumps into the hole, stays there for a little while and then gets out. He picks up the spade to fill in the grave but someone comes out of the house. The garden light goes on and frightens him, so he hides in the shadows. He leaves soon after when the light goes off, without saying goodbye. I sense his fear and shame and I feel it too.

After that, the images faded and I wasn't seeing through Beau's lenses any more.

I opened my eyes and met Clarrie's concerned gaze. Unable to believe what I'd seen, I sat down on the old garden seat Charles had placed near Beau's shelter, my head in my hands. Clarrie sat down beside me and put her arm round me.

'You saw him, didn't you?'

'Yes. But why would he *do* something like that?'

Chapter 17

Treasure Uncovered

Dinner that night was difficult to get through. I'd made Clarrie promise that she wouldn't say a word to Rowan about Theo being the traitor in our midst. I asked her to behave normally so as not to make him suspicious. My plan was to tell Charles what had happened and take guidance from him. He, after all, knew Theo best. Indeed, he'd been the one to defend him when I'd questioned Theo's presence in the house at all.

Clarrie said that now she knew what he'd done, she didn't want to spend an evening in the pub with him, so we agreed that she'd say she felt unwell and stay with me while he and Rowan went out.

Rowan and Theo did most of the talking at dinner. Once I'd made coffee I decided it was time for Clarrie's opening scene.

'How are you feeling now, Clarrie?' I asked pointedly.

Rowan's sticky toffee pudding came to a halt halfway to his mouth.

'Not too bad, thanks,' she said, doing a fair impression of a dying swan.

'What's wrong?' said Rowan, with a little boy lost look.

'Don't worry, Row. It's just a headache.'

My eyebrows prompted her for more.

'And I feel a bit queasy.'

'Are you sure you're up to going out tonight,' I said, feeding her a line.

'Maybe not,' she said weakly.

But Rowan urged her to rally.

'You must come, babe, that band's playing again. You said you loved them. Take an aspirin or something, they're good. Have you got any, Mum?'

'She's already taken some, darling, but they don't seem to be working.'

This was a lie, but was all in a good cause, so didn't count.

'I've got some painkillers, if it's bad,' said Theo.

Clarrie didn't answer, so I said, 'It's probably best not to mix them, Theo. But thanks anyway.'

Rowan finally gave in to persuasion and left his beloved Clarrie with me, to go carousing with Theo. The only channels on offer on Charles' TV were terrestrial, so it wasn't surprising there was nothing on the box to tempt him to stay in.

'He's under eighteen, so he shouldn't be drinking. You won't forget that, will you, Theo?'

I felt I had to mention it, even though neither of them would take a blind bit of notice.

'Don't worry, Sis. I'll take care of him,' said Theo, grinning at Rowan. 'It'll be Dr Pepper on the rocks.'

Once they'd gone, Clarrie and I relaxed. I told her to sit down while I cleared up in the kitchen, but she insisted on helping.

'So how's the assignment going?' I said. 'Is there much more to do?'

'Actually, I've got all I need on Beau now. I've made all the notes, taken all the pictures. I've just got to write it up when I get back. We'd been thinking of staying on an extra night or two – Rowan wanted to visit Charles in hospital. We like it here...Steve and his wife are so nice and Rowan gets on so well with Theo...'

Her eyes welled up, and I hugged her.

'I hate what's happened, too. It's hard on us, being the ones who found him out.'

'I know,' she said miserably, 'it's going to change how everyone feels about him. I'm worried Rowan will blame me for ruining his friendship with Theo.' She frowned. 'It seems so out of character – Theo seems such a nice person. You know, like wanting to get something for my headache.'

The offer of painkillers had reminded me of my conversation

with Theo in the dome when he'd revealed his fear of ending up in a wheelchair. With his muscular build it was easy to forget that he'd been forced to stop working because his body was failing.

'He's not as strong as he looks,' I said, 'but that doesn't excuse what he did.'

We both lapsed into silence as we finished up in the kitchen.

'Do you think there's any chance we've got it wrong, Clarrie?'

'No,' she said solemnly, 'because neither of us suspected him, so we weren't influencing the outcome.'

The phone rang and I went to answer it. It was Joe, one of Charles' friends, asking how he was and when he was expected home. When I came back Clarrie was more composed.

'It's probably better if you and Rowan go home tomorrow,' I said, in the voice I used when I was trying to tempt Oscar to take medicine. 'Once Charles hears what Theo did, it's bound to involve an argument, and you don't want to have to justify yourself to Theo, or anyone else, if he denies it. You might get caught in the crossfire.'

Clarrie looked relieved.

'What shall I say to Rowan, though?'

'Why don't you say you've had a call from home...your dad's short-staffed and needs your help?'

'Okay. I'll tell him at the farm, when we're on our own.'

She paused, as if debating whether to say what was on her mind.

'I've been thinking, Pandora. Even though what Theo did seems inexcusable, I shouldn't judge him, because I don't know the circumstances. He needs to explain his actions to you and Charles. Then you can make up your own minds.'

While I accepted the truth of Clarrie's words, the shame I felt at what my brother had done disposed me to keep his crime secret from the younger Jays.

'You're right. And as soon as we get an explanation I'll let you know – but it's still classified information as far as Rowan's concerned. Okay?'

She nodded, and then I remembered what I'd been meaning to ask her all evening.

'Why did you get me to tune in to Beau, by the way? I didn't expect that.'

'At the end of our session, Beau told me he wanted to show you what happened. He's a very special being, you know. I had a sense that he wanted you to be involved because something needs sorting out. A wrong needs righting.'

The palms of my hands became warm and tingly, always a sign that whatever was being said or done was on the right track.

'Amen,' I said. 'Ain't that the truth.'

I went off to marinate in a warm bath, and came downstairs in my dressing gown clutching the book I'd brought with me for emergencies.

It was strange not having my PC to hand, or a mobile phone. It was Tuesday now and Jay and I hadn't spoken to each other since he'd left for London on Sunday evening. I had no idea of his mobile number and kept forgetting to ask Rowan for it. I wanted to tell him about Clarrie's chat to Beau and get his take on it. And I badly wanted to hear his voice.

I thought of ringing Sharon, but I wasn't really in the mood. She'd be quizzing me about Rowan and Clarrie and I could hardly talk freely with Clarrie in earshot, on the sofa with Anubis, watching *Hotel Babylon*.

After an hour of my book, which was less riveting than I'd hoped, I said goodnight to Clarrie and was dead to the world when Rowan and Theo finally rolled in.

* * *

Once Clarrie and Rowan hit the road on Wednesday morning, I felt rather lonely. He'd called to say they were about to leave, but I was hoovering and didn't hear the phone, so all I got was a recorded message.

'Hi, Mum. Just to say we're off now. Clarrie said she told you we'd probably be going today because she had to get back. At least we've saved you paying for another night's B&B. See you soon. Love you.'

To take my mind off missing the kids, I busied myself making a fish pie for later. Unfortunately, the ensuing smell was so overpowering I felt obliged to scrub all the kitchen surfaces, and once I'd got going I couldn't stop. Having cleaned the cottage to within an inch of its life and completed my final task – polishing the windows until they gleamed – I was at a loose end, until I remembered Frankie's clothes. What would be the harm in sorting them into three piles: recycling, charity shop, and good enough to pass on to her friends? Charles would surely thank me for it.

So, armed with bin bags, I spread all of her clothes on the bed and began the task, watched by the goddess Isis from the wall above, her right eye keenly observing everything I did.

Some things I shed a tear over, like the priestess gown Frankie had worn to our handfasting, which she and Charles had produced, written and starred in, and which had involved silken cords to bind our hands together, and medieval costumes. I kid you not.

I put the handfasting gown into the 'unclassified' group, which I'd had to introduce in addition to the other three. Unfortunately, due to Frankie's somewhat eccentric taste, this was proving to be quite substantial. I'd been checking all the pockets along the way and had come across an assortment of miscellaneous items: throat lozenges, forgotten fivers, shopping lists, small crystals, etc.

I bundled the stuff to be recycled and the charity shop items into black bin bags, to be dropped off once I got permission from Charles. I decided to return the other two groups to the wardrobe and discuss them with Charles when he was in better health, but not before I'd inspected the inside for dust.

I ran my fingers round the inside of the wardrobe and my fingertips emerged grey and powdery so I got a wet cloth and set to work. I was attacking the left inner side when it started rattling and I realised it sounded different from the other side. On closer inspection, there appeared to be an inner panel with a keyhole that hadn't been visible in the packed wardrobe.

I remembered a slim key being one of the items retrieved from Frankie's pockets, so I tried it in the keyhole and it turned, opening the compartment to reveal a long, white, linen robe, the sort a person like Frankie might wear to a ceremony. A length of white pleated silk organza, which I assumed to be a shawl, was also draped around the hanger.

Fascinated, I examined the garment. It was embroidered in gold thread at the hem and neck with six-pointed stars which were made up of two triangles, one inverted, with a tiny ankh in the middle of each star. I wondered why she'd wanted to hide it. Maybe the pockets were filled with money she'd stashed away. I remembered the advice she'd been fond of giving me: 'No matter how close you are to someone, keep a property of your own, Pan, just in case it all goes belly up.' This cottage belonged to Charles, so maybe my mother had kept an escape fund, just in case.

The robe, did, indeed, seem to be weighted down at one side. I slipped my hand inside the pocket and drew out, not a bag of gold sovereigns, but a small, engraved chalice. Disappointed, I took it to the light of the casement window to study it more closely. The discoloured greyish metal was scratched and the engravings worn, but they appeared to be Egyptian.

I was scrutinising the designs, when a loud knock at the front door made me jump. Bundling the gown and the chalice back behind the secret panel, I locked it up and slipped the key into the pocket of my jeans.

I ran down the stairs, opened the door and found Pete standing there with a bunch of carrots, their greenery still attached.

'Hello,' I said, trying to sound normal. 'Come in.'

'Hello, Pandora,' he said, kissing me on the cheek. 'I wish they were roses, but I only grow veg on my allotment.'

I laughed and relieved him of his bouquet.

'These are much more useful, Pete. They're lovely. Cuppa tea?'

'Don't mind if I do, m'dear. I just stopped by the Cave to find out how Charlie is and Theo said you were here, so I thought I'd come and have a jaw. And if you want any company this afternoon, I don't mind coming with you to see him.'

I had nothing against Pete but his visit was disastrously mistimed. I'd been hoping for so long that Charles would confide in me about the break-in and I believed that revealing the identity of the grave opener was the key that would unlock his silence, so the last thing I wanted was the presence of another visitor.

Pete sat down at the kitchen table while I made us sandwiches. In less than an hour I'd be leaving for the hospital. I racked my brains for a reason not to take him with me, but try as I might, I failed to come up with a convincing excuse.

He was telling me he'd been shocked at how ill Charles looked.

'When did you go to see him?' I asked.

'First off, Sunday.'

'So you went with Theo and Rosemary, then?'

His face darkened.

'Hell, no. I went under my own steam. What she was doing there, God only knows.'

'But she took Theo, didn't she?'

'Yes, but she didn't have to, 'cos I offered him a lift meself.'

'That's weird. I asked Theo to let *you* know, but not to tell Rosemary because Charles wouldn't want to see her. Although,' I added, emphasising my words, 'I still don't know why they've fallen out.'

'I could tell you,' said Pete cryptically, 'but it'd be breaking his confidence.'

I was beginning to revise my view of Pete's unexpected appearance at the door. If he had information I was interested in, maybe he was a blessing in disguise.

'So if *you* didn't tell her about Charles being in hospital, who did?'

'Search me. Maybe that witch Dido saw it in her crystal ball.'

'It has to be Theo who told her,' I said, 'but why would he?'

'That young man's got himself mixed up with the wrong crowd, just like Rosemary. It's money, money, money with them. Everything else goes by the board.'

He stopped. I could see from his flushed face that he thought he'd told me too much.

'Max told me all about the dieting scam,' I said. 'I know Dido's real name is Tina. Her husband turned up out of the blue when we had lunch at Rosemary's and Theo seemed devastated.'

'He's a mug if he didn't see she was using him.'

Pete almost spat the words out. Unlike Charles, this man spoke his mind. I suppose the difference was that Charles was protecting Frankie, whereas Pete was free to let rip.

'How was she using him?'

'Let's put it this way, she's a woman who loves money and sex. So I'd say his wallet and his body in that order, to put it politely.'

'But what would he be giving her money for?'

'I don't know. I haven't figured that out yet. But believe me, she wouldn't be keeping him on a string for no reason.'

I relaxed slightly. Pete obviously hadn't realised that Theo had broken off all contact with her since her husband had come home.

'He's not seeing her now.'

Pete held my gaze and said, 'I'm saying nothing,' which, of course, made me pester him until he spilled the beans.

'That daft Circle of Isis had a meeting in Rosemary's garden last Saturday night. I was engaged in a bit of surveillance on the house,' he winked and began to talk out of the side of his mouth, like a private eye, 'for your stepdad, as it 'appens, and I saw Theo go in. So the suspect in question is still active.'

'The bloody idiot,' I raged. I wanted to get hold of my brother and give him a good shake. 'Don't tell me he followed her home for a threesome,' I hissed.

'Calm down,' said Pete, with more than a hint of disapproval in his voice, suggesting that Pete liked his ladies ladylike. 'No, I followed him back here. He came back alone, just before midnight. I was going to report all this to Charles on Sunday, but with her bloody ladyship there, I didn't get the chance. I had to go back to see him on Monday afternoon.'

My mind was doing cartwheels now, trying to work out what Charles knew and when he'd been told it. According to Pete, Charles would have known that Theo had returned to the Circle when we visited him together on Monday evening. And he'd had every opportunity to tell me about Theo's involvement in the Circle on Tuesday afternoon, so why hadn't he? Didn't I have a right to know about my own brother?

By now it was ten to two – time to set off to the hospital.

'Pete, I've got something to tell Charles that you should hear, as you're acting as his private eye.' He puffed with pride at this. 'Let's go, and we'll pick up where we left off when we get there.'

Chapter 18

Piecing Together

I played a CD of Amy Winehouse on the way to the hospital and Pete seemed happy to be serenaded by both of us. It had become clear to me that Pete was Charles' chief confidant, so any discussions would be best conducted among the three of us. When we got out of the car, I fairly ran to the ward in my eagerness to finally have an honest conversation with Charles about Theo. Pete did well to keep up with me and put a steadying hand on my shoulder as we passed through the doors.

'Remember, he's had a bad knock on the head, love. So go easy to begin with.'

I nodded and strode towards Charles' bed. He was awake, and broke into a smile when he saw us both.

'Hello, hello. Two for the price of one, I see.'

He and Pete nodded knowingly at each other, as old friends do, and I pecked his cheek.

I waited while Pete relayed town gossip and messages from their cronies. When at long last the chitchat came to a halt, I glanced at Pete and his eyes gave me the green light.

'Charles, do you remember we talked about Clarrie and Beau yesterday? Well, she did manage to communicate with him and he told us who was in the paddock that night.'

I'd purposely kept my tone soothing; nevertheless, Charles turned white and his chin quivered slightly. Pete leaned over and patted his arm.

'Who was it?'

His voice had reverted to the wheezy croak it had been on Monday evening.

'Beau identified Theo as the one who disturbed the grave.'

Both Charles and Pete gasped and stared at each other open-mouthed. I was so glad Pete was there, because he'd been a rock to Charles ever since Frankie had died and his presence softened the blow.

'So, please,' I said, with the beseeching air of a *Big Issue* hawker, 'will you tell me what you know about the Isis Circle because,' I said pointedly, 'I now know that's the common link between Theo, Rosemary and Dido.'

Charles wore a stunned expression. Poor man. He was probably trying to work out what lies to tell me so I'd retain glowing memories of my devious mother and brother.

'She knows about Dido and her husband and the diet-pill scam,' said Pete quickly.

Sighing, Charles brushed some imaginary crumbs from his bedclothes, avoiding my gaze.

'I didn't want to upset you, Pandora. You've got enough to worry about with that big house to run and Jay's children coming and going. Then, the shock of your mother dying and discovering you had a half-brother...and Jay...how could I add my troubles to all that? It wouldn't have been fair.'

My eyes filled with tears and I blinked them away, wondering, in passing, why Jay had been included in the list. My heart ached for this poor old man who, I was convinced, had landed up in a hospital bed because of the stress surrounding the break-in at the cottage and the disturbance of the grave.

'How many times have you advised people not to bottle things up, Charles?' I said, trying to control my voice. 'I want you to tell me everything. And that includes the break-in. This time I won't take no for an answer.'

Pete cleared his throat and gazed keenly at his friend, who was reaching for a tissue to dab his eyes.

'You-you're right, my dear,' Charles stuttered. 'I should have told you what was going on.'

His tears made mine flow even faster and Pete, making the most of our mutual wallow in woe, grabbed his chance to expedite proceedings.

'What say I tell her, Charlie? I found out most of it, anyway.'

Given a mournful nod by Charles, Pete proceeded to reveal what his gumshoe activities had uncovered. He started with a quick recap of the Tina and Gavin Bull debacle when they'd fled from their salon in Guildford after being caught charging the earth for phony diet pills, following which Dido opened a salon in Glastonbury, hubby having disappeared to the other side of the world until the heat died down. Soon after she arrived, she started the Circle of Isis.

Rosemary, Frankie and some of their clique of healers, shopkeepers and kooks had joined the Circle, meeting once a week, either at Dido's salon or Rosemary's house. There were about twelve regulars. Once a month, at the full moon, they'd hold a special ceremony. With her sultry looks, Dido soon became a local queen bee, but when Pete heard from a mate about the scam the Bulls had pulled, Charles took a dim view. He asked Frankie to leave the Circle, but she refused. Pete paused in embarrassment when he got to this part of the story and Charles filled in the gap.

'I'm afraid we argued quite a lot about it, Pandora. It was beyond my comprehension that your mother – or Rosemary, for that matter – would want to consort with such a woman, but she seemed to have some sort of hold over them. Anyway, when Theo turned up, his presence in the house brought us closer. I suppose your mother was grateful that I welcomed him.' His eyes grew dim again as he remembered and he whispered, 'You take over now, old man.'

Pete nodded sympathetically and carried on with the story. He told me that soon after Frankie had died, Charles had received a phone call from Rosemary, offering to speak at the funeral and asking him over for a meal. When he returned home from that visit, he found that someone had searched the house.

'It wasn't immediately obvious,' said Charles. 'But when I

went to bed I noticed that some of the bedroom drawers were slightly open and when I looked inside, the contents had been rearranged. I went back downstairs and they'd done the same thing to all the cupboards and any piece of furniture with storage space.'

'Did they break a window to get in?' I asked.

'No. The back door was unlocked, hadn't been forced. I assumed I'd forgotten to lock it...'

As he talked, my mind's eye focused on Dido coming downstairs on the day of the funeral and her words as she'd said goodbye: 'Don't forget, Charles, if you find anything that belongs to the Circle, let me know.' Then she'd looked at Rosemary and given a slight shake of the head as if to say, *No luck.*

'Charles,' I said. 'Do you remember what Dido said as she left, after the funeral?'

He seemed to be struggling to remember, possibly due to his recent concussion. Pete had chosen not to join the funeral party after the burial, so he couldn't throw any light on the antics of the two women either.

'Is it possible that Rosemary created a diversion so Dido could go upstairs?' I said. 'When I saw her coming down, I assumed she'd been to the bathroom but she could have used the downstairs loo. She had no good reason to be up there.'

'Unless she was snooping around for something,' said Pete.

'Who did you originally suspect of breaking in?' I asked Charles.

His face cleared and he pursed his lips.

'Definitely a Circle member or one of their cohorts. I blamed Rosemary most of all. I was convinced she'd got me out of the way on purpose, for someone else to search the house.'

'And now Theo's been exposed,' said Pete, 'he's got to come under suspicion for the break-in as well. Specially as he didn't even have to jemmy his way in. If he'd been a bit more careful putting things back, you'd never have noticed.'

I caught Pete's eye and he winked at me.

'It would have taken him ages,' I said, trying not to smile at the image of butterfingers Theo tipping out drawer after drawer and attempting to replace the contents neatly. Then a thought occurred to me. 'Why couldn't he have searched the house in the daytime when you were at Gaia's Cave?'

There was an awkward pause before Charles answered. 'Because after I woke up and found your mother dead in bed beside me, I hardly left the house.'

The memory of this caused him to break into a racking sob and Pete and I both looked away while he dug into his pyjama pocket for a handkerchief to cover his face.

Pete shook his head.

'He took it real bad. I got him as far as the registrar's to register the death and that was about it. Took to his bed after that.'

Charles blew his nose loudly as a sign he was back in the game. 'What I can't understand, is why he left Frankie's grave open,' he said. 'He'd have got away with it if he'd filled it in immediately.'

'He's obviously got completion issues,' sniggered Pete, inappropriately.

'Beau said he was disturbed,' I answered.

'He's that all right,' said Pete.

'No, I mean that someone came out of the house while he was about to shovel the earth back in, so he took off.'

'Well it wasn't me,' said Charles. 'But Jay was in the house that night.'

'Jay the smoker who had a bad night's sleep,' Pete said, his mind working like a well-oiled machine. He caught my admiring gaze and looked bashful.

'Full marks, Sherlock,' I said. 'Jay said he woke up with backache and went outside for a smoke. Does the garden security light work, Charles?'

He nodded.

'That's the answer, then.'

We were all quiet for a few moments, fitting this piece of the jigsaw into what we had of the picture so far.

'But what would he have done if you'd called the police?' I said.

'If you remember, that's what Jay and I wanted to do, but Theo put Charlie off,' said Pete, his eyes hardening at the memory, 'telling him he'd have his privacy invaded.'

'That'd be why he arrived back from that Dido woman's bed early – so he could talk me out of making it public,' said Charles in a resigned tone.

'He's a pretty cool customer, that's for sure,' said Pete.

We all nodded and sank into further reflection.

Theo's profession of ignorance of the machinations of the Circle members, when we'd sat in the car after visiting Charles on Monday evening, was the next irregularity to grab my attention.

'Pete, you said that Theo's still going to the Circle, didn't you? And you told Charles this on Monday afternoon?'

Pete nodded and Charles looked suitably guilty.

'So, Charles,' I said, my voice sharp with irritation, 'I still haven't worked out why you've been protecting Theo. You never told me he went to the meetings or that he's still going. That means he's still got a foot in both camps. Why didn't you set me straight?'

'I didn't want to worry you. This is Glastonbury business, Pandora. Pete and I can deal with it.'

I sighed. I was hitting my head against a brick wall. Maybe I should just go home and let them all get on with it. Say goodbye for good to my rogue brother and focus all my energies on the saplings and their father.

A wave of despair crashed over me. Beau had contacted me so I could right a wrong, but if Charles insisted on excluding me, what hope did I have?

The two men had resumed chatting in low voices. A trolley came round selling papers, magazines, drinks and chocolate bars, so I bought myself and Pete plastic cups of tea and a Twix each to dunk. Charles, who got his tea and biscuits free, bought a *Daily Messenger*. When he saw my surprise, he looked sheepish, protesting that he liked it for its sports coverage.

'So, to sum up,' said Pete, revelling in his role of private eye. 'Theo searched the house without finding whatever he was looking for. Then Dido and Rosemary tried again at the funeral and found nothing, so they must have given him orders to search the coffin, in case it'd been buried with Frankie, God rest her. They're all members of the Circle, so it's probably something they use at their ceremonies.'

Charles raised his fine head, with its recently coiffed hair (courtesy of yours truly). 'That theory certainly sounds credible. What's not so clear, if we assume Theo got embroiled with the Circle because he fell for Dido, is why's he gone back there now he's found himself a new filly?'

'Blimey, that's quick,' said Pete, with a titter. 'Who is it? Has he shown her his giant ass yet?'

'Her name's Tegan. They met at my place. And, yes, she has met Beau,' I said, trying to look disapproving, but failing.

Feeling some action was necessary after all this talk, I turned my attention to Charles.

'Do you think it'd do any good if I spoke to Theo this evening? You can be there as well, if you like, Pete. We'll ask him outright what he's playing at.'

Pete's eager expression suggested he was up for it, but Charles poured cold water on the idea.

'And offer what evidence, exactly? If you quote the word of a dumb animal, he'll laugh in your face. And attending their meetings is no crime, particularly as he goes straight home afterwards.'

There was a little woodpecker in my head hammering for

attention, so I brought my inner eye to bear on the situation, which showed me a picture of Theo in the dome, speaking to me about his diagnosis. Professionally, I should always observe patient confidentiality but that day he was being my brother, telling his sister a key piece of information about himself. *Blow it,* I thought. *I'm going to tell them.*

'Has Theo ever mentioned to either of you why he retired from film work?'

'He said something about an injury,' said Charles, puzzled. 'Why?'

'A spinal injury. There's some neurological damage which explains why he couldn't grip the coffin rope properly. He's been told his condition's degenerative.'

'Now then,' said Pete, his eyes gleaming. 'This is more like it. We may be on the trail of summat.'

'Ever since he told me he'd been going to the Circle meetings,' I continued, 'I've been asking myself why a man like him, with no interest in the esoteric, would do that. I think the answer is – because it's a healing circle.'

Charles looked thoughtful and Pete pleased.

But the woodpecker hadn't finished.

'When you knocked today, Pete, I'd been sorting out Frankie's clothes.' I saw Charles stiffen. Assuring him that I hadn't thrown anything away, I continued with my tale. 'I found a hidden compartment in her wardrobe where she kept a white linen robe. Would that be the one she wore to the Circle?'

'To the full moon ceremonies, yes,' said Charles gruffly. 'I never opened her wardrobe, so I had no idea there was any compartment...'

His voice trailed away and I read his misery. This was something else that Frankie had kept from him.

'Inside the pocket I found a small metal chalice.'

'That's what they wanted,' said Pete.

'They'll get it over my dead body,' growled Charles.

Scanning the small ward, I saw that most of the other visitors had gone. We had only ten minutes of visiting time left so Charles quickly formulated a plan, announcing that he and Pete would confront Theo next week, once he was out of hospital. He was particularly insistent that I should take the chalice home with me because he didn't want Theo to find it.

'Would you do one more thing for me, Pandora, before you leave?'

I nodded.

'I'd like you to remove the picture of Isis from my bedroom and dispose of it. Don't keep it yourself in case...' He stopped, exchanging a glance with Pete. '...You having a bonfire any time soon?'

'I'll take care of it, don't worry,' said Pete, tapping the side of his nose.

'And, Pandora, can I prevail upon you to put the picture of St Michael in its place? You'll find it on the wall of my study. I'm in need of some protection and he's never failed me yet.'

Hm, I thought, *sounds as if Charles blames the magical goddess for his bad luck.*

Having secured Charles' permission to dispose of Frankie's old clothes, I drove back to the cottage with Pete in companionable silence. We'd done enough talking for one day.

After a quick stop to remove Isis from the bedroom wall, I dropped Pete and the picture off at his place. I had no feelings of regret about it being destroyed. In fact, I'd have destroyed it myself, if necessary. This morning, when I'd taken the goblet to the window and held it to the light, I'd felt a strange, almost painful, sensation in my spine. When I turned around I got the impression of a venomous energy which seemed to emanate from the picture.

On the short drive back to the cottage, I contemplated the approaching evening with Theo – the last hurdle to clear before I could head back home first thing tomorrow, leaving the secrets and lies far behind.

* * *

Pulling off my boots, I poured myself a welcome glass of wine. Pete's *Daily Messenger* lay on the kitchen table, so I picked it up and took it into the living room. Tabloid newspapers were my guilty pleasure.

About five minutes into it, I realised it was yesterday's. I carried on reading the feature articles until I came to the Showbiz section where, splashed across the page, was a picture of an attractive couple leaving a London nightclub. They were laughing and he had his arm round her waist. He was an older man, tall, dark and still handsome, and she was a stunning blonde in a Grecian top and figure-hugging leather trousers. The headline said: *James Jay and Gaby Laing bond at the Lazy Lizard club*. There followed a short paragraph about them reviving their careers by currently collaborating on an album.

I closed the newspaper and thrust it in the bin, jagged daggers of anger and jealousy gouging at my heart. Searching feverishly for my last remaining roll-up, I took several deep drags to calm me down. I was fully aware of how suggestive the tabloids could be without actually libelling anyone. The word 'bond' could insinuate anything from a boogie in a nightclub to full-on sex, although presumably not in full view of the dancing public. No wonder Charles had included Jay in my list of stress-inducing factors. He must have seen this article yesterday, after he'd devoured the sports news.

With no way of contacting Jay, I'd have to wait till I got home tomorrow to ring him. I could only hope the desolation that engulfed me would have subsided by then.

Chapter 19

Phoenix Rising

I'd calmed down a bit by the time Theo came in, with the help of another large glass of wine. Incorporated in my 'transformation' contract had been an undertaking to eat healthily and avoid alcohol so, like a good acolyte, I'd removed all red meat from my diet, given up drink and gone a bit macrobiotic. But this had only made me miserable. In the end I decided that loving myself was more important than striving in vain for spiritual perfection, especially as it's twice as easy to love others when happy oneself. So I returned to my former regime of everything in moderation, which suited me fine. This had been Jay's cue to tease me by quoting Oscar Wilde: 'Everything in moderation, including moderation.'

What was life without the occasional bag of salted nuts and a soothing tipple, I thought, as I sipped and nibbled, especially when faced with evidence of potential adultery on the part of one's best beloved.

My good cop had tried to reason with me: *It's only a picture, after all, sensationalised by a tabloid hack. Jay's probably been ringing your mobile so you can have a laugh about it.*

But my mother's voice injected her usual dose of candour into this imagined scenario: *Why couldn't he ring you here? He knows the number.*

Resolving to temporarily let Jay drop off my worry list, I concentrated on getting through dinner with my devious brother. This wasn't as hard as I'd imagined. When I asked him about his day, Theo actually made me laugh with some of his dry observations on the customers who entered Gaia's Cave and the therapists who worked upstairs.

After a decent interval, I made an excuse that I was tired, and left him watching pre-recorded back-to-back episodes of *The Wire*. Despite the soothing presence of St Michael the Archangel on the wall above me, sleep proved impossible so I raided my bag for emergency sleeping tablets, prescribed after Frankie's death. Consequently, I woke later than intended next morning, to the sound of Theo closing the back door on his way out.

Blearily making for the kettle, to irrigate the desert in my mouth with some tea, my eye was caught by a small purple box on the kitchen table accompanied by a tiny gift card from Gaia's Cave. Inside the box, on a cushion of white satin, lay a golden, oval pendant depicting a phoenix rising. The bird's engraved wings tapered upwards, curving to form an inner oval which enclosed the bird's neck and upper body, its head bent backwards, its beak pointing up. This inner oval gave the impression of a chick inside an egg, ready to peck its way out. So within the image of resurrection there dwelt an image of new life.

The card said: *Thanks for riding to the rescue. Love, T x*

In the following few minutes, the two forces of aversion and affection campaigned for supremacy. But hadn't this been the theme of my relationship with my brother so far? Never being sure whether he was a goodie or a baddie, my opinion of him had constantly ebbed and flowed. After Beau's revelation, it sank to rock bottom, yet today he enchanted me with this golden phoenix, a bird associated with Enoch, erstwhile ruler of Phoenicia, land of the phoenix – the person who'd taught me to take note of signs and portents. Did this symbol of rebirth signify my life was going to change again?

After a hasty breakfast, I packed my things, including the chalice and the key to the secret panel. When I opened the car boot to deposit my holdall, staring back at me were the four black plastic bags full of Frankie's clothes, waiting to be delivered to their fate.

So much for my plans for an early start, I thought, as I drove to the supermarket car park, where I fed the oldest of my mother's clothes into the recycling bank. While there, I did some shopping for Theo, feeling much warmer towards him since his gift of gold. After dropping off the wearable clothes at a charity shop in the town, I returned to the cottage with some provisions, which included Theo's favourite – bacon and sausages. *I'm not doing it all for him,* I told myself. *It's so there's something for Tegan when she comes at the weekend.*

I couldn't leave without saying goodbye to Beau. When he saw me coming, he ambled over to meet me. I was still smarting from the Gaby and Jay business and he seemed to sense that I needed comforting, standing meekly until I'd finished hugging his neck.

I remembered that I had something to tell him.

'I believe we know now why Theo did it.'

Concentrating on an image of the chalice, I said, 'That's what he was looking for. And now we've got to find out why.'

Beau stood very still, then nuzzled my hand, so I took that to mean he appreciated being kept in the loop. And, just as importantly, that there was an apple in my pocket with his name on it. Theo had filled the hay rack with barley straw and left clean water, so once Beau had finished munching, I led him down the lane to Flossy so he wouldn't be on his own. I said goodbye with a final scratch behind his ears and told him I'd be back soon.

* * *

Pulling up in the courtyard of Four Seasons, I breathed a sigh of relief, happy to back in my safe haven.

As I passed by the kitchen door on my way upstairs I called out 'Hello' to Sharon. She was pleased to see me but her attention was directed at a magazine recipe for some bright red cakes, clipped on to a skirt hanger, hooked over a cupboard doorknob. She was peering at it and muttering under her breath.

'Time for new glasses, Sha?' I said.

'Migosh. You may be right. I could have sworn it said table-spoons but it should have been teaspoons.'

'Of what?'

'Cider vinegar and baking soda.'

'I thought that's what you cleaned ovens with.'

Resolving to steer well clear of these cakes, I left her to it and broke into a trot, taking the stairs two at a time and rugby tackling my black bag which was lying on the bed where I'd left it. I fished out my basic cell phone – what Rowan called my 'dumbphone' – which suited the technophobe in me.

I scanned the Inbox for texts. There were some from Rowan at the beginning of the week, until it had sunk in that I didn't have my phone with me. But nothing from Zac.

There was one missed call from Jay on Tuesday afternoon but he hadn't left a message. Their nightclub sortie must have been on Monday night, so he probably *had* been phoning to put me in the picture.

There was only one recorded message. It proved to be from Mary, a client who'd wanted a session on Wednesday, so I rang her immediately to explain why I hadn't got back to her, and to say I wouldn't be available till after Easter.

'Can you possibly fit me in tomorrow?' she pleaded. 'I'm exhausted. I really need a boost.'

So I booked her in for ten o'clock the next day. I'd been missing my peaceful intervals of contemplation and it would give me an excuse to spend some time alone in the dome after she'd gone, so I could zap my own feelings of jealousy and anger.

I'd mulled the problem over on the drive home and decided not to mention the newspaper picture to Sharon. With three kids on the premises, it wouldn't be right to cause an atmosphere. It wasn't as if Jay and Gaby had been snapped in bed together. All he'd done was put his arm round her waist, hadn't he?

All the same, a niggling earworm kept slithering round my audio system.

Jay and recording studios have always been a bad combination. Add a busty blonde to the mix and he's potentially a tinderbox in danger of combustion.

Having dealt with my phone, I went downstairs to the study to open the post and answer emails. There I found a large envelope adorned with the Oven Ready logo – a sketch of an old-fashioned chef, with red cheeks, chef's hat, a moustache and a big smile on his face, carrying a cake on a baking tray. It contained some papers and a covering letter from Portia, dated the day before.

When I read the line: *Mr Willoughby has asked me to send you the enclosed documents,* with no mention of me coming into the office, I concluded that he'd interpreted the deafening silence from Glastonbury as a knock-back from yours truly and this letter was a covert signal that he intended to confine our relationship to the strictly professional from now on.

You know it's for the best, my sensible head counselled. *You can't be up in arms about Jay and Gaby one minute, and longing for a rendezvous with an old flame the next.*

But my heart was curling up with disappointment and I had to force myself outside to see Midnight and the goats, so I wouldn't dial his number there and then.

I was just going out the back door, when I heard Sharon calling out for me to wait for her. As we walked, she updated me on the comings and goings of the young Jays.

'Willow and Cherry have been helping Hugh,' she said, smiling at my surprise. 'His two boys are on their Easter vacation and Jay's paying them to do a bit of casual work around the place.'

'So who's paying the girls?'

'They're doing it for love, honey. And if I was their age, with two six-foot hunks around the place, so would I.'

We were laughing about that when we saw Rowan and Clarrie standing in Midnight's field holding hands, their free hands on her neck.

I'd been on the point of asking Sharon if she'd heard from Jay, but, seeing them in the distance, she launched into an extended riff on the subject of Rowan.

'He hasn't left that girl's side since they came home...'

She went on to express several degrees of astonishment that he hadn't contacted Tom, or any of his other friends, since he'd got back. She was still expanding on this theme when we reached the perimeter fence. Before I could stop her, she called out to them.

They dropped their hands and walked towards us with Midnight following close behind.

'Hi, Mum,' said Rowan, a big grin on his face, climbing the stile. 'Clarrie's been teaching me how to talk to Midnight.'

'Sorry to interrupt you,' I said, squinting apologetically at Clarrie. She glanced towards Sharon and shook her head.

'No problem...'

Midnight had put her head over the fence in greeting and Sharon reached for her nose and started rubbing it vigorously.

'Don't do that,' said Clarrie quickly.

Sharon dropped her hand in alarm.

'Do you think she was going to bite me?'

'No. Sorry.' Clarrie's face had turned pink. 'She wouldn't do that. She just doesn't like having her face touched.'

Sharon looked bemused, so I changed the subject.

'What did Midnight say to you, Rowan?'

'Well...'

He turned to Clarrie, who answered for him.

'You were right, she is lonely. She remembers when the other ponies were here...'

'Oh, poor old girl,' I whispered. 'Rowan's probably told you – Jay gave Dixie away when Cherry went to university. He kept Raindrop and Midnight but not long afterwards Raindrop had to be put down. It was awful.'

'Was he a dapple grey?' said Clarrie.

'Yes,' said Rowan, his doe eyes wide with admiration.

'Midnight gave me a picture of Raindrop. She still misses him.'

We all fell quiet then, even Sharon, who must have been wondering what the hell was going on.

'Clarrie can communicate with animals,' I said, bluntly. 'It's a gift.'

'Really?' said Sharon. Our eyes met for a moment and I was convinced she was thinking: *Isn't one weirdo in the house enough, already?*

'Can you ask Midnight whether she likes sharing the barn with Bonnie and Clyde?' I said hastily.

Clarrie paused for a few moments.

'Yes. But they're a pair so they favour each other. She feels a bit left out.'

'I can empathise with that,' said Sharon, cleverly conveying in five words that she sometimes felt excluded when Jay and I were together.

'So, have you two been asking the whole menagerie what star rating they give this hotel?' I asked, trying to lighten the mood.

'We've only got as far as Midnight,' said Rowan. 'Clarrie had to write up her notes on Beau first.'

'But I'll gladly come back tomorrow, if you like,' said Clarrie. 'I'll do three categories: health, wellbeing and diet.'

'Great.'

I'd been wondering how to get Clarrie on her own, to fill her in on the latest in the Theo saga and to let her know that Charles believed her. Now I had an excuse.

'Come with me, and I'll show you the computer. Then you can do it here if you like.'

On the way back to the house, I asked Rowan what he'd experienced when he'd tuned into Midnight and he said he hadn't seen any images, but he'd thought of Raindrop, and felt sad.

'I know what to get you for your birthday, now,' I grinned, 'a DVD of *Doctor Dolittle*.'

Sharon took the cue and started singing, 'If we could talk to the animals...'

'Ha, ha, ha,' said Rowan, in a mock-hollow voice, as he patted my head. This was easy for him, as he was nearly as tall as Jay.

'Have you decided what you're doing for your birthday?'

Rowan's sixteenth birthday was on March 25th – the same day as mine. This year it fell on the Tuesday after Easter, only twelve days away.

'I'm not sure. I'll see what Clarrie wants to do.'

Sharon grunted her disapproval.

'What's wrong with paintballing with your friends?' she asked sharply. 'You enjoyed it last year.'

We'd reached the back door and I continued down the hall with Clarrie, as Sharon and Rowan gravitated towards the kitchen.

I briefly gave Clarrie a tour of my computer, giving her my password, and explaining that I was seeing a client tomorrow and if I wasn't around she should just let herself into the study.

'On the subject of Theo,' I said, closing the door. 'You haven't mentioned anything to Rowan, have you?'

'No, No,' she replied. 'When he asked me what we'd been doing with Beau, I said you wanted me to give him a health check. How did Charles react to the news?'

'Don't worry, he accepted it. He thinks Theo might have been searching for a small chalice that I happened to find when I was clearing out my mother's wardrobe, probably used by a...a group she belonged to. When Charles comes home, he and his friend Pete are going to speak to Theo and ask him to explain himself.'

'Wow,' said Clarrie, her eyes large. 'Serious stuff.'

'Afraid so.'

'They must have wanted that chalice badly to open the grave

for it.'

I was glad she'd said 'they' and not 'Theo'. I'd begun to hope he'd been simply a pawn in the game rather than a prime mover.

I could hear footsteps approaching so I spoke quickly.

'I'm going back on Monday to collect Charles from hospital. I'm not looking forward to the fallout, but I want to hear Theo's explanation.'

Clarrie looked solemn, no doubt thinking of her role in the affair.

'Thanks for your help, Clarrie,' I said, in a low voice. 'It got us closer to the truth...'

At that moment Rowan opened the door, his hand on his throat.

'Ugh, Grandma's been trying to poison me. Those cakes are gross.'

Leaving Clarrie dispensing sympathy, I went upstairs to my bedroom, having picked up the letter from Oven Ready Productions which I'd left on my desk. I didn't want Rowan catching sight of it and asking awkward questions. I'd gone upstairs with the idea of ringing Jay but, instead, decided to complete the documents, so I sat down at the dressing table and waded through them. When I finished, I went downstairs and slipped out the front door to walk to the post box, a short distance from the end of the drive.

Doing this raised my spirits. I imagined Portia opening the letter the next morning and reporting to Zac that she'd heard from me, in response to which he'd ring me and I could explain to him about being incommunicado. Then we'd be friends again.

On the walk back I considered whether I should forget about contacting Jay today. There was always the danger of losing control and accusing him of getting too friendly with Gaby. The risk of having an argument and him coming home tomorrow all frosty and withdrawn finally decided me. I'd leave it. Another night's sleep and a session in the dome tomorrow should, with any luck, give me a new perspective on the matter.

As I let myself in the front door, my phone was ringing. It had a retro ringtone with added amplification (necessary because I was in the habit of leaving it all over the house), and unmistakably mine. I'd left it on my desk when I'd been looking for an envelope, so I sprinted into the room, just managing to answer before it went to voicemail.

'Hello. Andy?'

'Yes, this is she.'

He responded with a hearty guffaw, followed by, 'How you doing?'

My heart had given a great leap when I heard his voice and I had to sit down, because my knees had gone all weak.

'It's so good to hear you. I couldn't contact you. I left my phone at home and...'

Against my will, I'd started to cry.

'It's all right, babe, Sharon told me. I tried to ring you.'

He waited for me to recover myself but I still couldn't speak coherently.

'I wanted to tell you about, (sob) about Th-Theo...And ask you...'

Jay broke in, sounding worried.

'Why you crying, darlin'? What's happened to Theo?'

'Nothing. I-it's what h-he's done.'

'Hold on a sec.' I heard voices in the background which gradually faded. After what seemed like an age, he returned. 'Gaby and the team have just left the building for a farewell drink.'

The mention of that name ignited a flame of anger in me which miraculously dried up the tears, allowing me to proceed without further weeping, but with a certain amount of concealed gnashing of teeth.

'Are you joining them?'

My voice was still shaky and his answer was soothing.

'No, darlin', got a bit of finishing-up to do. Tell me about Theo.'

My heart lifted and I began to feel better.

'We think Theo opened the grave because he was searching for a sort of goblet. It's all connected to the Circle Frankie went to. Charles and Pete are going to face him with it next week.'

There was silence at the other end of the line.

'Jay. Are you still there?'

'Yeah, just trying to get my head round it. Let me wind things up here. I'll be home tonight.'

Chapter 20

Making Up

As soon as Jay rang off, I spread the news that he'd be home today instead of tomorrow. While Rowan looked pleased, Sharon appeared flustered.

'Omigosh,' she wailed, 'I'm going to my book club tonight so I've told the kids to cook pizzas for themselves.' She glared at me accusingly. 'I like to have an occasional break from cooking.'

I was so high on the prospect of a reunion with my sexy genarian, that I refused to be drawn into a *who does most around the house* contest.

I had a cursory forage in the fridge but only for show. I'd been cleaning, washing, ironing and cooking non-stop for three days in Glastonbury, and I certainly wasn't hanging around as short-order cook for teenagers who were perfectly capable of feeding themselves for one evening.

'Jay and I can go out,' I said, noting Sharon's expression of disapproval, but still too happy to let it get to me.

I called Jay and we decided to meet at Giovanni's, our favourite local restaurant. He reckoned he'd be there by eight-thirty. Before he rang off, I asked if he had to go back to the studio and, to my relief, he said that everything was wrapped up and the job finished.

Jay was already sitting at our table when I arrived. He stood up when he saw me and kissed me softly on the lips.

'Mm, you smell nice,' he said, briefly nuzzling my neck.

'So do you,' I said, thinking that the last person who'd nuzzled my neck had been a bit hairier and heftier than my old man. And a quadruped to boot.

Jay was looking incredibly fanciable, his honey-coloured skin smooth and moisturised. He must have found time to visit an expensive barber in London, because his hair was skimming his collar at just the right length.

I was glad I'd put on my new V-necked peplum dress in a fetching shade of teal. It was a dream to wear, an ingenious construction which managed to sculpt and enhance in all the right places. It fitted so comfortably, I could eat what I wanted without undoing any fastenings.

A waiter appeared, pulled out the chair for me, and took our drinks order.

'Nice dress,' said Jay, eyeing my embonpoint.

'I thought you'd like it,' I said, pushing my shoulders back so he'd get the full effect.

'Outstanding,' he grinned. 'And I haven't seen that before,' he added, as he leaned across for a better view of the pendant around my neck.

I'd found a gold chain in my jewellery box the perfect length for the phoenix to rest just above my cleavage – a cleavage, it has to be said, that wouldn't be half as prominent were it not for the interior architecture of the dress.

'Theo gave it to me.'

Jay's fingers brushed my breasts lightly when he let go of the medallion and we stared at each other across the table, saying nothing. This happened to us every so often. In my case, I can only describe it as being overwhelmed by love for him. And I can only compare it to the sort of wholehearted love you have, as a child, for a pet – one you rush home from school to see and who breaks your heart when, inevitably, it dies.

I'd never asked Jay what went on in *his* head when we had these 'moments'. Maybe for him it consisted mostly of sexual desire.

'So what's the gen on Theo,' said Jay, breaking the spell.

In between ordering our food and drink I told him everything, pausing only while we wolfed down Tuscan soup and toasted bread like characters in a Henry Fielding novel. By the time our spaghetti alla vongole arrived, he was as wised up as I was.

'Are you surprised?' I asked, when I'd finished.

'Not as much as you. I never trusted the sexy abbess. They had their heads together at the funeral...it was obvious he was hooked. When he stayed out tomcatting, I guessed who it was. She used him to do her dirty work.'

'You know it was you who spooked him that night.'

Jay's sleepy eyes opened wide.

'Me?'

'Beau said when the garden light came on, Theo ran away. You must have activated it when you went into the garden for a smoke.'

'Blimey, so now it's my fault Frankie spent her first night in the ground minus a coffin lid...'

I stifled a giggle.

'You do believe Clarrie spoke to Beau, don't you? She showed me how to communicate with him and I saw it too...'

Jay adopted a barrister-like expression.

'I call Beau, the Baudet of Poitou, to the witness box, with a bag of hay and a court interpreter. Failing that, can someone channel St Francis of Assisi?'

I laughed.

'How does a heathen like you know about St Francis?'

'He was the original Dr Dolittle, wasn't he?'

'Possibly. But ever since the Vatican demoted St Christopher, I take it all with a pinch of salt. My granny was outraged when they said he never existed.'

'Don't tell Sharon,' he said, refilling my glass, 'she's still got his medal clipped to the back of the SUV sun visor.'

I waited for him to go on, but he was concentrating on his pasta.

'So, do you believe Clarrie or not?'

'Yeah.'

I wanted more than that, so I stared at him, to signal I was waiting for a proper reply. He gave a rueful shrug.

'Babe, I believe whatever you and Clarrie say, but what's Charles gonna do when Theo denies it?'

'If he denies it he'll be calling Beau a liar.'

'No, my sweet. He'll be calling you and Clarrie liars.'

I shook my head. Surely even Theo wouldn't sink that low.

'What do you think we should do, then?'

'Put Theo in the dome and torture the truth out of him with your gong.'

I tried to scowl at this, but the twinkle in his eye made me smirk. We'd nearly finished our second bottle of wine, so further cogent discussion was becoming less and less of a prospect.

An alarm bell rang in my brain then, and I knew the time had come to either have it out with Jay about his nightclub jaunt with Gaby, or tell him about my new job. Knowing it would be foolish to wage both battles at the same time, the competitor in me chose the one that would put him on the back foot. But that was not before my conscience hurled an accusation at me.

Secrets and lies – you're as bad as your brother.

Okay, I'm keeping this job offer secret for now, but when have I lied?

You kept quiet about the column, the job and Zac – sins of omission, just as bad as lying.

Drowning my conscience with a swig of Amarone, I took aim and fired.

'I saw you in the paper with Gaby...'

I paused, bereft at the memory of them looking like a couple in that picture. An involuntary muscle spasm pulled at the left corner of his mouth, indicating that I'd rattled him. But his reply was composed – possibly even rehearsed.

'Don't worry, babe, it was staged. Advance publicity for the album, that's all.'

'But you had your arm around her waist and the headline

made it sound as if you were an item.'

He took my hand across the table and stroked it soothingly.

'If we'd been at it, d'you think we'd have been posing for the paparazzi?'

I clutched at his hand like a drowning woman, willing myself to stay calm. Out of the corner of my eye I saw a waitress hovering with the dessert menu but Jay asked her to give us a minute and she disappeared.

'Don't worry, darlin',' he crooned, 'women always see chicks like Gaby as a threat. But she's a mate. End of.'

His defence of her, and the suggestion that I, one of the 'women', would be older and less attractive, moved me to withdraw my hand swiftly. I thought back to the first day Gaby had come to Jay's studio at Four Seasons and the mystery of why they'd been approaching from the opposite direction to the Feathers, where they'd said they were going for lunch.

'You never did tell me where you'd been that day when our cars passed.'

His face darkened.

'That's because you made some crack about me being in her hotel room.'

Still deprived of an explanation, I floundered on.

'And when we all had dinner together, you never took your eyes off each other.'

'Wow,' he said, his eyes flashing, 'the accusations are coming thick and fast now. As it happens, she's started having problems with her hearing.' His voice was low and angry and a black dread gripped the pit of my stomach. 'She asked me to keep it to myself – if people in the industry knew, she'd be binned off.'

I sat motionless, wondering why, if she'd been lipreading, she hadn't hung on my every word, as she had Jay's.

'You've got a trust issue that needs sorting, Andy. Otherwise...'

It seemed as if he was going to say more, but he stopped.

Suddenly the enormity of what could be happening to us hit me like a blow in the solar plexus and I covered my face with my hands. Jay must have grasped it too, because after a silence which felt like a lifetime, he backtracked.

'We did have lunch at the Feathers,' he said, with a sigh. 'But she'd left a demo CD at her hotel so we went to pick it up afterwards. I waited in the car. Simple as that.'

'I still wish you'd told me that when I asked you in the first place,' I said, patting at the stray tears on my cheek with my napkin. 'You didn't use to be so touchy.'

'You wait till you make sixty, babe. You won't know what hits you...'

I gave him a long look which I'd copied, some years ago, from a Spanish friend. It consisted of widening one's eyes and filling them with a sympathetic, loving expression then almost closing them for an instant, in a slow-motion blink. It usually worked wonders on the recipient, be it man, woman, child or beast.

'Come on, Jay. You're gorgeous. And you look better now than you did five years ago.'

He straightened up, looking pleased.

'That's all down to you, Andy...'

At that moment our waitress reappeared to take our dessert orders.

'Do you think we should get a cab home?' I said, when we'd polished off our cognac coffees. I'd acquired the *carajillo* habit in Spain and Jay had become a willing devotee.

'Probably,' he said, waving his credit card at a passing employee.

When the waiter returned with it, Jay told him we'd be leaving our cars in the car park. And so it was, that we staggered out of a taxi, letting ourselves into the house as quietly as possible, so we wouldn't be waylaid by any sober family members ready for a chat.

We tiptoed upstairs and while I hung my coat in the dressing-room, Jay took off his clothes at what seemed to me like lightning pace. When I was drunk everything seemed to happen in the blink of an eye. I expected him to undress me, as he usually did, but this time he seemed happy to concentrate on my lips and neck. I sat up in bed and undid the side zip of my dress so I could pull it over my head, but he stopped me.

'Leave it on for a minute. I like the way it pushes up your breasts.'

I complied, always grateful that Jay never referred to my breasts as 'tits' or 'boobs'.

After five minutes or so of Jay 'appreciating' my cantilevered bosom, I staggered to the bathroom and undressed, eager for some bare skin action. I was ready, and so was he, yet he insisted on delaying, as per the instructions on the Tantric Sex for Beginners webpage that had become his manual. He'd placed a bath towel on our lovely new bed while I was in the bathroom, and when I came out I saw that he was holding a small bottle of sandalwood oil.

'I'll oil you first,' he said, as I lay down on my front.

He straddled my body and slowly rubbed the oil on to my back and shoulders, then my buttocks and the backs of my legs. Even though his penis lightly brushed my body as he worked, I was almost asleep by the time he whispered to me to turn over, when he did the same to my neck, breasts, stomach and the front of my legs. At no time did he caress my body in an overtly sexual way; his hand movements were more effleurage than erotic.

When he'd finished, we swapped roles and I did the same for him. I was supposed to push my hands forward on his skin in a fan-like movement and not linger too long in one place. This proved easy when I was doing his back but when he turned over, it was tempting to alter the rhythm slightly and apply a little more pressure to certain sensitive places in the hope he'd be overcome with passion and get on with it. His manhood, or 'lingam' as he liked to call it now, had subsided slightly. Like me, he'd relaxed when his back was being stroked, so when I worked my way down his front, I pressed my fingers on his erogenous zone a little more firmly than I had on his back. Once this had achieved the desired effect, I massaged the front of his legs and he lay there, glistening.

'You're all ready for the barbecue now, big boy,' I said, breathy and mock-sexy. 'Get ready for some heat.'

'Something tells me you're not taking the sacred tantra seriously,' said Jay, amused. 'It's not the barbecue that's important – it's the long, slow, marinating of the meat.'

I leant over him and he reached up to kiss my breasts. I lowered myself on to him and started to move my whole body to complete the massage. We were like two seals, slipping and sliding all over the place.

When I'd slithered enough I whispered, 'Are you ready yet?' and he replied by flipping me on my back and locking loins.

'Yes, yes,' he gasped, as he reached a climax moments later.

Unsurprisingly, after all the shilly-shallying, my G-spot had failed to synchronise on this occasion. But I wanted my easy-going Jay back, so anything I could do to exorcise his grumpy doppelganger, was worth the sacrifice of an orgasm or two.

'Did the earth move for you, babe?' he asked, once he'd got his breath back.

I hesitated, wondering whether to lie, but as he'd asked me outright, I decided to do a George Washington.

'Not this time,' I breathed, embroidering the truth by adding, 'I got too relaxed. Must have been the wine.'

'Come on, then,' he said, manoeuvring me on to my front, covering what he now called my 'yoni' with one hand, and doing his best to cup my breasts with the other.

Jay was expert at this. He knew the map of my body better than I knew it myself, and in no time I'd scaled the heights and lay waiting for him to finish showering so I, too, could delubricate.

Soon we were both back in bed and he moved in for a cuddle. His tattoo, a few inches above his left wrist, bore a heart, which I traced with my finger. The name tattooed beneath was 'Andy'.

'Has anyone ever thought you were gay?' I said.

'What?'

'Maybe you should have paid a bit more and gone for "Pandora".'

Jay clasped my hand.

'Actually, it came in very useful on one or two occasions. Some ladies don't like taking no for an answer. But show them that and they back off.'

Jay had drunk more than me that evening, evident from what he'd just revealed, so I seized the moment.

'When was the last time you had to fight someone off?'

'Well,' he yawned, 'not exactly fight off. But it was an invitation. Definitely. Not too long ago.'

I shifted up in the bed and cradled his head to my chest.

'I love you, J-J,' I whispered. 'I'll always love you.'

I kissed his eyes, nose, cheeks and the tips of his ears as if he were a cherished baby.

'Who was it, darling? I won't be cross.'

'Promise?'

I knew I'd be furious with the wanton hussy, but he'd already said that he hadn't succumbed to temptation, so it *was* true, up to a point, because it wouldn't be him I'd be cross with him.

'I promise.'

'Gaby. Last night. I suppose it was her way of saying thanks.'

I had to exert every last ounce of control to stop myself from shouting my rage from the rooftops. And, contrary to what I'd just promised, my anger wasn't all directed at her. What did the stupid idiot expect if he'd been to a nightclub with her and emerged with his arm round her waist?

'Did you go out with her again last night, then?'

Blood pounded in my ears, but I forced my voice to stay calm and low.

'Yeah. We went out every night, but never on our own. There was always a few of us. It's what you do when you're working together. She wanted me to go back to her place for a nightcap.'

'How did you get out of it?' I asked silkily. 'Did you show her your tattoo?'

Jay laughed. I was still cradling his head so he couldn't see my face.

'Wouldn't have worked, darlin', she knows I call you Andy. Nah, I told her I gave all that up years ago. Anyway,' he nuzzled my breasts like a contented child, 'why settle for a burger when you've got fillet steak at home?'

I felt like telling him to stick the barbecue metaphor where the sun don't shine, but stroked his hair instead.

'Will you be seeing Gaby again?'

'Well, we both might.'

'What do you mean?'

'We offered to have her cats if she went on tour, didn't we?

'Don't worry, darling,' I said, breathing gently in his ear, which had always been high on his list of top turn-ons. 'Leave it to me and Sharon. We'll deal with it.'

Chapter 21

Orchestrating Easter

Jay was at the kitchen table eating the full English I'd just prepared him. Sharon and I sat the other side, watching in admiration as he packed it all away.

'Is there any more toast?'

Catching our amused glances he said, mock seriously, 'A man needs to line his stomach before a day tilling the soil.'

'So you're working with Hugh today?' said Sharon. 'You might find it a bit crowded out there. You know his two boys *and* Willow and Cherry are helping out.'

'The more the merrier, I'll find something for 'em all to do, don't worry.'

It was lovely to see Jay in such a good mood, raring to resume his role of feudal lord of the manor, and I gave his back a little pat as I put more toast on the table.

After woofing this down, he got up and kissed Sharon, then me. As he walked to the door I remembered what I had to arrange, and called after him.

'Can you find out who wants to spend Easter in Glastonbury? I need to confirm numbers with Steve.'

Jay looked blank.

'He's got the farmhouse down the lane from Charles. It's where Rowan and Clarrie stayed.'

'What's it like?'

'Fine. It's a new annexe with three double rooms. You're coming, aren't you, Sharon?'

'Sure I am. I don't mind driving down...'

She eyeballed Jay, to check he'd be with her.

'When is Easter?' he said, completely at a loss where most religious festivals were concerned.

'Good Friday's a week today.'

'And when are you going?' he asked, sounding peeved.

I'd already told him this last night, so I guessed he was suffering from a touch of alcohol-induced amnesia. *If he doesn't remember this,* I thought, *he's probably forgotten he let drop that Gaby propositioned him.*

'I'm collecting Charles from hospital on Monday. I was hoping you'd come down on Thursday or Friday.'

At that moment Willow wandered in and helped herself to coffee.

'Willow and Cherry can share a room. Sharon, you'll have one to yourself.'

'What's this, Mum?'

While I was explaining it all to Willow, Jay made for the back door.

'Yeah, course I'll come. You in the garden today, Will?'

'Oh,' Willow said distractedly. 'Yes. I'll be there in half an hour, Dad.'

'Don't forget our cars are still at the restaurant, Jay.' He was so eager to get out into the fresh air that I almost had to shout. 'I can't pick mine up – I've got a dome appointment.'

'No probs, darlin', Hugh can take me and one of the boys. Give your keys to Willow.'

I blew him a kiss and turned back to his daughter, who'd taken her coffee to the table and sat down.

'What do you want for breakfast?' I said, feeling guilty that Sharon, Jay and I had all fled the nest last night and left the chicks to it.

'Ooh, French toast with cinnamon, please.'

'Make that two, please, Mum,' said Cherry, appearing in the kitchen in her Disney princess pyjamas.

I assumed frying-pan duties and was all ears as they answered Sharon's questions about Hugh's boys. The way Willow and Cherry giggled when they talked about them said it all.

'So what are they doing for Easter?' said Sharon.

I liked her line of interrogation – it would give me a clue as to what the girls might be planning.

'They're going to see their mum in Paris.'

Cherry paused, looking at Willow.

'They've asked us if we want to go with them.'

Sharon and I mulled this over in silence.

Finally Sharon said, 'Me and Pandora and your dad are visiting Charles, so if you two want to join *us*, you're welcome.'

I put myself in the girls' place – Easter in Paris with a hunk, or Somerset with the old folks? It was a no-brainer.

Cherry jutted her jaw, refusing to be sidetracked.

'They said their mum's got plenty of room.'

'And I'd have a chance to practise my French,' said Willow, pleadingly, looking at me.

I wasn't sure what to say. Cherry was old enough to do her own thing, but Willow was still only seventeen and not very worldly-wise.

Luckily, Sharon took the reins. 'What have you told them? Have you said you'd go?'

'I said we'd ask Dad, and he'd probably say yes.'

Sharon fixed Cherry with a hard stare. She'd lived in this house for the last seven years, since Debbie had left, following the pony-girl incident. She'd become the dominant female two years later when Debbie had died. So she didn't care to be bypassed now they were old enough to want to go their own way.

'Tell you what. I'll have a word with your dad and Hugh, and see what they think.'

'Okay, Gran,' said Cherry, with an exaggerated sigh, as Sharon bustled off to make sure all arrangements would be closely coordinated and monitored before any descendant of hers would be setting foot on French soil.

Twenty minutes later, Sharon still hadn't returned from her

summit talks. It was nine-thirty and Mary was due at ten. I usually spent at least half an hour in the dome beforehand, running through the client's notes and chilling out, but today I was too hung up on where the girls were spending Easter. If they weren't coming to Glastonbury, I had Tegan in mind for the third room. I felt a duty of care for her – as a client, and because she'd met Theo through me. Now that they were getting close, she needed to know what he'd done, so she could decide whether to continue with the relationship. And if it all went belly up, at least I'd be there to comfort her.

The girls were in the middle of telling me which bits of Paris they most wanted to see, when Sharon reappeared, a broad smile on her face.

'It's all arranged. Hugh spoke to his wife – ex-wife – on the phone. It was news to her you two were going as well...'

'That's because I told them not to say anything till I'd asked Dad,' said Cherry, with more than a hint of irritation. 'He's been away all week.'

'Whatever,' said Sharon, cutting in. 'Anyway, their mother says it's okay. She's going to let us know when you get there and when you leave, so no hanky-panky please, missy. And you don't let Willow out of your sight. You clear on that?'

While Cherry glowered at Sharon, Willow, bless her, beamed.

I shot them a thumbs-up and excused myself, thankful that they'd be well away from what might prove to be a rather tense time in the Charles Lockwood household. I was dreading the showdown between him and Theo, and the reverberations, whatever they might be.

* * *

Oscar and I arrived at the cottage just after eleven on Monday morning. This time I'd brought plenty of supplies with me to fill the fridge and freezer so I wouldn't be forever traipsing to the shops.

Just as I'd finished packing the stuff away, Tegan came in the back door with Milo at her heels. She was wearing a collarless grey wool jacket with her jeans tucked into Ugg boots. Her hair was encircled by a narrow grey and cream bandana, tied at the front. She looked great.

'Hi, Pandora, Theo told me you were coming today. I was hoping I'd see you before I left. Let's put the kettle on.'

'Hey, lovely to see you,' I said, kissing her and petting Milo.

The two dogs sniffed each other. Reassured that they were already acquainted, they ran off into the back garden.

'How did the Palm Sunday procession go? Did Beau behave himself?'

'He was perfect, beautifully behaved. The kids loved him. Here, have a look.'

Producing her phone, she showed me some video footage of Theo leading Beau towards the church door where the vicar waited, the congregation waving their palm fronds enthusiastically. Theo's face had an expression of serenity, bringing to mind a modern-day Christ. The vicar then led them into the churchyard where Beau proceeded to graze among the headstones.

'Do you like Theo?'

There was no point in beating about the bush, seeing that she'd bared her heart and soul to me on several occasions in the dome.

'Yes, I do. We're on the same wavelength, mentally and physically.'

'You've left out spiritually.'

'I'm not sure about that. We haven't had any deep discussions. But then, half the time, I don't even know where I stand on that myself.' She laughed softly. 'Just as long as it's not Welsh Chapel. I had enough of that as a kid.'

'So what's the latest on Jeremy?'

'I've had a solicitor's letter saying I've got to leave the boat by the end of the month. I haven't been giving him any rent, so I can't blame him. I'll just have to find a flat.'

Tegan and flat hunting didn't seem to go together somehow. She was a water bird, a pink flamingo. I couldn't imagine her playing house on terra firma.

'But can you afford it? How's the supply teaching going?'

It was Monday morning. If she had any work, she'd surely be somewhere wielding a stick of chalk by now.

'Some schools are already on their Easter holidays. But I haven't actually done much teaching lately. I've been helping my friend Sophie in her craft shop. Milo likes that, 'cos I can take him with me and he doesn't have to go to dog crèche.'

She smiled wryly.

'Pandora, I really must get a grip...I can't keep blaming Jeremy. Now I'm over him, I've just got to decide what I want to do, where I want to go, and who I want to be with.'

I nearly said that she and Milo would be welcome to come and stay with us at Four Seasons, but I had a suspicion that the decisions she was referring to were linked to my brother. And once she heard what he'd done, maybe she'd want to sever all connections with him. And that might include me.

In the end, I asked her what her ideal career would be.

'Well, I studied art and design at college. I make a lot of my own clothes and I'd love to produce a clothing line.'

'That sounds like a plan. And I bet it'd be festival fashion. Yes?'

'You know me so well,' she grinned.

I had an image of a rotary washing line adorned with cropped tops, frayed denim shorts, fringed suede jackets and palazzo trousers.

'You could call it "Twirly".'

She gave a puzzled laugh.

'But it's just a dream because I haven't got any capital.'

We carried on chatting about this and that, and when I told her about Clarrie's case study on Beau, I made sure I mentioned her special talent: communicating with animals.

Once we'd had our second cup of tea, I looked around to see if Theo had left me a note.

'Does Beau need anything?'

'No, that's what Milo and I have just been doing. We've sorted Bobo out, haven't we, Milo? He's with Flossy now.'

Milo cocked his head, whimpering excitedly when he heard Beau's name.

'Sounds like a bromance.'

She laughed. 'Yeah, Milo certainly likes being with him; he didn't want to come away. Well, it's time we hit the road.'

'So what are your plans this week, Tegan?'

'I'm helping Sophie out tomorrow, Wednesday and Thursday. Theo said Jay and Sharon would be joining you at the weekend, so I'll probably see him some time after Easter.'

'Do you ever go back to Wales?'

Tegan probably wondered why I was conducting this interrogation just as she was trying to get out the door, but I needed to know if she was free to occupy the third farmhouse room, in the unlikely event she'd still be interested in Theo after finding out what he'd done.

'Occasionally. But there's only my dad, really, and he's married again. They're in Majorca at the moment.'

'So you're staying on the boat for Easter?'

Tegan nodded. She'd walked to the front door and was turning to say goodbye. For a moment I was tempted to drop a hint about Theo. But what could I say? *By the way, don't be surprised if the man you're in love with turns out to be a grave opener who, until recently, was sleeping with a married woman of the parish.*

I couldn't bring myself to rain on her parade, so I kept quiet.

'Okay, Tegan. Take care. Have a good journey. We'll speak soon.'

After waving them off, I went straight upstairs to check that Charles' room was shipshape for his homecoming. Either Theo or Tegan had put fresh sheets on the bed. Being the only double bedroom in the house, it had probably been their room of choice for the weekend.

I opened the secret panel in Frankie's wardrobe while I was there, and put the chalice back, placing the key in the pocket of the Man from Del Monte's jacket, in the other wardrobe, as arranged.

Downstairs, I took my newspaper to the sofa, to be swiftly joined by Anubis, who must have been hiding in the undergrowth waiting for Milo's departure. When Oscar ambled in from the garden, Anubis gave him a green stare, but maintained her position, right next to me. Poor old Oscar. I'd brought him with me so we could have some time together, and still there was a usurper on the scene.

When I got to the hospital a couple of hours later, Charles was already sitting in what he called 'the departure lounge' on the ground floor, clutching a hospital carrier bag with his worldly goods inside and some prescription drugs. Pinned to his jacket lapel was a sequinned Irish harp surrounding a clump of shamrock.

'I'm here, Charles,' I said unnecessarily. 'I hope you haven't been waiting long.'

He looked tired and grey around the gills.

'Don't worry, my dear.'

'Happy St Patrick's Day. I didn't know you had Irish blood.'

'Here,' he said, unpinning the harp and giving it to me. 'An Irish nurse insisted on giving it to me, but you've got more claim on it than I have.'

It was years since I'd worn shamrock, but I was more than happy to accept. It reminded me of my Irish granny, Doireann, who I was supposed to be called after. Except Frankie had transformed it into Pandora instead. Just plain Ann would have suited me, if I'd had any say in the matter.

'I rang this morning and they said to come about two...'

He laughed mirthlessly.

'That's to cover themselves in case the pharmacy's slow dishing out pills. The car park's so packed they try to stagger the pick-ups. I've been here since twelve o'clock.'

'That's disgraceful, I could easily have got here earlier.'

Charles prised himself from the hard, plastic waiting-room chair, and held on to my arm as we walked to the car park. I'd always known Charles as hale and hearty, his sturdy frame veering towards plumpness, yet today he seemed frail and his grasp weak.

I avoided any discussion of the nefarious activities of the citizens of Glastonbury on the drive back. There'd been too much of that lately. You'd think I'd never have forgotten my Wonder Woman responsibilities, but when death and disaster strike, the higher self can all too easily be sabotaged by the brain's primitive limbic system. Once an excess of emotion comes in the door, spreading justice, peace and light is apt to fly straight out the window.

* * *

My retuning came after Mary's sound healing session on Friday. I'd finished my sonic routine and put on her favourite music: Joaquin Rodrigo's *Concierto de Aranjuez, Second Movement*, which features a haunting cadenza for classical Spanish guitar: a slow flamenco of passion and regret. Later in the piece, the guitar is joined by the orchestra, bringing the music to a high point of intensity, the guitar ending with a peaceful arpeggio.

When Mary had gone, I sat cross-legged on the floor. Having spent two hours in the dome already, receiving the side benefits of the same sound bath as Mary, I was well primed, so I went straight into blazing the Violet Flame through every atom of my being, asking that my anger and sadness be transmuted by love and forgiveness into light, love and compassion. I followed that with some chanting my sound healing teacher had taught me, ending up with a breathing meditation.

I emerged from the dome counting my blessings and feeling at peace with the world. Yet something still impelled me to go straight to the study to check my phone for the call from Zac, which I'd been so sure would come. With a sinking heart, I saw that the voice mailbox was empty. Next I checked my emails, finding one from Portia which said thanks for returning the papers so promptly and they'd be in touch.

As I read it, a grey cloud of disappointment accumulated over my head. It was just about to engulf me, when Frankie came through.

Stop feeling sorry for yourself, Pandora. You'll have plenty of time to fraternise with the boss when you join the firm. Put all that on hold till you get your brother sorted out.

My irritation at her use of the word 'fraternise' had the welcome effect of putting the cloud to flight. Suddenly hungry, I was on the point of leaving the room, when I noticed something lying on the desk. It was Clarrie's neat document, entitled: *Report on the Health and Wellbeing of the Jay Family Animals.*

I skimmed through it and wandered into the kitchen to see if she was still on the premises so I could thank her. I found Jay and the girls there, eating their way through a stack of toasted sandwiches.

'Sit down,' said Sharon. 'Fill your boots. That woman looked like hard work.'

Sharon usually received my clients, since I tended to be in the dome when they arrived, and she always commented on them afterwards. I adopted my censorial face, but was unable to keep it up for long.

'Have you seen this?' I said, putting Clarrie's report in front of the girls and taking a seat next to Jay.

Cherry started speed-reading it, while Willow studied it over her shoulder.

'Have you read it yet, babe?' said Jay, grabbing my right thigh – mercifully out of sight of the other diners.

'She says Bonnie wants a kid, Midnight needs a boyfriend, the rabbits have asked for bigger premises and the chickens are being terrorised by a fox.'

'Sounds like *The Archers*,' said Jay. 'An everyday story of country folk.' His hand absent-mindedly massaged my knee. 'What are we supposed to do about it?'

Cherry had read the last page and handed it to Jay.

'Do you believe Clarrie can really find all that out by asking them?' she said.

'It depends,' replied Jay, straight-faced. 'If it means extra lettuce, yes. If it means forking out for a pony and a security guard for the silkies, no.'

The report had included a few minor dietary requests, which would be easy to implement. In the Health column, only Clyde was mentioned, for a broken back tooth which was bothering him. Under Wellbeing, however, there were a few more entries.

We already knew that Midnight felt lonely but had no idea that Bonnie felt broody, a situation we couldn't remedy, because poor old Clyde had been neutered. There were only two rabbits left now, but apparently they wanted a bigger run. The sad truth was, that the children had lost interest in them, and it was left to me, Sharon or Jay to feed them and clean them out.

The most dramatic entry was in the silkies column, where Clarrie had written: *Terrified of a fox who stalks their hen coop at night.*

When Jay got to that bit, he read it out, adding, 'Damn the expense, give the fox the rabbits. That'll kill two buns with one stone.'

In response, Willow and Cherry both screamed, 'Dad!' and Sharon pretended to box his ears, until he held his arms up in surrender.

Clarrie had also interviewed Oscar and Fritz. Fritz was at peace with the world; he loved everyone and had no complaints. Oscar, on the other hand, wasn't so happy. He'd missed me recently when I was in Glastonbury and he disliked having to share me with so many other people, including Fritz. He wanted some of our walks to be just the two of us.

When Jay read that out, both girls said, 'Aaah.'

Oscar had been given to me by Mike, my second husband and after his death, Oscar had been my consolation. At the sound of his name, he got up from where he was lying in the corner of the kitchen and now stood next to me, waiting for me to stroke his silky, grey body. Beneath his silver eyebrows, his big, brown eyes smiled at me and I whispered, 'We'll go out soon, sweetie, just you and me.'

'Anyway,' said Sharon, sensing that the comfort of our animal kingdom might be jeopardising her mini-break, 'who's going to look after the menagerie when we're all away at Easter?'

'That's a point,' said Jay. 'What's Rowan doing?'

'He's made plans to go to a music festival in Oxford,' I said.

Sharon and I had approved of this when he told us, because he and Clarrie were meeting up with his usual crowd, including Tom.

'Oxford's not that far. He won't be staying there, will he?'

'Probably not. Let me ring him,' said Sharon, and I waited around long enough to share her relief when Rowan accepted her cash offer to feed and water the livestock every day.

'Okay, then, that's settled,' said Jay. 'Now, all hands to the pump, young ladies. Those veg boxes won't pack themselves.'

It was strange going for a walk without Fritz, but he'd followed Jay and the girls to the vegetable garden, so he didn't even notice Oscar and me slip away. I drove to Oscar's favourite woodland and we walked until we were both tired out. It was just what I needed after the morning's Violet Flame blasting, and when we got back I felt more like myself again, before I'd been hit with the news of my mother's sudden death.

From there, Oscar and I went straight to the hut, where he dozed while I composed my dispatch. Then we went indoors, where I typed it up and emailed it off. I'd written about Clarrie and how she communicated with animals (without revealing her name, naturally). I thought Polly's readers would be pleased with that, as any mention of my menagerie always generated a good response in the comments section.

I had one last thing to do before I allowed myself to relax, so I went in search of Sharon and found her tidying up in the TV room, which was equipped like a mini-cinema. It was mostly the kids and Jay who used it; Sharon and I were happy with the smaller TV in the sitting room.

'What's that for?' she said, when I gave her a hug.

'Sit down a minute,' I said, steeling myself for the task ahead.

'What's happened?' she wailed, alarm written all over her pink face.

'I just need to tell you a couple of things. First of all, Gaby made a pass at Jay on the last night they were in London.'

'Oh my gaad,' she said, her jaw dropping. 'I knew it. I never trusted the way she looked at him that first week when she was here...'

Sharon would probably have shared more of her observations on Gaby, but I didn't want to hear anything that might prey on my mind, so I talked fast.

'It's okay, he didn't take her up on it.'

Sharon's eyes narrowed and I knew she was thinking: *Well, he would say that, wouldn't he?*

'But how did you find out, Pan?'

'He told me last night. He'd had more to drink than me. I don't think he remembers what he said.'

Sharon had collapsed back in her chair and her eyes had gone misty. Poor old girl. She was seventy-six and, at that moment, looked every minute of it.

'Look, we didn't argue, and I'm not going to dwell on it. So don't worry about us splitting up again or anything like that. I just wanted to let you know in case Gaby ever rings the house. Jay gave her the impression we'd board her cats if she goes on tour. We'll have to make some excuse about the dogs or something. I don't want any contact with her, Sha, that's why I'm telling you. Otherwise, I wouldn't have worried you with it.'

Sharon got out an embroidered hankie and blew her nose. I wasn't used to seeing her like this. I hoped she'd pull herself together, or else she'd be setting me off too.

'And there's something more you should know. It's about Theo.'

Her eyes widened.

'We're pretty sure Theo opened Frankie's grave in search of a chalice Frankie and her friends used at their meetings. Charles doesn't want to confront him until after he gets out of hospital, so the weird thing is, although a few of us know about it, Theo has no idea that we do.'

I could see Sharon was struggling to take this in.

'So when's Charles gonna speak to him about it? I hope it's before we get there. My goodness, there's me looking forward to a peaceful weekend in the country and it looks like it's gonna be a war zone.'

'That's why I'm glad the girls are going to France and Rowan's staying here. Please don't say anything to them, will you, Sha? Theo turning up in the first place was embarrassing enough, without the coffin business and all the other subterfuge on top of that...'

Sharon nodded sympathetically, but her anxious expression made me fear she was reconsidering her own plans for Easter.

'Please come, though. If the worst comes to the worst, Charles will just tell Theo to go.'

'And how would you feel about that, honey? You'd be finding

and losing a brother in the space of what, three, four weeks?'

We were sitting side by side in cinema seats, staring at seventy-five inches of blank screen, when she took my hand.

'That'd be tough on you. And just when he was getting on so well with the pink-haired Welsh girl. You liked the idea of the two of them pairing up, didn't you?'

I nodded, dreading the reappearance of the dull ache of loss which had been lurking in the shadows ever since my mother's death.

'Her name's Tegan. I was wondering whether to offer her the other room at the farm...'

'What, so she could comfort him when he was banished from Camelot?'

I had a picture of Charles as King Arthur and Theo as Galahad in search of the Holy Grail.

At that moment Fritz scratched at the door, a sign that his master had come into the house. I opened the door in time to see Jay striding up the hall.

'I've just been filling Sharon in on the Theo business, Jay. I thought I'd better prepare her...'

He paused at the door, possibly sensing that we'd been discussing more than just Theo.

'Okay, Ma?' he said uncertainly. 'You still coming?'

'You bet,' she answered, squeezing my hand. 'Wouldn't miss it for the world.'

Chapter 22

On Trial

On the way back from the hospital, I made a detour to the farm to pick up my room key from Steve's wife Jenny, who asked me how many others were coming, on which days.

'I'm a definite till Easter Monday. My husband and his mother are coming on Thursday or Friday and staying the weekend. And I'm not sure about the third room – but I'll be paying for it anyway.'

She was sweet enough to smile and say mildly, 'It's just so I know how much to get in for the breakfasts...'

'I promise I'll let you know as soon as I can.'

'So it's just one key at the moment? I think the room opening on to the patio would be best, as you're bringing a dog.'

I seized the key and thanked her, conscious of Charles waiting in the car. A few minutes later we arrived at the cottage, to a warm greeting from Oscar. Charles took a seat in the rocking chair, beside the woodburner. The room was warm and cosy, just what he needed.

'Aaah,' he sighed, 'so nice to be home. All I need now is a mug of hot chocolate and a toasted teacake.'

After fulfilling this order, I tucked a blanket round him and took Oscar out for a brisk walk by the River Brue, which tired us both out. He was eight now. Multiply that by seven, and it's the equivalent of fifty-six in human years. Which, coincidentally, was the age I was going to be next week – an age I couldn't believe, didn't feel, and definitely didn't want to be. Even worse, had been the discovery, via Google, that I was fourteen years older than Gaby, which meant Jay was *eighteen years* her senior.

How come, I thought, Jay considered it perfectly natural for a much younger woman to want to sleep with him, yet if a woman of my age was propositioned by a thirty-eight-year-old man, people would assume he was a gigolo?

When we got back, I parked in Charles' space in front of the cottage, his car having been reduced by a crusher to the size of a Rubik's cube by now.

I let myself in the front door and found Pete sitting the other side of the hearth from Charles.

'Happy St Patrick's Day!' he exclaimed, with a twinkle in his eye, as he went to the kitchen and poured me a cup of tea.

I took off my coat, detached the sequinned harp and its wilting clump of shamrock from the lapel, and put the whole lot in a bowl of water, so as not to offend St Patrick – who, as far as I knew, hadn't yet been removed from the Universal Calendar of Saints like his mate St Christopher.

I sat on the sofa and gratefully took the tea Pete brought me. Charles waited for me to take a sip.

'Pandora, we've come to a decision. Pete's going to stay here till Theo comes in, and then we're going to ask him, not *if* but *why* he was looking for the chalice. I'd like you to ring Theo now and get him to come home.'

'What reason should I give?'

'Tell him I want to see him. Then he can't refuse.'

'Can't you wait for him to come in at his usual time?' I said, wishing I didn't have to be his go-between.

'That would add at least another hour, and interfere with dinner.'

Being in hospital had institutionalised Charles, it seemed. There were matters of almost criminal gravity to be discussed, but they mustn't get in the way of a hot dinner served on the dot.

'Okay.'

I got my mobile out of my bag – this time I'd double-checked I had it before leaving – and dialled Theo's number.

'Hi, Sis. How's things? Did you like the pendant?'

That threw me. I should have contacted him to say thanks, but

I hadn't, for fear of being tempted to warn him of the cross-examination that faced him.

'It's lovely. How did you know the phoenix is special to me?'

'I didn't. I just liked the design.'

I could hear Charles sighing loudly in the background, muttering that it wasn't supposed to be a social call.

'Well,' I continued, giving the patient a cool stare, 'Charles is back home and looking forward to a square meal.'

'Good. So what can I do for you?'

My mind went blank for a moment, so I ad-libbed.

'Do you like sea bass?'

I caught Charles exchanging raised eyebrows of irritation with Pete. When he saw I was observing him, he did a winding-up signal with his hand.

Theo had already begun telling me how he liked his sea bass cooked, so I politely waited till he'd finished.

'Charles wants me to tell you it's okay to come home now.'

'Excuse me?'

I knew I hadn't put it very well so I tried again.

'He said you should finish early and...'

I trailed off and Charles got up, more nimbly than I thought possible in his condition, and snatched the phone.

'Hello, Theo. I'll see you here in fifteen minutes. Yes. Bye.'

I was tempted to ask Charles why he hadn't done that in the first place, but as I'd recently recalibrated to stay positive and keep the peace, I held my tongue.

As the time got nearer to Theo's arrival, I went upstairs and sat on the bed in the small spare room for a think, while the two gents downstairs spoke in undertones to each other. I heard the rattle of the bike as Theo came round the side of the cottage, then came the sound of the back door opening and closing and Oscar's excited greeting. When the commotion died down, Charles' querulous summons came wafting up the stairs.

'Pandora. Can you come down, please?'

His tone held a tacit *It's no use hiding up there* postscript.

Pete and Charles had repositioned themselves on the sofa, Theo had taken the chair Pete had vacated and I had no option but to sit the other side of the hearth in the rocking chair.

When I saw that Theo was holding a steaming mug of coffee, I got a small table and placed it by his side. He nodded his thanks and surveyed us all quizzically.

'So what's up, folks?'

Charles wasted no time.

'Theo, we have reason to believe that you may have done something you now regret. I'm going to tell you what we know, and I'd like you to give an explanation for your behaviour.'

Theo sat like a statue, his face impassive, the only clue to his distress, the faint rattle of the mug as he put it down on the wooden table, ignoring the coaster I'd provided.

'We know that you opened your mother's grave, and that's why you didn't want me to call the police.'

Charles paused to measure Theo's reaction, but no emotion was yet apparent on his features.

'We also have an idea what you were looking for. And we suspect that your membership of the Circle of Isis is connected to all of this. Have you anything to say in your defence?'

When Theo spoke he reminded me of a character in a Wild West movie. I could almost see his hands reaching for his holster.

'Seeing as you're acting like some kind of attorney, what evidence do you have for these accusations, exactly?'

Charles looked resigned and embarked on what I presumed would be the 'Beau as witness' story.

'You were seen in the paddock that night...'

A plan had formed in my mind when I was upstairs, which I immediately put into action. It required interrupting Charles before he could say any more.

'Jay saw you. He came out for a cigarette. The garden light went on and he saw you running away. He kept quiet because he thought it would upset Charles and me too much. And, as far as he could see, no harm was done anyway.'

I had no idea whether Charles and Pete would approve of this mangling of the facts, but it was a risk I had to take, given that the evidence of a dumb animal was never going to yield a confession, no matter how much the accused doted on the dumb animal.

The three of us leaned forward, holding our collective breath to hear what Theo would say.

'Yeah, I did it,' he said, slumping in the chair. 'But don't think I haven't hated myself every minute of every day since then.'

Tears had started free-falling from his eyes and he was wiping them away roughly with the palms of his hands. I fetched some kitchen paper and knelt in front of his hunched figure, dabbing at his cheeks.

'Don't cry, Theo, it's all right.'

'It's not all right!' he shouted, brushing my hand away. 'Nothing's all right.'

He was holding his chest, as if this would stop the wrenching sobs which seemed to spring from deep in his gut.

Pete found a bottle of whisky and poured everyone a tot. Theo managed to take a few sips and finally regained some control.

'We're not here to hound you, son,' said Pete, in a kind voice. 'We know the Bull couple are probably up to no good and it looks to me as if you've been sucked into some dodgy dealings. We were hoping you'd throw some light on what's going on.'

'Then, maybe, we could start making plans to put a spoke in their wheel,' added Charles.

Theo straightened up in his chair and expelled air from his mouth as if blowing out a large candle.

'I've been a fool.'

'Go on,' said Charles.

'When Frankie took me to a Circle meeting, right away Dido made a play for me. Told me she was separated. We started...'

'Sleeping together,' said Charles, eager for him to get to the point. 'Yes, yes, I didn't think you were stacking shelves in Morrisons when you stayed out all night. Just tell us who asked you to search the house and grave.'

Theo's head jerked. Nobody had mentioned the house but it was plain from his guilty expression that he'd done that too.

'Dido. When Frankie died she really started working me. She wanted a chalice that Frankie found in a field. It didn't look much...but Frankie always protected it as if it was something special...took it home after the meetings. Dido asked me to look for it in the house but I couldn't find it...'

He stopped when Charles cut in, angrily. 'Did it ever occur to you to ask me man to man if I knew where the bloody thing was? It would have saved us a lot of trouble,' he said, glancing in my direction.

Theo winced.

'No, sir. Dido and Rosemary thought you'd hidden it. Dido said it was because you hated the Circle.'

'Poisonous bloody woman, in pursuit of an equally poisonous chalice,' spat Charles. 'For all the trouble it's caused I'd toss it in the Brue if I had my way. In fact, I wish I had.'

Charles lapsed into stony silence and Theo took the opportunity to visit the downstairs loo.

My brain cells had been working away in the background, and now they were alerting me to why Theo hadn't wanted me to rush to Charles' side when he'd first had his accident.

As he walked back into the room, I barked a question at him.

'Did you search the house again when Charles was taken into hospital?'

'Guess so,' he muttered, avoiding my gaze.

'And is that why you dug his garden over, because you thought the chalice might be buried there?'

His reluctant nod induced such a burst of anger in me that before I knew it, I'd gone for him like an enraged pit bull, my hand delivering an eye-watering slap to his cheek, throwing him off balance and leaving him sprawled on the floor.

'If you disturb one more clod of earth on this property,' I screamed, 'I swear, I'll bury *you!*'

Even through the red mist that engulfed me, I noticed a fleeting look of approval cross Charles' face. The loss of his wild garden hadn't gone down too well with him when he'd discovered it this afternoon.

Pete rushed forward to pull me away.

'Now, now,' he said, guiding me back to my chair, still rocking from the force of my exit. 'It's all water under the bridge. What's done is done.'

My whole body was shaking with fury. *I'm supposed to be above all this,* I kept telling myself, but still the acid anger flowed in my veins. Meanwhile, Theo had sat back down again, his head bowed, the picture of misery and remorse, nursing his stinging face.

'You knew all along they were looking for the chalice, didn't you, Charles?' I said, turning on him. His lack of surprise when I'd told him and Pete about it in the hospital hadn't escaped me.

He glared at me warily, confirming my dawning suspicions that he hadn't welcomed my investigations. If I hadn't got Clarrie involved we wouldn't be sitting here now. In fact, it was only my status as Frankie's daughter which had forced him to this point. The realisation of this cleared my head. It was time he was forced to show his hand.

'You knew, didn't you, Charles?' I repeated, accusingly, fixing him with a stare as hard as granite.

He shot me a dirty look and answered grudgingly.

'I guessed that's what they wanted.'

He looked at Pete apologetically.

'I've always kept quiet because it shouldn't have been in our possession.'

Aha, I thought. *You old devil. All this time I thought you were protecting Theo, but you were actually protecting yourself.*

'No worries,' said Pete, like the good and faithful friend he was. 'So how did you come by it?'

'Well,' said Charles, relaxing. 'The year before last, Frankie insisted on borrowing a metal detector from Ralph and going to Cress Field. Said she'd had a dream of something buried in a field of sheep.'

'Where's Cress Field?' I asked tersely.

'It's adjacent to the Chalice Well Gardens, just beyond the Well Head,' answered Pete.

'Metal detecting is against all the rules, of course,' Charles continued, 'but we went early in the morning, so there was no one around. Frankie did her trance thing and went straight to the spot. The chalice was only buried eight inches down.' Charles scratched his head and looked pained. 'Should have taken it to the Chalice Well Trust, but Frankie wouldn't let it go. She convinced herself it was the cup that Christ drank from at the Last Supper.'

'The same one that Joseph of Arimathea used to collect Christ's blood,' volunteered Theo, in a subdued voice. 'Frankie said he came to Glastonbury and buried it beneath the wellspring.'

'But we didn't find it *beneath* the Chalice Well, did we?' snapped Charles.

'The area round the Tor was under water a couple of thousand years ago,' declared Pete. 'It's possible it shifted when the water subsided.'

'Shifted my backside. Yes, the Tor did use to be surrounded by a lake, and there may or may not have been a chalice buried under the well, but the one we found most certainly isn't it.'

'Rosemary seemed pretty convinced it was genuine. She said she felt Joseph's presence when she touched it,' said Theo, trying to ally himself with the good guys.

The pink stain I'd dealt his cheek had subsided but I was still simmering.

'Can we please stick to facts, Theo,' said Charles, falling into schoolmaster mode. 'I'm getting hungry. Just tell us as quickly and succinctly as possible why the Circle so desperately needs the chalice, and why you're still involved with that shower!'

Theo looked puzzled.

'He means why are you still involved with that useless lot,' Pete translated.

Taking Charles' hint, I stalked into the kitchen to put the oven on but left the door open so I could hear Theo's reply.

'Okay, you want it succinct, you got it. They planned to hold a ceremony at Rosemary's this coming Friday. They've got an old manuscript with a recipe for the elixir of life. It says it should be performed "with a blood sacrifice" and "a goblet taken from the earth" to catch the blood – namely, Frankie's chalice. I started going to the meetings because Frankie said this elixir would fix my back. If there's a way of being able to ride again, I want in on it.'

Taking a moment to digest all this, Charles retaliated.

'Do you honestly believe in that mumbo-jumbo, boy? You, of all people, raised in a Baptist home, poles apart in your beliefs from your mother...and your sister, too, come to that... (I could almost see his black schoolmaster gown and hear his cane swishing.) ... The only possible explanation is that you're bewitched. And that's why you're still sniffing round that awful woman.'

Theo's tone became indignant.

'That might have been true once, but whatever the hell spell she put on me, it's over. And if you think I'm gonna let that witch Dido and her old man turn out more snake oil so they can make a bundle, you're crazy.'

Touché, I thought, against my will.

Charles stared thoughtfully at Theo while Pete topped up their glasses with whisky.

'So you heard about the phony diet pills, then?' said Pete.

'Yeah, Max told me.'

'When did you see Max?' Charles asked.

'Friday night, when I went to the meeting. He's on vacation from college.'

'So where was Dido when you had this conversation?'

'She'd gone home,' his face darkened, 'with her husband.'

'Has anyone told Rosemary about them yet?'

'Yes.' He glanced across at Pete, who winked at him. 'It was Rosemary who asked me to stay on, after the meeting. Someone had been in touch with Max and said he should let his mother know she was keeping bad company, so he'd shown her the article that day.'

'I wonder who that was,' I said, observing a wily look passing between the two older men.

'Well, love, if we waited for divine intervention we could be here till Christmas,' chuckled Pete.

I took that to mean that Pete had commandeered Max as part of his and Charles' plot to scupper the Circle and felt cheered to have him on board.

'Can we let Theo speak, please,' said Charles. 'Theo, just tell us what action, if any, Rosemary took, so we can coordinate our efforts.'

'Okay, boss,' said Theo, a smile beginning to fight its way through to his lips. 'Rosemary said she'd guessed that Dido had pressured me to find the chalice but stayed with it because she believed that the end justified the means.'

'And what would that be exactly?' I said, to no one in particular, brushing aside Charles' instruction to keep quiet. 'Eternal youth? Wouldn't that get rather boring after a time?'

'Two questions,' said Pete, talking over me. I detected that he disapproved of my hostility towards my brother and Charles, but I was still too annoyed to drop the cold shoulder treatment just yet. 'Was she in on the coffin opening and where did the manuscript come from?

'No to the first. The manuscript she found in an old book on alchemy she got from the Speaking Tree Book Store. It was taped between the book and its jacket. The title's something like: "a rejuvenating and healing elixir".'

'Sounds like something you can get from any Chinese herbalist – without shedding a single drop of blood,' said Pete.

'Or disturbing a grave,' added Charles, and Theo's shadow of a smile promptly vanished.

'I can just see his fancy piece Dido selling it as an anti-ageing panacea on the internet and making a fortune,' I said, caustically.

Theo looked forlorn. 'Tell me about it. She asked me to go into business with her to mass-produce the stuff, once the prototype was produced. She's planning a health drinkcalled the Grail Elixir of Youth and a whole range of creams and stuff to sell to beauty salons.'

'She's never been known for her authenticity in the past,' said Charles. 'Why start now?'

Theo shook his head. 'She said that advertising it as "blended at the full moon, using an ancient formula", would make for better publicity and we'd be able to charge a fortune for the product. Maybe as much as Crème de la Mer. That was when I had a rethink about investing. When I told her I was out, she went cold on me.'

'And then, by coincidence, hubby turns up?' ventured Pete, and Theo nodded.

'You know what I think?' I said, addressing Pete and ignoring the other two. 'I think she truly believes it'll work and she wants to use it on herself, so she's desperate to follow the recipe to the letter. But she'd be quite happy to palm the punters off with fake rubbish.'

'That was my take on it, Sis.'

His pleading eyes searched mine and I blanked him.

'You've had a lucky escape, mate,' said Pete.

'But Frankie and Rosemary and most of their friends seemed pretty genuine,' he said, like a bewildered child. 'They looked at it from a healing perspective. At first, I thought Dido did too...'

He looked desolate, so I fed him his next line in the interest of getting the whole story straight.

'You told her you'd had a riding accident, your condition was incurable and you were likely to end up in a wheelchair, and she promised to fix you with this elixir.'

'How do you know how bad my condition is?' he said, his eyes full of confusion.

I could have continued not speaking to him for ever if I'd wanted. It'd been my standard reaction to disloyalty and hurt feelings in the past. But I was supposed to know better now, so I forced myself to look in his direction.

'You told me when we were in the dome.'

He shook his head as if he had no recollection of it.

'So, just to recap, this cure she promised you, that's why you kept going to the meetings even after her husband came back and you'd stopped sleeping with her?' asked Pete, ever the detective.

Theo took a deep, shuddering breath and nodded. All this honesty after weeks of secrets and lies was evidently proving pretty strong medicine to take.

'And I didn't want her to think she meant that much to me...'

'So, are they making the elixir without the chalice or not?' asked Pete.

'They intended to. They were going to use an old goblet that Rosemary had. She planned to bury it for a short period to fulfil the condition in the recipe.'

Charles harrumphed.

'That's a case of keeping to the letter of the law but not the spirit of it. Anyway, it makes no difference. It's all nonsense. Alchemists have been trying for centuries to produce a potion for eternal youth; I hardly think it's going to happen in Rosemary's back garden under the apple tree.'

'So what's Rosemary's take on it now Max has spilled the beans?' said Pete.

'She's furious that they thought they could use the Circle as a cover to get rich quick. We figured we'd been screwed over.'

'So what's Rosemary going to do now?'

'It's done. She cancelled the ceremony. She called all the members and told them she suspected Dido and her old man wanted to manufacture the elixir commercially. And as it'd come to light that someone had searched Frankie's house and grave for the chalice,' Theo lowered his eyes when he said this, 'she was disbanding the Circle.'

'You say she rang all of them,' said Charles sarcastically, 'did that include Gav and Tina, alias Dido, and their lackeys Cynthia and Ralph?'

Theo was interrupted by a knock on the door, which I answered.

On the doorstep stood Rosemary, her normally calm face pale and taut.

'Hello, Pandora, Theo said you'd be home today. Charles,' she said, looking past me, 'I have an apology to make. Can I come in?'

'I suppose so,' I heard him sigh. 'Pandora, is there enough dinner for five, because if I don't eat soon, I'm going to need an intravenous drip.'

Chapter 23

All For One and One For All

I took Rosemary's coat and Charles signalled her to sit down. The dauphinoise potatoes were already cooking, so next I sliced some lemons and laid them, with some crushed garlic and dill, in a baking dish. I oiled and seasoned all the fillets of sea bass I'd brought with me, rested them on top and placed them in the oven. If Rosemary decided to stay, she and I would have to be content with one each.

'Before you begin your apology,' Charles was saying, 'I want you to answer a question.'

Rosemary must have indicated she would, because he kept talking.

'You deliberately broke the crystal skull to cause a diversion so your evil little friend could search my bedroom. How then, does that make you any better than her?'

This was strong stuff, so I suspended my preparation of the vegetables to hover in the doorway.

'That's one of the things I've come to apologise about, Charles. But, believe it or not, breaking the skull *was* an accident. Yes, I did lift it, to see if the chalice was behind it, but it just fell out of my hands.'

Charles got up, went to an open cabinet packed with memorabilia, and came back with a silver goblet, tarnished with years of black sulphide.

'What you saw was Pandora's christening gift from her godparents. Satisfied?'

Rosemary flushed and wrung her hands. Charles went on.

'On the same day, when Dido came downstairs, she looked at you and shook her head, so you must have known what she was doing.'

'Yes, and I can't tell you how much I regret that. But in my defence, I was convinced that the chalice was necessary to produce something that would really benefit those who need it – someone like Theo, for example.'

'Someone like Theo who, that night, opened his mother's coffin, you mean?' snapped Charles. 'After performing a forensic examination of every cupboard in the house.'

Looking as if he'd had enough aggravation for one day, Theo said he was going upstairs to freshen up before dinner.

'Rosemary,' said Pete, in a calmer voice than Charles. 'When you cancelled the ceremony, did you give the Bulls the same message as the others?'

'More or less. They weren't happy, as you can imagine.'

'Did you mention that you knew about their dubious past?' said Charles.

Rosemary shook her head.

'I didn't want to get into a slanging match. But then,' said Rosemary, her face flushing at the memory, 'Dido said she intended to contact the members and hold the ceremony at her place, but I said that all of them, except Cynthia and Ralph, had been as shocked as I was at Frankie's grave being disturbed, and had agreed we should disband.'

'So that's how it's been left?'

'Yes. I don't see how she could do it, anyway. I've got the manuscript, which I never showed anyone. And the real chalice is missing...'

There was a pause while the two men exchanged glances, then Pete spoke. 'I'm curious. Were you really in the dark about Gav and Tina Bull being con-artists?'

'Of course.' Rosemary's cheeks grew pink with indignation. 'How could you think otherwise?'

But Pete wasn't satisfied with her denial.

'I mentioned it to Max shortly after she came to town, and he never told you?'

'Not till last Friday, no. I only see him occasionally...since he went up to Manchester.'

I felt the time had come to stick up for the poor woman.

'I can vouch for that. Max only remembered on the day we went to lunch. He showed me the newspaper coverage online. He said he wouldn't say anything to his mother because she was already upset enough.'

Rosemary gave me a grateful smile and I wondered if she'd be grateful enough to talk about Frankie's involvement in the Circle of Isis.

'Now we're being open with each other, Rosemary, can you tell us why the chalice was so important to the Circle?'

Rosemary fixed her eyes on Charles, but he turned his head away.

'It made our remedies and skin treatments much more effective. The first time I used it, I realised how powerful it was. I only had to put a small amount of the preparation in the chalice, then add it back into the mixture, for it to work its magic.'

'And the Circle itself? I'm trying to get to the bottom of why Frankie was so secretive and why she never mentioned it to me.'

Rosemary coloured, glancing at the two older men. 'Dido set it up as a means of restoring and retaining youthfulness and beauty.'

Charles and Pete both let out groans of derision.

'You see? That's the typical reaction women get from men if we want to maintain our looks and stay attractive. Yet it's the logical extension of keeping fit and healthy. If only they'd accepted it would work for them too, we might have welcomed them more. But one look at a beauty tincture and they were out the door.'

'It's hardly rarefied metaphysical work for the good of Mother Earth and humankind, is it?' mocked Charles. 'It's a question of standards, Rosemary, standards.'

Well, standards or no, I wouldn't have minded a basinful of

that, I thought. It'd save me a fortune at the Xanadu Salon de Beauté. It was certainly true that Rosemary was wearing her years lightly, as was Dido.

Rosemary looked as if she'd found her inner Amazon and was about to biff Charles on the nose so I diverted her with a question.

'What did Frankie tell you about Theo?'

'That he'd had an accident and it was affecting his nervous system. She thought the elixir would help him. The whole Circle knew about the recipe I'd found, and we planned an elixir-creation ceremony, but I hadn't been able to get hold of all of the ingredients...'

'Have trouble finding a hemlock root, did you?' said Charles, scathingly. 'Or was it the baboon's blood?'

'For goodness' sake, Charles,' said Rosemary, rising to her feet. 'I came here in a spirit of reconciliation, but if you persist in insulting and bullying me, I'm going home. If this is what poor Frankie had to put up with, no wonder she was thinking of leaving you!'

A hush descended on the room as the blood drained from Charles' face.

'Dinner's ready in ten minutes,' I said, retreating to the kitchen. 'You're welcome to stay, Rosemary.'

* * *

Over dinner, Pete wondered out loud if it would be possible for all of us present to perform the ceremony at Rosemary's and produce some of the elixir on the coming Friday night. Then Rosemary would be able use it in her healing (at this, Theo looked enthusiastic) and if she saw any positive results, continue to make it for her clients.

When Pete had finished talking we all studied Charles. He'd been civil to Rosemary at dinner, despite what she'd let slip about Frankie. He seemed to have moved on from it, while I, on the other hand, had been wrestling with anger against my mother for keeping so much from me. Hard on the heels of the anger, came the twin spears of betrayal and jealousy. Jealousy because I suspected it was Theo's arrival which had given her ideas about leaving Charles – she may even have harboured thoughts of going to the States with him – and betrayal, because that would have meant she was leaving me as well.

What with all this and Gabygate on top, how many of these wounds can my heart take, I wondered, *before it buckles under the strain?*

'Does your manuscript specify the number of participants, Rosemary?' Charles asked, in a neutral tone.

'No, not at all,' she said, visibly brightening. 'There were twelve of us in the Circle, but any number would do. I had thought of doing it on my own, but, of course, group energy is always stronger. When the final ingredient arrived, just before Frankie died, the Circle decided to have a ceremony on March 21st, the feast of Ostara.'

She studied Charles' face. She must have perceived a glimmer of interest because she added, 'Everyone would receive a special blessing and a taste of the elixir. You, of all people, would benefit from that, Charles.'

'Bruised ribs and mild concussion will heal themselves eventually, Rosemary,' he grunted, but he was evidently considering it.

'What's Ostara, again?' I asked, glad to be stirred out of my gloom by a twinge of curiosity.

'It's a "she", actually,' said Charles, nodding at Rosemary to clarify.

'Ostara is a goddess who represents the dawning of spring. She's all about fertility and new life. This year her feast is on the same day as the equinox and the full moon, which makes any work three times more powerful.'

'Where's Max tonight?' asked Pete, swallowing the last

mouthful on his plate and sitting back in his chair with a satisfied sigh.

'At home, as far as I know. Why?'

'Would it be possible for him to bring the manuscript over so we could see it?'

Rosemary agreed in a flash and I left them to chat while I cleared the table and stacked as much of the washing-up into the small dishwasher as it would take.

I'd just made coffee and tea, when we heard a knock at the door. Max had covered the distance between Apple Blossom Cottage and our house in less than fifteen minutes.

'Hi, Pan-lid,' he said, looming in the doorway, and I immediately cheered up. Bowing extravagantly, he added, 'I come at your command.'

'You didn't waste much time, did you, Maximus?'

I took his arm and led him into the dining room to join the others. Somehow, a round table seemed more appropriate than easy chairs, in view of the strategic manoeuvres that were about to be discussed.

Max kissed his mother and held his hands up in greeting to Charles, Pete and Theo.

'Welcome, Max,' said Charles, more genial now that his blood sugar level was up where it should be. 'Take a seat. Thanks for coming. We thought you should be included as you've been in the thick of it lately, so to speak. Have you got the manuscript?'

Max reached inside his hoody and retrieved a dog-eared scroll which he handed to Rosemary.

Next to the cafetiere and teapot, I set a tiered cake stand, bearing small macaroons of many colours. There wasn't a matching bit of china in the place: the cups and saucers, like the plates, were all different shades and patterns, but I liked the effect. It made a change from the clinical white favoured by Sharon. Thinking of Sharon reminded me that she and Jay, and possibly Tegan, would be around on Friday, which would have to be factored into the equation.

'Shall I go and get it now, Charles?' I said, leaving the beverage dispensing to them.

'Yes, do. We need delay no more.'

I saw Theo and Rosemary exchanging quizzical glances and remembered that even Theo didn't know we'd found the chalice. I began to feel excited, my better self finally re-emerging and hoping that soon we'd all be on the same side.

I went upstairs, took the key from Charles' jacket, and removed the chalice from behind the secret panel, wrapping it in one of Frankie's silk scarves on my way downstairs. Placing this object of so much deception in the centre of the table, I pulled the scarf away to reveal what lay beneath, drawing gasps from Rosemary and Theo. Pete and Charles, taking delight in their amazement, broke into wide grins.

'Is this the famous chalice?' said Max. 'I expected it to be all gold and shiny. It's kind of dull.'

'That's because it's made of base metal,' said Charles. 'Pewter, probably.'

'Where did you find it?' said Rosemary.

'Behind a false panel in Frankie's wardrobe.'

I looked at Theo as I said this, wondering if now he'd remember his 'vision' in the labyrinth when he'd seen Frankie pointing at 'a hidden door'. But there was no sign of recollection in his eyes.

'Is there any chance it's the real cup that Christ drank from?' said Theo, still in search of the true Grail.

Charles got up and went to his den, where he kept all his books and jottings. He finally found what he wanted, and came back with a photocopied picture of a drinking vessel made from dark red agate set on a golden stem with two gold handles and a quartz base.

'This one's kept in Valencia Cathedral and it's certainly old enough to be the cup that Christ drank from at the Last Supper.

Of course, the stem and the base would have been added after His death. I'd say, of all the contenders, this is the most likely to be the original chalice – Grail – whatever you want to call it.'

'Then why was Frankie so convinced the one she found was authentic?' asked Theo.

'You tell me. I showed her this picture...read her the article, but she wouldn't see sense. She could be so obstinate...'

'But just say this one *was* authentic, would that mean it was the actual Holy Grail that the knights of old went in search of?' said Max, picking up the chalice and examining the engravings.

Charles put on his 'man of letters' face. 'The Holy Grail has always been seen as something to seek or strive for. To some it's a concept – the search to find a higher meaning and purpose in life. To others it's the actual chalice Christ drank from at the Last Supper which collected the blood from his side, on the cross. Some say it's the elixir of life – a panacea capable of prolonging life, which the alchemists were always trying to create.'

'Wasn't Isaac Newton an alchemist?' said Theo. 'Didn't he try to turn lead into gold?'

'They share a birthday,' I said, seeing Charles' surprise at Theo's unexpected burst of learning. 'December 25th.'

'I know when Theo's birthday is,' said Charles, impatiently. 'It's the same as the one celebrated as Christ's, although His is far more likely to have been three months earlier. December 25th was the last day of the Roman festival of Saturnalia – settling on that as Christ's date of birth was purely arbitrary.'

He paused for a moment to recapture the thread of his discourse. His body was still recovering from the accident and what he really needed was hot milk and an early night.

'The mystery of the Eucharist, when the priest changes bread and wine into the body and blood of Christ, is the greatest alchemy of all. The Roman Catholics call it "transubstantiation". They believe they're receiving the essence of Christ when they take communion.'

I immediately received a picture of a class of seven-year-olds, the girls in white dresses and veils, the boys in white shirts and short, grey trousers, taking their First Holy Communion one Sunday in May. We'd had to fast from the night before and been warned, under pain of mortal sin, not to allow our teeth anywhere near the host. My friend Cece and I were under the impression this wafer was somehow miraculously absorbed into our bodies, until we passed the scholarship, had our first biology lessons, and realised that Our Blessed Lord's fate was to be consumed by hydrochloric stomach acid, the same as the bacon and egg we'd eaten for our communion breakfast straight after Mass.

Returning to the present, I heard Rosemary contributing to the grail glossary.

'The Holy Grail cup is also a symbol of the womb, which contains the waters of life, another term for sexual energy.'

Charles harrumphed.

'Yes, I know the theory of raising the kundalini, but let me tell you now, we're not getting involved in any sex magic.'

Rosemary's voice rose. 'That's not what I meant and you know it. I was going to say that being a symbol of the feminine vessel of conception, the Grail represents our human genetic heritage.'

Max rescued the situation by focusing on our very own reproduction model.

'Why are the symbols on this chalice Egyptian?'

At ease in his role as chief egghead, Charles obliged with an answer. 'Egypt became a Roman province in 30 BC so their goods would have been distributed throughout the Roman Empire.'

'And what do they all mean?'

Naturally, being a stickler for research, Charles had the answer. On the back of the picture of the Valencia chalice, he had sketched the symbols engraved on the Cress Field chalice and made notes, which he began to read aloud. 'The eye of Horus symbolises protection and good health. The ibis symbolises

Thoth, god of wisdom and scribe to the gods. The ostrich feather he holds in his mouth symbolises Ma'at, the goddess of balance, justice and truth: the feminine counterpart of Thoth.'

The name Thoth rang a bell with me. Hadn't my old friend Enoch spoken of him, when I'd first asked him if he was the Enoch of the Old Testament, great-grandfather of Noah.

I answer to Enoch, which means 'initiate' or 'anointed one'. I am known by many other appellations – among them Thoth, by the Egyptians, Hermes by the Greeks, Mercury by the Romans and Merlin by the Celts.

'Hello, Enoch', I whispered under my breath and I thought I saw a tiny spark hover above the humble chalice which Max was in the process of handing to Theo.

'And the other two symbols?' asked Theo.

'The looped cross is called an ankh – symbol of eternal life.'

I was trying to remember where I'd heard that word recently when Rosemary spoke. 'It's a symbol associated with Isis.'

Charles chose to disregard her remark, barely taking a breath before continuing. 'And the flower is a lotus. At night the lotus closes and sinks under water and at dawn it rises and opens its petals. It's a symbol of long life, good health, and rebirth.'

'The lotus is Quan Yin's symbol,' said Rosemary. 'She carries "the water of life" in her vase, the elixir which brings peace to her followers.'

'Is "vase" a euphemism by any chance?' asked Charles irreverently.

'Ask her for the recipe,' quipped Pete. 'We can compare it with yours.'

Rosemary blinked in exasperation, and continued.

'She assists with the releasing of feelings of resentment and sadness because holding on to them harms us and prevents us being at peace.'

'That sounds like forgive and forget to me, not a bad idea in the circumstances,' said Pete.

'Well, being the goddess of loving kindness and compassion, it's on the cards that's what she'd advise,' said Charles smugly.

Nodding in Rosemary's direction, he added, 'Her Egyptian equivalent is Isis. Although Isis is, shall we say, capable of darker acts. She has many aspects, one of them being the goddess of destruction.'

I sighed. Charles was determined to run Isis down, whereas I'd begun to see that tough love had its place, even though it had left me feeling guilty as hell. 'We could all do with some of Quan Yin's loving kindness tonight,' I said, with feeling.

On impulse, I took hold of Max's hand, who was sitting on my left and Theo's, on my right. Then Theo took hold of Pete's, who took hold of Charles', who was forced to take hold of Rosemary's, who was already holding Max's.

I knew this round table was the right place for us, I thought, as Rosemary started intoning Quan Yin's mantra and we all gradually joined in, including Oscar.

After our chants of *Om mani padme hum* had faded, Rosemary asked us to remain with our hands joined while she sought guidance. Then she began to speak. 'I've been told that we should go ahead with the ceremony, but that we must include Dido and her husband ...'

'What!' cried Charles. 'Are the gods mad?'

'Ssshhh,' I exclaimed. I wanted to hear what our elders and betters 'upstairs' had to say. 'Go on, Rosemary.'

'Saint Germain came through. He told me that the elixir is sacred and may only be made or administered by the pure in heart. Two drops are to be placed on each tongue. The drops will burn like acid the flesh of anyone who is black of heart and seeks to misuse the precious gift of the elixir.'

She stopped speaking and opened her eyes, then gazed searchingly at each of us in turn and came back to me.

'He said the one who carries the Violet Flame must protect the elixir, if necessary. It appears to be you, Pandora. You have a lot of violet light in your aura.'

'I can guarantee she packs a punch,' said Theo next to me, under his breath.

Paying no heed, on the grounds he'd deserved a slap, I imagined myself as Flame Girl in superheroine costume, with gauntlets, boots, goggles and helmet, carrying a violet flamethrower.

'How appropriate,' said Charles. 'He, who discovered his own elixir of life, has provided us with the means of protecting ours.'

'So why do you think Saint Germain wants the Bulls at the ceremony, Mum?' said Max.

'I should think it'd be to test if they have a bad reaction to the elixir. If they do, that'll make it unsaleable, so no use to them, personally or commercially.'

Charles went to his den and came back with pen and paper. 'Okay, everyone, now we've got the go-ahead from above, let's devise an action plan. First of all, does everyone consent to being part of the group on Friday?'

We all said yes and then he agreed certain details with Rosemary regarding the starting time and what she'd include in the ceremony. At Charles' request, she read out what the recipe demanded.

'The title of the recipe is: "A Life-Prolonging Elixir with Rejuvenating and Healing Properties". It says it should be made at full moon, then there's a list of ingredients.'

She recited the names of the ten ingredients, which included anise, wormwood, tartaric acid, colloidal silver, violet petals and elderflower.

'They'll be mixed with alcohol and honey. I'll probably use vodka because it's not as strong-tasting as brandy. The recipe says to keep the mixture for four weeks before straining it and after that small amounts can be taken using a dropper, because it's incredibly potent. But, as you've just heard, we've had the go-ahead to have two drops each on the night.'

Rosemary rolled up the manuscript and placed it in her bag.

'Is that all?' said Pete, stroking his chin.

'There's a standard warning about the body needing to adapt to the elixir's strength and for the dosage to be adjusted accordingly, but I can do that for Theo when the time comes.' She paused, no doubt wondering why we were still looking expectant. 'And for anyone else who wants to use it.'

'I still don't think you've told us everything.'

Rosemary's eyes flicked from side to side, avoiding Pete's beady eye.

'What happened to the blood sacrifice that young Theo here was telling us about before you came?'

'Is that right, Mum?' said Max, sounding shocked.

'It's the word sacrifice that's got you all going,' said Rosemary, defensively. 'That was the first thing I checked out when I found the manuscript.'

Charles had begun to drum his fingers on the table so Rosemary hurried on.

'Sacrifice might have been acceptable in the old days, but of course we won't be doing any sacrificing.'

I thought I detected a flicker of disappointment in Pete's eyes.

'All we have to do is choose someone to prick his or her finger and place a few drops in the chalice. Then I'll pour the blood into the mixture in the jar.'

'And so we'll all be drinking a minute amount of someone's blood,' I said.

'Yes.'

'A bit like taking holy communion – the body and blood of Jesus Christ.'

'Yes, Pandora, we get the symbolism,' said Charles impatiently. 'Good Friday and all that.'

'Well, in that case,' I said, 'Theo should be the blood donor because he's played Christ already.'

Everyone looked at Theo, whose smile indicated he was happy to oblige.

'Yeah, with Beau. On Palm Sunday.'

'That's settled then,' said Charles, moving on.

'Hold on a sec,' said Pete, metaphorically donning his gumshoe dirty raincoat again. 'If you never showed the manuscript to anyone, how come Theo knew about the blood sacrifice?'

'I've no idea,' said Rosemary, in a more-in-sorrow-than-in-anger tone. 'I assume someone must have read it when I wasn't looking.'

Theo looked as if he wanted to be anywhere but here.

'Well, Theo?' said Charles, his eyes as piercing as any hawk's.

'Okay. It was Dido. I swear I wasn't involved. She told me she deliberately went early to a meeting. Rosemary let her in and went upstairs to change. She searched the place, found the recipe in a desk and copied it.'

'Fantastic,' said Charles heavily. 'So now we know she's got the recipe, there'll be no chance of getting them to join up with us.' He shook his head at Theo. 'Why've you been letting us waste our time?'

'Sorry,' said Theo, his face assuming a *What can I do right?* expression. 'I thought maybe having the chalice would swing it. And Rosemary's got a regular outside altar, Dido's only got a table in the salon.'

The room remained silent for a few moments, while we reassessed the situation. Rosemary was the first to speak.

'Theo's right about the chalice being important to Dido. She's seen the power it has.'

Charles wasn't convinced. 'How are you going to persuade two raging Bulls, furious with you for disbanding the Circle, to show up?'

'Plus, what motivation would we have for asking them?' added Pete.

Rosemary's eyes lit up.

'There might be a way of tempting them. I could ask them to take the roles of spring god and goddess as part of the Ostara celebration – as they're the only couple among us.'

'What does that involve, exactly?' said Charles, all set to disapprove.

'Nothing much. There'll be some seed planting,' said Rosemary sharply.

'So we might see some sex magic after all,' sniggered Pete, to Rosemary's annoyance.

The idea of a spring god planting his seed, prompted me to mention that Jay was coming.

'Actually, Jay and Sharon will be here. I'll have to ask them if they want to join in.'

'Well,' said Charles, 'we'll need some outside help with the special effects. I suppose they could be deployed in that area.'

'Special effects?' said Pete. 'I thought this was going to be bona fide magic?'

'We require some artillery in reserve in case the Bulls cut up rough. I want to put the fear of God in them so they give up any idea of making money from the elixir. We can get Jay and Sharon to do some noises off, maybe get some dry ice for effect, that sort of thing...'

At the mention of dry ice, I noticed that Theo became more attentive.

'Do you have any expertise with special effects, Theo?'

'Me? No. I was thinking of Tegan. She's registered with a performers' agency. Maybe she'd know something.'

'And she can walk on stilts,' I added. 'She'd be great. Though I don't think we'll need her juggling skills.'

'Can you get her down here for Friday, Theo?' said Charles, disregarding my attempt at humour.

Theo appeared slightly fazed.

'I asked her but she said she thought it'd be a little crowded with the family here...' He shot me a glance, his eyes troubled. 'And she doesn't know what I did. That might make a difference.'

'There's a room at the farm she can have,' I said gently. 'I'll ring her later and ask her if she wants to come – unless you want to ring her?'

'No. No, you call her. Then let me know what she decides.'

'Do you want me to tell her about your search for the chalice and how Dido, uh, tricked you?'

'Yeah, would you?'

He was looking sad again.

'Okay, darling.'

The 'd' word had slipped out before I knew it, and I felt myself blushing. Catching my eye, Pete gave me an approving wink, and inside my head, a voice sounding suspiciously like my mother's, crowed: *There's enough love to go round for everyone, Pan. Don't limit yourself to the Jay clan.*

Shortly after that, Charles, whose first day out of hospital appeared to have pushed him to near exhaustion, drew the meeting to a close, saying that we'd reconvene on Thursday or Friday, depending on which day Jay and Sharon arrived. Rosemary was tasked with getting in touch with Gavin and Dido, I had to find seven black sheets, and Max two black robes. His friend's father owned a fancy dress shop, and he was pretty sure he could get the dry ice from him as well.

As we gathered at the front door, Pete said, 'Remember, comrades, from now on, it's all for one and one for all!'

And we all echoed that as we went our separate ways.

Chapter 24

Baiting Bulls

The first thing I did when I got to my room in the B&B was to ring Jay to see when he and Sharon would be coming down.

'It'll be Friday, babe. The veg boxes have to be packed on Thursday. My little helpers are jumping ship so it's all down to me, Hugh and Sharon.'

I explained about the ceremony and my role as Flame Girl, and that if the Bulls could be persuaded to come, he and his mother were pencilled in for some haunting. When he heard this, he laughed his head off.

'Do you think Sharon will go for it?' I giggled.

'The question is, would the sexy abbess and her old man fall for a ghost who's eaten all the pies?'

'Why not? She could be wreaking revenge on behalf of all the fat people they'd scammed.'

We were both chortling at this thought until interrupted by the sound of crockery breaking, followed by Sharon's voice coming through, loud and clear.

'Pandora, is that you? Why's James laughing? He's just knocked over the tea I made him.'

I forced myself to sound grown-up and serious.

'Hello, Sharon, nothing really. I'll let him explain. I was just ringing to check when you're coming. It'd be handy if you can get here on Friday morning. When are Cherry and Willow leaving?'

Luckily, my mention of the girls distracted her, and after a few minutes of gossip about them and Rowan, she let me go, assuring me that they'd be in Glastonbury by noon on Good Friday, minus Fritz, Hugh having volunteered to have him at his place. As she was about to go, I remembered the items Rosemary had asked for, which were pretty impossible to find at short notice in the middle of Somerset.

'Can you see if you can get hold of seven black sheets please? Get cheap singles. They're not going on beds.'

'What on earth do you want them for, girl?' said Sharon.

She only ever called me 'girl' when I exasperated her.

'It's for a ceremony that Charles wants to attend...celebrating spring. If you can't get black, any dark colour will have to do. Thanks. Bye.'

Feeling like a wayward teenager, I rang off before she could argue with me.

Next on my list was Tegan. She answered immediately and I launched straight into a confession on Theo's behalf. She listened so quietly that I had to check every so often to see if she was still on the line. But when I got to the bit about Theo's accident, and how it had left him, she uttered a deep sigh of sympathy. I went on to outline our plans for a ceremony on Friday evening, so that Rosemary could start using the elixir for healing. And that her 'guinea pig' would be Theo. I also mentioned my brother's dalliance with Dido, but emphasised that it happened before he'd met her.

'So you see, Tegan, we're all batting on the same side now, and we'd love you to come down for the weekend. Theo, especially, wants to see you.'

'It's a lot to take in, Pandora,' she said, in a small voice.

'Well, you don't have to decide now,' I said, trying to quash my impatience. 'You can think it over and get back to me tomorrow, maybe? Or would you rather call Theo?'

I knew Theo would be pacing the floor till he got an answer, but it'd be wrong of me to rush her into the wrong decision. To be honest, even though he was my own flesh and blood, after what he'd done, I still wondered whether he was good enough for her.

'Actually, I noticed on Palm Sunday, when we walked to the church, that he dragged his feet on the way back.'

Hearing this, despite my uncertainties, my heart rose, glad that she'd homed in on Theo's health rather than his nocturnal misdemeanours. There was a long pause while I waited for her to speak.

'I wouldn't be much of a person if I gave up on someone who was sick, would I? After all, he didn't actually hurt anyone...'

'Only Charles and me.' Damn, the words had slipped out before I knew it. 'I mean, we were upset at the time, but it's been resolved now.'

'Did he really ask you to ring me?'

'Yes, yes. Are you coming, then?'

I'd had enough pussyfooting around. I wanted my brother put out of his misery, one way or another.

'Yes. I can come on Friday morning.'

'Great. That's when Jay and Sharon are coming. That's settled, then. At last I'll be able to tell the farmer's wife how many rashers to buy in for breakfast.'

She laughed her light, tinkly laugh.

'Can I bring Milo?'

'Why not? I've got Oscar here with me.'

At the mention of his name, Oscar raised his head and grinned.

'Okay. I'll ring Theo now.'

'Excellent. By the way, can you bring your stilts?'

'What!'

'I'm serious. Now go on, ring Theo. He'll explain.'

When she rang off, I knelt and gave Oscar a hug. If this had been a hotel room, I'd have had a gin and tonic and some chocolate to celebrate. But in the absence of a minibar, I broke open an emergency packet of jelly beans I had in my case, and scoffed the lot.

* * *

Rosemary rang Charles the next morning to tell him that the Bulls wanted to see him to discuss the ceremony. In response to this, Charles summoned Pete, who was there when Oscar and I popped in to say good morning.

Pete was in the middle of telling Charles that he'd heard from a 'contact' that Gav had set up a hairdressing chair in Dido's beauty salon, and had been charming the local dowagers out of wads of cash with his 'unique hair-thickening treatment', already branded and packaged as 'Grail Hair Elixir'. His chats to customers, after enquiring about their holiday plans, had revealed that he and his wife were very happy in Glastonbury and intended to release a range of beauty products which would be 'extra special'.

'They don't hang about, do they?' I said. 'Did he mention a miracle cure?'

'Not as I've heard,' muttered Pete. 'But it's only a matter of time...'

'Anyway,' said Charles. 'They want to come this evening, at half past seven. I'd like the two of you and Rosemary to be here. It's best if Theo keeps out of the way. So we'll eat about six. Is that all right, Pandora?'

'Yes. And it's two for dinner,' I said firmly. I didn't want Charles inviting Pete and Rosemary again. I'd noticed there was still a good bit of washing-up from the night before waiting for me in the kitchen.

Charles seemed to catch my drift and nodded.

'Come at seven, Pete. I'll tell Rosemary to get here then, so we can go over what we'll be saying to them. Rosemary told Gavin on the phone she thought she'd acted a bit hastily, so we'll follow that line. It won't take long, but we need to be on the same page.'

'Right, boss,' said Pete obediently.

I wandered upstairs to see if Charles' bed needed making and decided to ring Theo, who was at the shop.

'Hi, Sis. How you doing?'

'How are *you* doing, more like. Have you spoken to Tegan?'

When he answered, I could hear the smile in his voice.

'Yup. You did a good job. I don't know what you said to her, but she's on the team.'

'I'm happy for you.' Something made me add, 'And I mean that most sincerely.'

He laughed, even though he probably had no idea I was using the catchphrase of a popular TV host. One significant thing my brother and I failed to share was a common cultural background. That this was neither his fault nor mine, provoked in me a sudden surge of resentment against our mother.

'See you later, Sis.'

'Before you go, Theo. The Bulls are coming tonight at seven-thirty and Charles thinks it's better if you're not around. Is that okay?'

'Yeah, fine. I can arrange something with Jake.'

Jake was Sonia's son, a local artist, who helped out at Gaia's Cave occasionally.

'Okay. I'll give you a ring when they've gone to let you know the coast's clear.'

Downstairs, the men seemed happy enough. Having unloaded and reloaded the dishwasher, I quit the kitchen and took Oscar to the river.

* * *

So here we were again, six people seated around Charles' dining-room table, except that tonight Theo and Max's places had been taken by Dido and Gavin.

The rest of us had decided, in our pre-meeting parley, that we'd be nice as pie to them, in the hope they'd agree to join us on Friday night. This despite a further, shocking, piece of intelligence that Pete had brought to the table – one which left us all stunned, and Charles quivering with rage.

'Brace yourself, Charlie-boy,' Pete had said after we sat down at the table. 'Ralph was in the Flying Horse last night talking to Joey and the lads. He'd had one too many. Anyhow, they were saying as how you'd come out of 'ospital and Ralph, he says, "It doesn't do to cross Cruella." And Joe, he says, "What d'ya mean?" And Ralph says, "She told Cynthia she put a hex on him"...'

Pete stopped because our expressions told him that we all believed, without a shadow of a doubt, that Dido, alias Cruella, had, indeed, placed a curse on Charles.

'Did you know anything about this, Rosemary?' I said, experiencing a sudden hot spurt of anger.

Rosemary's reply was as fiery as mine.

'Don't insult me, Pandora. Of course I didn't!'

I believed her, but I was left with a strong sense of exasperation that she'd allied herself with that woman in the first place.

Seeing how pale Charles had become, I began to doubt that he'd see this meeting through. He was still in some pain from his bruised ribs and hadn't been outside the cottage since he'd come back from hospital. I also questioned the advisability of his attending the al fresco Ostara ceremony, in case it proved too much for him, but he protested vigorously.

'Nonsense, Pandora. And I fully intend to go out for a walk tomorrow. I'll be fine by Friday.'

I made a note to keep him to that. The wind was cold, but as long as the weather stayed dry, Oscar and I would drag him out.

'Anyway,' he steamed on, 'if you think I'm going to let those two charlatans terrorise me, you couldn't be more wrong. This just makes me more determined to run them out of town. As for the hex, I don't believe it touched me.'

'But, Charles, it *did* get to you,' I argued. 'She shot arrows of anger against you. As a result, you got stressed, lost your concentration, and ended up wrapped round a UPS van.'

While I was sounding off, it came to me where the word

'ankh' had cropped up.

'You had a bad dream in hospital, didn't you? An Egyptian figure holding an ankh...wasn't there a snake as well?'

He nodded. His tone was level, but his cheeks were afire with indignation.

'It didn't escape me at the time that someone might be using the shadow side of Isis to, shall we say, put the fear of Goddess into me. That's why I told you to get rid of her picture.'

'I set light to her in the garden that night, goddess or no,' said Pete, gleefully. 'That's what they used to do with witches.'

Rosemary, who was wearing a horrified expression, failed to return my amused glance.

Charles' eyes had gone cloudy when he'd been railing against Isis and the Bulls, but they cleared when he reached forward to touch the chunk of rose quartz crystal he'd placed in the centre of the table.

'My answer to their so-called hex is to decree that no negative force can touch me. I invoke Archangel Michael's sword of protection and ask him to protect my home and all here present.'

We waited while Charles intoned this decree three times, and then Pete spoke up.

'Let's hear it for St Mick,' he said, and we all gave Charles and Archangel Michael a polite round of applause.

We spoke a little more about winning the Bulls over and then I went upstairs to the bathroom. As I emerged, I heard a car draw up, so I raced downstairs, where, to my dismay, I found Rosemary smudging the rooms with a smoking bunch of sage. Snatching it out of her hand and causing sparks to fly in all directions, I threw it out the back door.

'Charles has already taken care of that,' I whispered forcefully. 'I don't want them to think we're protecting the space because we fear them.'

She heaved a deep, reproving sigh, but when I motioned her to answer the knock at the door, she did so, saying, 'Hello.

Welcome.'

Conducting them to the dining room, she sat them down.

'I think you know Pete, a friend of Charles.'

I took my seat at the round table and drank in the sight of the beautiful couple. Gavin was as immaculate as he'd been when he'd turned up at Rosemary's house, his hair carefully tousled and his shirt as white as snow. Dido wasn't dressed as a sexy abbess today – maybe that outfit had been her funeral garb. Today she, too, wore a crisp white shirt, with tailored black trousers which showed off her slim but shapely figure. *That's her beauty salon wear*, I thought, as I watched the couple link hands and place them on the table to demonstrate how united they were.

'Help yourselves to water.' I'd placed a carafe of water on the table in the hope it would pre-empt any irritating requests for herbal tea.

'So...' said Charles, smiling through his teeth. 'As Rosemary's already told you, Pandora found the chalice while she was sorting out her mother's clothes. And as we're now in possession of both the manuscript and the chalice, in a spirit of conciliation, we'd like to invite you to our Ostara celebration, when Rosemary will make the healing elixir.

'There will only be eight people present: yourselves, Rosemary, of course, Max, Pandora, Theo, Pete and me. As the Circle of Isis has been disbanded, we will not be extending the invitation to the other members. I think Rosemary has already mentioned that we'd like you, the only couple among us, to represent the god and goddess of spring.'

He paused to gauge their reaction, but their faces were impassive.

'It will take place at eight p.m. in the garden of Apple Blossom Cottage. The weather forecast promises a break from the cold weather, so we should be all right. Nevertheless, I advise warm clothing. Does anybody want to add anything?'

The four of us shook our heads. Our eyes were on Dido and Gavin, waiting for them to speak. Neither of them had said anything more than 'hello', or 'pass the water', up to now.

'It's very kind of you to ask us to join you,' said Dido, her tone matching Charles' in its studied politeness. 'But I happen to have a copy of the recipe. Let's face it, that's what we're all interested in. By the time of the April full moon, I'll have all the ingredients, so I'm quite happy to wait till then and make it on our own, if it's all the same to you.'

Remembering what Rosemary had said about Dido's faith in the chalice, I played my ace.

'Am I correct in assuming that you want to start producing the elixir so you can create a range of products?'

Dido's eyes wavered. That's what she'd told Theo when she was inveigling him to invest, so I was letting her know that I was aware of what had been going on between them. And from the way her colour heightened, I had a strong impression that her relationship with Theo wouldn't go down too well with Gav.

'Well,' I continued, 'you might have the recipe, but you don't have an ancient chalice that's been buried for centuries, so any elixir you make won't be the real thing.'

Dido regarded me with an expression of contempt. 'I doubt if anyone could prove that.'

Dido was wearing her hard-nosed businesswoman mask, but by the way the fingers of her free hand had crept towards her face to massage the fine lines on her forehead, it was obvious that she desperately wanted the end product to be genuine so she could use it on herself.

'It's time I said what I came here to say,' said Gavin, in response to the disapproval that had flickered across our faces at Dido's words. 'After a certain person here present,' he said loudly, scowling at Pete, 'has been blackening our reputations...'

Pete started to object but Gavin stopped him in his tracks by raising his hand in a silencing gesture. And from the way Pete flinched, I sensed that Charles had simultaneously aimed a kick at his ankle – as a reminder of our agreement to keep schtum on anything too inflammatory.

'...and a certain other person, without a by-your-leave, behind our backs disbanded the Circle that Di had put her heart and soul into,' at this point he glared at Rosemary, 'do you honestly think we'd agree to take part in your pathetic charade?'

Dido seemed nonplussed by this, as if her dreams of eternal youth had been dashed forever.

For a minute or so you could hear a pin drop. It seemed that our careful avoidance of sensitive topics like the diet-pills scam, copying the recipe on the sly, and ransacking the house and coffin for the chalice, had only achieved stalemate.

Gavin and Dido pushed their chairs back and got up to leave, causing my heart to sink to my boots. My eyes met Rosemary's, who looked even glummer than I felt.

Charles had got to his feet in time with the Bulls.

'I was about to say that Rosemary has recently channelled some additional information on the elixir from Saint Germain which would increase its potency, but if that's your decision, so be it. You can't say we didn't give you the chance...'

He omitted to include the warning, 'The drops will burn like acid the flesh of anyone who is black of heart and seeks to misuse the precious gift of the elixir', but as he was dealing with the sort of person who thought a hex was okay, he'd surely be excused.

Gavin had started walking towards the door, but Dido put a hand on his arm.

'Would you consider letting us have some of the elixir, Charles?' Her next words seemed to be choking her, but she forced them out, 'In the spirit of conciliation.'

'Don't you trust your own brew, Dido?' murmured Rosemary, *sotto voce*.

Sensing victory within his reach, Charles fired the next salvo.

'To be frank, Rosemary holds the key to this whole business.

Without her, you've just got a common-or-garden herbal tonic, a spurious copy, which is all you'll ever be able to produce. But with the information she's channelled, plus, of course, the chalice, we could well produce what the manuscript promises: "a life-prolonging elixir with rejuvenating and healing properties". I know which one I'd rather have.'

By now, Dido's mouth had twisted to one side and I saw how near she was to not being beautiful any more. Gavin had stopped moving towards the door and, as sometimes happens, I caught his thoughts and realised that he, too, wanted the elixir to extend the life of his own good looks.

Dido put her mouth to her husband's ear and whispered something, after which he gazed deep into her eyes and whispered, 'If that's what you want, angel.'

Seizing the advantage, and probably keen to get the pair off his property, Charles strode towards them saying, 'That's it, then. We'll see you at Rosemary's at eight o'clock on Friday.'

'Hold on a sec, mate,' said Gav. 'How much of the stuff do we get? It's gotta be worth our while.'

Charles redirected this query to Rosemary.

'Just a little on the night. The mixture has to infuse for four weeks and after that I'll share it out.'

'So how much are you making on Friday?'

'Two pints.'

Gavin looked puzzled.

'So what's that in millilitres?'

'Divided between eight people,' said maths wizard Charles, 'roughly 140 mls each.'

'Which is a lot,' said Rosemary quickly. 'It's so potent, you'd only be using three or four drops a day.'

'Is that for personal use?' Gavin asked.

Rosemary nodded.

'But what about adding to a face cream, for example? Any idea how much should go in?'

Rosemary shook her head.

'It'd have to be trial and error. But don't all products have to be tested first?'

'Don't worry, hon,' said Dido to Gav, in an undertone. 'We can always go down the homeopathic route.'

'You mean dilution well past the point where none of the original substance is present?' said Charles.

Ignoring him, Dido finally addressed Rosemary directly.

'Wouldn't it make more sense to increase the quantity?'

'I'm not a factory. I had to send off for some of the stuff, and there's only enough for two jars. In any case, I can make more at subsequent full moons. I'll need to, if it works, because I'll be wanting it for my patients.'

'So we can buy some from you every month. Is that a deal?' said Gav, still in negotiating mode.

Faithfully obeying Charles' orders to agree to almost anything up front just to get them to the ceremony, Rosemary said yes to that.

The Bulls conferred, then Gavin spoke the words which were music to our ears.

'Okay, we'll come. Do we have to bring anything?'

'No,' said Rosemary, her eyes shining in triumph. 'Just yourselves.'

Chapter 25

Rehearsing Ostara

Charles, Jay, Sharon, Oscar and I stood at Rosemary's door at two o'clock on Good Friday afternoon, having walked to Apple Blossom Cottage in the spring sunshine. The Met Office had kept its promise and the temperature had turned much milder.

Like the weather, Charles was also showing a marked improvement, the challenge of the coming evening bringing a glint to his eye and a spring to his step.

Sharon had been nagging me on the way over. 'Are you ever gonna tell me why I had to bring these black sheets, Pandora?'

I was unable to enlighten her, because I didn't know myself.

Tegan, Milo, Pete and the stilts had gone on ahead in his van. She and Milo had travelled down to Glastonbury with Jay and Sharon in the end, as her car had been playing up, which had been handy in terms of checking them all into the B&B at the same time. Theo was at the shop but planned to meet us later at a restaurant in town, after which we'd make our way back to Rosemary's for the ceremony.

Max let us in, giving Jay a big hug.

'You must come and see this,' he said, bubbling with excitement.

We went into the garden via the conservatory and found Tegan dressed in a flowing black costume with long, tight sleeves and a black cowl which she'd pulled up over her hair. She was prancing around on stilts as if she'd been born with them on. Milo was tearing around the garden enjoying all the new scents and got even more excited when Oscar joined in.

'Tegan,' I shouted. 'Where did you get that costume? I expected to see you in striped trousers and a top hat.'

'I've worn worse than that,' she laughed. 'I've been a dancing flame, butterfly, giant bride, all sorts. This is supposed to be a vampire's outfit. A friend from the agency let me borrow it – they don't get much call for vampires at Easter.'

'Can we see what the stilts look like?'

Tegan obligingly lifted her skirt to show us the stilts strapped to her legs and shoes.

'Get those leather kneepads,' Jay said. 'Very natty.'

We heard the sound of hands clapping and turned to see Rosemary summoning us back into the conservatory. 'Shall we let Tegan have a practice with the climbing frame while I run through the programme for tonight?'

'Climbing frame?' I repeated, expecting Rosemary to elaborate, but by then she'd hurried inside, urging people to sit down so she could start.

Once we were all seated, Rosemary stood in front of the French doors and gave us a rundown of the evening, which would begin with her casting the circle in a clockwise direction, described by Rosemary as 'deasil'.

'I didn't know she was bringing her car,' Jay quipped, from the table behind me.

Fortunately, his wisecrack didn't reach Rosemary's ears.

'On no account,' she was saying, 'should any member leave the circle until the end of the ceremony, when I uncast it.'

Those of us who'd been party to this sort of shenanigans before, knew that it entailed asking the guardians of the north, south, east and west to protect the space, and placing coloured beeswax candles, anointed beforehand with what Rosemary called 'goddess oil', at the four points. Novices like Jay and Sharon, however, needed guidance on these things, as even though they wouldn't be at the actual ceremony, they'd be watching from inside the house for their cue to start haunting.

Sharon had proved surprisingly amenable to the task. Jay had shown her the articles on the Bulls, using the link Max had sent me, and she was raring to take them down.

Rosemary was warming to her theme. 'After that, I'll start with the equinox balancing ceremony. I'll have one white and one black candle on the altar. Each of you will put on a black sheet – thank you for bringing those, Sharon. I'll get Max to cut holes in them for your heads. Had it been summer, some of you might have chosen to be naked underneath, but at this time of year, I'd advise wearing thermal underwear and warm sweaters.'

Sharon shuddered at the word 'naked'. 'My gud, if I'd been told what they were for, I'd have got the polycotton ones.'

'What sort did you get, Sha?' I said, pretty sure that I'd asked her to get cheap ones.

'They only had silk or polycotton, so I got the silk. Don't worry, I put them on your account.'

'That's all right then,' I said, under my breath.

I caught Pete's eye and he winked at me. Earlier, when we'd met up in Charles' cottage, he'd been quite jolly with Sharon. He must be one of those skinny men who likes big women. To my surprise, she'd been quite skittish back.

'Er, can we get back to the programme, please?'

Rosemary had spent the morning at the dental practice and was definitely still in dentist mode: *Let's get this cavity filled and move on to the next one*, rather than high priestess figure, which she'd morph into later in the day.

'One by one, you will come forward and kneel before the altar and I'll ask you if you want to experience the rebirth of spring. Then I'll sprinkle you with salt, pass incense over you, show you the burning white candle and, finally, sprinkle a little water over you. When I tell you to "Step forth out of the darkness into the light", you have to take off the sheet and move to the edge of the circle.'

'This kneeling,' said Pete. 'Is it important? Only my joints aren't what they were...'

'Tell me about it,' said Sharon. 'When I kneel down beside my bed at night to say my prayers, I just have to use the bed as a springboard to get up again.'

The image of Sharon on her knees praying for Rowan's lost sports kit to turn up, then somersaulting on an oversprung mattress and landing like a gymnast on wobbly pins, set me off so much I had to almost stuff a tissue in my mouth. Behind me, I heard Jay and Max suppressing guffaws as well.

'Ever thought of praying for new kneecaps while you're down there, Ma?' said Jay, managing to control his vocal cords so his observation sounded almost sincere.

Fortunately, Sharon was too busy making sympathetic eyes at Pete to take any notice.

'Well, if you *really* can't kneel, Pete, you'll just have to stand.'

Rosemary was beginning to sound snappy, so everyone went quiet.

'During the second part, I'll get the Bulls to perform their rites of spring, while I make up the elixir.'

I saw Pete exchange a sly grin with Sharon at the mention of 'rites' and had to force my fingernails into the palm of my hand to forestall another fit of giggles.

'Once this is done, there'll be the final, third part – a healing ceremony where you'll receive just two drops each on your tongue. I'll move deasil round the circle making sure that Dido and Gavin go last, because they're the ones most likely to fail the purity test and spit it out. So whoever's standing to the left of them, will go first. Is that clear?'

Nobody said it wasn't, so Jay put up his hand.

'What happens next? When do *we* come in?'

'I'm going to let Charles take over now,' said Rosemary. 'I need to rest and prepare myself. I always call upon my own guides and guardians before any ceremony, today it's particularly important to call in the big guns as well. I'll see you all at eight o'clock. Come earlier if you like. Max will let you in.'

Once Rosemary had left the conservatory, the atmosphere changed from unruly classroom to police incident room. I almost expected Charles to produce a whiteboard or start filling the wall with pintacks and string, so seriously did he take his role as chief tactician. After calling Tegan in from the garden, he cleared his throat and took the floor, having first distributed to each of us a schedule of the evening and a pen for making notes.

'So let's go over the logistics. Jay and Sharon, you can either chance it and cross the garden while Rosemary's mixing the potion, or you can position yourselves out of sight behind the altar at half past seven.'

Sharon let out a yelp. 'Unless that garden's got under-turf heating and cable TV, thanks, but no thanks.'

Charles beetled his brows and continued. 'In that case, wait till the Bulls are doing their thing, then come down in your costumes, which are upstairs for you to try on before you go. It's too obvious if you come out via the conservatory, so you'll have to go out the front door and round the side of the house. Max is going to ensure the side gate won't be locked. You must let yourselves into the garden as quietly as you can...'

'I've oiled those hinges, specially,' said Pete, looking towards Sharon for approval, who rewarded him with a warm smile.

'Quite,' said Charles, a little put out that his friend seemed more concerned with impressing Sharon than letting him continue uninterrupted.

Jay had looked doubtful when Charles had been describing their entry into the garden and I didn't blame him. I had an image of Sharon waddling across the grass and stuffing herself behind the altar with great huffing and puffing.

'What about the dry ice?' asked Pete.

'Max has procured some. It's being delivered later this afternoon. Tegan, you've dealt with dry ice before, I understand.'

She nodded. 'It'll need a few gallons of water. And you have to wear gloves to handle it because it's so cold.'

'Thank you, Tegan. There'll be three empty cauldrons out of sight, behind the altar. The dry ice will be next to them, in three separate polystyrene containers. We'll place several flasks of hot water beside the cauldrons, so whoever sets it up, will just need to put the ice into the cauldrons and empty the water on to it. There'll be watering cans for topping up if needed. Warm would be better, but cold still works.' Charles paused and addressed Jay and Sharon. 'Do you think you can handle that?'

'You sure there's room for the two of us behind the altar without being seen,' said Jay, looking at Charles and casting a quick glance at Sharon.

'Just about. One of you could hide behind the tree, if you prefer.'

Jay looked relieved on that score but still unconvinced on another.

'So you want us to get from the side gate to behind the altar and not be seen by the Bulls? I'm not sure that's possible...'

'You shoulda got midgets, Charles. He's too tall and gangly and I'm too Rubenesque,' said Sharon, twinkling at Pete.

Jay put on a faux hurt expression and continued. '...Unless they had their backs to us, but that's not something Rosemary can guarantee, is it?'

Charles shook his head. He'd attended enough of these events to know that there was little about full moon celebrations that could be guaranteed. 'Can't promise anything, but if you wait till they're doing their spring deities impression, they should be facing away from you. I'll mention it to Rosemary. We'll have to trust in her.'

'I don't mind starting the dry ice off,' said Tegan. 'I'll be out there anyway. As long as I have something to sit on while I'm waiting.'

It was good of her to volunteer for extra duties. I suppose, being so loved up with Theo, she'd agree to almost anything to help his healing along.

'Note that down, please, Max. A garden chair or some blankets behind the altar and a pair of gloves. Once the dry ice is going, Tegan, you'll have to head for the climbing frame and get your stilts on. Then you'll be ready to loom over the altar as soon as they've drunk the elixir.'

Jay and I exchanged glances: the climbing frame mystery had been solved.

'Okay,' said Tegan. 'Oh, and one other thing, Charles, I don't have to say anything, do I? I'm not sure I can do an angry goddess voice.'

'Don't worry, my dear,' said Charles, smiling benignly, 'there'll be a megaphone behind the tree which Jay can project his famous voice into.' Seeing Jay's expression of horror, he added, 'All we need is a touch of countertenor, I'm sure you've got the range. If Tegan blacks her face, she won't look particularly male or female. Anyway, in the absence of a *castrato*, you're all we've got.'

'I get it,' said Jay. 'You want me to do a Bee Gee impression. No problem. How about "More Than A Woman"?'

There was general tittering, but Tegan took it more seriously.

'Oh, I used to love the Bee Gees. I played "Smoke and Mirrors" so much, I wore out the cassette.'

'Any more requests?' said Jay with a big grin, and we started listing our favourite Bee Gee songs.

Charles soon began tapping his foot impatiently. I almost expected him to cry 'Order! Order in the House!' but instead he fixed Jay with a gimlet gaze.

'Can we continue discussing the logistics for this evening?'

With an effort, Jay wiped the grin off his face. 'So what's Sharon supposed to be doing while I'm on the megaphone?'

'She was originally down as sound effects,' said Charles, with more than a tinge of resignation in his tone.

I concentrated on keeping a straight face as I imagined her woo-wooing in time to Jay's impression of Barry Gibb in full falsetto.

'She could keep the dry ice going. If it doesn't get enough

water, it dies down,' said Tegan.

Sharon was sporting a sulky pout. It was written all over her face that busting the baddies wasn't sounding half as much fun as she'd imagined.

'What's the worst noise you can make?' asked Jay. 'Apart from when you're singing along to Capital Gold.'

'Can you imitate a clap of thunder?' said Pete.

Unfortunately for their budding relationship, Sharon failed to see the joke. 'I hate to be a party pooper, but this is beginning to sound unworkable to me.'

'Hold on a minute,' said Max. 'I might have something...'

He left the room, reappearing, a couple of minutes later, with a tin horn a good two feet long. When he blew it, everyone put their hands over their ears.

'That's enough, Max,' said Charles, going all schoolmasterly. 'That's loud enough to bring down the walls of Jericho. I don't think it's suitable.'

'Oh, I don't know,' said Jay, picking it up for a closer look. 'If we can't frighten them, at least we can blow their brains out.'

'Remind me to bring ear plugs,' Charles muttered, but seeing Jay was serious, he added something to his notes. 'So that's Jay on megaphone and horn,' he said.

'It's called a vuvuzela,' said Max. 'My dad sent it to me from Africa.'

'I'll play it but don't ask me to spell it for you,' said Jay to Charles.

Sharon was feeling neglected and her face could only be described as a sour puss. 'I thought you were getting something for me.'

Max picked up a small digital recorder from the table.

'How about a screeching barn owl?'

He flicked a switch and a series of blood curdling screams rent the air.

'That's it,' cried Charles. 'By George, he's got it. Okay, Sharon,' he said reaching again for his pen and paper, 'I'll put you down for screeching and cauldron duties.'

Still sulking, Sharon appeared in two minds whether to commit to these responsibilities. Taking her silence for assent, Charles moved on. 'We've also got some firecrackers which a friend of Max's has agreed to let off in the next door garden.'

'Our neighbours are away for Easter, I'm sure they wouldn't mind,' said Max, looking sheepish. 'Chris can get into their garden. But I'd rather you didn't mention it to Mum beforehand.'

We all assured him we wouldn't and Charles continued. 'As you know, the whole aim of this operation is to ensure that the Bulls give up all notion of getting access to the elixir and selling it for profit – in their case, huge profit. So we've literally got to put the fear of God in them. Agreed?'

We all mumbled our agreement. And then Sharon piped up.

'Have you thought, Charles, what you're going to do if the elixir *doesn't* affect them badly. Suppose they take the drops and just walk back to their places?'

The room waited expectantly. I suppose this was something we'd all considered, but had pushed to the backs of our minds.

Charles' lips had tightened to the point of disappearance at Sharon's words. 'My answer to that is to go ahead and frighten the hell out of them anyway. We already know they're shysters. Their goal is to make money under false pretences – Dido said as much on Tuesday night. And call it revenge for the hex, or what you will, but I intend to thwart them if it kills me.'

'Hear hear. That's the right decision, old boy,' said Pete, patently relieved that his evening wouldn't be deprived of circus skills, dry ice and fireworks.

Smiling in acknowledgement of his old friend's allegiance, Charles turned to Max.

'Perhaps you'd like to take Jay and Sharon upstairs to try on their costumes and then, Jay, we'll go through your script.'

I followed them upstairs because I was dying to see their

costumes. They were black and floor-length, with extra long sleeves to ensure no flesh was exposed. The hoods even had a mesh face to protect the wearer's identity. The outfits would give near invisibility on a dark night. But Rosemary's garden would be lit with candles on the altar and at the edge of the circle. What's more, the full moon would be bright if it was a clear night, so Jay was right about the danger of detection.

'Ooh,' warbled Sharon, 'I love it. Black's so slimming. And two deep pockets for biscuits.'

I inspected the label, which read 'Grim Reaper' – exactly what they both resembled.

'All you need is a scythe,' I said in a low voice to Jay.

'All the better to SLAY you with my dear,' he replied, following up with a Hammer House of Horror laugh.

'Sssh, You'll disturb Rosemary.'

Jay waited until Sharon had finished admiring herself in the mirror, taken the robe off, and gone downstairs.

As soon as she left the room, he pounced, giving me a bear hug which nearly squeezed the life out of me, followed by a kiss which took my breath away.

'Are you trying to kill me,' I gasped when I surfaced for air.

He laughed.

'Just getting into character.'

I broke away from him and slipped Sharon's Grim Reaper robe over my head.

'How do I look?'

'It does nothing for you, madam,' said Jay, in his *Are You Being Served* voice. 'In my opinion, you'd suit something from our Flame Girl range. We've got a figure-hugging red and yellow number in your size. Did you know her special power is generating heat?'

'I don't need a costume to do that.'

He gently removed the Grim Reaper and went in for another clinch.

'Missed you, baby,' he breathed in my ear. 'Any chance of some coitus uninterruptus this afternoon? If we can shake Sharon off.'

In our younger days, we'd probably have closed the door and had a quickie. But since Jay had gone tantric, sex had turned into a series of slowies. Not that I was complaining, but I couldn't see much prospect of love in the afternoon on this busy Good Friday.

'The only way we'll shake her off is if we set her up with Pete,' I whispered back. 'And then it'd have to be his place because I wouldn't want them in the next room to us.'

Sharon's voice floated up the stairs. 'Are you two coming?'

'Chance'd be a fine thing,' said Jay.

Downstairs, Charles collared Jay so Pete offered us a lift back to the B&B. Tegan and Sharon hadn't had time to properly unpack, and we all felt in need of a rest.

'Bye, Charles. We'll see you at the restaurant at six.'

'I won't be long, darlin',' said Jay, giving me a melting look.

I fluttered my eyelashes ironically, knowing that the odds were I'd be fast asleep by the time he got away from Charles.

* * *

Back at the farmhouse, I had a bath and lay on the bed in my dressing gown. Rosemary had instructed us all to have a salt bath before the ceremony, to cleanse and protect ourselves. She'd even given us each a small bag of salt, just to make sure. I'd explained that we were eating out, so fitting the bathing in might be tricky, and that Tegan's room only had a shower.

'Well, you'll just have to have it this afternoon. She can use your bath, can't she? And remember, no alcohol.'

As if on cue, there was a tap on the door. I let Tegan in and we joked about feeling like giant chips and Oscar licking most of it off my legs anyway.

Tegan and I had been wondering if the dogs would be all right this evening. We couldn't take them with us, so on the way in, I'd warned Jenny we'd be leaving them in our rooms. She said she'd have taken them into the farmhouse, but she and Steve were going out, so she suggested putting both dogs in the same bedroom with the television on low.

Tegan emerged from the bathroom, all pink and salty.

'See you later, Pandora.'

Seeing her standing there, clutching the small plastic bowl she'd used to carry her salt, reminded me of an odd dream I'd had the night before.

The scene was spread out below me, giving a bird's-eye view. Theo and Tegan were walking beside a meandering river. The countryside was lush and abundant. Ahead of them a tiny figure appeared on the horizon, getting bigger by the second. When she materialised in front of them, I perceived her to be a small woman of oriental appearance dressed in a white robe which covered her head. She held in her hands a beautiful jade vase and took from her pocket a drinking bowl into which she poured some liquid. She gave the bowl to Theo first, then Tegan. She waited while each of them drank from it. Then she was gone, leaving the bowl on the ground where she had stood.

Tegan picked up the bowl and the scene changed to that of a barren wasteland where a fierce wind was spiralling sand into a multitude of mandalas, which disappeared almost as soon as they were formed. Their heads bowed, Theo and Tegan strained to move forward in the face of the wind. Tegan bent down and scooped some sand into the bowl.

As soon as she had done this, she was back by the river, this time on the other side, returning from whence she came. From my elevated position, I saw Beau walking to meet her. He gave Tegan a gentle nudge with his great head, and she stopped and emptied the bowl of sand into the river.

The dream had been playing in my mind on and off all day, but I still couldn't recall whether Theo had been with them.

Chapter 26

Spilling Blood

Charles and Jay had split the bill and were waiting for their change. The restaurant tab wasn't bad considering there were six of us. Normally, our crew would have yielded a fair bit of profit, but Charles had insisted that we all, even the special effects team, laid off red meat and drank water or fruit juice.

I'd been a bit twitchy beforehand in case Sharon harangued Theo with a good telling-off, but she'd limited herself to a relatively mild, 'I hope you're thoroughly ashamed of yourself, young man,' and seemed satisfied by his admission of guilt and request for forgiveness.

Charles looked at his watch. 'Quarter past seven. I'd better ring Rosemary to say we're on our way.'

He made the call at the table, receiving two messages in the process.

'She says don't forget to switch off your mobile phones as you enter the house and she hopes you've remembered to protect yourself with the salt baths.'

'Did you have one, Theo?' I asked, channelling my mother hen.

'Certainly did, Sis. Stopped off at the cottage specially. Charles gave me my orders and I followed them to the letter.'

When he said this, he smiled first at me and then Tegan, and she snuggled in closer to him. Since their reunion, they hadn't moved more than an inch away from each other. They looked so sweet together it made my heart sing.

'Omigosh!' wailed Sharon. 'I knew I'd forgotten something. That damn bed was too comfy. What am I gonna do?'

'I expect you're glad *you* managed to have your salt bath when you did,' I said softly to Jay.

This made him smile. He'd finally got back from Rosemary's at four-thirty, hoping for some afternoon delight, to find Tegan in our room. She'd come to collect Oscar for a walk and I was explaining how to get to the river. By the time she and the dogs got going, it was twenty to five, and in the meantime Jay had stretched out on the bed fully clothed, and was snoring gently.

At five o'clock I ran his bath and woke him up.

'What? Who are you? Where am I?'

I laughed, knowing that he knew very well where he was.

'I've drawn your bath, and placed the toothpaste on your toothbrush, if you please, sir.'

Jay liked a bit of role play.

'What's this, Armstrong?' he said, sternly, slipping easily into his lord of the manor impression. 'I cannot take a bath alone. You know my doctors strictly forbid it. Off with your clothes, and assist me into the water.'

'You know we're leaving for the restaurant at quarter to six, don't you?'

'Oh gawd. We'll have to be quick then.'

Jay tore off his clothes and made for the bathroom.

'The salt's in, Jay,' I called. 'Just swish the water around so it dissolves.'

I was just about to join him when there was a knock on the door. It was Jenny.

'Hello. Sorry to disturb you. My youngest boy's just turned up. As they do,' she said, sounding pleased. 'He wasn't due till tomorrow. Anyway...' She scoured the room for Oscar. 'Where's your dog?'

'He's gone out for a walk with Milo.'

She looked puzzled.

'And Tegan.'

'Ah. What time are you going out? Ryan says he doesn't mind having them. He likes dogs.'

'Quarter to six,' I said. 'That's really kind. And, of course, we'll pay him for dog sitting. We'll bring them over when Tegan gets back. Thanks ever so much.'

As I said goodbye, I heard Jay calling. I opened the bathroom door to find him in the bath, wearing my pink shower cap, his arms open.

'Come to me, baby.'

'We've only got half an hour before we go out. It takes me longer than that to get ready.'

He stood up in the bath.

'I'm ready now. Let's play find the soap.'

I perceived that he was, indeed, exceedingly ready.

'Tegan's due back any minute with Oscar. Then we've got to take the dogs to the farmhouse...'

Jay, by now draped in a towel, carried me to the bed and began to make love to me.

'That bath's too small anyway,' he gasped, as he climaxed all too quickly. 'Wow, I needed that.'

I put my mouth to his ear and whispered, 'Jay, you've forgotten something.'

'What, darlin'?'

'You didn't say "thank you, mam" after the wham bam.'

The penny dropped and he said, 'Sorry, petal. Was I too quick? Would you like me to...?'

He was just poising himself to ignite my hot spot, when there came a snuffling at ground level as two doggy noses sought to find out what was going on behind the green door.

I jumped up like a scalded cat and pushed Jay back into the bathroom. Finding my dressing gown, I slung it on and opened the door to Tegan and the canines.

We finally reached the restaurant at six-fifteen, which was why we were now running a little later than intended. We'd spent the first half of the meal filling Theo in on the meeting. He was really keen to see Tegan on stilts but seemed doubtful about the special effects.

'Do you think all that smoke and mirrors stuff will fool them? Dido's a tough cookie. And if she can plant hexes on people, who's to say she won't call up a demon of her own?'

Charles had remained calm. 'That's the whole idea of casting a circle, Theo. Rosemary will do her best to make it a safe place. We've just got to hope her best is strong enough to deter any negative entities Dido might have up her sleeve.'

* * *

'Did I hear you saying you didn't have your bath?' Charles asked Sharon as we piled into the people carrier. 'In that case, you'll have to drop us off and go back and have it. I'll get hold of a front door key from Max and you can let yourselves in. If you wait till after eight o'clock there's no danger the Bulls will see you. Assuming they come, of course.'

This plan seemed to suit both Jay and Sharon. So they dropped us off at Apple Blossom Cottage, picked up a house key from Max, and headed off back to the B&B.

Charles was eager for Tegan to get dressed, blacked up, and into the garden before the Bulls arrived, so she dragged herself away from Theo and went straight upstairs to change. Theo, Charles, and I joined Pete in the conservatory. Soon after that, Max appeared and told us that the altar was prepared and Tegan and the dry ice were in place.

'Good, so everything's on track. There's nothing we have to do now, but wait,' said Charles. 'And pray they show up.'

I sat down next to Theo, feeling sad for him that he'd been parted from Tegan. They had so much to say to each other, they must have been dying to be alone together.

There was a loud knock at the door and we all held our breath. Max went to answer it and when Dido and Gav came into the room, the tension palpably subsided. For me, however, this was soon followed by an intense anxiety that the plan would come terribly unstuck.

I imagined an unconvincing Tegan being mocked by the Bulls; Sharon getting wedged behind the altar and causing a fuss, or munching biscuits so loud she'd be heard; Jay's falsetto and the vuvuzela making us laugh hysterically with nerves. Not to mention the damage Gavin might do to my friends and family if he lost his temper. He looked like a man who worked out.

Dido had on a replica of the linen robe I'd found in Frankie's wardrobe. I was taken aback when I saw that she was wearing the pleated organza as an overgarment, draped over one shoulder and fastened at the waist with a red stone brooch in the shape of an ankh, the flow of the material giving the appearance of two wings crossing her lower torso.

She sneered when she saw me staring. 'Haven't you ever seen ritual Isis wings?'

I wanted to say I'd seen similar wings, outstretched, in a picture she'd used to curse my stepfather, but I bit my tongue and shook my head.

Gavin was more casually dressed in Hugo Boss jeans and a classic polo neck jumper. The rest of us, knowing that we'd be wearing a black sheet for some of the time – more than enough dressing up for us lot – had on warm jumpers and trousers.

After some muted hellos, we didn't speak, which was acceptable, given that we were supposed to be meditating upon our impending rebirth. *But I've already had one rebirth, haven't I?* I said inwardly. *This is an annual rebirth to celebrate spring, dear one,* I heard in reply. *Your phoenix rebirth was more profound and lasting.*

At eight o'clock, Charles led us outside, where he told us to stand on the patio. We watched as Max took a folding table into the garden, followed by two wooden chairs, which he placed facing away from the path that Jay and Sharon would have to take to get behind the scenes.

The impressive altar was made of stone and had once stood in a church. Rosemary had bought it years before from a reclamation yard. When they'd delivered it, her ex had told the men to put it in front of the apple tree, not realising that practitioners of natural magic would usually have placed their altar in the centre of any circle. It was too heavy to move once the men had gone, so it had remained there ever since. On this occasion, it suited our purposes perfectly because the passage between the tree and the altar was just wide enough to hide the cauldrons and their custodians.

Rosemary came out and greeted us, having turned off the conservatory lights, leaving the house in darkness. She was dressed in the long, white robe which I recognised as her usual priestess gear, over which she'd put a pale green, sleeveless chasuble decorated with a silver pentacle. She told us to stay on the patio while she cast the circle. This she did by ritually carving out a large circle with a small white-handled dagger, invoking the spirits of the four directions and placing a coloured beeswax candle, sheltered by a candle holder, at each direction, to protect and bless our work.

I was fairly familiar with the drill. A green candle inscribed with the symbol for the earth element stood at the north, a red candle with a symbol for fire at the south, a yellow candle depicting air at the east, and a blue candle representing water at the west. Following this, she sprinkled sea salt all around the inside of the circle to cleanse and sanctify the space.

While this was going on, I feasted my eyes on the altar. Either side of the large, central tabernacle, Rosemary had strewn Easter lilies, bright yellow forsythia, tulips, pussy willow and lilac. Placed in front of these, on the left, were pots of crocuses, violets, hyacinths, narcissi and miniature daffodils. Between the pots lay pale-hued crystals: rose quartz, amethyst, agate, moonstone and aquamarine. On the far left sat a statue of a moon-gazing hare. And what a full, bright moon there was to gaze at, on such a cloudless night.

To the right, Rosemary had positioned a basket of eggs,

flanked by a flagon of milk and a large jug of clear honey, next to a pink cardboard cake box. In the centre of the altar, in front of the tabernacle, stood the small chalice. Either side of it were two pillar candles: one black, one white. To the far right, stood two large empty jars and a glass jug full of colourless liquid which Rosemary had told us would be vodka. I assumed the pots of herbs and additional ingredients were tucked safely away in the tabernacle.

'I'm now going to welcome you into the circle one by one,' Rosemary was saying. 'I'll ask you "How do you enter the circle" and your reply will be *"In the light and love of the Mother Goddess and Father God".'*

She beckoned Charles forward from the patio and, one by one, all seven of us took our places within the circle she'd created. Rosemary lit both of the pillar candles, along with some pungent incense sticks, and began to recite an ode to Ostara, goddess of spring. When this was complete, she moved towards the pile of black sheets which had been placed, rather haphazardly, in a hessian sack to one side of the altar.

'Put these on, please.'

Gavin and Dido were positioned to Theo's right, so Rosemary called him forward first, asking him to kneel down on the soft foam kneeling pad someone had thoughtfully provided. I caught Pete's eye and he gave me a discreet thumbs-up, just visible under his black silk sheet, so I assumed he was the foam donor.

'Let us celebrate the feast of Ostara by welcoming the vernal equinox, when light and dark are equal. Spring is a season of buds and newborns, of beginnings and fresh starts. As Mother Earth wakes from her slumber and welcomes new life, so let us be reborn into the light and love of Isis and Ostara.'

That's her insurance against offending the great mother goddess, I thought, registering that Rosemary had managed to slip in a mention of Isis.

Rosemary had got to the part where she asked Theo whether

he wanted to experience the rebirth of spring and step out of the darkness into the light, and he'd replied 'I do', sounding for all the world like a bridegroom.

I thought of Tegan, concealed behind the altar listening to this, waiting to set off the dry ice. And I wondered whether Sharon and Jay had arrived back yet and were at the upstairs bedroom window, watching out for their cue to sprint downstairs, through the side gate, to join Tegan at the back of the altar, before she went off to the climbing frame to put on her stilts.

Rosemary was now sprinkling salt over Theo, saying, 'Take this blessing from the earth for you are reborn in the eyes of the gods.'

Next she waved an incense stick over his head.

'Take this blessing from the air, may the wind carry all good things to you.'

This was followed by the lighted white candle.

'Take this blessing from the fire of the spring sun.'

Finally, she sprinkled water on his head.

'Take this blessing from water, bringing growth and abundance into your life.'

Rosemary bent to whisper an instruction in his ear, so when she told him to: 'Rise and step out of the darkness into the light!' he obediently got to his feet and started tugging at his black sheet. Unfortunately, his mass of dreadlocks must have somehow expanded since he put it on, because no matter how hard he and Rosemary tugged, it wouldn't budge.

Avoiding Pete's gaze, I chewed my cheeks to stop the laughter gurgling up. I hoped, if they were watching, that Jay and Sharon wouldn't laugh too loudly, in case Dido and Gavin, now regarding the spectacle with unconcealed disdain, heard them and got suspicious. They were probably wishing Rosemary would hurry up and get on with the main attraction so they could go home and start getting younger.

Rosemary produced a pair of scissors, which did the trick, freeing my brother from the darkness and propelling him into the light at last.

Giving him a moment to compose himself, Rosemary spoke the words she wanted him to repeat.

'I am opening, newborn, through the luminous love light of Ostara.'

Unfortunately, Theo fluffed his lines.

'I am newborn through the...the voluminous opening...of the love life of Ostara.'

This caused one or two of us to start sniggering, probably from nerves. In an attempt to recapture the solemnity of the occasion, Rosemary addressed us all sternly.

'As the theme of the equinox is balance, please meditate on the balance you wish to find in your own life, and how you can work towards inner harmony.'

Rosemary must have guessed that we didn't want to loiter over the first course of the ceremony, so she picked up speed, going clockwise round the circle. This made Dido and Gavin the last two rebirthings, as planned, thus setting a precedent for them being the final two for the healing ceremony, which would take place once the elixir had been created.

As soon as Gavin had cast off his black sheet, declaring himself reborn in a bored monotone, Rosemary announced it was time for the god and goddess of spring to take their places.

Pulling the wooden chairs further forward into the centre of the circle, she motioned the Bulls to sit down. Max positioned the folding table in front of them and Rosemary trekked back and forth from the altar with a plate of small honey cakes, a jug of milk, some picnic beakers, two flower pots, two packets of seeds, two miniature trowels and some potting soil.

While she was doing this, I was squinting out of the corner of my eye in anticipation of Jay and Sharon making their dash across the garden, but they must have been quick because I didn't see a thing.

I tuned back in to Rosemary, who was addressing the Bulls.

'I now crown you god and goddess of spring.'

As she spoke these words, she placed a posy of spring flowers on the heads of Dido and Gavin.

The pair sat there stony-faced, but brightened up when Rosemary announced, 'And now I ask the Circle to celebrate Ostara's feast in dance,' motioning us to cavort around them as they welcomed the season of fertility by planting their seeds in the pots provided.

Watching us self-consciously dragging our feet in a sullen sardana, the two of them exchanged smug smirks. Rosemary, who hadn't seen fit to warn us that we'd be called upon for ecstatic dancing duties, busied herself at the tabernacle, thus avoiding our disgruntled glares.

By the time she turned round, we'd all ground to a halt, including the seed planters. She then asked us to approach the table, one by one, to receive a beaker with a miserly inch or two of milk in it and a honey cake, dispensed with zero eye contact by the god and goddess.

Once we'd polished off the riches of spring, Rosemary asked Max to move the table to the side of the altar, and Dido and Gavin to return to their places in the circle. She then began her preparation of the elixir. Murmuring an incomprehensible incantation, she placed the herbs and other ingredients in the two jars, two-thirds of which she filled with vodka, topping up with honey. Finally, she gave the contents of each jar a good stir.

With most of the work done, she called Theo to stand in front of her. Taking the small dagger from her pocket, she passed it through the white candle flame and plunged it into a bowl of water. Satisfied it was clean, she took hold of the chalice and asked Theo to hold it in his right hand and to be prepared to catch the drops of blood when she cut the middle finger of his left hand.

Chanting an invocation, Rosemary stabbed at Theo's finger, but the dagger simply bounced off his skin. Charles walked forward to examine the blade.

He tried it on his own finger, but it scarcely broke the surface.

'This wouldn't cut butter. It's a ritual dagger, for God's sake. What are you thinking of, Rosemary?'

'Shall I go and get something sharper?' I said, looking for an excuse to go inside and check that Jay and Sharon had left the bedroom.

'We can't break the circle now we've built up the energy,' said Rosemary, sternly. 'Going back and forth from the circle would dissipate it.'

'Here, give it to me,' said Theo, grabbing the dagger and hacking at his finger tip.

'No!' I cried.

But by then a spurt of blood had flowed into the chalice and the tip of Theo's finger had opened half an inch.

I ran over to the altar and got some of the ribbon that Rosemary had used to tie the flowers and bound it tightly round his finger. As the blood began seeping through the ribbon, Rosemary's eyes fixed hungrily on it.

'I think you've got enough now, Rosemary,' I said sharply, wishing I had some garlic to hang round Theo's neck. 'Why don't you finish the elixir so we can get to the *finale*,' emphasising the last word so she'd get a move on.

I glanced at the other members of the circle to catch their reaction to Theo's bloodletting. Charles, Pete and Max were looking worried, Dido looked as if she thought Rosemary was making a proper pig's ear of it and she would have done much better, and Gavin was examining his nails for soil.

Rosemary proceeded to stir some blood into each jar, pouring some of the mixture out of each jar and swilling it round in the chalice, which she then elevated above her head, as if offering it to be blessed by a deity. She did this for each jar, pouring the contents of the chalice back into the jar once she had offered it up. After muttering a further incantation over the two jars with her back to us, Rosemary captured some of the liquid with a dropper, then, like a fire-eater, opened her mouth and allowed two drops to settle on her tongue.

Having waited a few moments to confirm that she wouldn't burst into flames and be damned to kingdom come, she siphoned more of the elixir into the dropper, rested it in the chalice, and approached Theo.

'You are a child of the gods and I ask them to bless you. May this sacred elixir heal and revitalise your body and blood.'

She motioned Theo to open his mouth and then carefully released two viscous drops on to his tongue.

'Repeat the last three words,' she commanded.

Theo complied.

'Body and blood.'

'Put it on his finger,' I hissed, the words bypassing my brain and shooting out of my mouth, as sometimes happened.

She wasn't sure, and looked at Charles for guidance. He made a *why not?* movement with his shoulders, so she let two drops fall on to the blood-stained ribbon at approximately the site of the cut.

I was next, then Pete, Charles and Max, all of us in tune with the elixir, with no adverse reactions. The taste was strong and aromatic, but not unpleasant. Those two small drops infused my whole body with a welcome sensation of heat, as the evening was becoming chilly.

Dido stepped forward.

Intoning the blessing, Rosemary let the elixir drop on to Dido's eager tongue. After that, all hell broke loose.

Chapter 27

Dea ex Machina

Tegan was right on cue with the dry ice, because as soon as Dido had clutched her mouth in agony, swirls of fog rose up around the altar.

Gavin rushed to his wife's side, shouting, 'Do something, somebody!'

Turning on Rosemary, he growled, 'You conniving bitch. You've doctored it, haven't you? You just couldn't bear the thought of us having any.'

Theo was the first to rush forward to get between Rosemary and Gavin, closely followed by Max.

'Calm it down, buddy. You saw she had the same as we had. Nobody's trying to poison anybody. Got it?'

Dido was meanwhile spewing the contents of her stomach in all directions, her body heaving and convulsing.

Charles placed his hand on Gavin's arm, adopting a reasonable, almost medical, tone. 'It's obvious she's had a bad reaction to it. There was a warning on the recipe, if you remember.'

Gavin shoved his arm into Charles' solar plexus to release his hold. 'Get your hands off me, you self-righteous old windbag! Fuck the warning on the recipe. Get a doctor, you clowns.'

Charles dropped his head like an angry rhino and, for a moment, I thought he was going to charge Gavin, so I rushed to his side and led him back to his place in the circle, making him sit on the ground until the pain subsided.

It was Rosemary who saved the day. She'd been busy rummaging in the tabernacle, from which she brought forth a tincture and a glass of water which she thrust at the gasping Dido.

'Here. Rinse out your mouth with the water and then drink this.'

Dido, her once immaculate robe now spattered with vomit, snatched the water, swilled it round her mouth and spat it out. Leaving a little in the bottom of the glass, she let Rosemary add the tincture and drank it down.

How prescient and proper of Rosemary to have prepared an antidote, I thought, and my former good opinion of her began to revive.

'Go and sit down with her,' Rosemary ordered Gavin. 'It'll take a little while to work.'

But Gavin just stood there, one arm round his wife, the other hand clenched in a fist, looking round to see which of us deserved the first punch.

At the sound of Charles coughing, I looked his way, to find him fixing me with an intense stare, mouthing the words 'violet flame'. At once it came to me that I was supposed to be in charge of security, so I mentally created a giant bonfire of violet flame and encased Gavin in it, giving him a good blast, hoping to neutralise as much as possible of his volcanic aggression.

After a minute or so, muttering under his breath, he complied with Rosemary's command, leading his wife to a chair and supporting her while she fought to gain control of her breathing.

The rest of us had moved to join Rosemary in front of the altar. We formed a small circle, huddling together so the other two wouldn't hear us.

'What's happened to Tegan?'

'Wasn't she supposed to appear by now?'

'Where are the sound effects?'

'Did you leave the side gate open for Jay and Sharon?'

It appeared that the only success had been the dry ice, and even that was rapidly running out of steam.

'Tegan must have set it going, so where is she, and why isn't Sharon topping it up?' I said, becoming increasingly more agitated at the apparent dereliction of duty on the part of our three special effects artists.

'Keeping the cauldrons bubbling is the least of our problems,' said Pete, nodding towards the Bulls.

We all regarded the lovely couple. Gav was rubbing Dido's back; she had stopped being sick and was breathing normally again. They had their heads together and seemed to be plotting something. When they saw us observing them, they sprang into life.

'I don't know what you did to me, Rosemary,' she snarled. 'But if you think this farce changes anything, you're mistaken.'

'Yeah,' jeered Gav. 'You think a bit of fake fog scares us?'

Dido got up and her husband joined her.

'We're taking the elixir as compensation. And if you try to stop us, I'll call the police and say you gave me something that nearly killed me. At the very least, you'll be struck off the General Dental Register.'

For some reason, the last few words tickled my funny bone. I suppose it was the juxtaposition of alchemy and dentistry – two fields one wouldn't normally bracket together.

We watched in disbelief as Dido, followed by Gavin, approached the altar and reached for the jars.

Before I even had a chance to fire up my violet flamethrower, there came a roll of thunder, accompanied by a fierce wind which catapulted the flowers from the altar and extinguished every candle flame. At the same time, black clouds came from nowhere to entirely obscure the effulgent moon. I looked around but could barely see anyone else in the pitch dark.

Above the altar, though, something was swirling. Whether it was fog from the dry ice or some ghostly ectoplasm, each wisp and plume was slowly building into a moving image of a female face, two enormous wings billowing out behind her. But the image didn't stop there. Gradually, a fist materialised and in it, a mighty sword.

Just when I'd begun to suspect that it might be some fantastic festival showpiece that Jay had secretly commissioned, the vision spoke.

'I come in answer to the call of the spirit of the Fountain of Life. I am Nemesis, daughter of the night, sent by Mother Isis to dispense justice. Who is Priestess here?'

She didn't sound a bit like a Bee Gee so it definitely wasn't Jay speaking.

Rosemary stepped forward and knelt down, Pete having swiftly placed the kneeler in position for her.

'Tell me who among them has drunk of the sacred infusion with an impure heart,' she boomed.

Rosemary pointed at Dido, still in the same pose, reaching for the jar. She moved not a muscle, and it dawned on me that she was frozen to the spot. Gavin had stepped back from the altar, his face a white blob of fear in the darkness.

'There is imbalance here which I am obliged to redress. Tell me, Priestess, know you of some infidelity by persons here?'

The way Nemesis had honked these words was far worse than any vuvuzela.

Rosemary answered a faint 'yes'.

'Speak.'

Rosemary nodded towards Dido, saying simply, 'She.'

'Is her lover here?' cried the goddess.

In reply, Rosemary reluctantly pointed at Theo.

'Who, then, is he who was wronged?' bellowed Nemesis.

Rosemary indicated Gavin, whose face, in the darkness, burned puce with rage.

I suppose my flamethrower could have intervened, but I reckoned Nemesis had it all well under control so I held fire.

'Awaken!'

So saying, the goddess directed her sword at Dido, who miraculously came to life.

'I command you, by the light of heaven, to speak the truth. Did you

lie with this man?'

To my amazement, Dido whispered, 'Yes.'

'Thereby wantonly deceiving the one to whom you were conjoined in marriage?'

Dido gave a further whispered assent. Nemesis then pointed her sword at Theo.

'Did you shamelessly deceive this woman's husband?'

My chest filled with sisterly pride as Theo answered firmly and clearly. 'No, mam, I did not. She was living alone and told me she and her husband had separated.'

The evil eye that Gavin had been giving Theo swiftly transferred to Dido, who was on her knees, beating her breast and moaning – without even the comfort of a soft foam kneeling pad.

Aiming her sword at Dido once again, the goddess delivered her judgement without delay.

'Your secret is out. You have betrayed two men who loved you. And by so doing have lost the love of both. For this crime, I decree your loss punishment enough.'

Dido stopped moaning and threw herself on to the earth in obeisance to the spectre who had acquitted her. But Nemesis hadn't finished with her yet. The substance which formed her features writhed into a massive scowl.

'But for the greater crime of misusing the magic of Mother Isis, it is decreed that you are forever forbidden to perform any ritual in her name, and forever prohibited from access to the Fountain of Life.'

That's what you call retributive justice, I thought, in awestruck admiration of the goddess, swiftly replaced by alarm at her next move. She was pointing her weapon at my brother again.

'You have experienced loss and suffering. To restore equilibrium, the spirit of the Fountain of Life will support you in your quest for wholeness. Go in Peace.'

At that moment, the clouds disappeared, and with them, Nemesis. Once again the garden was bathed in moonlight, the wreckage of the whirlwind which had preceded the apparition, proof that we hadn't dreamed it.

'How cool was that?' said Max, after a few seconds, breaking the spell she had cast on us.

'Was she for real?' said Theo, rubbing his eyes.

As one, our gang walked towards the altar to inspect the passage behind it. All we saw were the cauldrons, none of them giving off any vapours, and the blankets and gloves Max had left for the special effects team.

'I wonder what happened to Tegan,' said Theo, worried.

'And Jay and Sharon,' I said, equally worried. 'As soon as we're dismissed, I'll see if they're upstairs.'

Sensing we were ready to mount a search party, Rosemary called us back to our places.

'I'm going to uncast the circle now,' she said, ignoring sobbing Dido and glowering Gavin. 'It's important to do this, so please, everyone, stay in the circle until I've finished.'

'But you can talk among yourselves,' added Charles.

So while Rosemary moved anticlockwise round the circle ('widdershins' in her parlance), saying thanks and *au revoir* to the spirits of the four directions and collecting the fallen candles extinguished by the wind, I had a word with Dido.

'If you need a ride home, or if you want to go to a hotel, I'm sure Pete will give you a lift.'

'That might be an idea,' she sniffed. 'I don't particularly want to be alone with Gavin right now.'

I beckoned Pete over and explained the situation.

'That's it, everybody,' said Rosemary. 'You can leave the circle now if you want. Or you can stay and help me clear up.'

I noticed that she, Charles and Theo were staying pretty close to the two jars of elixir, just in case Gav decided to risk incurring the wrath of Nemesis by doing a runner with them.

'We can get going now, if you like,' said Pete, kindly.

Dido looked well and truly crushed. Formerly our arch-enemy, she was now a blubbing wreck, a pitiable creature who'd incurred the wrath of the gods, her dirty deeds having boomeranged back on her big time.

Telling Theo to wait for me, I went into the house. On my way upstairs, I heard a sound, turned, and caught a glimpse of Gavin on his way out. *Good riddance to bad rubbish,* I thought, as the door slammed shut.

When I got to the bedroom, I found the room empty and Jay and Sharon's costumes unworn, still folded neatly, as they had been earlier in the afternoon.

I ran downstairs and let myself out the front door. I wanted to check if the side gate had by mistake been locked, but it opened easily. Charles, Max and Theo were helping Rosemary clear the altar and tidy up the ground which was scattered with twisted garlands of spring flowers, cracked eggs, broken glass, crystals, plants, pots and trampled honey cakes. Even the moon-gazing hare had been swept from its perch. Only the elixir had escaped unscathed. I called to Theo, who came to join me.

We walked past the apple tree, into the shadows further back in the garden, to the climbing frame, which must have been a relic from Max's earlier days.

'Hello, Tegan,' I said. 'We wondered what had happened to you.'

She was sitting on the ground with her back to the frame. Her stilts lay close by, at angles to each other. Her long skirt bunched around her like a nest. Theo put out his hand to help her up.

'I can't get up, Theo,' she said in a shaky voice, tears running down her cheeks and leaving a grey trail on her blackened face. 'I fell off the climbing frame when I was putting my stilts on. It feels like I've broken my ankle.'

* * *

That night and the next morning, the phones were buzzing between all of us. Everyone wanted to know how Tegan was, where Sharon and Jay had got to, the whereabouts of the firecrackers, whether what we'd seen had been real or staged, etc., etc. So it was decided by Charles and Rosemary that we should meet at hers for supper, to get to the bottom of what had really happened.

When the ambulance had come to take Tegan away, I'd given Theo my keys so he could collect my car from the B&B and follow her to hospital. It turned out her ankle wasn't broken, but badly sprained.

She appeared at breakfast, in the main farmhouse, looking tired but happy, with Theo by her side. By then she'd changed out of her vampire costume, but her black make-up had proved hard to shift, giving her an eerie grey pallor. I had to explain to Jenny that my brother had brought her home from hospital in the early hours so, out of the goodness of her heart, she gave him breakfast as well. To save any awkwardness, we'd agreed not to mention stilts, just to tell her that Tegan had tripped on a paving stone.

When Theo and Tegan arrived at Rosemary's for supper, a cheer went up as she hobbled in. Rosemary produced a padded footstool and she sat in an easy chair while Max brought her a tray of food.

'What did you tell them at the hospital, love?' said Pete.

'I told them I was an entertainer at a party.' She managed a weak smile. 'Everybody accepted it, to my surprise.'

'They're used to it,' said Max. 'You get all sorts around here at festival time.'

'So didn't you ever get up on the stilts?' asked Rosemary. 'You managed it without any trouble when you practised yesterday afternoon.'

'No I didn't. I feel so awful that I let you down...'

We all murmured that of course she hadn't.

'...I was on the frame putting on my left stilt when it slipped out of my hands. I reached out for it and overbalanced. Next thing I knew I was lying on my side and my ankle was killing me. Jay and Sharon hadn't turned up, so there was no one to help me. I didn't dare call out because that would've given the game away.'

'You'd better tell everyone what happened to *you*,' I said to Jay, as he started apologising for the umpteenth time to Tegan for not being there.

'Ah, well. Thereby hangs a tale. We got back to the B&B, Sharon went to have a bath, and I asked her to give me a knock when she was ready.'

'And he fell asleep,' Sharon said, accusingly.

'And you locked yourself in the lavatory.'

'Bathroom,' she corrected him. 'And how was I to know the darn lock would snap off when I turned it? If you hadn't fallen asleep, we might have made it.'

'Anyway,' said Jay wearily. 'I woke up about nine o'clock, went to find Sharon and couldn't get into her room, so I knocked for Steve, but he'd gone out.'

'But his son Ryan was there. He had Oscar and Milo in the farmhouse with him,' I explained.

Two tails, one beside me and one beside Tegan, thumped at this mention.

'Yeah, but he didn't know where they kept the spare keys, and his parents had their phones switched off. Anyway, he found one in the end. We got into the bedroom, but couldn't open the bathroom door, so he had to go and find a screwdriver.'

'Lucky I didn't die of cold,' said Sharon. 'I only had a towel to cover me.'

'Hope it was a good size bath sheet,' said Pete.

Seeing Sharon's offended expression he managed to rescind his *faux pas*.

'I like a woman with a bit of meat on her.'

This sounded like a backhanded compliment to me but seemed to please Sharon no end.

'Anyway,' continued Jay, 'I managed to unscrew the fitting without breaking the door down, but it was getting on for ten by then, so Sharon went to bed and I hung around waiting for someone to switch on their phone so I could explain why we hadn't turned up, and see when you lot wanted picking up.'

'It's a shame you and your mother missed our celestial visitor,' said Charles.

'Yeah, Andy told us all about it.' Jay pretended to look serious by stroking an invisible beard. 'Sounds to me like you were all high. What exactly went into that elixir, Rosemary?'

'Did you put any peyote in it, Mum?' said Max, grinning.

'No need,' she said. 'Nemesis was the real thing. Of that I'm a hundred per cent sure.'

Tegan's eyes were wistful. 'I wish I'd seen what you saw. All I can remember is falling down. And then Theo and Pandora turning up.'

'I rest my case,' said Jay, his thumbs hooked in his shirt like a QC summing up. 'Tegan didn't hear or see anything and she was the only one there who didn't drink the potion.'

Charles shook his head. 'That's not true, actually. Gavin Bull didn't take the elixir, but he still had the same experience as us. Hence him losing his temper good and proper after Nemesis exposed his wife as an adulteress.'

'Most biblical, old man,' said Pete, chuckling. 'In fact, it was Rosemary who grassed her up, but Nemesis forced Dido to confirm it. She was like a zombie when I dropped her off. Like she'd had all the life sucked out of her.'

'I wonder what Dido and Gavin will do next,' I said. 'They can't carry on working together, surely.'

Pete adopted a conspiratorial air, looking over his shoulder as if checking for eavesdroppers.

'Well, it looks as if he's done a bunk. A mate o' mine, Chalkie, he's got the caff next door. He said Gavin came in this morning and paid his tab – told him he was off back to Australia. Next thing, he puts a sign on the door: "Closed due to unforeseen circumstances". Chalkie said all day long he had women coming into his caff asking him where the Bulls were.'

'Wasn't Dido there either, Pete?'

'No sign of her, apparently. If it's still shut next week, we can consider our work done.'

'So where did you take her last night?'

'The Flying Horse. They do rooms. She didn't want to go home. I don't blame her, the mood he was in.'

'It's a shame he couldn't forgive and forget,' I said, feeling inexplicably sad.

I'd always imagined the pair of them leaving town together. A marriage break-up hadn't been in the plan. Jay caught my eye and winked. He knew I hated couples splitting up. (All except him and Debbie, of course. Even though I'd heard about that some time after the event, I'd still felt a warm glow.)

'By the way, Max,' said Jay, 'what happened to the firecrackers?'

'What firecrackers?' said Rosemary. She was only teasing because she must have heard us discussing them in the midst of the drama when nothing was going as planned.

Max looked embarrassed. 'What a complete dead loss they were. Chris said he tried to light them but they fizzled out.'

'Less of a fusillade more of a damp squib, then,' said Pete, and Sharon gave a girlish peal of laughter.

'But did he say he'd seen the goddess?' asked Jay.

'No. When he heard Dido coughing, he tried to light the first batch, but the bangers were soaked through, even though he'd kept them in a polythene box. He couldn't see any point in hanging around in the cold, so he went home.'

'You didn't tell him what we saw, did you?' said Charles.

Max shook his head.

'Good. Keep it to yourself, Max. What goes on in the circle, should stay in the circle.'

Jay nodded sagely. He used to say the same thing about what happened on tour.

Charles surveyed the room. 'Well, I think, between us, we've shared all our information. It only remains for me to say how grateful I am to all of you for your help, first of all in solving the mystery of Frankie's grave...' When he mentioned her name, his eyes filled tears and so did mine. '... And for helping to produce the elixir – which is what she was working towards herself, just before she died.'

I caught Theo's eye when Charles said this, remembering his experience in the labyrinth when he'd sensed Frankie's presence, telling him to finish what she'd started.

Hope you're happy now, Mum, I said silently.

Charles had paused to collect himself and now he produced a small package, covered in Christmas paper, and handed it to Rosemary. 'Apologies for the wrapping. It was all I had.'

When Rosemary unwrapped the chalice, she expressed her delight by first bursting into tears and then giving Charles a big hug, which he seemed to appreciate.

'I know I doubted its authenticity and effectiveness,' said Charles, once he and Rosemary had disengaged. 'But it was recognised by the spirit of the Fountain of Life, which is all that matters.'

'I don't know what to say,' she sniffed, 'except please don't tell the Chalice Well Trust I've got it.'

Amid laughter, Charles made his final announcement. 'And, of course, we mustn't forget the part Rowan's friend, Clarrie, played in all this. A young woman, sadly, I didn't get to meet. I hope you'll pass my thanks on to her, Pandora.'

'You can thank her yourself, if you like, Charles,' said Jay.

I looked towards the door, half expecting a giant cake to be wheeled in, out of which Clarrie would leap. After the night before, nothing would ever surprise me again. But there was no sign of her.

'Andy and Rowan, our youngest, have both got a birthday next week,' Jay went on, 'so Sharon and I thought we'd have a party at our place, a week today. You're all more than welcome to join the celebrations.'

This was news to me. I wasn't sure I was ready to 'celebrate' my fifty-sixth in public, but I liked a good party, so I played the game and beamed in Jay and Sharon's direction. Nevertheless, a naughty little thought crossed my mind that this might be Sharon's way of ensuring Rowan's birthday was an occasion for family and friends, rather than simply a night out *à deux* with Clarrie.

'That sounds like just the thing to bring us all back down to earth,' said Rosemary.

'I'd have thought a party in a pop star's house would be the one place we could get high as a kite,' said Pete, imitating being spaced-out by half-closing his eyes and waggling his head.

'I was never a pop star, mate. My roots are rhythm and blues,' said Jay reprovingly. His music was one of the few subjects he took seriously.

'Sorry, old man,' said Pete, winking at Sharon. 'I can see I touched a nerve.'

News of the party was the signal for general chatter – Jay asking Max if he'd be bringing a girl, Sharon giving Pete directions to Four Seasons, Charles comparing notes with Tegan about the hospital. But Rosemary still had something to say, so she stood up and raised her voice to get our attention.

'Can I just announce something while you're all here? Those of you who want to claim your share of the elixir should let me know and I'll give it to you, or post it off to you, when it's ready in four weeks' time. If anyone isn't bothered, I can always use their share to treat Theo.' She smiled. 'We've already had one successful result.'

Like a model, Theo held out his left hand and waggled his middle finger. We moved closer to inspect it.

'You can't even see the join,' said Pete, whistling in wonder.

Sure enough, the deep cut had healed, in less than twenty-four hours, without the faintest scar.

'I was wondering, Rosemary, if you could put some on Tegan's ankle?' Theo said this awkwardly, as if shy of appearing to hog the elixir.

Rosemary paused and did her trick of cocking her ear, to hear what 'them upstairs' had to say.

We all fell silent while she downloaded whatever it was they were telling her. This was new territory for us, too. Maybe one day *we* would need some urgent treatment, and how wonderful it would be to have an instant remedy.

'Theo, they say that your finger healing was exceptional because of the presence of the goddess Nemesis and the power she brought with her. As the recipe said, the true potency of our elixir will not be realised until the time of the next full moon – four weeks. When it is administered, its effect will be cumulative, not instantaneous.'

Rosemary opened her eyes to indicate she'd finished channelling.

'Sorry, Tegan. They're saying the elixir's still "cooking" and we shouldn't disturb it until it's ready.'

While empathising with Theo and Tegan's disappointment, I wasn't surprised. As I'd learned from Enoch, with the physical world being of a much denser vibration than the spiritual world, the window for miracles doesn't open very often. Unless, of course, like the yogis in the East, said to be able to raise the dead, we can lift our own vibrations to such a lofty level that we can tap into the power of divine cosmic energy, as Christ had.

'Never mind,' said Sharon, taking her mobile from her bag. 'Why don't you say a prayer? Let me google "circus performers".'

'I thought you'd given the internet up for Lent, Sha,' I said, trying to head her off.

'Well it's taking me to a Catholic website, so I guess I'll get a dispensation.'

Tegan had no idea what she was talking about. But Sharon's smartphone had yielded what she wanted.

'The patron saint of circus performers is St John Bosco. Says here he used to juggle and do magic and acrobatics to keep the younger members of his congregation interested.'

Tegan started giggling and Sharon observed, dryly, 'Take my word for it, young lady, speak to him right, and he'll be just as effective as any pagan magic circle.'

Chapter 28

Blowing Out Candles

Our sitting room was large enough for any family party, but Jay, Sharon and Rowan had invited so many people to the birthday celebrations that we had to have an emergency marquee erected in the garden, complete with heaters and chandeliers. It had a dance floor and a DJ, and tables decorated with pink and blue hyacinths in tall, chalice vases. When the florist delivered these, I did a double-take, and Sharon said, 'Jay specially requested those vases.'

I did another double-take when Theo and Tegan arrived. His hair was clipped at the back and sides, with short curls on the top, taking years off him.

'Don't look so surprised, Sis. It's how I used to wear it when I was working.'

'Yeah,' gurgled Tegan. 'He showed me an old photo and I loved it, so he let me cut it for him.'

Theo gazed at her like a moon-struck calf. 'I remembered what you said to Pandora on the first day I met you, "New life, new look".'

'Now you've shed your dreads, you look like Beau again,' I said.

My words broke into his love rapture and he turned back to me.

'On that subject, Sis, how'd you like to have him here to keep Midnight company?'

'Oh my God, this is my dream come true. I would like that more than anything in the world. I love you,' I shrieked, planting a kiss on his cheek.

Of course, it was partly the drink talking, but at least the champagne had prompted me to tell my little bro at last that I did love him.

'When are you bringing him over?'

'Probably the end of next week? I wouldn't mind another crack at Pan's labyrinth,' he said, to my delight.

'Come for the weekend and stay as long as you like,' I cooed.

Jay had dragged himself away from Max, Rowan and his friends, to join us.

'I've just had the best birthday present I could ever wish for, Jay. Guess who's coming to live with us?'

Jay's brow wrinkled.

'Two legs or four?'

'Four.'

'Theo and Tegan?'

Theo laughed. 'No, just the opposite. Me and Tegan are off to the States and Beau's coming here.'

My heart plummeted to my Jimmy Choos. Why did life give me the perfect animal companion with one hand, and take away my brother with the other? I knew Theo couldn't stay longer than six months, but I'd expected him to stay until the last possible day.

Tegan came closer, speaking just to me, while Jay and Theo were talking. 'After everything that's happened, he felt uncomfortable living with Charles, and now I've left the boat, we've been staying at Steve's B&B. He asked me to go to the States with him last night. Perfect timing, see?'

I thought of the dream I'd had of Tegan and Theo, lost in a wasteland, and hoped there wouldn't be troubles ahead for them.

Jay was giving Theo a sideways hug.

'I'll miss you, man.'

The look they exchanged was brief but intense. Both men had been deserted by mothers who'd put thousands of miles between them and their sons, which was why having a woman who loved them unconditionally was so important to them. And they recognised that hunger in each other.

'That's Beau taken care of, so where's Milo going?'

Jay was always tuned in where our furry friends were concerned.

Theo smiled his shy smile. 'Seems like you're in for another birthday present, Sis.'

'I hope that's all right, Pandora,' said Tegan, and I kissed her in reply.

Jay put his arm round my waist.

'Looks like we got two new arrivals, momma. Must be all that rebirthing you did.'

I smiled, suppressing the sinking feeling I had of my primary flight feathers being pruned just as they'd begun to grow back.

I still hadn't got round to telling Jay about my invitation to join the *Straight Talking* panel. Sharon had been so tired this week, after her weekend in Glastonbury, that she'd been rising late and retiring early. Consequently, I'd been caught up in the logistics of family life and party planning, only just delivering my dispatch to Polly on time.

Being a great believer in signs and portents, I'd almost convinced myself I was being 'told' not to take on anything new. Much as I loved Beau, the news that we were welcoming two more creatures into the fold, was pointing me towards taking a rain check on Zac's job offer. Which, effectively, would be saying no. A rookie like me, especially *at my age*, would be unlikely to be given a chance like this again.

We sat down at a spare table – the place was filling up rapidly – and Theo and Tegan told us their plans. Theo's house in Los Angeles was rented out, so they'd be staying with a cousin until it was free. Tegan had applied for a visa, which wouldn't entitle her to work, but according to Theo she could probably find a place as an unpaid apprentice in a design studio.

'LA's a great place for Tegan to get some experience in the fashion industry. My family know a lot of people. They'll have some contacts in the business.'

It sounded as if Theo's family were the equivalent of minor royalty in La-La Land.

'So when are you going? I thought you'd be staying on for Rosemary's elixir sessions.'

'Actually, I've already had some of her regular energy healing.'

He sounded apologetic and we both knew why. When I'd recommended Rosemary, that day we climbed the Tor, he'd reacted as if I'd asked him to put his head in the lion's mouth.

'And?'

'And the plan is, we hang around for another three weeks, till the elixir's ready. Rosemary's gonna give me the first full dose, just to make sure there's no bad reaction...'

'If there is,' said Tegan. 'I might get to see Nemesis after all. That should be exciting.'

We laughed. The ceremony had been only eight days ago, but it seemed like an age away now.

'So if everything goes well, Rosemary will send me what I need.'

'The spirit of the Fountain of Life will support you in your quest for wholeness', I said, quoting Nemesis. 'Just hold that thought every time you take it.'

A mood of quiet reflection descended on the four of us. I was wondering whether Theo really would get better and I sensed that Tegan and Jay were thinking the same.

It was Theo who broke the silence. 'We've invited Rosemary and Max to come over in the summer.'

He must have caught my disappointment that he hadn't asked me first, because he added, 'You can come visit any time you like.'

'That sounds great,' said Jay. 'I've got some pals across the pond. Wouldn't mind looking 'em up.'

'I see Sharon and Pete are burning the floor. If it wasn't for this,' Tegan said, pointing to her ankle, 'I'd be up there with them.'

Rowan and his friends had commandeered the dance floor and were dancing in a circle, waving their arms in the air, shouting the words of the song. I waved to Clarrie and she waved both arms back. Sharon and Pete were attempting a spirited jive in the middle of the circle, which owed more to enthusiasm than expertise. She was wearing a Frankie dress, acquired, along with a number of others, when I'd shown her the remaining garments in my mother's wardrobe. It was a black floral number, sleeveless with a cowl neck, which she'd said would be a 'new departure' for her.

'I see Sharon's got her bingo wings out,' said Jay, shaking his head.

In the further reaches of the marquee, Charles was doing his rounds of the tables in the manner of a priest at a church hall hop. When he got to us, he sank down into an empty chair and accepted a glass of champagne gratefully.

'Did you see anyone you know, vicar?' said Jay.

Luckily Charles didn't hear the last word, but the rest of us did, and we had to avoid catching each other's eyes.

After a good gulp of bubbly, Charles answered. 'Yes, I did. Ashley and Linden are in great form. They were talking rugby with two lads who told me they're working here in the Easter vac.'

My heart sank on behalf of Cherry and Willow, who'd probably imagined a romantic evening with their swains until their older brothers stepped in and distracted them with sports-oriented man-talk.

'They're Hugh's boys,' I said.

'They seem pretty pally with Cherry and Willow.'

My heart rose again. Maybe the girls would win out in the end.

'The four of them spent Easter together, don't you remember, Charles? I told you. They went to Paris, otherwise they might have been with us in Glastonbury, which would have been a bit awkward, in view of all the shenanigans.'

Charles looked a bit blank, understandable considering the bump on the head he'd suffered. 'Oh yes. So you did.'

'Any more news from the front?' Jay asked.

He'd changed the subject to cover Charles' memory lapse and I patted his knee in a gesture of thanks.

Jay had spoken to Charles on the phone earlier in the week and he'd said that Chalkie had seen Dido coming and going from her flat above the salon. She must have cancelled the rest of the appointments because no more clients came.

'Harry from the estate agents says she's put the salon up for sale.'

'The sad demise of the sexy abbess,' said Jay.

'You're right,' sighed Charles. 'Even though I couldn't stand the woman, revenge has a bitter aftertaste.'

'Even Nemesis said she'd been punished enough, didn't she?' I said. 'For the adultery part of it, at least.'

'She sounds like she's got her head screwed on, that Nemesis,' said Jay, getting up and disappearing in the direction of the marquee entrance.

Minutes later he was back with, of all people, Gaby Laing, who was wearing a pale orchid cocktail dress with a bejewelled bustier, held up by the slimmest of spaghetti straps. I looked past her to see if any significant other was trailing, but the way she was clinging to Jay's arm indicated otherwise. What on earth had he been thinking of, inviting her to my birthday party?

'Happy birthday, Pandora.'

She bent down and gave me an air kiss, almost choking me with the weapons-grade perfume emanating from her bosom.

Over her shoulder I flung indignant eye signals at Jay, but he was looking everywhere except at me.

Thrusting a present into my hand, she purred, 'I hope you like it. I know you're a dog person.'

She stood over me, so I had to open it. Inside was a square of silk, reminiscent of those horsey headscarves the queen used to wear, only with Scottie dogs. Scotties were a breed I disliked, ever since one had nipped Oscar on the nose and drawn blood. I wouldn't be seen dead in such a scarf.

'Thank you,' I said tightly. 'You shouldn't have.'

Jay pulled out a chair for Gaby and sat down next to her.

'Gaby's got some good news.'

'Really?'

This time our eyes met and he winced as I thrust several daggers into his pupils.

'Yeah. Fantastic news,' she gushed. 'A tour promoter's approached my management. They want me to be support act on a Sammy Wilson tour.' She paused. 'And they want Jay as well.'

My blood ran cold at the last six words. Finally, I managed to defrost my tongue.

'But I thought you and Jay only recorded two songs together?'

'That's right, but my record company's decided they're the best two tracks. The promoter thinks so too. And they want him on guitar for the other numbers. If he doesn't sign, I could lose the contract.'

My eyes met Jay's, which held the same soulful expression as Oscar's when he was waiting for the last piece of my steak, which I always gave him. I knew he wanted this badly, but suppose Gaby asked him to sleep with her again? Would he be able to say no?

I searched my mind for an indisputable reason which would prove to everyone it was a bad idea for him to go.

'But you've never been a supporting act before...'

'No, but this time the billing wouldn't be James Jay and the Jaylers. This is different, like having a cameo part in a film. I can do it without losing face.'

Embarrassed, he glanced at Gaby, realising that he'd indirectly insulted her for desperately grabbing at support-artist status. Her face revealed nothing, so fixed was her rictus smile.

Tegan, Theo and Charles had been listening to this with interest. I looked to them for backing but they all seemed fascinated by Gaby. Sensing this, she pressed home her advantage.

'It's a great opportunity to showcase Jay's writing. For him, it's not really about the tour, it's about getting other artists to see what a good writer he is. But I know Jay won't go without your say-so. Go on, Pandora. Say yes, *please*, for *his* sake.'

I looked around the table at their faces, willing me to agree. Jay was the only one aware of the real reason I didn't want him to go on tour with Gaby. The crafty devil knew that if he'd asked me this when we were on our own, I'd have said 'no way José'.

My hands were trembling and I could feel my lip pout in frustration. Recognising the signs, Jay led me to the dance floor where he held me so tightly I could hardly breathe. It was a slow song and, out of habit, I put my arms around his neck and rested my head on his shoulder.

Jay sang a few bars of the music in my ear. Luckily for him, it happened to be a love song. He knew how to win me over. When he stopped singing, he whispered, 'I get what's bugging you, babe. But it ain't gonna happen. Trust me.'

'When do you leave?' I sniffed, knowing when I was beaten.

'End of May. Rehearsals first, followed by two weeks on tour. We start in Manchester, finish in London.'

'But Sammy's still a big name. He must be touring Europe as well.'

'Yeah, well. They haven't offered her a spot on the international leg. He's playing Germany, Paris, Amsterdam – the usual, but she's not known enough there. They'll get local bands.'

He bent down, lifted my chin and kissed me on the lips.

'Between you and me, this is her last chance. What with her dodgy hearing and being a bit, you know, passé, she's dead lucky to get it. And it's good money. I'd be mad to turn it down.' He waved his arm at the mass of people queuing at the buffet, provided by outside caterers, naturally, and at the bar beside the buffet table, dispensing free booze. 'This doesn't come cheap.'

'You're not regretting the party, are you, Jay? Because, honestly, I didn't expect it. I would have been happy with a takeaway – just us and the kids.'

'Easy, tiger,' he said, ruffling my hair (the hair I'd paid a hefty sum for Franco to treat, so that when I moved my head there was movement and swing rather than a thatch which stayed close to the roof). 'One has to keep up appearances, doncha know,' he said, sounding like Burlingon Bertie and making me smirk.

Still holding hands, we returned to the table. Gaby was bending Theo's ear about the music business in the States and Tegan was looking restless. The more Gaby leaned forward, the more restless Tegan looked.

'So what's the verdict?' said Charles. 'Does Jay go to the ball?'

I hesitated for a second. Did I love Jay so completely that I'd agree to something every atom of my being was screaming at me to deny him? I wasn't absolutely sure of the answer to that, but I decided this time a tactical withdrawal would be the dignified option.

'He'd never forgive me if I said he had to stay home and dig the garden,' I answered, managing a faint smile.

'Great,' cried Gaby, leaping up and kissing Jay on the cheek.

I watched closely to see how much he'd enjoyed it, but he stepped back and surreptitiously wiped his face with a paper napkin, which reassured me more than a bit.

Jay got another bottle of champagne from the bar and charged our glasses.

'To Andy. Happy birthday, my darling.'

I was touched. I'd expected him to toast the tour, not me.

'Well,' said Gaby, once she'd emptied her glass. 'I'll love you and leave you. I'm on my way to a hen do. Everyone I know's getting married. In a couple of years I expect they'll all be getting divorced.' She focused her gaze on Theo. 'Who knows what's the longest sentence in the English language?'

My brother looked puzzled, as did all of us except Jay, who answered, 'I do.'

There was silence for a few seconds, while we waited for him to say what it was, then it slowly dawned on me that he'd already given us the punchline. It was the marriage vow, 'I do'.

Tegan gave Jay a cool stare while he explained the 'joke' to Theo, and Charles pursed his lips.

Seemingly oblivious to how flat her joke had fallen, Gaby got up to go, pausing by my chair.

'By the way, Pandora, can you have my cats when we're on tour? It'd take a weight off my mind.'

Sharon and I had agreed to say no if Gaby ever took Jay up on his offer. But now he was included in the tour, I could hardly refuse.

'Er, well, if you can't get anyone else. Although we'll have three dogs by then.'

'No probs, chuck. I'm sure you'll keep your eye on 'em good style.'

Flushed with victory on all counts, she swept out of the marquee followed by Jay, who walked her to the exit. I was hoping that they weren't saying something like, 'we managed to swing it' when Rosemary, Pete and Sharon turned up at our table.

Charles got more chairs and they sat down. 'Correct me if I'm wrong, but wasn't that the hussy who tried to seduce Jay?' said Sharon, fortissimo.

'Why don't you shout a bit louder, Sharon, I don't think the people at the back heard you,' I snapped.

Everyone's ears were flapping now, so I sat still and reflected, while she told the others what Gaby had suggested to Jay.

'I'm not surprised,' said Tegan. 'I reckon she's a right man-eater.'

Then my mother decided to join in.

Pandora, listen to me. If you let him and his floozie walk all over you, you're no daughter of mine. What's happened to your backbone, girl? For heaven's sake, get a grip. You're letting history repeat itself.

I sighed. Was I never to have any peace – from the living or the dead?

When Jay returned to the table, the conversation died. This time it was me who filled everyone's glasses with champagne.

'I've got an announcement to make, too.'

I took a deep breath, my gaze spanning everyone at the table and coming to rest on Jay. 'I'm going to be a panellist on a new daytime TV show called *Straight Talking*. I start in two weeks' time.'

At first, nobody spoke, then everyone fired questions at me while Jay listened in silence. I told them about my anonymous weekly column and how I'd been headhunted because of it. As a finale, I delivered my studio audition story.

When I finished talking, Jay got up from the other side of the table and bent over me, in a manner reminiscent of a *mafioso* delivering the kiss of death.

'Nice of you to tell me, Andy,' he murmured as he skimmed my cheek with his lips.

'You weren't around,' I murmured back. 'And I didn't make up my mind till just now.'

He straightened up, standing beside my chair, seeming unsure what to do or say.

'By the way,' I said, looking up at him. 'Tell Gaby, now I've decided to take the job, she'll have to make other arrangements for her cats.'

Jay stared back at me with an unfathomable mix of expressions, which I hoped included a degree of admiration.

They say be careful what you wish for. Maybe being a mother wasn't what I'd been sent to earth to do. And maybe Jay had thought he wanted me as a mother for his kids, when all the time what he really wanted was the superheroine that Enoch had created.

I touched the phoenix pendant at my neck that Theo had given me. Too late to go back now. My spreading wings had fanned the flames. One phase of life was ending and a new one about to begin.

'Can I have the birthday girl and the birthday boy over here please?' the DJ boomed, and the crowd looked around to see where we were.

Rowan broke away from Clarrie and his friends to escort me to the dance floor, where the cake ceremony was about to take place. With ironic birthday cheers from drunken teenagers ringing in my ears, I began to feel sick at the possibility of my age being exposed to the assembled masses.

Actually, it wasn't too bad in the end. A waiter wheeled forward an enormous cake composed of two circular layers, one large and blue and the other small and pink. There were sixteen gold candles for Rowan round the perimeter of the blue layer and one gold candle in the centre of the pink cake for me. I heard the DJ wish Rowan 'Happy sixteenth' and held my breath until he made a joke about never revealing a lady's age, when I was able to inhale again.

'Thanks for sharing your party with me,' I whispered to Rowan, as the DJ led the throng in a chorus of "Happy Birthday" while they lowered the lights and Rowan puffed his way through the candles.

'Happy Birthday, Mum,' said Rowan. 'Don't forget to make a wish.'

'I wish...I wish all the changes ahead will be for the best,' I whispered, as I blew out my solitary candle, hoping, with every atom of my being, for coming events to spin into a happy-ever-after.

Good luck with that one, Pan, you'll certainly need it, said Frankie, as the revellers whistled and cheered.

Further Reading

Lauren Artress (2006) *Walking a Sacred Path: Rediscovering the Labyrinth as a Spiritual Practice* Riverhead Books U.S.

Dielle Ciesco (2013) *The Unknown Mother: A Magical Walk with the Goddess of Sound* Roundfire Books

Elizabeth Clare Prophet (1997) *Violet Flame to Heal Body, Mind and Soul* Summit University Press

Also by this author

Transforming Pandora – showcased by The People's Book Prize 2014

Pandora, 51, childless, and still beautiful, is attempting to come to terms with her husband's death. Having a history of being drawn to the esoteric, yet remaining a healthy sceptic, she reluctantly attends an evening of clairvoyance and raises a spirit who sets her on a new path…

…inventive and accomplished use of language and assured handling of the different elements of the story, make for a great read.

Lois Keith, author of *A Different Life* and *Out of Place*

This charming novel blends romance with spirituality. Carolyn Mathews is a talented writer, adroitly balancing the emotional and spiritual themes that drive this multi-layered metaphysical romance. A rich cast of characters supplement the basic love story and keep the plot moving. Whether you're looking for romance or spiritual guidance, this well-written novel of love and rebirth satisfies both.

P. J. Swanwick, *Fiction For A New Age*

Well-written and engaging, Transforming Pandora is an enjoyable read. I highly recommend it.

Alice Berger, *Berger Book Reviews*

Carolyn Mathews has a background in English Language materials writing and teaching, with an interest in the spiritual, and an awareness of how ridiculous that can seem to others.

978-1-78099-745-2

At Roundfire we publish great stories. We lean towards the spiritual and thought-provoking. But whether it's literary or popular, a gentle tale or a pulsating thriller, the connecting theme in all Roundfire fiction titles is that once you pick them up you won't want to put them down.